John Glyde

The New Suffolk Garland:

A miscellany of Anecdotes, Romantic Ballads, Descriptive Poems...

John Glyde

The New Suffolk Garland:
A miscellany of Anecdotes, Romantic Ballads, Descriptive Poems...

ISBN/EAN: 9783744787048

Printed in Europe, USA, Canada, Australia, Japan

Cover: Foto ©Andreas Hilbeck / pixelio.de

More available books at **www.hansebooks.com**

THE

NEW SUFFOLK GARLAND:

A

MISCELLANY OF ANECDOTES, ROMANTIC BALLADS,
DESCRIPTIVE POEMS AND SONGS, HISTORICAL
AND BIOGRAPHICAL NOTICES, AND STATISTICAL RETURNS

RELATING TO

THE COUNTY OF SUFFOLK.

With an Appendix,

CONTAINING THE

HISTORY OF THE REFORM STRUGGLE IN IPSWICH IN 1820; OR THE
CELEBRATED ELECTION OF LENNARD AND HALDIMAND.

COLLECTED, COMPILED, AND EDITED BY

JOHN GLYDE, JUN.,

AUTHOR OF "SUFFOLK IN THE NINETEENTH CENTURY,"
"SOCIAL AND MORAL CONDITION OF IPSWICH."

IPSWICH:

PRINTED FOR THE AUTHOR, ST. MATTHEW'S STREET.
LONDON: SIMPKIN, MARSHALL, AND CO.
AND SOLD BY ALL BOOKSELLERS.

1866.

PREFACE.

The "Garland" which we here offer to public notice scarcely needs a Preface. It may be as well, however, to remark, that all the persons noticed in the volume have been either natives of, or residents in the County of Suffolk; and that as we have dealt with hundreds of dates, events, and persons, it has been almost impossible to avoid trifling errors; but we can honestly say that we have laboured to be truthful in statement and exact in detail.

To enumerate the many volumes to which we are indebted for this miscellaneous collection would occupy more space than we have at our disposal. Several of the old Ballads have been selected from the old "Suffolk Garland"; the "East Anglian"; "Notes and Queries"; the Fitch MSS. in the British Museum; the twenty-eight volumes of Fitch MSS. in the Ipswich Museum, as well as the files of the "Ipswich Journal" and "Suffolk Chronicle," have been freely used; and the unrivalled collection of Suffolk books and MSS. in the possession of W. P. Hunt, Esq., of Ipswich, has been kindly placed at our disposal. Our thanks are especially due to the Rev. Hugh Pigot for the loan of materials, and also to those authors and publishers who have granted us the freedom to select from their publications whatever seemed most suitable for our purpose.

The gathering of the materials for the present volume has been the work of several years, and since the announcement of its intended publication, no amount of research has been considered unprofitable or irksome.

We had intended to give a return of the gross estimated rental, the rateable value, and the amount expended for the relief of the poor during the year ending Lady day, 1864, for every parish in the county of Suffolk, and the clerks of twelve Unions in this county had kindly furnished us with returns for that purpose; but as we could not obtain such returns from the Unions of Bosmere, Hartismere, Mutford, Thingoe, and Woodbridge, we were at last reluctantly compelled to abandon this part of our plan.

We hope that this volume of miscellanies will be welcomed as an addition to Suffolk Literature, and by local readers become numbered with that pleasant class of books which Horace Walpole describes as " lounging books, which one takes up in the gout, low spirits, ennui, or when one is waiting for company."

To those Ladies and Gentlemen who have kindly given their names as subscribers to prevent our risking a loss by publication, we tender our hearty thanks.   Had not our materials extended to fifty pages more than we promised in the Prospectus, we should have had great pleasure in giving a list of our Patrons.

JOHN GLYDE, Jun.

Ipswich,

December 1st, 1865.

CONTENTS.

Appendix.

I.

Anecdotes and Biographical Reminiscences.

Anecdotes and Biographical Reminiscences.

DR. WHATELY was Rector of Halesworth at the time he was appointed Archbishop of Dublin. Directly after his consecration he was sworn in of the Irish Privy Council, where his "odd ways" excited much comment. The weather was cold, and the Archbishop's manner seemed quite as cool as the atmosphere in which he was placed. At the Privy Council he used to stand the whole time before the fire, with his coat tail separated and pulled forward, whereby he received a considerable share of heat, to the exclusion of many right honourable gentlemen, who felt rather chilly. It was in reference to this act, and to the circumstance of a noble lord, afflicted with baldness, who put on his hat for warmth, that Master Gould wittily observed : "A bishop keeps uncovered that which ought to be covered, and a peer keeps covered what ought to be uncovered."

Having accepted an invitation to dine with Lord Anglesey, at the vice-regal lodge, it is almost incredibly told of him that having arrived before the bulk of the guests, he drew over an arm chair to the fire and stretched to the uttermost his legs, until their heels seemed to repose upon some object of *virtù* on the mantel-piece. The Archbishop was pleased with the inmates of the vice-regal lodge, and often repaired

there of a morning to enjoy himself in converse with those
that belonged to the privileged circle. It was diamond cut
diamond between the parties, but Whately in strength of
wealth was like the mine of Golconda. In working the
mine, his Grace would give way to his accustomed eccentric
vigour of movement, and no less than four or five chairs
were sometimes dislocated in succession by the energy with
which, during animated talk, the Archbishop was in the habit
of making his chair spin round on one leg. A council of
ladies was held, under the presidency of the Marchioness, to
consider what steps should be adopted to arrest the wholesale
destruction of her papier mâché and other fragile furniture,
and Lady Anglesey took credit to herself for the firmness
with which when the Archbishop appeared on the following
day, she pointed out for his use a powerfully built chair, with
legs like the balustrades of Dublin Castle. The Marchioness
remarked that the uniform frankness of Dr. Whately invited
a corresponding frankness.

At a dinner of the late Provost Lloyd's, his Grace was the
lion of the party, and he exhibited many of the attributes of
that formidable animal. The company were however surprised
at a strange way he had of raising his right leg and foot,
and doubling it back over the thigh of the left one, and
grasping its instep with both hands, as though he were
strangling some ugly animal. He did this repeatedly during
the evening, especially while telling some good stories, to
which he did ample justice; and during the process, the foot
thus raised, or rather strangled, was always in the lap of
Provost Lloyd, on whose right-hand side the Archbishop, as
the guest of the evening, sat. The Chesterfield suavity of
the Provost's face, while his fine black small-clothes were
subjected to such treatment, was not quickly forgotten.

Even at the Board of Education the presence of the Duke
of Leinster, Lord Plunkett, the Lord Chancellor, Mr. Baron
Greene, and other great guns, was often not sufficient to prevent Dr. Whately indulging the odd habit of placing his legs

on the very table round which they sat. Throwing his chair backwards and making it rest entirely on the two hind legs, he used to counterbalance the sedentary occupation of a diligent attendance by creating the exercise incidental to making his body oscillate like a pendulum. For many years after his Grace's retirement from the Board, a breach in the carpet used to be pointed out as the result of this extraordinary chair exercise.

At Oxford, he would lecture his pupils lying on a sofa, "with his legs over the end."

BISHOP BLOOMFIELD AND THE QUAKER.

Dr. Bloomfield, whilst rector of Bishopsgate, made himself very popular, and managed the vestry meetings of this immense parish, which contained more than 10,000 inhabitants, with great tact and good nature. On one occasion a Quaker who attended refused to take off his hat at a vestry meeting held in the church. Dr. Bloomfield, finding that the disciple of George Fox would not comply with his desire to uncover, proposed to the meeting a resolution—"That the beadle be directed to take off Mr. ——'s hat," which was accordingly done, and the Quaker thus quietly submitted.

IMPULSIVENESS OF GAINSBOROUGH.

Gainsborough's nature was generous, impulsive, enthusiastic. When Thicknesse stopped him on his way to the theatre, and told him the story of the friendless and forsaken woman, the tear started to his eye, he " *could not* " go till he had contributed to her necessities. Like Honeywood, in Goldsmith's play, his bounty not unfrequently partook of weakness. Money and pictures were bestowed inconsiderately. He presented twenty drawings to one lady, who was so ignorant of their value that she pasted them on the wall of her dressing-room, and gave Colonel Hamilton the " Boy at the Stile," for playing a solo on the violin. His impulsiveness was occasionally attended with unpleasant results. Being very much struck with Velasquez's portrait of the young

Duke of Asturius, now in the Dulwich Gallery, he said to the servant of its possessor, Mr. Agar, "Tell your master I will give him a thousand pounds for that picture." The message was delivered, and Mr. Agar, thinking the offer advantageous, sent Gainsborough word that he might have the painting on those terms. Gainsborough, very much confused, was compelled to acknowledge that however he might admire it, he could not afford to give so large a sum.

JEMMY CHAMBERS AND THE LADIES.

Mr. G. W. Fulcher, having mentioned to Bernard Barton that he thought of giving a portrait of Jemmy Chambers, the poet, as a frontispiece to his *Ladies'* Pocket Book, Bernard Barton thus wrote in reply :—" Ladies are somewhat fond of pet oddities. An old, tattered, weather-beaten object like old Chambers, is the very thing to take their fancies. Why, when the poor wretch was living, and had located himself hereabouts, his best friends were the ladies. When they stopped to speak to the old man, to be sure they would get to windward of him as a matter of taste, for he was a walking dunghill, poor fellow, most of his wardrobe looking as if it had been picked off some such repositories; and his hands and face bearing evident marks of his antipathy to soap and water. Yet, though he was the very opposite of a lady's lap dog, curled, combed, washed and perfumed, he had his interest—and it was pretty effective too—with the sex. His wretched appearance was sure to appeal to their compassion : the solitary, wandering life he led, his reputed minstrel talent, some little smattering of book learning, which he would now and then display—in short, I might write a regular treatise, giving very philosophical reasons why Chambers was quite a lady's man."

BERNARD BARTON AND POLITICS.

" Politics of any sort, or of all sorts, are not to my taste ; but those connected with electioneering tactics are the most loathsome. I would as soon turn in three in a bed with two like Jemmy Chambers, as go through the endurance of an election at Ipswich or Sudbury. Believe me this is no "*façon de parler*," for I should be truly sorry a dog of mine, for whose respectability I felt the least regard, should be put in nomination for either place."

THE HANDSOME MILLER.

When Constable, the artist, was about sixteen years of age, he was employed in his father's mills, where he performed the duties required of him carefully and well. He was remarkable among the young men of the village for muscular strength; and being tall and well formed, with good features, a fresh complexion, and fine dark eyes, his white hat and coat were not unbecoming to him; and he was called in the neighbourhood the " handsome miller."

CONSTABLE'S GENEROSITY.

It may be doubted whether, under any circumstances, he would have become a rich man by his own exertions; for although he was an early riser, frugal in his habits of living, and not addicted to any vicious extravagance, either of time or money, yet of neither was he an economist. Both were always too readily at the disposal of others. It was as difficult for him to say no to a borrower, as to shut his door against a lounger; still less could he ever resist an appeal to his charity; and if a book or print he wanted came in his way, the chances were that he would buy it, though with the money that should pay for his next day's dinner. He was well aware of this want of resolution, and often formed plans of economy, but failing in a constant and steady adherence to them, they seldom proved of much real advantage to him.

THE BISHOP OF CLOYNE.

The Honorable Frederick Augustus Hervey, son of the Earl of Bristol, was in January, 1768, Bishop of Cloyne; but a

vacancy occurring in the see of Derry, the most valuable
bishopric in Ireland, he was promoted to that see. The
Bishop was amusing himself in feats of activity, with some
of the young men attached to the castle, trying which could
jump the furthest, when a note was put into his hands,
announcing his promotion. On reading this, he exclaimed,
"he would jump no more; he had beaten them all, for he
had jumped from Cloyne to Derry."

GAINSBOROUGH'S "GIRL AND PIGS."

Gainsborough's picture of "Girl and Pigs" attracted great
attention at the Academy exhibition. "The expression
and truth of nature," says Northcote, "were never surpassed. Sir Joshua was struck with it, though he thought
Gainsborough ought to have made her a beauty." Reynolds,
indeed, became the purchaser of the painting, at one hundred
guineas; Gainsborough asked but sixty. During its exhibition it is said to have attracted the attention of a
countryman, who remarked, "They be deadly like pigs,
but nobody ever saw pigs feeding together but one on 'em
had a foot in the trough."

CRABBE AS A YOUTH.

Crabbe delighted in verse from the earliest time that he
could read. He was of a very mild and obliging disposition,
and being the most patient of listeners, he was a great
favourite with the old dames of the place. Like his own
"Richard," many a friendly

> " Matron woo'd him, quickly won
> To fill the station of an absent son."

He admired the rude prints on their walls, rummaged their
shelves for books or ballads, and read aloud to those whose
eyes had failed them, by the winter evening's fire-side.
Walking one day in the street, he chanced to displease a
stout lad who doubled his fist to beat him, but another boy

interfered to claim benefit of clergy for the studious George. " You must not meddle with *him*," he said; " let *him* alone, for he ha' got larning." At an early age—in his tenth year— Crabbe was placed by his father at a boarding-school at Bungay, hoping that the activity of his mind would thus be disciplined into orderly diligence. The first night he spent at Bungay he retired to bed, he said, with a heavy heart, thinking of his fond, indulgent mother. But the morning brought a new misery. The slender and delicate child had hitherto been dressed by his mother. Seeing the other boys begin to dress themselves, poor George, in great confusion, whispered to his bed-fellow, " Master G———, can you put on your shirt? for—for I'm afraid I cannot."

Whilst at this school he had a very narrow escape for his life. He and several of his school-fellows were punished for playing at soldiers by being but into a large dog-kennel, known by the terrible name of the " black hole." George was the first that entered, and the place being crammed full with offenders, the atmosphere soon became pestilentially close. The poor boy in vain shrieked that he should be suffocated. At last, in despair he bit the lad next to him violently in the hand. " Crabbe is dying! Crabbe is dying!" roared the sufferer, and the sentinel at length opened the door and allowed the boys to rush out into the air. After he arrived at manhood, Crabbe remarked on this affair, " A minute more, and I must have died."

CLARKSON AND POETRY.

Bernard Barton had addressed some appropriate verses to Thomas Clarkson, on his labours in the cause of phil- anthropy, and he writes, " I had a note from Catherine Clarkson, thanking me for the lines, which she says she shall treasure up for herself; but her good man is so little of a poetical amateur that when he had a similar tribute once forwarded to him in the form of an ode, the poet was forced *to promise him a prose translation*."

LORD THURLOW AND LORD LOUGHBOROUGH.

Lord Thurlow disliked and made light of Lord Lough-borough, as attested in some good stories. Once, when the latter Lord was making a considerable impression in the House of Lords, on a subject which Lord Thurlow had not studied in detail, the latter was heard to mutter, "If I was not as lazy as a toad at the bottom of a well, I could kick that fellow Loughborough over, heels over head, any day in the week." It was this ceaseless antagonism between Thurlow and Loughborough which led George III to say in a letter to Lord Eldon, just after he had been raised to the woolsack, "The king felt some pleasure at hearing that the Lord Chancellor sat the other day on the woolsack between Rosslyn (formerly Loughborough) and Thurlow, who ever used to require an intermediate power to keep them from quarrelling."

Lord Thurlow told George IV (who repeated it to Lord Eldon) that "the fellow (Lord L.) had *the gift of the gab* in a marvellous degree, but that he was no lawyer," adding, "In the House of Lords I get Kenyon or somebody to start some law doctrine, in such a manner as that fellow must get up to answer it, and then I leave the woolsack, and give him such a thump in his bread-basket that he cannot recover himself." Dr. Johnson, in comparing the two, says:—"I never heard anything from Loughborough that was at all striking; and depend upon it, sir, it is when you come close to a man in conversation that you discover what his real abilities are. To make a speech in a public assembly is a knack. Now I honour Thurlow, sir. Thurlow is a fine fellow; he fairly puts his mind to yours."

THOMAS TUSSER.

Tusser at one time lived at "Brames Hall," Brantham. The common opinion relating to him is that he impoverished himself by experiments, and died poor. Fuller, in his "Worthies" says, that "He traded in oxen, sheep, dairies, grain of all kinds, to no profit. Whether he bought or sold, he lost, and when a renter, impoverished himself and never enriched his landlord. He spread his bread with all sorts of butter, yet none would stick thereon. That his stone which gathered no moss was the stone of Sisyphus." In Peachern's "Minerva," a book of emblems, printed in 1612, there is a device of a whetstone and scythe, with these lines :—

> They tell me, Tusser, when thou were alive,
>   And hadst for profit turned every stone,
> Whene'er thou camest thou could never thrive,
>   Though hereto best could counsel every one,
>   As it may in thy husbandry appear,
>   Wherein afresh thou liv'st among us here.
>   So like thyself a number more are wont
> To sharpen others with advice of wit,
>   When they themselves are like the whetstone blunt.

BISHOP BEDELL.

At the time the Rev. W. Bedell (afterwards Bishop of Kilmore) was lecturer at St. Mary's Church, Bury St. Edmund's, he had as his colleague the Rev. Samuel Southeby, a man of very opposite pulpit abilities. Of Mr. Bedell it was said, "that he made the most obscure passages of Scripture very plain ;" and of Mr. Southeby, "that he made the plainest portions of Scripture obscure."

PROFESSOR HENSLOW.

When Professor Henslow was presented to the rectory of Hitcham, he found himself pastor over a large, scattered, and neglected population. His predecessor in the pulpit was a man of a very different stamp to the Professor. He was an easy going clergyman, whom the farmers and labourers deemed " a jolly good fellow." At his annual tithe feast, he took great delight in seeing the farmers indulge themselves beyond the bounds of temperance. He always sang the first song, the burden of which was—

> " He that drinks stong beer, and goes to bed mellow,
>   Lives as he ought to live, and dies a hearty fellow."

The sentiments thus endorsed by the parson, were loudly cheered by his parishioners ; and as may be supposed, under such a shepherd, the moral and spiritual condition of the flock was at a low ebb.   Although Professor Henslow introduced some excellent plans for social improvement, he had to labour for several years amid much opposition before he saw among his parishioners that amount of industry and self-respect which he could look upon as a reward for his labours.

REV. JOHN CARTER.

This puritan divine had a fair share of humour. He said a traveller should have swine's belly, an ass's back, and a merchant's purse. His meaning was that he must put up with all sorts of diet, bear all kinds of injuries, and be prepared for heavy expenses.

He died calmly, and without a struggle, on the sabbath morning of the 22nd February, 1634, having the day previously expressed his intention to preach twice on that day. He would have no funeral sermon, and left orders to be buried, not in the church, but in the churchyard, under a common tombstone, on which the following inscription was placed :—

HERE
UNDER THIS STONE LYETH
HID A RICH TREASURE,
THE PRECIOUS DUST OF THAT
HOLY MAN, THAT BURNING
AND SHINING LIGHT,
MR. JOHN CARTER, FIRST
PASTOR OF BRAMFORD,
AND AFTERWARDS OF
BELSTEAD, IN SUFFOLK,
WITH ESTHER, HIS FAITHFUL COMFORT,
BOTH OF THEM
WAITING FOR A BLESSED
RESURRECTION.

ROBERT BLOOMFIELD.

Soon after the publication of " The Farmer's Boy," Bloomfield's fame was so great that his company was courted, and himself "lionised," in London society. Blue-stocking ladies invited him to their soireés, and aristocratic men enveloped him in a patronising atmosphere. The humble shoemaker was often drawn from his garret in Coleman's Alley, to the gilded saloons in Belgravia—he left the awl and the lapstone to dine off plate and porcelain. He was caressed, flattered, and, in some instances, extravagantly praised. The Duke of Grafton invited him to his mansion. The Earl of Buchan desired a pair of shoes made by Bloomfield's own hands. Many other titled men applauded and rewarded, but most of them treated Bloomfield as a prodigy, or a toy which would yield amusement. Sir Charles Bunbury, however, with all his sporting predilections, remained a true friend of the poet. Bloomfield's financial position having greatly improved, he removed to better lodgings, and eventually took a house in the City Road, where, in addition to his regular trade as a shoemaker, he manufactured and sold Æolian harps, many of which were purchased by persons desirous of helping the poet, and who thus delicately diminished the obligation which a pecuniary gift might have been supposed to create.

BISHOP AYLMER.

Aylmer, Bishop of London, was well known for his oddity of speech; and on some occasions he was equally odd in his conduct. Whilst he was at court, in 1578, he found her Majesty, Queen Elizabeth, suffering very severely from tooth-ache. Extraction had been advised by the medical attendant as the only remedy, but the Queen was very averse to the operation. To encourage her to submit, Aylmer sat down in her presence, and had one of his own teeth drawn, though, being an old man, he had not a tooth to spare.

LADY SARAH BUNBURY.

Lady Sarah, the youngest daughter of the second Duke of Richmond, was born in 1745, and it is said that when sixteen she refused an offer of marriage made her by George III., but that she ultimately accepted him. Kensington traditions describe Lady Sarah as making hay in the fields, then bordering the road, and exchanging a word or two with the young prince, as he rode by. But the royal lover deceived her, and she, instead of being bride at his wedding, was only a bridesmaid. Lady Sarah was speedily consoled, for the year after the union of King George and Charlotte, she married, at the age of eighteen, the sporting baronet, Sir Thomas Charles Bunbury. Subsequently, at the mature age of thirty-six, Lady Sarah married, in 1781, the Hon. George Napier, son of Francis, fifth Lord Napier; and the first child of which she was the mother, was the "Sir Charles Napier," the hero of Scinde.

DR. BLOMFIELD AND NEWMARKET RACES.

While Dr. Blomfield was rector of Chesterford, it was the permanent annoyance of every Easter day, that a stream of carriages was passing through the village, giving it the appearance and too much the reality of a noisy fair, while conveying the racing men of the day to Newmarket. The aristocratic sporting men would drive up to the inn in open carriages, playing at whist, and throwing out their cards, would call to the waiter for fresh packs. To remove the scandal, the Jockey Club were induced, after great pressure, to alter the first day of the meeting to Easter Tuesday. Bishop Howley, at the desire of Dr. Blomfield, applied to the Duke of York, but the duke declined to alter his practice of going on a Sunday, saying, "Though it was true he travelled to the races on Sunday, *he always had a Bible and Prayer Book in the carriage !*"

THAT "FELLOW" GAINSBOROUGH.

George III. had marked at the Academy's annual exhibitions the beauty of Gainsborough's works, and before the painter had been many months in London, he received a summons to the palace. It was soon known that the King and Queen had sat to Gainsborough. Peers and Commoners were not slow to follow the royal example. Commissions for portraits now flowed in so fast, that with all his rapidity of execution and untiring industry, he was unable to satisfy the impatience of some of his sitters. One gentleman lost his temper, and inquired of the artist's porter, in a voice loud enough to be overheard, "Has that fellow Gainsborough finished my portrait?" Ushered into the painting room he beheld his picture. After expressing his approbation, he requested it might be sent home at once, adding, "I may as well give you a cheque for the other fifty guineas." "Stay a minute," says Gainsborough, "it just wants the finishing stroke;" and snatching up a back-ground brush, he dashed it across the smiling features, indignantly exclaiming, "Sir, where is my *fellow* now?"

SIR THOMAS HANMER.

Sir Thomas Hanmer was one of the most independent men that ever sat as a representative for the county of Suffolk. He was the Gladstone of his age. Like him, he was one of the most graceful and accomplished speakers of his day; like him, he was implicitly trusted by the High Church party; like him, the ascendancy of the Church of England outweighed in his mind the divine right of kings, and the legitimate succession to the Crown. As a politician, he was exceedingly cautious and reserved. Pope appears to stigmatise him as a Trimmer, in the lines—

> "Courtiers and patriots in two ranks divide:
> Through both he passed, and bowed from side to side."

But there does not appear to be good ground for the censure. He cared not for office, but he evidently liked to be the head of an independent party; and patriotism with him consisted mainly in upholding the landed interest, and the ascendancy of the English Church.

After he retired from Parliamentary duties and political

struggles, he resided chiefly in the country, occupying his
time by literary pursuits, and amusing himself by gardening.
His garden at Mildenhall was celebrated for the quality of
its grapes, and Sir Thomas used to send every year, hampers
filled with these grapes, *and carried on men's shoulders, to
London* (nearly seventy miles), as his offering to the queen.

In private life Sir Thomas Hanmer was much respected,
and he would have gone to the grave happy as well as
honoured, if it had not been for his unfortunate second
marriage. It was said of him that he married an old woman
for love and a young woman for money, and was not very
fortunate in either of them. The elopement of his second
wife, the vexatious claims of her child, and the book which
Mr. Hervey published, tended to embitter the last years of
the baronet's life. He is said to have been strict but just
towards his tenants, and they respected him ; kind and liberal
towards the poor, and they loved him. Traditional information as to the personal appearance and manners of Sir
Thomas, exhibits very forcibly the minutely true touch in
that line of Pope—

"There moved Montalto with *superior air.*"

The Baronet in his latter days is described as a portly old
gentleman, of a very stately carriage, accustomed to walk
solemnly to church twice on every Sunday, followed by all
his servants, and moving from his iron gates to the porch of
the church between two ranks of his tenants and adherents,
who stood hat in hand, bowing reverently low, while the
great man acknowledged their salutations by a few words and
dignified condescension.

HONEST TOM MARTIN.

Honest Tom Martin, the antiquary of Palgrave, lost his
wife in 1731, ten days after she had been delivered of twins,
leaving him, who was domestically a helpless man, surrounded by a family of six children. The antiquary, however,

soon repaired this loss, as well as he was able, by marrying
Frances, widow of Peter Le Neve, Norry king-at-arms, then
living at Great Witchingham. There is a well authenticated
anecdote which proves this *courtship* to have been a very
curious affair. Mr. Martin was acting as executor to the late
Peter Le Neve, when one morning, having been intently occupied in looking over the MSS. of his deceased friend, he
was summoned by the widow to dinner. He raised himself
suddenly, and throwing himself back in his chair, stretched
out his arms, and as it were yawned out, " O yes, O yes,
who'll have me and my six children ? " " That will I, Mr.
Martin, if I like those which I have not seen, as well as those
which I have seen ; " and they were married so shortly after
that event that Sir James Burrough, Master of Caius, had
not had time to have his mourning completed for the lost wife,
before he heard of the approaching nuptials with the second.
By this marriage, Mr. Martin came into the possession of a
very valuable collection of English antiquities and pictures.

LORD CHEDWORTH.

Lord Chedworth was in the habit of wearing top-boots,
and he wore them so bare that almost any person would have
been ashamed of them. When *new* boots were sent home,
he was accustomed to set them on one side, and get his man-
servant to wear them a short time, to prepare them for his
own feet. Sometimes the man would tell his Lordship that
he thought the boots were ready, but his Lordship would
generally reply, " Never mind, William, wear them another
week."

His Lordship's legal attainments and well-known generous
disposition caused him, whilst he resided in Ipswich, to be
frequently consulted by tradesmen and others in indigent
circumstances, for legal advice. The applicants were ushered
into the library, where, surrounded by books, they found
him seated at a table. The chairs and furniture of the room,
like his Lordship's clothes, had not merely seen their best

c

days, but were comparatively worthless, and the old *red cloak* which invariably enveloped his shoulders, made him look more like a gipsy hag than a peer of the realm.

THE LAST EARL OF DYSART.

Wilbraham Tollemache, the last Earl of Dysart, was most devotedly attached to his Countess, who died September 14th, 1804. The Earl continued to wear mourning for her until the day of his death, and for many years her place at table was arranged as if she was expected to occupy it. One day there was more company than he had anticipated, and he quietly took the place himself, and ever afterwards made use of it.

The Earl chiefly divided his time between the mansion at Helmingham, and the beautiful Marine Villa at Steephill, in the Isle of Wight. Ham House, in Surrey, he only occasionally visited, as he seemed to have a dislike to that charming spot, and sometimes called it the *death* house, as all the family died there, and singularly enough he died there himself. He usually came to Helmingham in March, and stayed until the end of August, exercising all the bounty of an old English gentleman. A yeomanry volunteer corps was raised about 1799 at the expense of the Earl, and whenever they met for exercise there was always " open house at the hall." Upon one grand field day the Dowager Countess presented the corps with a pair of colours. The Earl was Colonel ; but although he had his uniform made he invariably attended in mourning. One day he complimented one of the men, named Noble, who beat the great drum, by saying, " Noble, you played well." The man answered, " I know it, my Lord ;" and this became a bye-word in the district for years afterwards.

MRS. ELIZABETH COBBOLD.

Miss Elizabeth Cobbold, a lady well known as one of the leaders of the literary, artistic, and fashionable circles in Ipswich, during the first quarter of the present century, married in her twenty-third year, William Clarke, Esq., of Ipswich, a gentleman twice her own age, by whose death she became a widow within six months of her marriage. Her sentiments towards Mr. Clarke, and her indifference to the remarks which the disparity of years had occasioned, may be collected from the following lively verses, which she addressed to him on St. Valentine's day, soon after their marriage :—

" Eliza to William this valentine send,
  While every good wish on the present attend ;
  And freely she writes, undisturb'd by a fear,
  Tho' prudes may look scornful, and libertines sneer.
  Tho' talkers and tale-bearers smiling may say,
  ' Your geniuses always are out of the way ;
  Sure none but herself would such levities mix
  With the seriousness suited to grave twenty-six.
  A wife send a valentine! Lord, what a whim!
  And then, of all people, to send it to him—
  Make love to her husband ! my stars, how romantic !
  The girl must be certainly foolish or frantic !
  But I always thought so, else what could engage
  Her to marry a man who is twice her own age ?'
  While the tabbies are thus on my motives enlarging,
  My sentiments, William, may read in the margin.
  On the wings of old time have three months past away,
  Since I promis'd ' to honour, to love, and obey,'
  And surely my William's own heart will allow
  That my conduct has ne'er disagreed with my vow.
  Would health spread her wings round my husband and lord,
  To his cheeks could the smile of delight be restor'd,
  The blessing with gratitude I should receive,
  As the greatest that mercy benignant should give,
  And heedless of all that conjecture may say,
  With praise would remember St. Valentine's day."

OLIVER CROMWELL'S GRANDDAUGHTER.

Mrs. Bridget Bendish, the daughter of Bridget Cromwell, the Protector's eldest daughter, and Commissary General Ireton, resided for many years at South Town, near Yarmouth. During her childhood she lived for a long time at her grandfather's home, and became a special favourite of his. When she was only six years of age she has sat between his knees when he has held a cabinet council even on very important affairs. Some of the council objected to her being present, when he said, " There was no secret he would trust with any of them which he would not trust with that infant; " and to prove that he was not mistaken, he has told her something as in confidence, and under the charge of secrecy, and then asked her mother and grandmother to try and obtain it from her. All their efforts to extort it proved useless. She held steady against promises, bribes, and threats, and became at a very tender age a proficient in the art of keeping secrets. During her whole life she was an eccentric and enthusiastic woman, and thoroughly idolised the memory of her grandfather. During a violent fever, and at a time when it was thought she was not sensible of what was passing around her, her aunt, Lady Fauconburg, and other persons, were one day in her bed-room, and her Ladyship, though Oliver's daughter, did not resent things said by some present in dishonour to Cromwell's memory. Mrs. Bendish, to the astonishment of all, raised herself up, and with great spirit, said, " If I did not believe my grandmother to have been the most virtuous woman in the world, I should conclude your Ladyship to be a bastard ; for I wonder how the daughter of the greatest man that ever lived can not only sit with patience, and hear his memory ill-treated, but seem herself to assent to it."

REV. WILLIAM LAYTON.

Anecdotes are said to be the best illustration of character, and there are a number afloat relating to the bachelor life, the artless disposition, and the inclination to eccentricity of the Rev. William Layton, who was for many years rector of St. Matthew's, Ipswich. He had all the simplicity of character which usually accompany gifted minds, and was often sadly annoyed at little things. He could not bear the creaking of a door, and when such a noise grated on his ear, he was sure to ask for oil and feather, which he instantly applied to remove the nuisance; and the sight of a book "dog's eared," irritated him very much. Though by no means a rigid Sabbatarian, he had a great dislike to seeing things exposed for sale on a Sunday. One morning, before service, whilst walking at the end of the Butter Market, he saw a sheep's head hanging out for sale. With his stick he lifted the sheep's head off the hook, laid it on the pavement, and walked on without further notice. A stall for the sale of vegetables and fruit, near the King's Head Inn, was a terrible eyesore to the reverend gentleman. It was simply a shutter in the old-fashioned style, hinged on at the bottom of the window, and transformed into a stall by a leg which, resting on the ground, kept it at the height of a table. One Sunday morning, the parson with his foot knocked away the support of the shutter, and down went the apples and vegetables, seriously inconveniencing and annoying the greengrocer. Mr. Layton's scruples of conscience did not prevent his employing a baker to provide him with a hot dinner on Sundays. The greengrocer knowing this, resolved on giving a "Roland for an Oliver." He watched for the parson's dinner that day, and just before it reached home he thrust some fine ribs of beef off the board on to the pavement, and marched off, chuckling with glee at having thus balanced accounts with his clerical neighbour.

SIR HARVEY ELWES, THE MISER.

Sir Harvey Elwes lived at Stoke, near Clare, the most perfect picture of human misery that ever existed. He succeeded Sir Jervaise Elwes, a generous and well-disposed gentleman, who had "lived beyond his means," and had in consequence so burthened the estates, that when Sir Harvey inherited the property he found himself nominally possessed of some thousands a year, but really with an income of *one hundred pounds per annum*. On his arrival at the family seat, at Stoke, Sir Harvey declared that he would never "leave it

till he had entirely cleared the paternal estate," and he lived
to do it, and to realize above *one hundred thousand pounds* in
addition.

The miserly disposition was constitutional in Sir Harvey.
In his youth he was considered likely to become a victim to
that great English malady, consumption, and was even given
over as lost. He did not, however, lose his life, but he lost
his constitution and power of enjoyment. Yet, strange to say,
his penurious mode of living and regular habits sustained
him to a patriarchal age. His passions were as dormant as
his constitution. He was timid, shy, and diffident in the
extreme; of a thin, spare habit of body, and without a friend
on earth. He had no acquaintances, possessed no books, had
no desire for reading, and, in fact, for more than sixty years,
lived almost alone. With the true avaricious spirit, he loved
to see and handle his gold; the hoarding up and the counting
of his money was his delight—the ringing of his guineas his
greatest joy. The next to that was *partridge setting*, at which
he was so great an adept, that he and his man have been known
to take *five hundred brace of birds* in one season! Sir Harvey's
household consisted of one man and two maids, and they, as
well as himself, nearly lived upon partridges and fish from
his own ponds. What they could not eat he turned out
again, as he never gave anything away.

FUNERAL OF A CLERICAL RATIONALIST.

The arrangements for the funeral of the Rev. James Ford,
which were made according to his own directions, exhibited,
to a certain degree, that tinge of eccentricity which pervaded
his character, and that freedom from conventional habits,
which throughout life distinguished his career. But they are
more worthy of notice for their strong protest against the
pompous and extravagant funeral trappings, which charac-
terize the present age. Mr. Ford was buried three days after
his decease, in a plain oaken coffin, without inscription, which
was borne by twelve labourers of his parish, each in a new

suit of clothes left for the purpose. No pall was used, but in place of it a very handsome table cloth, which, after the service, was presented to the officiating minister. According to strict orders left under his own hand, the mourners followed in coloured clothes; and his own servant, who was also his clerk, was presented with a new suit, not of black, but of livery. No hat-bands or scarfs were given away, but in lieu of these funeral trappings the sum of £50 was distributed, in amounts of ten shillings each, to one hundred of the poor of the parish.

CONSTABLE AND THE FIELD MOUSE.

Leslie, in writing of Constable's conversation, remarks, " I remember to have heard him say, 'When I sit down to make a sketch from nature, the first thing I try to do is *to forget that I have ever seen a picture;* ' " and it is related as a curious proof of the stillness with which he used to sit whilst painting in the open air, that one day a field mouse was found in his pocket.

SIR JOHN SUCKLING, THE POET.

Sir John Suckling, the poet, whose gay and easy ballads are familiar to every lover of poetry, and whose "Sessions of the Poets" has been imitated by numberless writers, was one of those wealthy cavaliers in the reign of the first Charles, who risked their fortunes and their lives in the royal cause. His frankness of manner, gracefulness of person, and elegance of address, soon rendered him famous at the luxurious court of Charles. His love of amusement and taste for display were so great that one of the entertainments which he gave at his house is said to have cost him several thousand pounds. With this love for amusements Sir John unhappily combined pursuits of a more odious character. He became enamoured of play, and was soon known as one of the best bowlers and card players in the kingdom. It is said that he was so enraptured by the fascination of play

that he would frequently lie in bed the greater part of the
day with a pack of cards before him, to obtain by practice
the most perfect knowledge and management of their powers.

ADVERTISEMENT FOR A WIFE.

A man named Thomas Sadler, who resided for many years
in the parish of St. Peter, Ipswich, was after the decease of
his mother advised by some of his boon companions to ad-
vertise for a wife. He in consequence sat down and penned
the following poetical epistle, which was inserted in one of
the Ipswich newspapers :—

"ADDRESS TO THE SUFFOLK FEMALES.

" Wanted immediately as a wife
And a partner throughout life,
One that is in temper mild--
As meek and gentle as a child ;
One that's healthy, young, and strong,
And will not vex me with her tongue ;
One that's not o'er nice in dress,
No more than humble cleanliness ;
One that's not o'erwhelmed with care,
Nor e'er will drive me to despair ;
One that won't abroad be straying,
Nor know no bed but what we lay in ;
One that's not o'erwhelmed with riches,
Nor e'er will want to wear the breeches,
But with me, in my humble state,
Strive to be happy, in whatever fate
May on us fall in this short life,
Meanwhile that we are man and wife ;
For swift the hours of pleasure fly
When love's entwined with constancy ;
But when once sullied by a jealous strife,
Slow moves the hours of a bitter life.
A virtuous wife is an honor to her birth ;
A discontented wife is a hell on earth.
Now any lass whose will incline,
And wish to know where she may find

The man who is so much inclined
To enter in this happy state,
I my abode will now relate.
> I a native am of Ipswich town,
> My name in here I won't put down,
> But if to find me out you are inclined,
> Come over Stoke, and there you will me find,
> In a house where I was born and bred,
> Well nigh unto the Boar's Head.

In the columns of the same journal, a week after the insertion of the above, the following reply appeared :—

"ADDRESS TO THE SUFFOLK BACHELOR.

"SIR,—

> "A young lady from Norfolk has read your petition,
> And is highly concerned at your woful condition,
> But the reason for that you yourself have betrayed,
> Your head is too nigh a Boar's Head, I'm afraid ;
> And so, if from Suffolk you look for a wife,
> Get away from that hog for the rest of your life,
> For what Suffolk female, though ever so poor,
> Would look for a husband so nigh to a Boar ? "

"THE SENSE OF THE PARISH."

In 1822 Dr. Whately, the future Archbishop, accepted the pastoral charge of Halesworth, in Suffolk. Whilst residing there he seems to have known more of the plagues than of the "recreations" of a country parson. Rector Whately wanted on one occasion to divert a footpath. Probably he did not know what a violation of all public notions of right he was contemplating. His churchwardens came to him half in alarm, half in triumph, to tell him that "the sense of the parish was dead against him." Whately was a little amazed, but having made up his mind to his discomfiture, went to his vestry plainly to say so, talked the matter over with a good deal of geniality, and just a little "chaff"; and it appeared the "sense" of the parish consisted after all of a bumpkin sort of landowner, a gossiping apothecary, and three patriots fresh from the public-house.

ARCHBISHOP WHATELY AND THE AIDE-DE-CAMP.

The caustic way in which Archbishop Whately snubbed a young aide-de-camp who at one of the castle levees asked, apropos of Dr. Murray, who wore a cross: "What was the difference between a Roman bishop and a jackass?" was very characteristic. "One wears the cross upon his back and the other upon his breast," explained the aide-de-camp. "Do *you* know the difference between an aide-de-camp and a donkey?" ask Dr. Whately. "No?" said the other, interrogatively. "Nor I either," was the reply.

LORD THURLOW'S START IN LIFE.

Thurlow had travelled the circuit for some years with little notice, and with no opportunity to put forth his abilities, when the housekeeper of the Duke of N—— was prosecuted for stealing a quantity of linen with which she had been entrusted. An attorney of little note and practice conducted the woman's case. He knew full well that he could not expect hearty co-operation by employing any of the leading counsel. It was a poor case, and a low case, and it could not be anticipated that they, "the foremost men of all the Bar," would set themselves tooth and nail against the Duke, who in himself, his agents, and his friends, made the greatest part of every high, legal, and political assemblage in the county. The attorney looked round, therefore, for some young barrister who had nothing to lose, and might have something to win, and he fixed upon Thurlow, who read over the brief with the highest glee, and had an interview with the prisoner. As he entered the Court, he jogged the briefless one, and said, in his favourite slang language—"Neck or nothing, my boy, to-day; I'll soar or tumble." The opening speech of the eminent counsel for the Duke, and the evidence, completely convicted the woman; but Thurlow, by his withering cross-examination of the witnesses, his sneers at the Duke and Duchess, and his powerful address to the jury upon the "grovelling prosecution," triumphed. The woman was acquitted, and from that day the powers of Thurlow in voice, sarcasm, gesture, and all the superior intonations of brow-beating, which raised him to the most dangerous pinnacle of legal greatness, became known, and rapidly advanced him to fame, and caused the grand-children of his father to be enrolled among the established peers of the realm.

CRABBE'S SIMPLICITY OF CHARACTER.

Whilst Crabbe was on a visit, during the autumn of his days, to Mrs. Hoare, of Hampstead, Mrs. Joannie Baillie, for whom he had a high esteem, sent him one day the present of a black cock, and a message with it, that Mr. Crabbe should look at the bird before it was delivered to the cook, or something to that purpose. He looked at the bird, as desired, and then went to Mrs. Hoare in some perplexity, to ask whether he ought not to have it stuffed instead of eating it. She could not in her own house tell him that it was simply intended for the larder, and he was at the trouble and expense of having it stuffed, lest Mrs. Joannie Baillie should think that sufficient respect had not been paid to her present.

In June, 1819, the "Tales of the Hall" were published by Mr. Murray, who for them and the remaining copyright of all Crabbe's poems, gave the munificent sum of £3000. When Crabbe, who was staying in London, received the bills for this amount, Moore and Rogers earnestly advised him to deposit them without delay in some safe hands—but no; he must "take them with him to Trowbridge, and show them to his son John. They would hardly believe in his good luck at home, if they did not see the bills." On his way down to Trowbridge, a friend at Salisbury, at whose house he rested (Mr. Everett, the banker), seeing that he carried these bills loosely in his waistcoat pocket, requested to be allowed to take charge of them; but with equal ill success. "There was no fear," he said, "of his losing them; and he must show them to his son John."

COMPLIMENTS TO JOHN CONSTABLE'S ART.

When Fuseli was looking at Constable's picture of "Salisbury Cathedral," at the Academy exhibition, in 1823, he said, "I like de landscapes of Constable : he is always picturesque—of a fine colour, and de lights always in de right places ; but he makes me call for my great coat and umbrella." And the inimitable Jack Bannister, who sat as a model to Leslie for "Uncle Toby," called upon Constable in 1825, to request a landscape, as he said he had long desired one from which " he could feel the wind blowing on his face."

LYING GOES BY DISTRICTS.

Bishop Blomfield used to tell a story of one clergyman whom he had reproved for certain irregularities of conduct, which had been brought under his notice by his parishioners, and who had replied—"Your Lordship, as a classical scholar, knows that lying goes by districts : the Cretans were liars— the Capadocians were liars ; and I can assure your Lordship that the inhabitants of ——— are liars also."

CLERGYMEN ON DUTY.

Whilst Dr. Blomfield was Bishop, he said that intoxication was the most frequent charge against the clergy. One was so drunk whilst waiting for a funeral, that he fell into the grave ; another was conveyed away from a visitation dinner in a helpless state by the Bishop's own servants. A third, when rebuked for drunkenness, replied—"But, my Lord, I never was drunk on duty." "On duty !" exclaimed the Bishop ; "when is a clergyman not on duty ?" "True," said the other ; "I never thought of that."

BERNARD BARTON AND THE PLAYERS.

In 1822, there was a party of English actors performing plays at Paris. One evening, an actor of the name of "Barton" was announced, and some of the audience immediately called out, inquiring if it was the Quaker poet.

GAINSBOROUGH AND REYNOLDS.

When Gainsborough was lying on his death bed, he felt that there was one whom he had not treated with courtesy—it was Sir Joshua Reynolds. The president's unfinished portrait seemed to look reproachfully upon him; and the feeling that there was between them, the relationship of genius, induced him to write to Sir Joshua, expressing a desire to see him once more before he died. "If any little jealousies had subsisted between us," says Reynolds, "they were forgotten in these moments of sincerity; and he turned towards me as one who was engrossed by the same pursuits, and who deserved his good opinion, by being sensible of his excellence." It is a solemn scene, that death chamber—the two great painters side by side, forgetful of the past, but not unmindful of the future. Gainsborough says that he fears not death; that his regret at losing life is principally the regret of leaving his art, more especially as he now began to see what his deficiencies were, which he thought in his last works were in some measure supplied. The wave of life heaves to and fro. Reynolds bends his dull ear to catch Gainsborough's failing words— "We are all going to heaven; and Vandyke is of the company."

GAINSBOROUGH'S "BLUE BOY."

Sir Joshua Reynolds had maintained in one of his discourses, "that the masses of light in a picture should be always of a warm, mellow colour: yellow, red, or a yellowish-white; and that the blue, the grey, or the green colours should be kept almost entirely out of these masses, and be used only to support and set off these warm colours." To refute the President's objection to blue in the mass, Gainsborough, in 1779, clothed a full length portrait of Master Buttall in a dress approaching to cerulean splendour. The propriety of this has been the subject of much debate. Dr. Waagen remarks:—"In spite of the blue dress, Gainsborough has succeeded in producing a harmonious and pleasing effect; nor can it be doubted that in the cool scale of colours, in

which blue acts the chief part, there are very tender and
pleasing harmonies, which Sir Joshua, with his way of seeing,
could not appreciate." The author of " A Handbook for
Young Painters," however, says—" I agree with the opinion
of Sir Thomas Lawrence, that in this picture the difficulty is
rather ably combated than vanquished. Indeed it is not even
fairly combated, for Gainsborough has so mellowed and broken
the blue with other tints, that it is no longer that pure bleak
colour Sir Joshua meant; and after all, though the picture is
a very fine one, it cannot be doubted that a warmer tint for
the dress would have made it still more agreeable to the eye."

QUEEN CAROLINE AND THE REV. WILLIAM WHISTON.

The Rev. William Whiston was much esteemed by Queen
Caroline, consort of George II., who generously made him a
present of £50 every year from the time she became Queen;
and she usually sent for him every summer to spend a day or
two with her. Once, whilst at Richmond, she asked him
what people in general said of her. He replied that they
justly esteemed her as a lady of great abilities, as a patron of
learned men, and a kind friend to the poor. "But," says she,
"no one is without faults—pray what are mine?" He begged
to be excused speaking on that subject, but she insisting, he
said, " Her Majesty did not behave with proper reverence at
church." She replied, " That the king would talk to her."
He said, "A greater than kings was there to be regarded
only." She acknowledged and confessed her fault. "Pray,"
said she, "tell me what is my next." He replied, "When
I hear that your Majesty has amended that fault, I will tell
you of your next."

LORD KEEPER BACON.

Sir Nicholas Bacon lived at Redgrave Hall, and at this
seat Queen Elizabeth visited him in September, 1559, in
August, 1560, and in July and August, 1561. On one of
these occasions her Majesty remarked, " My Lord, what a

little house you have got here." He answered, "Madam, my house is well enough, but your Highness has made me too great for my house."

Lord Campbell, in enumerating some anecdotes to show that Lord Keeper Bacon was no contemptible jester, says of him, "Once, going the northern circuit as Judge, before he had the Great Seal, he was about to pass sentence on a thief convicted before him, when the prisoner, after various pleas had been overruled, asked for mercy on account of kindred. " Prithee," said my Lord Judge, " how comes this about? " " Why, if it please you, my Lord, your name is *Bacon*, and mine is *Hog*, and in all ages *Hog* and *Bacon* have been so near kindred that they are not to be separated." " Ay, but," replied the Judge, " you and I cannot be kindred except you be hanged, for *Hog* is not *Bacon* until it be well *hanged*." Unfortunately for the truth of Lord Campbell's anecdote, Sir Nicholas Bacon never officiated as Judge of Assize.

CHIEF JUSTICE HOLT AND A PRISONER.

It is related of Chief Justice Holt, that being once on the Bench at the Old Bailey, a fellow was tried and convicted of a robbery on the highway whom the Judge remembered to have been one of his old companions, at the time he was a wild youth. He was moved by that curiosity which is natural on the retrospection of past life, to know the fortune of those with whom he was once associated, and of whom he had known nothing for many years; he therefore asked the fellow what was become of Tom such a one, and Will such a one, and the rest of the knot to which they belonged. The fellow, fetching a deep sigh, and making a low bow, said, " Ah! my Lord, they are *all hanged but your Lordship and I.*"

BOYHOOD OF LIEUTENANT SHIPP.

Lieutenant Shipp, of the 76th regiment, was born at Saxmundham, and left an orphan at an early age. As he grew up to boyhood, he became known as a wild dog of unconquerable spirit—always ready to plan or to execute mischief. One morning, whilst playing marbles in "Love Lane," martial music from fife and drum struck on his ear. Instantly bagging his marbles, he scampered off to see the soldiers, whom he found to be a "recruiting party" of the royal artillery, who, decked out with flaunting ribbons, were trying to induce the Johnny Raws of the district to "enter the service of King George." The finery and the music were such attractions to his youthful fancy, that he, after due consideration, strutted up to the sergeant, and asked him if he would "take I for a sodger," to the great amusement of the company. It was not long after this adventure, that he went to live as cow-boy to a farmer in Saxmundham, whose heart was as cold as the hoar-frost, which sometimes blighted his prospects. The boy was so mischievous in his propensities, and the master so tyrannical in his inclinations, that the youngster tasted the lash almost as frequently as his supper. The recruiting party had upset the poor boy's brains, and the desire to wear his Majesty's livery was uppermost in his mind. The hoes and rakes were transformed into muskets, and the geese and turkeys into soldiers, to gratify the cow-boy's propensity for military exercises. He was always whistling "God save the King," or "The British Grenadiers," and was once caught riding the old sow, pitchfork in hand, singing at the same time, "See the Conquering Hero comes."

ONE QUAKER COOK.

The Rev. Charles B. Tayler, having applied to Bernard Barton for a cook, the poet writes in reply:—"I am requested to say that we are quite unable to recommend thee a cook of any kind ; as to Quaker cooks, they are so scarce that we Quaker folk are compelled to call in the aid of the daughters of the land, to dress our own viands, or cook them ourselves as well as we can. But what, my dear friend, could put it into thy head to think of a Quaker cook, of all nondescripts ?

Charles Lamb would have told thee better: he says he never could have relished even the salads Eve dressed for the angels in Eden—his appetite is too highly excited 'to sit a guest with Daniel at his pulse.' Go to! thou art a wag, Charles; and this is only a sly way of hinting that we are fond of good living. But, perhaps, after all, more of compliment than of inuendo is implied in the proposition. Thou thoughtest we were civil, cleanly, quiet, etc., all excellent qualities, doubtless, in women of all kinds, cooks not excluded. But, my dear friend, I should be sorry the reputation of our sect, for the possession of those qualities, should be exposed to the contingent vexations which culinary mortals are especially exposed to. 'A cook whilst cooking is a sort of fury,' says the old poet. Ay! but not a Quaker cook, at least in the favourable and friendly opinion of Adine and thyself; we are proud of that good opinion, and I would not risk its forfeiture by sending one of our sisterhood to thee as a cook. Suppose an avalanche of soot to plump down the chimney the first gala day—'twould be Cookship *versus* Quakership whether the poor body kept her sectarian serenity unruffled; and suppose the beam kicked the wrong way, what would become of all our reputation in the temporary good opinion of Adine and thee? But all badinage apart; even in our own Society there are comparatively few who are in the situation of domestic servants, and I *never remember but one in the peculiar office referred to.*

DRESS AND FURNITURE OF SIR HARVEY ELWES.

Sir Harvey Elwes's predecessor had been so lavish in dress that the new Baronet found lots of clothes, which he undertook to wear up; and it is believed that Sir Jervaise's garments were used by Sir Harvey until the day of his death. He was generally seen with a black velvet cap pulled over his face, so as to form a good shade to the eyes; a worn-out, full-dressed suit, and an old great coat, with worsted stockings drawn up over his knees. He rode a thin, thorough-bred

D

horse, and " the horse and its rider " both looked as if a gust of wind would have blown them away together.

The furniture in the mansion at Stoke was most sacredly unique. Not a room was painted, not a window repaired. The beds were all in canopy and state, but the miserable Baronet let the worms and moths have undisturbed sway, and the roof of the house was more adapted to the climate of Italy than that of England. The fuel consumed in the house was supplied by his woods ; and if a farmer in the neighbourhood called, Sir Harvey would strike a light in a tinder-box, that he kept by him, and putting one single stick in the grate, would not add another until the first was nearly burnt out. When the day was not fine enough to tempt him abroad, he would walk backwards and forwards in his old hall, to save the expense of a fire ; and after taking a basin of *water gruel* in the evening, he went to bed, to save the unnecessary extravagance of a candle.

ADVANTAGES AND DISADVANTAGES OF TRAVELLING.

In a letter from Marseilles, Mrs. Barbauld, in 1785, thus amusingly sums up the advantages and disadvantages of travelling :—

ADVANTAGES OF TRAVELLING.	PER CONTRA.
A July sun and a southern breeze.	Flies, fleas, and all Pharoah's plague of vermin.
Figs, almonds, etc., etc.	No tea, and the very name of tea-kettle unknown.
Sweet scents in the fields.	Bad scents within doors.
Grapes and raisins.	No plum pudding.
Coffee as cheap as milk.	Milk as dear as coffee.
Wine a demi sous the bottle.	Bread three sous the halfpenny roll.
Provençal songs and laughter.	Provençal roughness and scolding.
Soup, salad, and oil.	No beef, no butter.
Arches of triumph, fine churches, stately palaces.	Dirty inns, heavy roads, uneasy carriages.
A pleasant and varied country.	But many, many a league from those we love.

PERSEVERANCE OF BISHOP BLOMFIELD WHEN A YOUTH.

The father of Bishop Blomfield was a schoolmaster at Bury St. Edmund's. Under his tuition, the future Bishop acquired the rudiments of latin; and at the age of eight, he was transferred to the Grammar School in the same town. He was at this time a very delicate boy, and subject to affections of the chest, for which the air of Bury was too keen. He used to climb up the stairs by the help of the banisters, and on account of his diminutive size, was nick-named by his schoolfellows *Tit* Blomfield. But he gave early promise of the ability and industry which marked his whole subsequent life; and during the ten years which he spent at the grammar school, he would often rise at four or five in the morning, in order to study modern languages, botany, and chemistry, in addition to his regular school-work. At the age of eighteen, he commenced his residence at Cambridge, as a pensioner of Trinity College, where he gained a scholarship in the following year. He soon found that the boys of Charterhouse and Eton were more than a match for him, and that if he were to retain the reputation which he had gained at school, he must work even harder than before. Accordingly, he began a system of reading, which overtasked his bodily, though not his mental powers, and the bad effects of which lasted, perhaps, throughout his life. He sometimes spent sixteen, and even eighteen hours out of the twenty-four over his books. He wrote every day a piece of Greek or Latin composition, and a translation from a Greek or Latin author, which latter he translated back again some days after, and then compared his version with the original.

At the end of his academical year, he was fortunately introduced to Mr. ——, afterwards Bishop Maltby, who gave him some good advice as to the method of reading which he should pursue. He, in consequence, re-commenced reading on the plan recommended by Mr. Maltby. At this period, his day was generally thus divided: rising in time for the early chapel service, which he never missed during his undergraduate life, except when prevented by illness, he began reading at nine, at twelve allowed himself two hours' recreation, walking or rowing, or occasionally a game of billiards; dined at two, the college dinner-hour, and returning to his books at three, read without interruption till twelve at night, and occasionally till three in the morning. Sometimes he alternated his work, one week sitting up till three, and the next rising at four. The remonstrances of friends or physicians, who warned him that he read too hard, were in vain; the objects which he had set before him he determined to gain, at whatever cost of ease, time, and health. A Bury friend, meeting him in the streets of Cambridge, during a long vacation, exclaimed, " Why, Charles Blomfield, I believe if you were to drop from the sky, you would be found with a book in your hand."

NOBLE CONDUCT OF LORD ROCHFORD.

A gentleman, whom Lord Rochford had made Consul at Messina, died in 1771, and gave his whole fortune, between £3,000 and £4,000, to his patron. But few gentlemen wanted money more than the Earl, yet he immediately gave the whole legacy to the testator's family.

DR. WHATELY'S CURE FOR A HEAD-ACHE.

Archbishop Whately, from his earliest youth, battled and balked all temptation to sloth. He knew that indolence begins in cobwebs and ends in iron chains, and he never spared either the sinews of his strong mind or the muscles of his strong arm; and when, as sometimes happened, a head-ache overtook him after some unusally severe intellectual effort, he used to refresh himself by manual labour. A friend of Dr. Field's says, "The first occasion on which I ever saw Dr. Whately was under peculiar circumstances. I accompanied Dr. Field to visit professionally some members of the Archbishop's household, at Redesdale. The ground was covered by two feet of snow, and the thermometer was down almost to zero. Knowing the Archbishop's character for humanity, I expressed much surprise to see an old labouring man in his shirt sleeves felling a tree 'after hours' in the demesne, while a heavy shower of sleet drifted pitilessly on his face. 'That labourer,' replied Dr. Field, 'whom you think the victim of prelatical despotism, is no other than the Archbishop, curing himself of a headache. When his Grace has been reading or writing more than ordinarily, and finds any pain or confusion about the central organization, he puts both to flight by rushing out with an axe, and slashing away at some ponderous trunk. As soon as he finds himself in a profuse perspiration, he gets into bed and wraps himself in Limerick blankets, falls into a sound slumber, and gets up buoyant.' "

Dr. Whately avowed a scepticism as regards drugs, and was very much of opinion with Dryden, that—

" Better to seek the fields for health unbought,
    Than fee the doctor for a nauseous draught."

The physic from the fields, and draughts of vital air, of which the Archbishop partook copiously, carried on his own face an advertisement of their potency, quite as effective and perhaps more truthful than the ubiquitous credentials of the Methuselah pill.

W. J. FOX AS AN ORATOR.

Though ungainly in figure, William Johnson Fox was very graceful in attitude; he stood with great ease, his folded arms crossed upon his breast, and the fore-finger of the right hand extended as an index; the upper part of the figure was thrown back, and the head slightly inclined forward. The most profound silence greeted his opening sentences, which were short, epigrammatic, and poured forth in a rich, mellow tone of voice. Perfect in articulation, and clear in voice, the words came vibrating on the ear with the sweet clang of a

distant bell.   Mr. Fox affected no quaintness, no singularity
of idiom; he adhered to pure English, seldom used words for
mere effect, and shrunk with fastidious delicacy from
unnecessary display.   His inflections were really musical.
As he proceeded he warmed with his subject, for though he
used little gesture, his figure dilated, his features worked, his
eyes seemed ready to burst with intellectual fire, and his
voice broke out like a trumpet call as he denounced some
social grievance, some iniquity wrought by the few at the
expense of the many.   Towards the conclusion of his discourse, he made use of long sentences ; but he was an artist
in words.   While constructing the first steps of his sentence,
his thoughts were moulding the remote conclusion.   His
eloquence was like an ionic temple—chaste and beautiful,
massive at the base, and having no useless ornament to
distract the gaze of the beholder.   In picturesqueness of language, in power of description, and in brilliancy of diction,
this self-taught man was equal to any orator of his day,
and his perorations were seldom paralleled.   As you read
the orations of this champion of English freedom and
instructor of mankind, you are enchanted ; but as Æchines
said of Demosthenes, "What would you have thought
had you heard him deliver them ?"

ROYAL INGRATITUDE.

Edward Rookwood, of Euston, a younger branch of the
Rookwoods of Stanningfield, and who with other Catholic
gentlemen of Suffolk, signed a protestation of loyalty and
a declaration against the Pope's deposing power, entertained
Queen Elizabeth in her progress through the county, in
1578.   Of this event a singular account is given by Richard
Topcliffe, to George Earl of Shrewsbury, in a letter published
in *Lodge's Illustrations of British History.*   In return for
Rookwood's hospitality, her Majesty, for no other reason
than because he was a Papist, not only joined in insulting
him in the grossest manner, but had him hurried off to

Norwich gaol, and fined him afterwards in a large sum for presuming " to attempt her real presence." The poor man ultimately died in the gaol of St. Edmund's, Bury, and his house and estate at Euston were sold to relieve the distress of the family.

DESTITUTE CONDITION OF MR. AND MRS. INCHBALD.

Soon after marriage, Mrs. Inchbald went with her husband to France, the wife that she might acquire a complete knowledge of the French language, the husband to prosecute portrait painting, in which he had made some proficiency. Their slender funds, however, were soon exhausted, and in the course of a few months they returned to Brighton almost penniless. So destitute was their condition, that on several occasions they went without either dinner or tea, and once they ate turnips in a field for a meal. They got to London by some means or other, and obtained an engagement for Liverpool. Here she made the acquaintance of Mrs. Siddons, who at that time washed and ironed for her husband and child, and lightened her domestic duties by *singing* away the hours. The future Countess of Derby was also there, taking a half benefit, neither of these ladies dreaming of the great honours that awaited them.

JOHN CONSTABLE'S HABITS.

Whilst Constable was staying at Petworth, in 1834, Leslie was an inmate of the same house, and it was the only occasion, he says, in which he had an opportunity of witnessing his habits. " Constable rose early, and had often made some beautiful sketch in the park before breakfast. On going into his room one morning, not aware that he had yet been out of it, I found him setting some of those sketches with isinglass. His dressing table was covered with flowers, feathers of birds, and pieces of bark with lichens and mosses adhering to them, which he had brought home for the sake of their beautiful tints. Mr. George Constable told me that while on a visit to him, Constable brought from Fittleworth Common at least a dozen different specimens of sand and earth, of colours from pale to deep yellow, and of ligh reddish hues to tints almost crimson. The richness of these colours, contrasting with the deep greens of the furze and other vegetation on this picturesque heath, delighted him exceedingly, and he carried these earths home, carefully preserved in bottles, and also many fragments of the variously coloured stone. In passing with Mr. G. Constable some slimy posts near an old mill, he said, " I wish you could cut off and send their tops to me."

Leslie says, " His very amusements consisted of study ; I do not think he ever read a novel in his life. It was on no narrow principle that he objected to works of fiction, but they did not interest him. I remember soon after the death of Mrs. Constable, when books were proposed to him as a relief to his mind, he said, " I should be delighted to read ' Tom Thumb,' if it could amuse me."

Again : " I have seen him admire a fine tree with an ecstacy of delight like that with which he would catch up a beautiful child in his arms. The ash was his favourite, and all who are acquainted with his pictures cannot fail to have observed how frequently it is introduced as a near object, and how beautifully its distinguishing peculiarities are marked.

In the winter seasons, after he could afford it, Constable frequently sent clothes and blankets to be distributed among the poor of his native village ; indeed, no feature of his character was more amiable than his sympathy with the sufferings of the humbler classes, and his consideration for their feelings in all respects. He possessed that innate and only real gentility of which the test is, conduct towards inferiors and strangers ; he was a gentleman to the poorest of his species—a gentleman in a stage coach, nay more— a gentleman at a stage coach inn dinner.

Writing to Mr. Purton, in 1836, Constable says, " We gladly avail ourselves of your and Mrs. Purton's kind invitation to dinner, and will be with you at four o'clock that day, John, myself, and the sailor, though for myself there is always an uncertainty. I like to be poking about my lumber, and loathe to go from home."

DR. WHATELY ON GAMING.

When the British Association for the Advancement of Science met at Belfast, in 1852, Archbishop Whately presided over one of the lectures, and was entertained at dinner by Mr. B——, with several of the northern great guns. The conversation turned on the subject of gaming, and the Archbishop asked any member of the company to state in what its moral offence consisted. One reverend gentleman maintained that gaming involved no moral transgression whatever, and ought to be regarded chiefly as a healthful relaxation for the over-tasked mind. Dr. H——, who had filled the Whately chair of political economy, advanced it as his opinion that the moral offence implied by the Archbishop consisted in prostituting to bad purposes the talents given by God for successful commercial speculation, in the same way as the commerce of prostitution degrades and checks marriage. "That is a very good answer for a political economist," replied Dr. Whately; "but my view is simply, that inasmuch as all gaming implies a desire of profiting at the expense of your neighbour, it involves a breach of the tenth commandment."

On another occasion, he said, " *The best throw with the dice is to throw them away.*"

KEEPING A PROMISE.

Hengrave Hall, and the Suffolk property acquired by Sir Thomas Kytson, was in the reign of Charles II. settled by the Countess Rivers upon Penelope, her third daughter. It is said that Sir George Trenchard, Sir John Gage, and Sir William Harvey each solicited Lady Penelope in marriage at the same time, and that, to keep peace between the rivals,

she threatened the first aggressor with her perpetual displeasure, humorously telling them that if they could wait
she would have them all in their turns—a promise which
was actually performed.   The gentleman first favoured was
Sir George Trenchard, of Wolverton, in Dorsetshire, who,
dying shortly after without issue, she married Sir John Gage,
Bart., of Firle, in Sussex; by him, who died in 1633, she
had nine children.   Lady Penelope remained a widow till
1642, when she married Sir William Harvey, of Ickworth,
grandfather, by a former wife, of John, first Earl of Bristol.
The lady survived all her husbands, and by her will, proved
in 1661, settled Hengrave upon her third son, Edward Gage,
who was created a Baronet by King Charles II., in 1662.

A NAVAL DUEL.—CAPTAIN BROKE'S COURAGE AND PERSEVERANCE.

In the spring of 1812, Captain Philip Broke, of the
Shannon, was the senior officer of a squadron cruising off the
North American coast.   The British ships had for some time
previous to this period been unfortunate in their encounters
with the Americans, and Captain Broke, indignant at the
defeat of his countrymen, burnt with a desire to prove, as he
was confident he and his ship's crew could prove, that the
victories gained by the Americans were the result of a
preponderance of force, in itself absolutely irresistible; and
that a British ship was as superior as ever to any antagonist
of equal size.   The Shannon was a fine frigate of fifty-two
guns, though some were only nine-pounders, and some even
smaller; and from the time that Captain Broke took the
command of her, he had carefully trained her crew in
gunnery, and in every exercise calculated to make them really
efficient in the day of trial.   It happened that in May, 1813,
the American frigate, Chesapeake, came into Boston, while
he was lying off that port, with another frigate, the Tenedos,
watching the American frigates President and Congress,
which, as he knew, were on the point of putting to sea.

They eluded him in a fog; and as, after their departure, the Chesapeake was the only vessel fit for service in the harbour, Captain Broke sent away the Tenedos, lest her presence should give the commander of the Chesapeake, Captain Laurence, an excuse for remaining in port, and then sent a formal challenge to that officer to meet the Shannon, "to try the fortune of their respective flags." No ships more nearly equal to one another could have been found in the navies of the two countries. What advantage existed on either side, was in favour of the Chesapeake. Her broadside weighed fifty-two pounds more than that of the English ship; her tonnage exceeded that of her antagonist by nearly seventy tons; her crew was the more numerous by a hundred and ten men—a superiority of no small importance in a conflict eventually decided by boarding. Captain Laurence did not decline the challenge. In the afternoon of the first of June, the Chesapeake was seen coming out of the harbour; and the whole populace of Boston had assembled on the pier to witness the combat, and to greet their countryman on his triumphant return. Captain Broke at once brought his ship into a favourable position, and then hove-to to receive his assailant. At half-past five the Chesapeake reached him. Neither ship had fired a gun till she came within hail; but then, as she hauled upon the starboard side of the British frigate, both ships steering full under their topsails, at the same moment opened their fire. Not more than two or three broadsides had been exchanged when the superior training of the British gunners began to show itself. The damage they had inflicted on the Chesapeake was already seen in its results. She was no longer steered with the necessary accuracy, but fell on board the Shannon, her mizen channels locking in with the main rigging of our ship. Captain Broke went forward to ascertain her position and condition, and observing that many of her crew were deserting her guns, gave the word to prepare to board. It was eagerly received. As the boarders swarmed up, the Shannon's boatswain

Mr. Stevens, a veteran who had fought in Rodney's great victory at Port Royal, lashed the two ships together, disregarding the sword cuts which the Americans showered upon him whilst thus engaged, and which cost him an arm, and in a moment Captain Broke himself led his men on to the enemy's deck. The ammunition of the Chesapeake, like that of all the other American frigates, had been curiously made up of novel missiles, such as long bars linked together, to cut the shrouds of an antagonist; and with a view to this particular conflict, in which they expected the British sailors to board them, they had recourse to a contrivance which the English had practised, though in a somewhat different manner, in the time of Henry III., but which had probably never since been seen on board a ship. They had prepared a quantity of unslaked lime, to cast in the eyes of their assailants; but they had worse luck with this device than we had on the former occasion, for a shot from the Shannon had struck the cask which contained it, and had scattered its contents over its owners. So that when the Shannon's boarders reached their deck, the Americans found themselves deprived of one resource on which they had reckoned, and had nothing to rely upon but their own strength and courage. A brief but terrible struggle ensued. Broke himself was desperately wounded by a sword-cut on the head, and a still more dangerous blow from the stock of a musket. His clerk fell dead by his side; his purser too, who, fired by the same enthusiasm that animated his shipmates, had volunteered to take the command of a party, was slain by a musket shot. In less than five minutes, fifty of our men fell; but the loss of the Americans was far greater. The Chesapeake's main-top was filled with riflemen, but a gallant young midshipman, of the name of W. Smith, with a small party, stormed their post, and drove them down, and then the Shannon's first lieutenant hauled down the Stars and Stripes, and hoisted the British Union Jack in its place. It was the last act of the gallant officer; he had already been severely wounded, and now while thus engaged he fell, shot through the head, it is believed, by a gun from his own ship, where the men who had been left behind were not aware that the conflict was over. Indeed, some of the American crew that had fled down the hold, still kept up a fire up the hatchways, till Captain Broke, who, in spite of his wounds, still remained on deck directing the operations, ordered some of his men to fire down below, on which they surrendered, and the Chesapeake was ours in fifteen minutes from the commencement of the contest. Her loss had been very heavy, and fully attested the gallantry of the crew, and the pre-eminent skill of Captain Broke's arrangements, both during and before the action. Seventy of her men were killed: her captain, her master, and two lieutenants being included in the number; a hundred were wounded. The hulls of both ships were severely damaged, the Chesapeake, in spite of the superior thickness of her timbers, being in this respect also the greatest sufferer; but so entirely had both ships agreed in keeping their fire low, that the rigging was almost untouched; and according to Captain Broke's report, " Both ships came out of action in the most beautiful manner, their rigging appearing as perfect as if they had only been exchanging a salute."

MRS. INCHBALD'S POLITICS.

The political principles of Mrs. Inchbald may be seen in her works, but her radicalism might be inferred from her intimacy with Godwin, Holcroft, and their friends. She rejoiced in the first triumphs of liberty in France, but was repelled by the horrors which subsequently attended the revolution. She visited Holcroft in gaol, and thought the Burdett riots combined the *sublime* and the *beautiful*. Even the Peninsula triumphs she did not enjoy; she doubted the possibility of Wellington beating Massina, and entered in her journal, " Glad to find the Tower guns fired yesterday for little boast." The howl of sedition and Jacobinism raised against one of her plays, in a treasury journal, the *True Briton*, she dexterously turned to account by replying in *Woodfall's Diary*, and in consequence of the attack the sale was immense.

CONSTABLE'S LOVE OF HUMOUR.

When Constable, the artist, had occasion to reprove a servant, or a tradesman, it was generally accompanied with a pleasantry. To the man who served his family with milk, he said, "In future, we shall feel obliged if you will send us the milk and the water in separate cans."

DR. WHATELY AND HIS DOGS.

Dr. Whately in his daily "constitutional" rambles was generally attended by three uncompromising looking dogs, the heads of which, if it were possible to draw together in a Shamrock form would forcibly suggest Cerberus. Richard Whately found, or thought he found in the society of these dogs far brighter intelligence, and infinitely more fidelity than in many of the Oxford men, who had been fulsomely praised for both. In devotion to his dogs Dr. Whately proved true to the end of his life, and during the winter season might be daily seen in St. Stephen's Green, Dublin, playing at "tig," or "hide and seek" with his canine attendants. Sometimes the archbishop might be seen clambering up a tree, secreting his hankerchief or pocket-knife in some cunning nook, then resuming his walk, and after a while suddenly affecting to have lost these articles, which the dogs never failed immediately to regain.

DR. WHATELY IN THE PULPIT.

Dr. Whately completely disregarded the graces of gesture in the pulpit. In his work on Rhetoric he lays it down as a very important principle that the orator should, in speaking, by concentrating his attention exclusively on the creation of the mind, entirely forget the outward man and manner; and he depreciated in the strongest manner all studied effect. Of this fallacious principle Dr. Whately was in his own person the intrepid illustrator, and the penalties attending its indulgence more than once overtook him. All Oxford was on one occasion convulsed with laughter, by the way in which Dr. Whately unconsciously permitted his outward man to run riot in the pulpit, during an extempore address. His thoughts had never before rolled forth in such vigorous volume. During the delivery of the sermon he worked his leg about to such an extent that it absolutely glided over the edge of the pulpit, and hung there till the conclusion of his homily. Time tamed this restlessness, and later in life Dr. Whately became almost impassive in his preaching.

ROBBING A MISER.

The most remarkable circumstance that occurred during the residence of Sir Harvey Elwes at Stoke, by Clare, was the quantity of money which some fellows who lived in the neighbourhood managed to transfer from the miser's custody to their own. As might be expected, such a notorious miser as Sir Harvey had but little faith in bankers, and having scarcely any connection with London, he always had three or four thousand pounds in cash in his house at a time; for even the loss of interest could not induce him to part with his gold. The "Thaxtead Gang" hearing of this fine chance, formed a plan to rob him. They ascertained the hour at which the old Baronet's servant went to the stable in the evening, and hiding themselves in the church porch, they fell upon him, and after some little struggle, bound and gagged him. They then ran up towards the house, tied the two maids together, and going up to Sir Harvey, presented their pistols and demanded his money. The Baronet, with all his love of money, behaved remarkably well in this transaction, and showed that if his passions were dormant, and his constitution shrivelled, his love for his man-servant was strong. When the fellows demanded his money, he refused them any clue to his valuables until they had assured him that his servant was safe. He then delivered to them the key of a drawer in which were fifty guineas. But they felt convinced that he had a much larger quantity by him, and again threatened his life unless he discovered where it was deposited. At length he showed them the place, and they turned out of a large drawer *seven and twenty hundred guineas*. These they packed up in two large baskets and actually carried off, thus effecting a robbery which for quantity of specie was never equalled. On quitting him, they said they should leave a man behind who would murder him if he moved for assistance. On which, having coolly taken out his watch (which they had not asked for), and said, " Gentlemen, I do not want to take any of you, and, therefore, upon my honour, I will give you twenty minutes for your escape. After that time nothing shall prevent me from seeing how my servant does." He was as good as his word. When the time expired, he went and untied the man; but though some search was made by the villagers, the robbers were not discovered. When they were taken up some years afterwards for other offences, and were known to be the men who robbed Sir Harvey, he would not appear against them. His lawyer, Mr. Harrington, of Clare, earnestly persuaded him to do so. "No, no," said he, " I have *lost my money*, and now *you want me to lose my time also*."

TRYING TO BRIBE A JUDGE.

On one occasion, when Baron Alderson went the Welsh circuit as judge, the defendant in an action which stood for trial in Cardigan, sent to him on his arrival in that town a statement of his case, with *a ten pound note enclosed !*

ACTING AND WRITING; OR, THE STAGE AND THE PRESS.

It was in the autumn of 1780, that Mrs. Inchbald first trod the London boards; she was, however, discouraged by secondary parts being assigned to her, and a low salary paid. Only £1 6s. 8d. was paid to her, and out of that sum she had to pay nine shillings a week for lodging. After a time her salary was raised to £2, and in April, 1781, the time of her highest salary, she received £3 a week; but this was only for a short time, and the amount afterwards was frequently low. She remained on the stage till 1789, but owed her favour with the public more to the beauty of her person, and her blameless reputation, than to her merits as an actress. Fortunately, she had the power to *write for the* stage, and she soon found this immensely more profitable than *acting on the* stage. She had begun to write dramatic pieces before her retirement, and the rejection of some dozen short pieces did not deter her from trying again. Ultimately, she became very successful. Her farce of the "Mogul Tale" brought her £105. For the comedy, "I'll tell you What," Colman paid her £300. For "Every one has his Fault," she received £700; and for many other pieces very handsome sums were paid.

GROG.

Until the time of Admiral Vernon, the British sailors had their allowance of brandy or rum served out to them unmixed with water. This plan was found to be attended with inconvenience on some occasions, and the Admiral therefore ordered that in the fleet he commanded, the spirit should be mixed with water before it was given to the men. This innovation at first gave great offence to the sailors, and rendered the commander very unpopular among them. The Admiral, at that time, wore a grogram coat, and was nick-named "Old Grog." This name was afterwards given to the mixed liquor he compelled them to take, and it has since universally obtained the name of grog.

QUEEN ELIZABETH'S VISITS TO SIR NICHOLAS BACON.

Queen Elizabeth visited the Lord Keeper Bacon at Redgrave Hall, Suffolk, on several occasions. At one of these

E

visits her Majesty remarked, " My Lord, what a little house
you have got here." He answered, " Madam, my house is
well enough, but your Highness has made me too great for
my house." The Queen also visited him at his house at
Gorhambury, and in consequence of her frequent visits
there, he added to that mansion a gallery of 120 feet in
length, and 18 ft. in breadth, with a piazza underneath, in the
centre whereof was a statue of Henry VIII., in gilt armour.
Her Majesty visited Gorhambury, May 18th, 1577, and
remained there until the 22nd. The cost of her entertainment
was about £577, besides the value of twenty-five bucks and
two stags. With the refined flattery characteristic of the age,
Sir Nicholas caused the door by which the Queen had entered
the gallery to be fastened up, so that no other step might
ever pass the threshold.

BISHOP AYLMER'S BLUNTNESS.

Bishop Aylmer was bold in speech, hasty in temper, and
blunt in words. Speaking of Queen Mary's Parliament,
that took the Pope's absolution from Cardinal Pole on their
knees, he said that they stooped upon their marrow bones to
receive the devil's blessing, brought them by Satan's apostle,
the Cardinal. The Popish clergy he called " spiritual
spiders," and Bishop Bonner he called " My Lord Lubber,
of London." Once, when addressing the judges, he said,
" Some in sport call you *drudges*, and not judges ; but I think
in good earnest it is contrary that you make yourselves lords,
and all others drudges." The under Sheriff he would call
the under thief, and the jury costermongers. He said,
between the high thief and the under thief, my lord (the lord
of the manor), and the costermongers (the choice of whom
was influenced by my lord), poor men got outweighed.

JOHN MOLE, THE ALGEBRAIST.

John Mole, the self-taught algebraist, was born at Old
Newton, near Stowmarket. His father was a farming bailiff,

but having a numerous family of children, was unable to give them the benefit of an education at school. John learnt the alphabet and a few easy lessons from his mother, and at the age of thirteen went as a servant to a farmer in his native village. Subsequently he removed to Mr. Harper's, of Downham Reach Farm, near Ipswich. He had now passed the age of manhood, and began to evince a predilection for his favourite pursuit. Having been sent one day with a waggon to the shop of a neighbouring carpenter for a load of timber to repair his master's premises, one of the workmen, who had heard something of Mole's being a calculator, asked him if he could tell how many cubical quarters of inches could be cut out of a solid foot of timber. Mole instantly replied that he could inform him how many cubical quarters of inches could be cut out of ten thousand solid feet. The carpenter betted him a trifling wager that he could not; but Mole soon satisfied him of his mistake, and won the wager. Some other questions were then started, one of which was, how many farthings there were in a million of moidores, of the value of twenty-seven shillings each ; these Mole readily answered, and in lieu of the wager he had won, asked the carpenter to teach him the method of multiplication. The carpenter asked him if he was acquainted with that of addition, which Mole told him he was not; he then showed him how to multiply a small number by twelve, and making two lines of the product, and the manner of adding them up.

This young arithmetician had previously made himself acquainted with numeration by setting down figures with chalk, and then asking some of his fellow-servants to read and decipher them to him. Having quickly mastered the rules of multiplication, and made a rapid progress in solving such questions as it would reach, he resolved to follow the bent of his inclination, and accordingly applied himself with diligence to figures. He soon acquired by his own exertion a thorough knowledge of the rule of three, and his residence

being situated within a short distance of Ipswich, he applied
to a Mr. Carter, who kept a school in that town, to teach him
during the summer evenings vulgar and decimal fractions,
and the extraction of the cube root. In the science of
algebra he was not indebted to any person for instruction,
but acquired his intimate knowledge of this difficult branch
of arithmetic solely by himself. Ultimately he commenced
keeping a school on his own account, was engaged by other
schoolmasters to teach algebra in theirs, published a treatise
on his favourite studies, and furnished essays to the magazine
literature of the day.

MR. CAPEL LOFFT STRUCK OFF THE LIST OF MAGISTRATES.

As a Magistrate, the well-known Mr. Capel Lofft was
indefatigable in the performance of his duties. When the
erection of a new gaol was decided upon for the Ipswich
division of the county, he interested himself very much in
its construction, and he obtained information and plans
which tended greatly to improve its salubrity. The year
1800 was destined, however, to put an end to his magisterial
career. A poor deluded girl from Hadleigh, was condemned
to death for stealing from a dwelling house to the value of
forty shillings! The facts of the case were peculiar, and
excited great interest in her behalf. Mr. Lofft and others
signed a memorial to the Sheriff for a delay of execution, in
order that the case might be laid before his Majesty, and
pardon solicited. William Pearson, Esq., of Ipswich,
happened to be under Sheriff that year, and he at Mr. Lofft's
urgent request consented to delay the execution for fourteen
days. A petition for remission of the sentence, numerously
and influentially signed, headed by the Duke of Grafton, and
supported by his Royal Highness the Duke of Gloucester,
was of no avail. That Mr. Lofft and his friends should
humanely interest themselves in trying to save the life of this
poor girl, caused the judge, Sir Nash Grose, Knt., to be
angry, and the Duke of Portland, who was Secretary of

State, to be indignant. The Duke ordered the sentence to
be carried out, and questioned the right even of the Sheriff
to delay the execution. On the 23rd April, 1800, this poor,
ignorant, misguided girl was executed at Bury St. Edmund's.
Mr. Lofft had exerted himself to the utmost; but there is
reason to believe that his Whig principles prevented his
humane efforts from receiving that attention which they
deserved, and grave doubts were entertained as to whether
the petition to his Majesty was ever introduced to his notice.
In this way was justice meted out to the people in the boasted
days of good King George! The affair was one of great
anxiety to Mr. Lofft, and although he had never attended an
execution, although he dreaded the approaching day almost
as much as if he himself were to be the victim, he nevertheless resolved to attend, and address a few words to the
assembled multitude. He obtained permission from the
under Sheriff, and at the place of execution he ascended the
cart and stood up to address the great black mass of human
beings that had been drawn together to see their fellow
creature strangled. The object of his sympathy, a short,
squaddy-looking young woman, about nineteen or twenty
years of age, of dark complexion, and innocent looking
countenance, was by his side. She was dressed in white,
with the exception of crape on her bonnet and arms. Mr.
Lofft spoke for about fifteen minutes in a most impressive
strain. Every one was eager to hear his explanations, and
there was a silence as if a thunderbolt had fallen among the
multitude. He commended the petitioners for interceding
in behalf of Sarah Lloyd, and considered the unhappy
woman as only an instrument made use of by a designing
villain to perpetrate the crime for which she suffered. His
heart was full of his subject, and his poetic temperament,
fired with indignation at the treatment he had received from
a Tory Government, caused him to excel himself on this
solemn occasion. His speech flashed with the lightning of
genius, thrilled the multitude, and the poor victim by his

side, though much agitated, gave evident signs of approving of what he said. A short prayer intervened, she was launched into eternity amidst the tears of the people, and Mr. Lofft, for his exertions, was, without intimation from the Government, struck off the list of magistrates.

WILLIAM HYDE WOLLASTON.

The eccentric but well-known natural philosopher, William Hyde Wollaston, resided at one time at Bury St. Edmund's. He was a man of singular habits, and was accustomed to carry on his experiments with very few instruments, and in the strictest seclusion. Even his most intimate friends were never permitted to enter his place of study. Dr. Paris relates that a foreign philosopher once called on Wollaston with a letter of introduction, and unaware of the philosopher's peculiarity, expressed an anxious desire to see his laboratory. " Certainly," was the reply, and the doctor immediately produced a small tray containing some glass tubes, a simple blow pipe or bent metal tube, worth a few pence only, two or three common watch glasses, a slip of platinum, and a few similar things.

It is also related that, shortly after Wollaston had inspected a grand galvanic battery, constructed by Mr. Children, he met a brother philosopher in the street. Seizing his button (which was, it appears, his constant habit when speaking of any subject of interest), he led the friend into a secluded corner, where, after looking carefully about him as if engaged in some strange mystery, he took from his pocket a tailor's thimble, which contained a galvanic arrangement, and pouring into it the contents of a small phial, he instantly heated a platinum wire to a white heat.

Wollaston had a great objection to his portrait being taken, though there is one fine portrait, by Jackson, of the eccentric philosopher in the meeting room of the Royal Society, the history of which is interesting. His family and friends knew his reluctance on this point; nevertheless, Mrs.

Somerville, the well-known authoress, who earnestly wished to possess a portrait of her friend Dr. Wollaston, many times asked when he would sit for his picture, to which he had invariably answered, " Never."

One day, however, when he was greeted with the same question, he said, " It is evident that I must either forego the pleasure of coming to this house, or submit; so I will submit." He added, " Let us separately write the name of the artist to be employed." This was agreed, and it turned out that both parties had named the same artist.

LORD THURLOW'S HABIT OF SWEARING.

In Lord Thurlow's time the habit of profane swearing was unhappily so common that Bishop Horsley and other right reverend prelates are said not to have been entirely exempt from it. But Thurlow indulged in it to a degree that admits of no excuse. Walking with the Prince of Wales on the Steyne at Brighton, they met Horsely, and entering into conversation with him, the Bishop said he was to preach a charity sermon next Sunday, and hoped he might have the honour of seeing his Royal Highness among the congregation. The Prince graciously intimated his intention to be present. Then, turning to the Ex-Chancellor, the Bishop said, " I hope I shall also see your Lordship there." The answer was: " I'll be d——d if you do. I hear you talk nonsense enough in the House of Lords; but there I can and do contradict you, and I'll be d——d if I go to hear you where I can't."

Sir Hay Campbell, when Lord Advocate, was arguing a Scotch appeal at the bar of the House of Lords in a very tedious manner, and said, " I will noo, my Lord, proceed to my seventh pownt." " I'll be d——d if you do! " cried Thurlow, so as to be heard by all present. " This House is adjourned till Monday next; " and off he scampered.

Sir James Mansfield used to relate that whilst he and several other legal characters were dining with Lord

Thurlow, his Lordship happening to swear at his Swiss valet when retiring from the room, the man returned, just put his head in, and exclaimed, " I wont be d——d for you, Milor," which caused the noble host and all his guests to burst out into a roar of laughter. From another valet he received a still more cutting retort. Having scolded this meek man for some time without receiving any answer, he concluded by saying, "I wish you were in hell." The terrified valet at last exclaimed, "I wish I was, my Lord; I wish I was!" But the happiest retort he ever received, conveyed to him a salutary hint of the ultimate consequences of his habit of swearing. He was one morning put into a great rage by finding that a cart-load of paving stones had been shot before his door, for the purpose of repairing the street. Observing au Irish pavior near the heap, he addressed him in a furious strain as the culprit, and ordered him to remove them. *Irish pavior :* " Where shall I take them to, please, your honour ? " *Lord Thurlow :* " To h——ll, and be d——d to you." *Irish pavior :* " If I were to take them to t'other place, your honour, don't you think they might be more out of your honour's way ? "

A SUFFOLK FEMALE ARTIST.

Mrs. Mary Beale, who distinguished herself as an artist during the reign of Charles, of licentious memory, is said to have been born at Woodbridge. She is acknowledged to have been a woman of cultivated taste, refined mind, and good morals; and her portrait painting, at a time when lordly rakes and courtly wantons were likely to be the best customers to a professional artist, doubtless placed her at times in a difficulty. Sir Peter Lely was the ladies' painter. Gascar, a French artist, was patronized by the Duchess of Portsmouth, and in compliment to her had many sitters. In the midst of such competition it was fortunate for Mrs. Beale that her moral worth attracted the attention of Archbishop Tennison, and he became her patron. The

Archbishop's portrait is the first instance of an ecclesiastic who, quitting the coif of silk, is delineated in a brown wig. The attention of Tillotson induced many of the clergy to sit to her. She painted a portrait of Ray, the naturalist, a very interesting one of Otway the poet, and another of Cowley. Lady Falconberg, Dr. Stillingfleet, Lady Elizabeth Howard, Sir Stephen Fox, Countess of Derby, Earl of Clarendon, Lord Halifax, Earl of Athol, Lady Northumberland, Earl of Clare, and Lady Stafford, were also among her sitters. She had £5 for a head, and £10 for a half-length in oil, which was her most common method of painting. Her income for pictures amounted in 1672 to £202, in 1674 to £216 ; in 1676 it rose to £429, but in 1681 it was down again to £209. Five of her portraits are at the Earl of Ilchester's, and five of her pictures are at Belvoir Castle. Each head is enclosed in a frame of stone colour, a mark that very generally distinguishes her works. Mrs. Beale's portrait, by herself, was in 1828 in the collection at Luton.

THE WAY TO CURE DROWSY CONGREGATIONS.

Aylmer, Bishop of London, in the reign of Queen Elizabeth, who could preach not only rhetorically but pathetically, whenever he observed the thoughts of his congregation to wander while he was preaching, used to take a Hebrew Bible out of his breast, and read a chapter from it. When the people naturally gaped and looked astonished he put it up again, and expatiated upon the folly of listening greedily to new and strange things, and giving small attention to matters regarding themselves, and of the utmost importance.

CALAMY'S REPROOF TO GENERAL MONK.

The Rev. Edmund Calamy was once preaching before General Monk, and having occasion to speak of *filthy lucre*, he said, " And why is it called *filthy*, but because it makes

men do base and *filthy* things ? Some men," said he,
" will betray three kingdoms for filthy lucre's sake." Saying
which he threw his handkerchief, which he usually waved in
his hand, at the pew in which General Monk sat.

AN INDEPENDENT M.P.

Whilst resident in Berkshire, Mr. Elwes, the miser, was
known as an impartial magistrate, and the prospect of a
contested election between two of the leading families of the
county suggested the idea of a third person, who might be
unobjectionable to both parties. The person thus proposed
was Mr. Elwes, and he was elected, being, perhaps, the only
person in modern times who obtained a seat in Parliament
for nothing, or for *eighteen-pence*, which is the sum he said it
cost him to get returned for the county—the expenses of the
election being defrayed by those who desired to avoid a
contest. At this period he was sixty years of age, and he
sat as member of the House of Commons in three successive
Parliaments, extending over a period of twelve years, and
gained the character of an independent member. During
the whole period he never asked or received a favour ; and
thus, wishing for no post, and desirous of no emoluments, he
held aloof from temptations which have led many a good
man astray. Mr. Elwes was never of that decided cast of
men that a minister would best approve. Though he, on
entering Parliament, joined the party of Lord North, he
would frequently dissent from the minister's measures, and
vote as his conscience led him. Hence many members of the
opposition looked upon him as a man " off and on," or as
they styled him, " a parliamentary coquette." It is remarkable that both parties were equally fond of having him as
a nominee on their election committees, and frequently he
was the chairman. The honours of Parliament made no
alteration in his dress ; but for the Speaker's dinner he had
an extra suit, with which the Speaker ultimately became
very familiar. Mr. Elwes always stayed out the debates,

and immediately after he *walked* off, without a great coat,
to the Mount Coffee House, to save the expense of a hackney
coach. Mr. Joseph Morley, and Mr. Wood, of Littleton,
who went the same way as Mr. Elwes, often proposed a
hackney coach to him, but the invariable reply was, that
"he liked nothing so much as walking." But when *their*
hackney coach used to overtake him, he had no objection to
ride, knowing that they must pay the fare.

GREY HORSES FOR THE JUDGE.

Baron Alderson, on one occasion, was met at Lancaster
by the Sheriff, on horseback, with a *cortege* of *eighty* persons,
all mounted on *grey* horses. The Judge was placed in a
coach drawn by six *greys*, and *seven* outriders were mounted
on *greys* also.

DAVID HARTLEY.

Mr. Burke was not the only tiresome speaker in his day,
as will be seen from the following anecdote, which Lord
North used to relate, as containing the best specimen of wit
he ever heard in the House of Commons.

One afternoon the opposition had come down to the House
to give the members battle on a very important point. The
business was opened by one of the ministerial party. Mr.
Burke was ready to rise the moment his antagonist sat down,
but on looking round he saw that Mr. David Hartley, who
sat a few benches behind Mr. Burke, was on his legs. Mr.
Hartley received the usual nod from the Speaker, and began
his oration. Mr. Hartley's eloquence was very wild in its
character, and as he kept pouring forth for three hours,
nearly every member that could get away left the House.
Mr. Burke sat writhing on the tenter hooks of impatience,
till at length Mr. Hartley stumbled on some idea which
made him call for the reading of the Riot Act. "The Riot
Act!" said Burke, starting up; "what does the gentleman
mean? Why, they are all dispersed already!"

THE ORIGINATOR OF "SAVINGS' BANKS."

For the "Savings' Bank" scheme, one of the best that was ever broached for the promotion of prudence and the encouragement of industry, we are indebted to Mrs. Priscilla Wakefield. She tried to establish a bank of this kind in Tottenham, in the year 1799, but it was 1803 before the plan came really into full operation. The express object was to provide a safe and profitable place of deposit for the *savings* of labourers, servants, etc., and the payments were made monthly. Mrs. Wakefield kept the books for some time herself, and six wealthy persons were appointed to act as trustees, each of whom agreed to receive an equal part of the sums deposited, and be responsible to the amount of £100 for the repayment of the principal, with interest. Any sum above one shilling was received, and, to encourage perseverance, interest at the rate of five per cent. was allowed for every twenty shillings which should remain a year with the trustees. There was no restriction as to the residence of the depositors, but the benefits of the institution were to be exclusively confined to the labouring classes, and she styled her banks, "*Frugality Banks.*" After her settlement at Ipswich, she had an interview with Henry Alexander, Esq., respecting the formation of a public bank in that town; and she wrote the rules for a bank that was founded at Witham.

PRAISE OF SIR NICHOLAS BACON.

Sir Nicholas Bacon, the father of Lord Bacon, was a generous patron of learning; and amidst all the drudgery of business and the cares of state, kept up his knowledge of classical literature. Almost all writers have sounded his praise. Pattenham says, that he was a "man of rare learning and wisdom." Sir Robert Naunton, who terms him "an arch wit," says that "he was abundantly facetious, which took much with the Queen, when it was suited with the season, which he was well able to judge." Fuller speaks of him as "a good man, a grave statesman, and a father to his country." Bishop Burnet calls him "one of the wisest ministers this nation ever bred." Macauley states that "Sir Nicholas Bacon was generally considered as ranking next to Burleigh;" and Lord Campbell remarks, "As a Judge the Lord Keeper gave the highest satisfaction; and it was universally acknowledged that since the time of Sir Thomas Moore, justice had never been so well administered in the Court of Chancery."

JOHN DAYE, THE PRINTER.

John Daye, the leading member of the typographic art in the sixteenth century, the printer and publisher of the works of Latimer, Archbishop Parker, and Fox, the Martyrologist, was born at Dunwich. He was on several occasions made Warden of the Stationers' Company, and in 1572 he obtained a lease, with power to erect a shop, in St. Paul's Churchyard; but some of his brother booksellers, apparently envious of his great success, interfered, and the Lord Mayor issued an order that the shop should not be erected. In consequence of this order, Archbishop Parker, on behalf of John Daye, applied to Lord Burleigh for his assistance, and the power of the great minister being joined with that of the Archbishop, the printer commenced the erection of his shop without interference.

The imprint of one of Daye's books, dated 1578, is— "Printed at London, by John Daye, dwelling over Aldersgate, beneath St. Martin's, and are to be sold at his long shop, at the north-west dore of Paule's."

Even at this period Daye appears to have been a wealthy man, as Archbishop Parker, in his letter to Lord Burleigh, says, that the envy of the booksellers, and the out-of-the-way situation of Daye's shop, prevented him from disposing of his stock, and that he had in consequence between two and three thousand pounds' worth on his hands. Permission to set up his shop was solicited, that he might the more readily, from his central situation, dispose of the books he published.

At this period, and for some years after this date, English books were printed in the type now called black letter. The Roman type was only occasionally used for quotations, etc., and the italic was still more rarely employed. Daye cast a new Italian letter for the Archbishop, and in 1574, he was the first as well as the only printer who had cut Saxon characters. In addition to his Saxon and Italian types, Herbert states that Daye brought the Greek to great perfection. Indeed, it is evident, from his position and his publications, that he was the most practical typographer of his time.

PRIESTLY AT NEEDHAM MARKET.

When Joseph Priestly was in his twenty-second year, he received a unanimous invitation from the congregation assembling at the Independent chapel in Needham-Market to be assistant minister, with a view of succeeding their aged pastor Mr. Meadows, in the event of his decease. The congregation, we may suppose, were not in very flourishing circumstances, for although they promised him an annual salary of forty pounds, they were not able to raise him more than thirty pounds a year. Things went on pretty comfortably during the early part of his ministry, but the absence of sermons on the great question of the triune Godhead, caused several of his congregation to suspect the soundness of his faith on the doctrine of the Trinity; and as Priestly was too sincere and candid a man to disguise his opinions, they soon discovered that he was an Arian. From this time his congregation decreased, and the salary fell so much short of the thirty pounds, that, had it not been for the aid which Dr. Kippis and Dr. Benson procured for him, he could not have lived upon his income. But he had learnt how to bear poverty without murmuring, and disappointments without fretfulness; and though his income only provided the necessities of life, he was far from unhappy at Needham Market. He was too poor to have many books of his own, but he had free access to the library of the kind-hearted Samuel Alexander; and he formed an acquaintance with the Rector of Stowmarket, and also with the Rev. Mr. Scott, of Ipswich.

Anxious to improve his pecuniary position, he proposed to open an academy and teach the classics, mathematics, etc., for half-a-guinea a quarter, and to board the pupils for twelve guineas a year. The people of Needham, however, seemed to consider that orthodoxy was as essential in a schoolmaster as it was in a preacher, and Priestly's project was a failure. He then offered to give scientific lectures to adults, and commenced with twelve lectures on the use of the globes, for half-a-guinea. His class consisted of only ten persons, and their payments amounted to little more than the price of his globes. His friends, knowing his pecuniary difficulties, recommended him to a congregation at Nantwich, in Cheshire, and to that place he removed in 1758, and left Suffolk for the remainder of his life.

The globes purchased as above mentioned, still exist. When Dr. Priestly left Needham Market, he went "to London by sea, to save expense," on his way to Nantwich, and it appears that he took the globes with him. He used them in his school, and on his removal to Warrington, in 1671, sold them to the Rev. John Houghton, who succeeded Priestly at Nantwich. Mr. Henry Dowson married the granddaughter of Mr. Houghton, and the globes are in his possession.

PORTRAIT OF PRIESTLY.

A carefully and well-finished portrait of Priestly, with full-bottomed wig and costume of a divinity student, was once placed in a window of a carver and gilder's shop, at Leeds, during the time that Priestly lived in that town. As he was passing one day, he stopped to look at it. A woman

happened to be doing the same, and on seeing him, exclaimed,
" Why, here's the fellow himself ! "

LORD THURLOW AND THE BISHOP.

Lord Thurlow once got into a dispute with a Bishop
respecting a living, of which the Great Seal had the alternate
presentation. The Bishop's secretary called upon him, and
said, "My Lord of ——— sends his compliments to your
Lordship, and believes that the next turn to present to ——
belongs to his Lordship." *Chancellor :* " Give my compliments to his Lordship, and tell him that I will see him
d——d first before he shall present." *Secretary :* "This, my
Lord, is a very unpleasant message to deliver to a Bishop."
Chancellor : " You are right; it is so; therefore, tell the
Bishop that I will be d——d first before he shall present."

BERNARD BARTON'S DREAM.

Writing to a dear friend, Bernard Barton said, " I have
not yet copied that trifle into thy book, but it shall be done
the first ten minutes I get. In the meantime I will put in
a curiosity—two stanzas composed in a dream the other night,
a thing I never did in my life before ; but I dreamt I was
dining with the Queen, who insisted on my writing in her
album out of hand, without study ; and on the dread emer-
gency, the muse put two stanzas into my head which I never
could have hammered out of it under such circumstances ;
so that on the whole I got off with flying colours. I woke
with the verses in my head, and wrote them down as a sort
of psycological curiosity. In themselves, of course, they are
not very striking ; but as made by a sleeping rhymer, they
are very tolerable. I do not care, however, to give many
copies, lest I should be saluted with the old taunt, " Behold
this dreamer cometh.' "

Some years later, the Poet writing to the same friend, says,
" Lord Northampton strongly urges me to print the dream
verses. Though he gave them years ago to his friend Lord

Monteagle, to present to the Queen, I should not wonder, if like me, he entertains doubts whether she ever really saw them. At any rate he considers them quite a literary curiosity, and as such worth preserving, and wishes me with a suitable note, not going into all the details of the dream, *now* to *print* them. They cannot, he says, be out of place in a book inscribed to the Queen; but the wording of a suitable note is a ticklish affair. It must not be done with levity, or familiarity, and it would be as absurd to be over grave or solemn about a trifle. Something bordering on the playful, mock heroic is the happy medium, could one do it. * * * Of course, neither he nor I dream of this dream ditty being of any worldly benefit to me; that would be dreaming wide awake; but we agree in thinking it worth preserving as a curiosity, and the object is to do this without taking improper liberties with ' La petite Reine ' on the one hand, or compromising one's proper self-respect on the other."

HOW " SCOGAN " BECAME A COURT FOOL.

Scogan, the Jester or Fool attached to the court of Edward IV., was a native of Bury St. Edmund's. His buffoonery has rendered his name famous among the " fools " of the English courts. His reputation as a Jester is so great that he is stated to have made half England merry with his jests. He was a student of Oriel College, Oxford, and is said to have been of good family, and one feels surprised that an educated man should have accepted an office which compelled him to wear motley, which certainly gave him wages and the freedom of the pantry, but it also provided an occasional whipping, and a bed with the spaniels. That Scogan was a learned, pleasant, witted gentleman at Oxford, is evident by Ben Johnson's notice of him in " The Fortunate Isles," as a *Master of Arts*, a fine gentleman, and a writer of ballads; but he appears to have associated with dissipated and facetious companions. Although he took honours at Oxford, he held the graduates in great contempt. His maxim was, that a merry heart doeth good like a medicine. As might be expected, he was not a very scrupulous tutor, and his irregularities were serious, for avarice induced him to help an unworthy candidate into the priesthood, for the bribe of a horse from the candidate's father. Even Oxford grew at last weary of Scogan's want of decorum, and the merry Suffolk punch was compelled to withdraw from the University. With no employment, and no funds, he applied to Sir William Neville to be employed as his "household fool." Whether Scogan desired to be a household fool because he was already laughed at for being one, and thought he might as well be paid, fed, and lodged, for being thus the object of sensibility, does not appear; but he was engaged, and shortly afterwards Sir William introduced him to Edward IV. The Knight took his jester to court, probably out of vanity, for it was not every wearer of "motley" that had the talent, wit, and education of this gentleman buffoon. He was not a mere low-comedy fool, but one of those jesters who grows dull in the country, brightens up town associations, loves good living, dislikes morning prayers, and has a turn for clever similes and smart sayings. Such fools as Scogan frequently quoted Latin, were apt at old proverbs, and verbose with old classical stories and tales. Scogan's fun, readiness of repartee, and love of coarse buffoonery, made him a favourite with the King, and the loyal Knight felt compelled to make him over as a retainer to his royal patron. Henceforward Scogan became the court buffoon of Edward, and a story is told of his standing a long time beneath a water-spout for a wager of twenty pounds—a large sum in those days, but not too large for the "Fool," who risked his life.

LORD THURLOW AND CRABBE.

Crabbe, the poet, soon after he made his first visit to London, became almost destitute. In his misery he wrote to Lord Chancellor Thurlow, enclosing him a short metrical effusion, hoping by that means to gain some pecuniary aid; but he received for answer a note, in which his Lordship "regretted that his avocations did not leave him leisure to read verses." The indignant bard wrote to the professed contemner of poetry some strong, but not-disrespectful lines, intimating that in former days the encouragement of literature had been considered as a duty appertaining to the illustrious station which his Lordship held. Of this remonstrance no notice whatever was taken for a long time. But Burke and Sir Joshua Reynolds having mentioned in Thurlow's presence the genius and the destitution of the new aspirant, and that he was about to enter the Church, Crabbe, to his great amazement, received a note from the Lord Chancellor, politely inviting him to breakfast the next morning. The reception was more than courteous, the Chancellor exclaiming, in a frank and hearty tone, "The first poem you sent me, sir, I ought to have noticed; and I heartily forgive the second." They breakfasted together, and at parting, his Lordship put a sealed paper into the poet's hand, saying, "Accept this trifle, sir, in the meantime, and rely on my embracing an early opportunity to serve you more substantially, when I hear that you are in orders." Instead of a present of ten or twenty pounds, as the *donee* expected, the paper contained a bank note for £100, a supply which relieved him from all present difficulties.

LORD BACON A MARTYR TO EXPERIMENTS.

During the last year of his life, Lord Bacon's love of scientific experiments was stronger than ever. In contemplation of a new edition of his "Natural History," he desired keenly to examine the subject of anti-septics, or the best means of preventing putrefaction in animal substances. "The great apostle of experimental philosophy was destined to become its martyr." It struck him suddenly that flesh might as well be preserved by snow as by salt. From the length and severity of the winter, he expected that snow might still, in shaded situations, be discovered on the ground. Dr. Wetherborne, the King's physician, agreed to accompany and assist him in a little experimental excursion. At Highgate they found snow lying behind a hedge in great abundance; and entering a cottage, they purchased a fowl, lately killed, which was to be the subject of the experiment. The philosopher insisted on cramming the snow into the body of the fowl with his own hands. Soon after this operation, the cold and the damp struck him with a chill, and he began to shiver. He was carried to his coach, but was so seriously indisposed that he could not travel back to Gray's Inn, and he was conveyed to the house of his friend, the Earl of Arundel, at Highgate. There he was kindly received, and, out of ceremony, placed in the state bed. But it was damp, not having been slept in for a year before, and he became worse. A messenger was despatched for his old friend and connexion, Sir Julius Cæsar, who immediately came to him. Next day he was rather better, and was able to dictate a letter to the Earl of Arundel, which proved his dying effort. A violent attack of fever followed, and early on the morning of Easter Sunday, 1626, he expired in the arms of his friend, Sir Julius Cæsar.

A JUVENILE COURTIER.

Queen Elizabeth was a frequent visitor of Sir Nicholas Bacon's, both at Redgrave Hall, in Suffolk, and at Gorhambury; and on these occasions was much attracted by the intelligence and gravity of his youngest son, Francis, afterwards Lord Chancellor Bacon. She used to amuse herself in conversation with him, and called him her "young Lord Keeper." One instance of his ready wit is remarkable. Being asked by the Queen the common question, *how old he was*, he replied, "Exactly two years younger than your Majesty's happy reign."

ARCHBISHOP TILLOTSON.

In 1685, Archbishop Tillotson avowed himself a warm advocate for affording charitable relief to the French refugees. On the repeal of the edict of Nantes, Dr. Beveridge, the Prebendary of Canterbury, having objected to reading a brief for this purpose, as contrary to the rubric, the Archbishop observed to him roughly, "Doctor, Doctor, charity is above all rubrics."

TITHE RECKONING.

The Rev. Mr. Lathbury, who was rector of Livermere, received a visit from a farmer who came to pay some arrears for tithes, and of whom he inquired concerning his family. The farmer's wife had just given birth to her tenth child, which he told the rector, adding jocosely, "As you have a tenth part of my other produce, sir, I suppose I must bring you my tenth child?" "No," replied the good pastor, "I am a bachelor, and cannot undertake the charge of an infant; but I can do what will, perhaps, be much more agreeable to you." He then returned the farmer the whole of his tithes, amounting to nearly one hundred pounds, towards the support of the child.

GENEROSITY OF LORD BROME.

Lord Brome, son of the Earl of Cornwallis, was aide-de-camp to King Ferdinand, in the German wars, at the beginning of George III.'s reign. He was then only ensign, but his father bought him a lieutenant-colonel's commission in General Napier's regiment, on condition of his allowing the last lieutenant-colonel, who was very old, and had a large family, an annuity of £300 a year during his life. This his Lordship continued to pay, and when he resigned his commission, he solicited the post for the Major of the regiment, who had been many years in the service, and had a large family. When the request was granted, he declared that he would still pay the annuity to the old lieutenant-colonel out of his own private fortune.

MRS. TRIMMER AN EARLY RISER.

Early rising was a distinguishing feature in Mrs. Trimmer's character. It was began in her youth, and neither the habit nor the love of it ever left her. When she resided at Kew, before her marriage, there was a rivalship between her and a friend who lived on the opposite side of the river, respecting early rising. The one who was up first would hang a handkerchief out of the window as a sort of triumph.

When Mrs. Trimmer became an author, the habit of early rising was particularly useful to her, as it gave her hours of quiet and retirement, which, with her numerous family, could not have been otherwise attained. While writing the Annotations on the Scriptures, she used frequently to rise at five, and sometimes at four o'clock, and that during a severe winter, to pursue her labours while the rest of the family were in bed. The fire in her study was prepared over night, and she put the candle to it herself in the morning, neither liking to disturb a servant at so early an hour, nor to be dependent on any one for her hour of rising.

In her youth these early hours were chiefly spent in committing poetry to memory, and in reading. She had a favourite closet, in which these studies were carried on, and she used to read aloud even when alone, especially poetry. Milton, Thomson, and Young, were amongst her favourite poets. She could repeat a great part of the "Paradise Lost," and of the "Seasons," and "Young's Satires" almost from the beginning to the end. She used to say that his Satire upon Women had been extremely useful to her, and had taught her to avoid many failings.

LITERARY HANDKERCHIEFS.

Bernard Barton, in one of his letters, dated 1845, wrote— "Are all those pocket-handkerchiefs gone imprinted with

Doddridge's mother teaching her boy Bible history, and a few of my verses appended? Methinks I should like a couple, if procurable. Tom Churchyard affects to speak disparagingly of this little incident, calls it a degradation, and says, if he caught a grub of a boy blowing his nose on one of his sketches, he would hide him. But this is all sheer envy: I am not sure that this is not ominous of my fame as a poet, as good, in a small way, as having a ship named after me. Anyhow, it may serve as a patent for my title to write *household verses*, when my lays are so appropriated to household uses."

SIR EDWARD COKE AS A JUDGE.

The conduct of Sir Edward Coke, whilst Attorney-General, was frequently open to the severest censure. The arrogance of his demeanour, and his oppression of individuals placed before him at the Bar, is said to be unparalleled. But, strange to say, whilst his conduct as Attorney-General was so reprehensible, his conduct as a Judge was in the highest degree meritorious. Although holding his judicial office at the pleasure of a king, and of ministers disposed to render courts of justice the instruments of their tyranny, he conducted himself with as much lofty independence as any who have ornamented the Bench. He opposed the Court of High Commission; he resisted the claim of the King to sit and try causes; he checked the arbitrary proceedings of the Courts of the Lord President of Wales, and of the Lord President of the North; and incurred the deepest displeasure of his Majesty, by denying the power of the Crown to alter the law by "proclamation." The King was in the habit of summoning the twelve Judges before him, occasionally, to school them a little, and increase their subserviency. At one of these "summonses," after steps had been taken to humble the twelve, the question was put to them, "In a case where the King believes his prerogative or interest concerned, and requires the Judges to attend him for their advice, ought they not to stay proceedings until his Majesty has consulted them?" All the Judges, except Coke, answered, "Yes! yes! yes!" But Chief Justice Coke said, "*When the case happens, I shall do that which shall be fit for a Judge to do.*" This sublime answer made the recreant Judges ashamed of their servility, and commanded the respect of the King himself. His independence led to his fall; and after he was deprived of his office of Chief Justice, he was one of the most useful members of the House of Commons, as his moral courage did not desert him; and in his profound knowledge of the Common Law of England, he stood unrivalled. To his exertions as a parliamentary leader we are in no small degree indebted for the free constitution under which it is our happiness to live. He appeared opportunely at the commencement of the grand struggle between the Stuarts and the people of England. It was then very doubtful whether taxes were to be raised without the authority of the House of Commons, and whether, Parliaments being disused, the edicts of the King were to have the force of law. There were other public-spirited men who were ready to stand up in defence of freedom, but Coke alone, from his energy of character, and from his constitutional learning, was able to frame and carry the PETITION OF RIGHT; and upon his model were formed Pym, and the Patriots who vindicated that noble law on the meeting of the Long Parliament.

SIR EDWARD COKE AS A STUDENT.

Sir Edward Coke began his legal studies at Clifford's Inn, an "Inn of Chancery," in 1571, and in the following year he was entered a student of the Inner Temple. Then it was that he commenced and persevered in a laborious course of study, of which, in our degenerate age, we can scarcely form a conception. Every morning he rose at three—in the winter season lighting his own fire. He read Bracton, Littleton, the Year Books, and the folio abridgement of the Law, till the courts met at eight. He then went by water to Westminster, and heard cases argued till twelve, when pleas ceased for dinner. After a short repast in the Inner Temple Hall, he attended "readings" or lectures in the afternoon, and then resumed his private studies till five, or supper time. This meal being ended, the *moots* took place, when difficult questions of law were proposed and discussed, if the weather was fine, in the garden by the river side ; if it rained, in the covered walks near the Temple Church. Finally he shut himself up in his chamber, and worked at his common-place books, in which he inserted, under the proper head, all the legal information he had collected during the day. When nine o'clock struck, he went to bed, that he might have an equal portion of sleep before and after midnight. The Globe and other theatres were rising into repute ; but he never would appear at any of them, nor would he indulge in such unprofitable readings as the poems of Lord Surrey or Spencer. When Shakspeare and Ben John-son came into such fashion that even " sad apprentices of the law " occasionally assisted in masques and wrote prologues, he most steadily eschewed all such amusements, and it is supposed that in the whole course of his life, he never saw a play acted, or read a play, or was in company with a player.

WHATELY AND THE TICKET-OF-LEAVE SYSTEM.

The ticket-of-leave system found little favour in the Archbishop's sight, and he lost no opportunity to make a cut at it ; and if he could contrive to make the sarcasm cut two ways, the joke was all the pleasanter. The Rev. Mr. M'Naught and others, having forsaken the Anglican church, joined the Dissenters, and finally came back to the Anglican church again. Dr. Whately quietly remarked, " I hope they are not going to send us ticket-of-leave clergymen."

WHATELY AND THEOLOGY.

At a dinner party at Dr. B——'s, Archbishop Whately mentioned that he had on that day received a long letter from a "Religious Inquirer" in America, who requested that Dr. Whately, as one of the highest theological authorities, would recommend him a good theological system. "My reply was laconic," remarked the Archbishop; "I told him that I knew no good system of theology."

"EXCUSE MY PREACHING."

"I hope your Grace will excuse my preaching next Sunday," said a parson, who was fonder of the cushions of his easy chair than of the cushions of the pulpit. "Certainly," said Dr. Whately, indulgently. Sunday came, and the Archbishop said to him, "Well, Mr. ——, what became of you? we expected you to preach to-day." "Oh, your Grace said you would excuse my preaching to-day." "Exactly; but I did not say I would excuse you *from* preaching."

"YOUR WIFE" AND "YOUR LADY."

On one occasion, when drawing the distinction between "your wife" and "your lady," Archbishop Whately told a good story in illustration. "Mrs. Whately," said he, "attracted by some goods in a haberdasher's window, went in and ordered them to be sent home. The trader, who was a more surly customer than the most petulant of his patrons, declined to do so. 'Sir, I am the Archbishop's lady,' said Mrs. Whately, much hurt and surprised. 'I didn't care if you were his wife,' retorted the hero of *counter* irritation."

MORAL COURAGE OF PHILIP, DUKE OF NORFOLK.

Philip, the eldest son of Thomas the fourth Duke of Norfolk, shone in the eyes of Queen Elizabeth for a short season, as a bright, particular star of her fancy, and then suffered the usual declination of favourite planets. He was charged before the High Commissioned Court of Star Chamber with conspiring to restore the religion of his

ancestors in the land, and suffered a money commutation
of £10,000 for the offence, seasoned, however, with the usual
punishment of confinement. He passed four years of solitude within the cheerless walls of his prison-house, and was
then brought into Westminster Hall for trial. "Hold up
thy traitor hand!" cried out one of the spotless judges of
the court. Norfolk raised it high in the air, and cried,
"Here is as true a hand as ever drew sword for the Queen's
mightiness, or ever came into this goodly hall." Condemned,
of course, without sufficient evidence, he was again sent back
to his imprisonment. During this second incarceration the
iron entered his soul, and in the last stage of a desperate
illness, urged by his own yearnings for liberty and a strong
desire to see the friend of his bosom, he begged of his
queenly prosecutor that his beloved wife might be allowed to
come to him. "Once attend the Protestant worship," was
the inhuman reply, "and not only shall thy prayer be
granted, but thou shalt be free." He refused the *boon*, and
died in prison, where he had rotted and chafed for more than
six long years. It has been said that neither his grief which
was intense, nor the ailments of his body which were many,
brought him to his end, but the common remedy used against
obnoxious subjects by their monarch—poison.

THURLOW AND THE CURATE.

A poor curate with some difficulty (it was supposed that
he gave the porter a fee) obtained admission into Lord
Thurlow's, and waited for him until he returned from the
Court of Chancery. When Lord Thurlow saw him he broke
out in his usual manner by abruptly and loudly asking him
questions: "Who are you? What do you want? How
came you here? What interest have you? Who sent you
here? What *Lord's name* do you come in? What *Lord's
name*, I say, do you come in?" "Indeed, my Lord," was the
answer, "I came to apply for the living of ——, but I have
no interest. I come in no Lord's name but the Lord of

Hosts." "The Lord of Hosts!" said the Chancellor; "the Lord of Hosts! Well, you are the very first parson that ever applied to me in *that* Lord's name, and I'll be —— if you shan't have the living!"

THE SHIP "BERNARD BARTON."

Some of the Woodbridge shipowners, resolving upon paying a tribute of respect to the memory of their poet, named a new schooner, in 1840, the "Bernard Barton." When voyaging up the Mersey, or the Humber, the captain had repeated inquiries as to what *place* or *person* his ship was named after; and the quaker poet was highly amused one evening at finding among the shipping list of some distant port, the arrival of the "*Barney Barton.*"

CRABBE'S LOVE OF PUNCTUALITY.

The poet Crabbe was a very punctual man in all his engagements, and felt much annoyed in being detained at the church, waiting for funerals. He once waited for a corpse a whole hour beyond the time appointed, and then went home to dinner; but just as he sat down the funeral train appeared. He rose in no pleasant mood, on which his son John said, "Father, allow me to bury the corpse." "Well, do so, John," he answered; "you are a milder man than your father."

JOHN CONSTABLE'S HUMOUR.

One year, when John Constable, the artist, was on the hanging Committee of the Royal Academy, he remonstrated with an exhibitor on the size of his frames. The artist defended himself by stating that they were precisely the same pattern as Sir Thomas Lawrence's. Constable replied, with his sly humour, "It is easy to imitate Lawrence in his frames."

MRS. INCHBALD'S GENEROSITY.

Mrs. Inchbald, even when her pecuniary resources were good, was noted for a shabby style of living. She invariably lived cheaply, lodged generally in poor neighbourhoods, and spared herself expenses in every possible way. She at one time, although in affluent circumstances, scrubbed her own stairs, sifted her own cinders, and was sometimes actually short of coal. But this penuriousness arose neither from avarice or sordidness. She grudged herself everything, yet was bountiful to her poor relatives and improvident friends. Her purse was ever open to the necessities of her parent, and the wants of every member of her own family. Whilst shivering at her own fire, she was giving large sums of money to keep others easy and warm ; and *she esteemed it her duty to support two sisters, instead of keeping one servant.*

LORD CHEDWORTH'S APPEARANCE.

Lord Chedworth was one of those persons that make an indelible impression upon most minds. Not because he was one of nature's aristocracy, but in consequence of his singular physiognomy ; strangers when passing him were sure to turn round to look more distinctly at "that queer little man." He was small and slight in stature, mean and insignificant in appearance, awkward in manner, careless in costume, and eccentric by habit. His countenance at times betokened imbecility, and although he had plenty of moral courage, he never exhibited a spark of physical courage. Timidity seemed interwoven into his very frame, and became the ruling principle of most of his actions. This feeling, joined with his mean-looking appearance, sometimes subjected him to very odd indignities. An occurrence of this kind happened to him in 1780. He paid a visit to the camp at Tiptree for the purpose of calling upon a relation, an officer in the Oxfordshire Militia. The soldiers on guard had orders not to admit mean-looking persons within the lines, and in consequence, *he refused to let Lord Chedworth pass!*

SUFFOLK LINKS AND GEORGE II.

In Suffolk, sausages are frequently called *links*. Once, when King George II. landed at Lowestoft, it was so dark by the time he reached Copdock that lights were thought necessary; the officer in advance inquired of the landlady at the White Elm if she had any flambeaux, or could procure any. Being answered in the negative, he ask her if she had any links. "Aye, that I have," said she, "and some as good as his Majesty, God bless him, ever eat in all his life!"

ADMIRAL VERNON, OF NACTON.

The fate of this gallant man was a peculiarly hard one, and such as would now be deemed as unjust as it was cruel. He fell a sacrifice to the writing of two foolish squibs, in the shape of pamphlets, against his employers; but they were smothered in their own smoke, went off without fire and without notice, scorching nobody but himself. He was nevertheless summoned to attend the Board of Admiralty, the pamphlets were shown to him, and he was desired by the Duke of Bedford to give a categorical answer, *Aye* or *No*, whether he was the author or publisher. He said he fully admitted the authority of Lord High Admiral, and as a naval officer owed all obedience to his orders, but that he looked upon the question now asked as one of a private nature, which he apprehended their Lordships had no right to ask him, and that he was not bound to answer it. The Duke said if that was the only reply he meant to give he might withdraw. The next day he received a letter from the Secretary to say the Duke of Bedford, having laid the pamphlet before the King, his Majesty had been pleased to direct their Lordships to strike his name out of the list of flag officers. There could be no excuse for this rash and tyrannical proceeding, as the wished for end might legally have been accomplished by a court-martial. Horace Walpole calls Vernon a silly, noisy Admiral, so popular that he was chosen into Parliament for several places, had his head painted on every sign, and his birth-day kept twice in one year. His fall, however, is not a singular instance of the fate that sometimes awaits vulgar popularity; but this is the last exercise on record of so harsh and summary a proceeding against a gallant flag officer. "To say he was a brave, a gallant man," says Chanock, "would be a needless repetition of what no person has ever presumed to deny him. His judgment, his abilities as a statesman, are unquestioned; and his character as a man of strict integrity and honour, perfectly unsullied."—*Barrow's Life of Earl Howe.*

THE DUCHESS OF HAMILTON.

Maria and Elizabeth Gunning, who appeared at the court of George II., one at the age of eighteen and the other nineteen, were two portionless girls of surpassing loveliness. "They are declared," writes Walpole, "to be the handsomest women alive; they can't walk in the park, or go to Vauxhall, but such crowds follow them, that they are generally driven away." They made more noise than any of their beautiful predecessors since the days of Helen. One day they went to see Hampton Court; as they were going into the beauty room, another company arrived; the housekeeper said, "This way, ladies, here are the beauties." The Gunnings flew into a passion, and asked her what she meant—they went to see the palace, not to be shown as sights themselves.

Elizabeth, the youngest of these fair sisters, became the wife of James Duke of Hamilton; he fell in love with her at a masquerade, and in a fortnight met her at an assembly made to show Lord Chesterfield's new house in May Fair. Duke Hamilton made violent love to her at one end of the room, while he was playing faro at the other end; that is, he saw neither the bank nor his own cards, which were of three hundred pounds each, and he soon lost a thousand. Two nights after, being left alone with her while her mother and sister were at Bedford House, the Duke grew so impatient that he sent for a parson. Doctor Keith refused to perform the ceremony without a license or ring—the Duke swore that he would send for the Archbishop ; at last they were married with the ring of a bed curtain, at half-an-hour after twelve at night, at May Fair Chapel. In less than three weeks, Maria Gunning followed her sister's example, and married Lord Coventry.

Nothing could exceed the curiosity excited by the beauty of the sisters, which interest was considerably increased by their splendid alliances. When the Duchess of Hamilton was presented at court, the crowd at the drawing-room was so great, that even noble persons clambered upon chairs and tables to look at her. When she went to her castle, it is said that seven hundred persons sat up all night, in and about an inn, in Yorkshire, to see her get into her post-chaise the next morning. Lady Coventry was equally run after. At Worcester, a shoemaker got two guineas and a half by showing, at a penny a head, a shoe that he was making for the Countess.

THE LATE MARQUIS OF HERTFORD.

One day, when the noble Marquis was going alone from Aldborough to Sudbourne, on the road he met a cart with one horse, deeply laden with coals, which, from the badness of the road, and the deepness of the ruts, was in great danger of being overturned. The Marquis endeavoured to pass it, when the carter, not knowing who the stranger was, said to his Lordship, " Come, ya might tie your horse to a tree, and come and help me." At this request the Marquis instantly stopped and dismounted, asking the carter what he should do to help him. " Why, lay hold here, and shove hard," was the ready reply, which being complied with, they together soon got the cart out of the difficulty. The Marquis then asked if there was anything more to do. " Why, no," said the carter, feeling his pocket. "If I had sixpence, I would give it thee; but if you *wool* go down to the Crown with me, you shall take part of a pot of beer." The Marquis declined the offer, and mounted. The countryman, however, observed, "Why, you ride a very good horse; perhaps we shall see one another again." "That may be," was the reply; "but it is not very likely; and here is half-a-crown for you to drink the Marquis of Hertford's health," and then rode on, leaving the poor fellow in fear and astonishment.

ARCHBISHOP SANCROFT.

"Pray, Mr. Betterton," asked the good Archbishop Sancroft of the celebrated actor, "can you inform me what is the reason you actors on the stage, speaking of things imaginary, affect your audience as if they were real; while we in the Church speak of things real, which our congregations receive only as if they were imaginary?" "Why, really, my Lord," answered Betterton, "I don't know, unless it be that we actors speak of things imaginary as if they were real; while you in the pulpit speak of things real as if they were imaginary." This clever answer is as applicable now as when the Archbishop put the question.

ROYALTY *v.* CONSCIENCE.

John Hervey, Esq., eldest son of Sir William Hervey, of Ickworth, was highly esteemed for his agreeable manners and polite accomplishments. He was M.P. for Bury St. Edmund's. The King loved him personally, and yet upon a great occasion he voted against the King's wishes, who reproached him severely. Next day, another important question falling in, he voted as the King would have him. The latter, taking notice of it at night, said "You were not against me to-day." He answered, "No, sir, I was against my conscience to-day." This was so gravely delivered that the King seemed pleased with it, and it was much talked of.

G

SCOGAN, THE COURT FOOL.

Scogan, the Court Fool in the time of Edward IV., was a native of Bury St. Edmund's, and the monarch was so well pleased with the jester that he furnished a mansion for his residence at Bury, as a mark of his royal consideration. Scogan's wife was a fine lady, who was desirous of having a page, who might precede her as she went in state to the church of St. Mary's. In fact, she intimated that it would be impossible to find her way to church without a page. " Poor lass ! " said the jester, one Saturday night, " you shall have a guide to church before the bells ring to-morrow morning." Accordingly, on the Sunday morning Scogan arose early, and had the road chalked which lay between his house and the church door. When church time came he led his wife to the threshold of their dwelling to see her new page, but the fastidious lady waxed so wrath at the practical trick played by her husband, that all his wit could hardly pacify her.

Scogan was fond of taking liberties with royalty. He had borrowed a large sum of money from the King, and when the time of payment arrived was not prepared to cancel the debt. After much thought upon the matter, he fell sick and pretended to die, and requested his friends to bury him in such a way as the King should encounter the funeral. They entered into the joke with great alacrity, put on the trappings of unmitigated affection, and in due time carried Scogan forth on a comfortably arranged bier. They contrived as directed to cross King Edward's path. The King, when he met the funeral procession, expressed his regret at the loss of his merry follower, and among other things remarked that he freely forgave Scogan and his representatives the sum for which the jester was indebted to him. The Buffoon, who had expected this act of release, immediately jumped up, thanked his illustrious creditor, and prudently called all present to bear witness to this royal act of grace. " It is so revivifying," said Scogan, "that it has called me to life again."

BISHOP STANLEY AND HIS ROOKS.

Bishop Stanley, whilst residing at Norwich, was sometimes spoken of as "Jackdaw Stanley," by those rev. gentlemen whose ease he incommoded. This unepiscopal epithet was thus derived. The Bishop was very anxious to establish a rookery in the palace grounds, and for this purpose he had conveyed from the Cathedral close a quantity of nests. He thus established a cawing colony in his own trees by depopulating those of others. Soon after, and while some of the citizens were yet annoyed at losing their favourite rooks, a few mischeivous boys broke into the Bishop's grounds and robbed the nests. One of the culprits was taken before the magistrates and charged with the theft, his Lordship being present in the court to urge the suit. When the young urchin was asked what reason he could assign why he should not be sent to gaol for the robbery, he boldly confronted the Bishop, and said that he did not take *his* rooks. "They warn't yours," said he; "*you stole* them from the Dean and Chapter; I took them from you." A peal of laughter followed this defence, and the duty-enforcing Bishop was after this often spoken of in the diocese as "Jackdaw Stanley."

GAINSBOROUGH'S LOVE OF MUSIC.

Gainsborough had an enthusiastic attachment to music. It was the favourite amusement of his leisure hours, and his love for this, the most fascinating of the arts, induced him to give one or two concerts to his most intimate acquaintances whilst living in Ipswich. He was a member of a musical club, and painted some of the portraits of his brother members in his picture of a choir. His love of music often seduced him from the easel, and caused him to lavish away his money and his pictures. He gave Colonel Hamilton, one of the first amateur violinists in England, the celebrated picture of the "Boy at the Stile," for playing a solo on the violin.

Gainsborough lived at Bath when Giardini first exhibited his then unrivalled powers on the violin. His excellent performances made the painter enamoured of that instrument, and he was not satisfied until he possessed it. He next heard Abel on the viol de gamba—the violin was hung on the willow, Abel's voil de gamba was purchased, and the house resounded with melodious thirds and fifths. Soon after this his passion had a fresh object—Fischer's hautboy; but though he procured a hautboy he was never heard to play on it. A year or two later, Gainsborough appeared in the character of King David. He had heard a harper at Bath—the performer was soon left harpless; and now Fischer, Abel, and Giardini were all forgotten—there was nothing like chords and arpeggios. Happening on one occasion to see a "theorbo" in a picture of Vandyke's, Gainsborough concluded, because, perhaps, it was finely painted, that the "theorbo" must be a fine instrument. He recollected to have heard of a German professor, and ascending to his garret found him dining on roasted apples and smoking his pipe, with his theorbo beside him. "I am come to buy your lute; name your price, and here's your money." "I cannot sell my lute." "No, not for a guinea or two; but you must sell it, I tell you." "My lute is worth much money—it is worth ten guineas." "Aye, that it is; here's the money." So saying he took up the instrument, laid down the price, went half way down the stairs, and returned: "I have done but half my errand; what is your lute worth, if I have not your book?" "What book, Master Gainsborough?" "Why, the book of airs you have composed for your lute." "Ah, sir, I can never part with my book." "Pooh, you can make another at any time. This is the book I mean; there are ten guineas for it, so once more, good day." He went down a few steps, and returned again: "What use is your book to me if I don't understand it? and your lute—you may take it again, if you don't teach me to play on it; come home with me, and give me the first lesson." "I will come to-morrow." "You must come now." "I must dress myself." "For what? you are the best figure I have seen to-day." "I must shave, sir." "I honour your beard." "I must, however, put on my wig." "D——n your wig! your cap and beard become you! Do you think if Vandyke was to paint you, he'd let you be shaved?"

ARCHBISHOP WHATELY AND BEGGARS.

Archbishop Whately, formerly Rector of Halesworth, was noted for his hospitable and generous disposition; but he was an inveterate foe to indiscriminate charity. He said, "I have given a great deal away, and I have no doubt often made mistakes; but there is one thing with which I cannot reproach myself: I never relieved a beggar in the streets."

CRABBE'S GENEROSITY.

His income at Trowbridge amounted to about £800 a year, but he was a mild man in the matter of tithes. When told of many defaulters, his usual reply was, "Let it be, probably they cannot afford to pay so well as I can afford to want it; let it be." His charitable nature caused him to be frequently imposed upon by fictitious tales of woe, which when he discovered, he merely said, "God forgive them; I do.

BISHOP BLOMFIELD'S RISE.

Blomfield when a boy, on being asked as to his views of a profession, replied, "I mean to be a Bishop," and he kept to his word. The Bishop's fortunes were built up by the munificence of various patrons. He boasted once, though rather *mal a propos*, to a poor clergyman who was grumbling, that he never had got a single thing he asked for, "And I never asked for a single thing I got." "But (says a writer in the *Saturday Review*) he might have added that he never refused anything that was offered him, when, perhaps, a little more severe sense of duty would have counselled some self abnegation. Quarrington, in Lincolnshire, was held with the curacy of Chesterford, in Cambridgeshire, then with the rectory of Dunton, a queer little place in Bucks, with seventy-two inhabitants, where the parish clerk was a female between seventy and eighty, who being unable to read when she stole the church communion plate, took it to the nearest pawn-broker, in ignorance that the name of the parish was engraved upon it. Then he held Great and Little Chesterford, with Tuddenham, in Suffolk. When promoted to the rich living at Bishopsgate, in 1820, and shortly after to the Archdeaconry of Colchester, he still retained Great Chesterford, and when elevated to the see of Chester, he still retained Bishopsgate. When a rather cross-looking picture of him was painted on his accession to the mitre, he said it might be supposed to be "inscribed without permission to the non-resident clergy of the diocese of Chester."

DR. BLOMFIELD'S EXTEMPORE SERMON.

Whilst rector of Great Chesterford, Dr. Blomfield preached *extempore* for the first and only time in his life, having forgotten his written sermon. His text was, "The fool hath said in his heart, There is no God." Anxious to know how he had succeeded, he asked one of his congregation on his way home, how he liked the discourse. "Well, Mr. Blomfield," replied the man, "I liked the sermon well enough, but I can't say I agree with you; I think there be a God!"

CRABBE'S DISTRESS.

When Crabbe wrote his pathetic letter to Edmund Burke, entreating aid from that great and gifted man, the poet was in the greatest misery. The pangs of hunger gnawed his physical frame, and the gloomy walls of a prison haunted his mental vision. So harassed was he by the miseries which he had endured, and the existing suspense, that after his delivery of the letter at Burke's door in the evening, he in the most agitated manner walked backwards and forwards on Westminster Bridge until daylight.

MAJOR MOORE ON POPULAR ERRORS.

The worthy Major Moore gave some entertaining lectures on "Popular errors" to the members of the Mechanics' Institutes of Ipswich and Woodbridge. These lectures held a sort of middle place between the solidity of studied discourses and the freedom of colloquial conversation, and were thus described in an unpublished letter of Bernard Barton's: " Major Moore gave us a fourth lecture on ' Popular errors ' the other night; and worn out and thread-bare as the subject one would think must be, he gave far the best lecture he has yet given to a crowded and applauding audience. None but *he* could have done it, and to no one but such a general favourite would the same auditory have gone for a fourth time to listen to the same subject. But the good Major, as Cuddie Hedrigge said of his old master, Henry Morton, has a face like a fiddle, and can make men dance to his tune. The simple fact is, that though he calls his subject ' Popular Errors,' he often ' travels out of the record,' as lawyers say, and brings in a variety of extraneous matter, and sometimes ' unpopular truths,' which makes his conversaziones very amusing, and at times instructive."

MRS. SHAWE, OF KESGRAVE.

The following extracts from letters of hers to Bernard Barton will convey a just impression of the strength of mind, homely freshness, as well as catholicity of judgment of this kind-hearted and truly benevolent woman.

" THE ANNUALS.

" I thank you for sending me your Annual, for which we can settle when we meet. But you could not have sent it to a worse person. I am an avowed enemy to the *class*. They are the coxcombs of literature, in their silken vests, pandering to our besetting sin of love of excitement and desultory reading."

" THOMAS CARLYLE.

" I agree in much that you say respecting Carlyle, and am often in a fever of irritation whilst I unravel his sentences : they are worse than a tangled skein of silk. But he is a suggestive writer. I like ' books of fact,' and ' books of suggestion,' and to do my own reasoning (*that is, when I can*)."

" PUSEYISM.

" What strange scenes at Oxford! I am convinced that there are thousands in the Church of England, who, though they would start at the word, ' transubstantiation,' attach a certain mystery and awfulness to the elements at the table of the Lord which they cannot fairly translate into any other phrase. But they have never thought upon the matter ; the same haziness of perception exists in the masses on the subject of baptsimal regeneration and apostolic succession. The Tractarians are turning all this into English, and we start to find ourselves on the threshold of Rome, instead of being, as we supposed, Protestants, living in hatred of the so-called Scarlet Lady."

The author of the above paragraphs died at Kesgrave, on the last day of September, 1856, her husband having preceded her to the world of spirits a bare twelve months. We have the best authority for the statement that Mr. and Mrs. Shawe paid away constantly *fifteen hundred pounds* per annum in charities, subscriptions, and annuities, before any portion of their income was appropriated to their own use.

REV. WILLIAM WHISTON.

The Rev. William Whiston, the celebrated mathematician, was at one time vicar of Lowestoft. In his memoranda, he says, " The parish officers came once to me to desire me to set my hand to a license for setting up a new ale-house in Lowestoft ; the justices, it seems, paying that compliment to the town, as not to set it up without the consent of the minister, and, I suppose, of the churchwardens also. My answer was short : ' If they would bring me a paper to sign to pull down an ale-house, I would certainly do it ; but I would never sign one to set up an ale-house.' At another time there came to me an order from Mr. Bachelor, who then acted in the Ecclesiastical Court as deputy to Dr. Pepper, Chancellor of Norwich, for reading an excommunication against a woman of my parish, who it seems had called another woman 'whore,' those courts not being able to proceed till such an excommunication was read in the parish church. Upon this I went and inquired of the sober people in the neighbourhood whether this imputation was believed to be true or false? The answer was, " that the accuser might have kept her tongue between her teeth, yet they doubted the thing was too true.' I then wrote to Mr. Bachelor that I was surprised to have an order for reading an excommunication against a poor woman for speaking what the sober people in the neighbourhood thought to be true."

MARGARET GAINSBOROUGH AND QUEEN CHARLOTTE.

Margaret Gainsborough, daughter of the celebrated artist, manifested many peculiarities, and was said at times to be subject to occasional aberrations of mind. She inherited all her father's fondness for music, and played exquisitely on the harpsichord. Queen Charlotte on one occasion expressed a wish to hear Miss Gainsborough's performance ; but the young lady was out of temper, and refused to gratify royalty.

CLARKSON AND HAYDON.

Whilst preparing for his great picture of the Anti-slavery Society Convention, Haydon had in London several interviews with Clarkson, and one morning, whilst breakfasting with him, he said, " Mr. Clarkson, those who have a great national object should be virtuous and see God daily, enduring, as seeing one who is invisible." " They should indeed," said Clarkson ; " it supported me. I have worked day and night, and I have awoke in convulsions after reading the evidence of the horrors of the slave trade." " Christianity," said Haydon, " is the power of God unto salvation. It is of heart and internal conviction, not of evidence and external proof." " Ah," said Clarkson, " what a blessing is the religious feeling! The natural man sees flowers, and hears birds, and is pleased; the religious man attributes it all to God."

In April, 1841, Haydon left London for Clarkson's residence, to paint his portrait, and in his journal we find the following notes of the visit: "I arrived at Ipswich at seven, and found Clarkson's carriage waiting. Got to Playford Hall about eight. Found the dear old man at tea with his niece and wife. Clarkson has a head like a patriarch, and in his prime must have been a noble figure. He was very happy to see me, but there is a nervous irritability which is peculiar. He lives too much with adorers, especially women. As he seemed impatient at my staying beyond a certain time, I went to bed and wished him good-night. I slept well, and the next morning walked in the garden and fields. He breakfasted on milk and bread (alone), and I breakfasted with Mrs. T. Clarkson upstairs. I promised to sketch him at ten, and at ten I was ready. He seemed much pleased by a letter from Guizot, wherein he had said that Soult and he meant to bring in abolition next year. Dear old man! no praise seemed lost on him.

"When all was ready, the windows filled, he said, 'Call in the maids.' In came six servant girls and washerwomen (it being washing day). 'I am determined they shall see the first stroke.' In they all crowded, timidly wondering. Clarkson said, 'There now, that is the first stroke; come again in an hour and you shall see the last.' We now began to talk. Clarkson showed no envy. He spoke of Granville, Sharp, and Wilberforce with affection and respect. 'But,' said the patriarch, 'they thought of the *slave*, I of the *slave-trade*.' I admired this distinction.

"I think Clarkson's intellects are unimpaired and shine through his infirmities. He told the whole story of his vision. He said he was sleeping when a voice awoke him, and he heard distinctly the words, 'You have not done all your work. There is America.' Clarkson said it was vivid. He sat upright in his bed; he listened, and heard no more.

Then the whole subject of his last pamphlet came to his mind. Texts without end crowded in, and he got up in the morning and began it, and worked eight hours a day till it was done—till he hoped he had not left the Americans a leg to stand on.

"Why was I not so impressed by my visit to Clarkson as I was by my visit to Wellington? Here was a man who in his Christian and peaceful object had shown equal perseverance, equal skill, equal courage, and yet I was not so affected. Clarkson has more weaknesses than the Duke. He is not so high bred. He makes a pride of his debilities; he boasts of his swollen legs and his pills, as if they were so many claims to distinction. The Duke did not let you see him in his infirmities. He was deaf, but he would not have let you see it if possible; he dined like others, ate like others, and did everything like others. Clarkson has the infirmity of asking questions about himself, as if he had forgot the answers, that he may elicit again the answers for the pleasure of hearing the repetition. The Duke—never. He is too much a man. Though Clarkson is a gentleman by birth, and was educated like one, he is too natural for any artifice. He says what he thinks, does what he feels inclined, is impatient, childish, simple; hungry, and will eat; restless, and will let you see it; punctual, and will hurry; nervous, and won't be hurried; charitable, speaks affectionately of all, even of Wilberforce's sons, whose conduct he lamented, more as if it cast a shadow over the father's tomb, than as if he felt wounded from what they had said of himself."

JAMES THE FIRST IN SUFFOLK.

> "King *Jamie* once in Suffolk went
> A hunting of ye deere,
> And there he met a *Burie* blade,
> All clad in finest gear."
>
> OLD BALLAD.

This monarch preferred the amusement of hunting to hawking or shooting. It is said of him that he divided his

hunting, his standish, and his bottle. The first had his fair
weather, the two last his dull and cloudy. One time, when
he was on a hunting party near Bury St. Edmund's, he saw
an opulent townsman who had joined the chase, " very brave
in his apparel, and so glittering and radiant that he eclipsed
all the Court." The king was desirous of knowing the name
of this gay gentleman, and being informed by one of his
followers that it was " *Lamme*," he facetiously replied,
" *Lamb*, call you him ? I know not what kind of *lamb* he is,
but I am sure he has got a good *fleece* upon his back."

THE DUKE OF GRAFTON AND THE CURATE.

The late Duke of Grafton, in hunting, was one day thrown
into a ditch; at the same instant a horseman, calling out,
" Lie still, my Lord ! " leaped over his Grace and
pursued his sport. When the Duke's attendants came up,
he inquired of them who that person was, and being told it
was a young curate in the neighbourhood, his Grace replied,
" He shall have the first good living that falls; had he
stopped to take care of me, I would never have given him
anything as long as he had lived." Of so much consequence
is it to hit the particular turn of a patron.

A WITCH AND A WIZARD.

Lord Chief Justice Holt resided at *Redgrave Hall*, Suffolk.
Once, when he presided in the Court of King's Bench, a
poor, decrepit old creature, equally bowed down by age,
poverty, and infirmity, was brought before him, charged as a
criminal on whom the full severity of the law might be
visited with exemplary effect. The terrors of impartiality
never sat on any Judge's brow with more impressive
dignity or threatening aspect than that of Judge Holt. The
trembling culprit was overwhelmed with her fears. The
charge was opened. " What is her crime ? " asked his Lordship. " Witchcraft." " And how is it proved ? " " She uses
a powerful spell." " Let me see it." The spell was handed

to the Bench. It appeared a small ball of variously coloured rags or silk, bound with threads of as many different hues; these were unwound and unfolded until there appeared a scrap of parchment, on which were written certain characters now nearly illegible from much use. "Is this the spell?" The prosecutor averred it was. The Judge, after looking at this potent charm a few minutes, addressed himself to the terrified prisoner: "Prisoner, how came you by this?" "A young gentleman, my Lord, gave it me to cure my child's ague." "How long since?" "Thirty years, my Lord." "And did it cure her?" "Oh, yes, and many others." "I am glad of it."

The Judge paused a few moments, and addressed himself to the Jury. "Gentlemen of the Jury, thirty years ago, I and some companions as thoughtless as myself went to this woman's dwelling, then a public-house, and after enjoying ourselves, found we had no means to discharge the reckoning. I had recourse to a stratagem: observing a child ill of an ague, I pretended I had a spell to cure her. I wrote the classic line you see on a scrap of parchment, and was discharged of the demand on me by the gratitude of the poor woman before us for the supposed benefit. Nature doubtless did much for the patient, the force of imagination the rest. This incident but ill suits my present character and the station in which I sit, but to conceal it would be to aggravate the folly for which it becomes me to atone, to endanger innocence and encourage superstition." The verdict may be imagined, and Judge Holt's address at this trial was one of the death blows which he gave to trials for witch-craft.

REV. JAMES FORD.

The Rev. James Ford, well known as the editor of the "Suffolk Garland," was for many years incumbent of St. Lawrence, Ipswich, and afterwards rector of Navestock, in Essex. He could not bear to see persons come into church when service had commenced. After he married, and whilst at Navestock, Mrs. Ford had frequently displeased him by inattention to this particular, and on one occasion, when she entered the church unusually late, he leaned over the desk, and said, " I wonder where you will be, madam, when the last trumpet sounds."

LORD THURLOW'S THUNDER.

The celebrated reply of Lord Thurlow to the Duke of Grafton, who had reproached him with his plebeian extraction and his recent elevation to the peerage, is described as superlatively great. He rose from the woolsack and advanced slowly to the place from which the Chancellor usually addressed the House, then, fixing on the Duke the look of Jove when he grasped the thunder—" I am amazed," he said, in a civil voice, " at the attack which the noble Duke has made upon me. Yes, my Lord "—considerably raising his voice—" I am amazed at his Grace's speech. The noble Duke cannot look before him, behind him, or on either side of him, without seeing some noble peer who owes his seat in this House to his successful exertions in the profession to which I belong. Does he not feel it as honourable to owe it to these, as to being the accident of an accident ? To all these noble Lords, the language of the noble Duke is as applicable and as insulting as it is to myself. But I don't fear to meet it singly and alone. No one venerates the peerage more than I do ; but, my Lord, I must say that the peerage solicited me, not I the peerage. Nay more, I can say, and I will say, that as a peer of Parliament, as Speaker of this right honourable House, as Keeper of the Great Seal, as guardian of Her Majesty's conscience, as Lord High Chancellor of England—nay, even in that character alone in which the noble Duke would think it an affront to be considered, but which character none can deny *me*—as a MAN, I am at this moment as respectable—I beg leave to add, I am at this time as much respected, as the proudest peer I now look down upon." The effect of this speech, both within the walls of Parliament and out of them, was prodigious. It gave Lord Thurlow an ascendancy in the House which no Chancellor had ever possessed ; it invested him in public opinion with a character for independence and honour, and this, although he was ever on the unpopular side of politics, made him always a favourite with the people.

ARCHBISHOP WHATELY'S HOSPITALITY AND WIT.

Sheridan, when asked what sort of wine he preferred, replied, " Other people's." It was not a joke which could come with truth from Dr. Whately, who seldom if ever dined abroad, and was never so happy as when presiding at the head of his hospitable table, round which every sort of good wine sped and flowed. No strait-laced whims ever penetrated these festive meetings. Conundrums and canons, logic and laughter, puns and parables, fell from the Archbishop in profusion. The fullest unreserve and the heartiest enjoyment reigned around. They were characterized by as much wit as wisdom. Fun, almost juvenile in its exuberance, was as often the order of the evening as logical puzzles or metaphysical speculations, and trying who should make the worst pun quite as frequently occurred as higher tests and tournaments of wit. At a farewell dinner to Dr. ———, Bishop elect of Cork, a bottle of rich old Waterloo port, instead of making a rapid circuit, rested before him : " Come ———," cried the Archbishop, from the head of the table, "though you *are* John Cork, you mustn't *stop* the bottle."

The reply attributed to the Bishop was quite in the Whatelian vein : "I see your Grace is disposed to *draw me out*. But though *charged* with *Cork*, I'm not going to be *screwed*."

" We are all most anxious to see you *elevated*," exclaimed the host.

"I leave to your Grace, as a disciple of Peel, the privilege of *opening the ports*," was the reply.

The Archbishop's points at dinner were often of a broadly humourous character, especially if he thought his presence imposed any feeling of awe or restraint. When a pause occurred, he would sometimes rouse the drooping embers by a touch of what he called "his hot poker." On one occasion, he cried out, "What is the female of a *mail* coach?" Several guesses were advanced, but not the right nail, until his Grace, amid convulsions of laughter, answered—"A *mis-carriage.*"

After he was attacked with paralysis, the Archbishop, whilst out for fresh air, leaning on the arm of his chaplain, was met by an old friend whose powers of pedestrianism had often been envied. "I hope your Grace is very much better to-day," said the friend. "Oh, I am very well indeed, if I could only persuade some strong fellow like you to lend me a pair of legs," was the reply.

"I should be only too happy to give you *my* legs, if your Grace has no objection to give me *your* head in exchange."

The Archbishop brightened up at this touch of wit and delicately conveyed compliment, and, laughing heartily, exclaimed, "What, Mr. ——, you don't mean to say that you are willing to exchange two *understandings* for one!"

Touching the word "either," Dr. Whately was asked whether *e-ther* or *i-ther* was the correct pronunciation. "*Ni-ther*," replied his Grace.

One of his last retorts conveyed a telling stroke of delicate irony: "They will begin to pelt me, now," said a freshly fledged Bishop, who sought consolation under the weight of a mitre, laden with some suspicion of a temporizing compliance on the education question.

"They have nearly given over that practice upon me," observed the Archbishop.

"Well, no one can say that I ever threw a stone at you," retorted the other.

"Certainly not," was the reply; "you only kept the clothes of those who did."

The Archbishop was very fond of making conundrums, and on the occasion of a meeting at the Famine Board, he asked his next neighbour, "Why Ireland was the richest country in the world? Because its *capital* is always *Dublin*" (doubling). And in reference to the Wicklow Railway, he asked, "Why it was the most unmusical line in the world ?" Answer—"Because it has a bray, a dundrum, and a still-organ upon it." To a person who, when asked a puzzling question, invariably closed his eyes in the intensity of his effort to solve it, the Archbishop said, "Sir, you resemble an ignorant pedagogue, who keeps his *pupils* in darkness."

"Why does the operation of hanging kill a man ?" inquired Dr. Whately. A physiologist replied, "Because inspiration is checked, circulation stopped, and blood suffuses and congests the brain." "Bosh !" replied his Grace, "it is because the rope is not long enough to let his feet touch the ground."

Among the "Evangelical" adherents of the Church of England, Dr. Whately was unpopular; his manners and habits tended to increase his unpopularity. They did not like to see their Archbishop sitting on the chains in front of his house in Dublin, smoking a long pipe, or (provided with a similar attribute), sauntering along the Donnybrook road, chewing the cud, not of tobacco, but "of sweet and bitter fancy." Dr. Parr was regarded as the greatest smoker of his day, but Dr. Whately boasted of being "*above Parr !*"

A man directed the Archbishop's attention to a valuable draught horse, as sagacious as he was powerful. "There is nothing," said the horse dealer, "that he cannot draw." "Can he draw an inference?" inquired Dr. Whately.

In hastening with a young clergyman to officiate at some religious ceremony in a neighbouring diocese, the chaplain, glancing at his watch, fell into a state of nervous agitation at their being so late. "My good young friend," said the

H

Archbishop, " I can only say to you what the criminal going to be hanged said to those around, who were hurrying him —" Let us take our time ; they can't begin without us."

He was never so strong as when making a pun.   In allusion to Lord Macaulay, who observed that "there was but one country in the world that presented the spectacle of a population of 8,000,000, with a church richly endowed for only 800,000 of that population," Dr. Whately said that the Irish Protestant Episcopacy was the poorest body of men, because they had only *one bob daily* amongst them."   Dr. Robert Daly, Bishop of Cashel, one of the most prominent polemics of his day, suggested this play upon his name.

A lady had the very bad taste to enter the Castle drawing-room in such ultra full dress, or rather undress, that more bust than *barège* was visible.   "Did you ever see anything so unblushing ? " whispered a custodian of the Great Seal, whose sense of decorum was outraged by the exhibition. " Never, since I was weaned," replied Dr. Whately.

In the course of a conversation or disquisition on Satan, he once startled his listeners by asking—" If the devil lost his tail, where should he go to find a new one ? " and without giving much time for reflection, replied, " To a gin palace, for *bad spirits* are *re-tailed* there."

" Pray, sir," he said to a loquacious prebendary who had made himself active in talking at the Archbishop's expense when his back was turned—" Pray, sir, why are you like the bell of your own church steeple ? "   " Because," replied the other, " I am always ready to sound the alarm when the church is in danger."   " By no means," said the Archbishop ; " it is because you have an empty head and a long tongue."

When Archbishop Whately was one day engaged in his gardening operations, a companion referred among other matters to the great revolution in the medical treatment of lunatics introduced by Pinel, who, instead of the straight waistcoat and other maddening goads, awarded to each patient healthful and agreeable occupation, including gardening and agriculture. " I think gardening would be a dangerous indulgence for lunatics," observed Dr. Whately. "How so ? " said his friend, surprised. " Because they might *grow madder*," was the witty rejoinder.

Soon after the introduction of the convict system into Ireland, a gentleman known and respected as an ardent advocate of reformatories, boasted to a friend who occupied a responsible office in the Irish government, that he held the system in such high estimation that he employed no servants in his house but those who had passed some time in a reformatory. The party so addressed was much struck by the information and its significance, and with suitable impressiveness he communicated both to the Archbishop. His Grace listened attentively to the recital, and at length quietly observed, " Your friend will waken some fine morning and find himself the only *spoon* left in the house."

Turning to a junior clergyman, he once asked, " What is the difference between a form and a ceremony ? The meaning seems nearly the same, yet there is a very nice distinction." Various answers were given. " Well," he said, " it lies in this : you sit upon a form, but you stand upon a ceremony."

A remarkable conundrum of his was, " Why can a man never starve in the Great Desert ? Because he can eat the *sand which is* (sandwiches) there. But what brought the sandwiches there ? Noah sent Ham, and his descendents mustered and bred (mustard and bread.) "

A VERY PARTICULAR PERSON.

When Mr. Vernon, in 1835, called at Constable's studio to see his pictures, he saw " Willy Lott's House," which was nearly completed, was very pleased with it, and became the purchaser. Prior to doing so, however, he asked Constable if the picture was painted for any particular person; to which Constable replied, "Yes, sir, it is painted for a *very particular* person—the person for whom I have all my life painted."

COWING A DOG.

When George Borrow was in Portugal, trying to circulate the Scriptures, his curiosity led him into some extraordinary places. "One day," he says, "whilst stumbling amongst ruined walls, he heard a tremendous bark, and presently an immense dog, such as those which guard the flocks in the neighbourhood against the wolves, came bounding to attack me, ' with eyes that glowed, and fangs that grinned.' Had I retreated, or had recourse to any other mode of defence than that which I invariably practise under such circumstances, he would probably have worried me; but I stooped till my chin nearly touched my knee, and looked at him full in the eyes; and as John Leyden says, in the noblest ballad which the Land of Heather has produced—

> ' The hound he growled, and back he fled,
>   As struck with fairy charm!'"

CRABBE AND HIS MASTER.

When Crabbe returned from London to Aldborough, he engaged himself as an assistant in the shop of a Mr. Maskill, who had lately commenced business there as surgeon and apothecary—a stern and powerful man. Mr. Crabbe, the first time he had occasion to write his name, chanced to misspell it *Maskwell;* and this gave great offence. "D—n you, sir," he exclaimed, "do you take me for a proficient in deception? *Mask-ill—Mask-ill;* and so you shall find me."

LET US BE INDEPENDENT OF FOREIGNERS.

The wit and sarcasm which shone conspicuously in the orations of William Johnson Fox, when agitating for the repeal of the Corn Law, were of great service to the cause. One of his best hits of this class was his reply to the Protectionist cry, that "we must not depend upon foreigners." He took a member of the aristocracy, and thus analysed his appearance, tastes, and modes of life, in order to show how much of all is of the true home growth. "A French cook dresses *his dinner for him*, and a Swiss valet dresses *him for dinner*. He hands down his lady, decked with pearls that never grew in the shell of a British oyster; and her waving plume of ostrich feathers certainly never formed the tail of a barn-door fowl. The viands of his table are from all the countries in the world; his wines are from the banks of the Rhine and the Rhone. In his conservatory he regales his sight with the blossoms of *South American* flowers. In his smoking, he gratifies his scent with the weeds of *North America*. His favourite horse is of *Arabian* blood, and his pet dog of the *St. Bernard* breed. His gallery is rich with pictures of the *Flemish* school, and statues from *Greece*. For his amusement, he goes to hear *Italian* singers warble *German* music, followed by a *French* ballet. If he rise to judicial honours, the ermine which decorates his shoulders is a production that was never on the back of a British beast. His very mind is not English in its attainments. It is a mere *pic-nic* of foreign contributions. His poetry and philosophy are from *Greece* and *Rome;* his geometry is from *Alexandria;* his arithmetic from *Arabia;* and his religion from *Palestine*. In his cradle, in his infancy, he rubbed his gums with coral from oriental oceans; and when he dies, his monument will be sculptured in marble from the quarries of Carrara. And yet this is the man who says, 'Oh, let us be independent of foreigners!' "

SIR CHARLES BUNBURY AND THE JEWELS.

In the *Ipswich Journal*, May 16th, 1778, the following anecdote is given :—

" *Bon Ton Anecdote.*—At the time when the black-legged

gentry of the turf were most importunate in their demands
on Sir Charles B——, he recollected that he might find a
temporary resource in his lady's jewels; and therefore, getting
the key of her cabinet, sent for a jeweller, unknown to her,
and told him he had a job for him, which he must execute
with the utmost expedition; and producing the baubles,
ordered him to go immediately and take out all the jewels,
and re-set them with paste. The man hesitated to comply
with his commands. Sir Charles d——d him for a fool, and
asked him why he did not go about it? "For a very good
reason (replied the jeweller), if your honour must know it:
because I have done the very same job for her Ladyship
already."

AN END TO TRIALS FOR WITCHCRAFT.

Among the many merits won by Chief Justice Holt, we
must not forget that of effectually repealing the acts against
witchcraft, although they nominally continued on the statute
book to a succeeding reign. Eleven poor creatures were
successively tried before him for this supposed crime, and the
prosecutions were supported by the accustomed evidence of
long fasting, vomiting pins and ten-penny nails, secret
teats sucked by imps, devil's marks, and cures by the sign of
the cross, or drawing blood from the sorceress—which had
misled Sir Matthew Hale; but by Holt's good sense and
tact in every instance, the imposture was detected to the
satisfaction of the jury, and there was an acquittal. One
of the strongest *prima facie* cases made out before him, was
said to have been that against the woman to whom many
years before he had given the cabalistic charm, which was
adduced as the chief proof of her guilt. At last, the Chief
Justice effectually accomplished his object, by directing that
a prosecutor who pretended that he had been bewitched
should himself be indicted as an impostor and a cheat. This
fellow had sworn that a spell cast upon him had taken away
from him the power of swallowing, and that he had fasted for

ten weeks; but the manner in which he had secretly received nourishment was clearly proved. He nevertheless made a stout defence, and numerous witnesses deposed to his expectoration of pins, and his abhorence of victuals; all which they ascribed to the malignant influence of the witch. The Judge, having extracted from a pretended believer in him the answer, that "All the devils in hell could not have helped him to fast so long," and having proved by cross-examining another witness, that he had a large stock of pins in his pocket, from which those supposed to be vomited were taken, summed up with great acuteness, and left it to the jury to say, not whether the defendant was bewitched, but whether he was *non compos mentis*, or was fully aware of the knavery he was committing, and knowingly wished to impose on mankind. The jury found a verdict of *guilty;* and the impostor standing in the pillory, to the satisfaction of the whole country, no female was ever after in danger of being hanged or burned for being old, wrinkled, and paralytic.

CHIEF JUSTICE HOLT AND FALSE PROPHETS.

Chief Justice Holt seemed to have had a high reputation among his cotemporaries for detecting false pretences of all sorts, and exposing those who put on an aspect of extraordinary sanctity. To a band of fanatics called the "Prophets," Holt had a particular antipathy. One of these, named Lacy, being beaten in a trial before him, complained of injustice. Calamy, the famous Presbyterian divine, relates that, he having repeated these complaints to Holt, "My Lord by this time was moved, and setting his hand to his side, cried out, '*An honest cause did he call it?* I tell you, sir, and you have full liberty to tell him, or any else you think fit, from me, that it was one of the foulest causes I ever had the hearing of, and that none but an arrant knave would have had the concern in it that Lacy had; for it was a plain design, in concert with a notorious jilt, to have cheated the right heir of a good estate upon his supplying her with money. If one that could do this may be allowed to set up for a prophet, the world is come to a fine pass.'"

Holt having some time after committed another of the brotherhood, called *John Atkins*, to take his trial for seditious language, the same Lacy called at the Chief Justice's house in Bedford Row, and desired to see him. *Servant:* "My Lord is unwell to-day, and cannot see company." *Lacy* (in a very solemn tone): "Acquaint your master that I must see him, for I bring a message to him from the Lord God." The Chief Justice, having ordered Lacy in, and demanded his business, was thus addressed: "I come to you a prophet from the Lord God, who has sent me to thee, and would have thee grant a *nolle prosequi* for John Atkins, his servant, whom thou hast sent to prison." *Holt, C. J..* "Thou art a false prophet, and a lying knave! If the Lord God had sent thee it would have been to the Attorney-General, for he knows that it belongeth not to the Chief Justice to grant a *nolle prosequi;* but I, as Chief Justice, can grant a warrant to commit thee to bear him company." This was immediately done, and both prophets were convicted and punished.

WHATELY'S OPINION OF WOMEN.

Archbishop Whately, when referring to women, whether in his writings or his conversation, was rarely complimentary. "Women," he said, "reason wrongly from right premises, sometimes rightly from wrong premises, and always poke the fire from the top." When disposed to be unusually gracious, he would sometimes pay them such dubious compliments as, "Woman is like the reed, which bends to every breeze, but breaks not in the tempest." With such provocation it is no wonder that Dr. Whately should have been no favourite with women, to whom, as Byron says, "revenge is sweet." In his sermons he never preached to the nerves—he appealed to the understanding; and his congregations, therefore, contained more cloth than crinoline. A few years before his retirement from the Board of National Education, he was requested by a literary lady, who, however, wore petticoats long enough to conceal her "blue stockings," to meet her by appointment at the Model School in Marlborough street, and act as her *cicerone* in exploring it. The invitation was accepted, and two hours full of interest passed. When the Archbishop and the lady, face to face, were going home in a cab, his Grace suddenly broke through a brown study, by exclaiming, as he fixed his eyes stedfastly at Miss ————, "I'm beginning to think that you are a man!" The lady was embarrassed. The Archbishop repeated the remark, adding, "I never in the whole course of my life knew a woman keep an appointment before."

It is evident that, notwithstanding his avowed admiration of the gifted woman who was his wife, Dr. Whately held no very high opinion of ladies, intellectually considered; and such jokes as "the difference between a looking glass and a lady consists in one reflecting without speaking, and the other speaking without reflecting," were always welcome at his fireside.

SIR EDWARD COKE A RIOTER.

Sir Edward Coke felt very acutely the loss of the Lord Chief Justiceship, and after his deprivation he tried to regain the favour of Buckingham, the King's favourite, by marrying his daughter, Lady Frances, only fourteen years old, who was a very rich heiress, to Buckingham's elder brother, Sir John Villiers, who was nearly thrice her age, and exceedingly poor. Sir Edward's wife, however, Lady Hatton, became frantic with rage, when she heard of the proposed match, not so much at her disapproval of Sir John Villiers, as on account of such an important family arrangement having been made without consulting her. When the first burst of her resentment had passed over, she appeared more calm, but this arose from her having secretly formed a resolution to carry off her daughter, and marry her to another. The same night, Sir Edward still keeping up his habit of going to bed at nine o'clock, soon after ten o'clock she sallied forth with the Lady Frances from Hatton House, Holborn. They entered a coach which was waiting for them at a little distance, and travelling by unfrequented roads, they arrived next morning at a house of the Earl of Argyle's, at Oatlands, then rented by Sir Edward Withipole, their cousin. There they were shut up in the hope that there could be no trace of the place of their concealment. While they laid hid Lady Hatton not only did everything possible to prejudice her daughter against Sir John Villiers, but offered her in marriage to the young Earl of Oxford, and actually showed her a forged letter purporting to come from that nobleman, which asserted that he was deeply attached to her, and that he aspired to her hand.

Meanwhile, Sir Edward Coke, having ascertained the retreat of the fugitives, applied to the Privy Council for a warrant to search for his daughter; and as there was some difficulty in obtaining it, he resolved to take the law into his own hands. Accordingly, the Ex-Chief Justice of England mustered a band of armed men, consisting of his sons, his dependents, and his servants, and himself putting on a breastplate with a sword at his side, and pistols at his saddle bow, he marched at their head upon Oatlands. When they arrived there they found the gate leading to the house bolted and barricaded. This they forced open without difficulty, but the outer door of the house was so secured as long to defy all their efforts to gain admission. The Ex-Chief Justice repeatedly demanded his child in the King's name, and laid down for law, that, " if death should ensue it would be justifiable homicide in him, but murder in those who opposed him." One of the party, gaining entrance by a window, let in all the rest; but still there were several doors to be broken open. At last Sir Edward found the object of his pursuit secreted in a small closet, and without stopping to parley, lest there should be a rescue, he seized his daughter, tore her from her mother, and placing her behind her brother, rode off with her to his house at Stoke Pogis, in Buckinghamshire. There he secured her in an upper chamber, of which he himself kept the key.

COKE AS ATTORNEY-GENERAL.

Sir Edward Coke filled the office of Attorney-General for twelve years, and unscrupulously stretched the prerogative of the Crown, showing himself for the time utterly regardless of public liberty. He perverted the criminal law to the oppression of many individuals; and the arrogance of his demeanour was unparalleled. His brutal behaviour on the trial of the Earl of Essex, and his insulting language at the trial of Sir Walter Raleigh, are disgraceful to him as an advocate. He on all occasions exhibited a desire to obtain convictions for any offences, and against any individuals, at the pleasure of his employers; and he became hardened against all the dictates of justice, of pity, of remorse, and of decency. He gave the greatest satisfaction to Lord Burleigh, and to his son and successor, Robert Cecil, so that legal dignities which fell were within his reach; but fond of riches rather than ease, he despised being made a judge, and thus was unwilling to be "forked up to the bench," which with a sad defalcation of income, offered him very little increase of dignity; for till the elevation of Jeffreys, in the reign of James II., no common-law judge had been made a peer. Coke's salary as Attorney-General was only £81 6s. 8d.; but his official emoluments amounted to £7,000 a year; and Lord Campbell says, that "his private practice besides must have been very considerable."

DR. MESSENGER MONSEY.

The eccentric Dr. Messenger Monsey commenced the practice of medicine at Bury St. Edmund's. He was the son of a Norfolk clergyman, received his education at St. Mary's Hall, Oxford, and studied physic under Sir Benjamin

Wrinch, at Norwich. A "fortunate accident" was the occasion of his leaving Bury. Lord Godolphin, grandson of the Duke of Marlborough, being on a journey to his seat at Gogmagog, near Newmarket, was taken exceedingly ill. The only medical aid next at hand was at the town of Bury. Dr. Monsey was called in, and found so successful in his applications, as not only to reinstate his Lordship in a comfortable degree of health, but to engage also throughout life the warmest gratitude of his noble patient. Lord Godolphin found with surprise his rural physician to be a man of candour, of cheerfulness, of literary talents, and of convivial wit, and felt strongly disposed to patronise one so very superior in all respects to the situation in which he found him. Upon his Lordship's recovery, his offers were so very liberal and kind, that Dr. Monsey could not hesitate to accompany his patron to town. A vacancy occurring in Chelsea Hospital, by his Lordship's interest he was appointed, in 1742, Physician to the Royal Hospital; but so necessary had the doctor's company become to his patron, that he was to be allowed to reside as usual at St. James's, which he did till his Lordship's decease, when he removed to Chelsea, where he died, December 26th, 1788, at the advanced age of ninty-four. Monsey was also the companion of Sir Robert Walpole, who used to call him his "Norfolk Doctor." He was a great billiard player. Sir Robert said one day to him, "I don't know how it is, Monsey, but you are the only one I can't beat." "They get places," replied the Doctor; "I get a dinner and praise." As a physician he was skillful and benevolent, and much respected by all the pensioners, particularly for his marked attention to them. But his reputation rests principally upon his wit, in which he bore a great resemblance to Dean Swift. "The exuberance of his wit (says Boswell), which like the web of life, was of mingled yarn, often rendered his conversation exceedingly entertaining, sometimes indeed alarmingly offensive, and at other times pointedly pathetic and instructive.

The following anecdote is said to be well attested. "He lived so long in his office of Physician to Chelsea Hospital, that the reversion of his place had been successively promised to medical friends of the various Paymasters-General of the forces. Looking out of his window one day, and observing a gentleman below examining the cottage and gardens, who he knew had secured the reversion of his place, the Doctor came down stairs and accosted him with, "Well, sir, I see you are examining your house and gardens that *are to be*, and I will assure you that they are both very pleasant and very convenient. But I must tell you one circumstance—you are the fifth man that has had the reversion of the place, and I have buried them all; and what is more," continued he, looking very scientifically at him, "there is something in your face that tells me I shall bury you too." The event justified the prediction; and what is more extraordinary, at the time of the doctor's death there was not a person who seems to have even solicited the promise of a reversion.

On the morning of the day of his death, being at breakfast, he said to his attendant, "I shall entirely lose the game;" and upon her asking him what game, he replied, "The game of *a hundred*, which I have played for very earnestly many years; but I shall lose it now, for I expect to die in a few hours."

A WARM ANXIETY.

One evening, whilst Nelson was waiting before Copenhagen, in 1801, he received a letter from Sir Hyde Parker informing him that a Swedish squadron was at sea. Sir Hyde was off Bornholm, about twenty-four miles from Copenhagen. The wind was foul; but the moment Nelson received the letter he ordered a boat to be manned, and though it was nearly dark, set out to row to his Commander-in-chief, to be in time for the battle which the news seemed to announce. He was suffering from severe indisposition; the night was bitterly cold; yet so eager was his hurry that he would not even stop to get a great-coat. When in the boat they offered him a cloak, he refused it, saying, " his anxiety for his country kept him warm."

AN EXAMPLE FOR WIDOWS.

In the year 1799, a tenant of Mr. Way's, at Hasketon, near Woodbridge, died, leaving a widow with fourteen children, the oldest of whom was a girl under fourteen years of age. He had rented fourteen acres of pasture land, on which he kept two cows. These cows, with his little furniture and clothing, were all the property he left. The parish of Hasketon was within the district of the Nacton House of Industry, and the Directors of that establishment offered to relieve the widow, by taking her seven youngest children into the House. When this was proposed to her, she replied, in great agitation, that she would rather die in working to maintain her children, than part with any of them; or she would go with all of them into the House, and work for them there; but if her landlord would continue her in the farm (as she called it), she would undertake to bring up the whole fourteen without any help from the parish. She was a strong woman, about forty-five years old, and of a noble spirit; happily, too, she had to deal with a benevolent man. He told her she should continue as his tenant, and hold the land for the first year rent free; and at the same time, unknown to her, he directed his receiver not to call upon her afterwards, thinking with even that indulgence it would be a great thing if she could maintain so large a family. But this further liberality was not needed. She brought her rent regularly every year after the first, held the land till she had placed twelve of her children in service, and then resigned it to take the employment of a nurse, which would enable her to provide for the remaining two for the little time longer that they needed support, and which was more suited to her declining years.

PUNCTUALITY.

The most industrious disposition often proves of little avail for the want of a habit of very easy acquirement—punctuality, the jewel on which the whole machinery of successful industry may be said to turn.

When Lord Nelson was leaving London on his last expedition against the enemy, a quantity of cabin furniture was ordered to be sent on board his ship. He had a farewell dinner-party at his house, and the upholsterer, having waited upon his Lordship with an account of the completion of the goods, was brought into the eating room, in a corner of which his Lordship spoke with him. The upholsterer stated to his noble employer that everything was finished and packed, and would go in the waggon from a certain inn at *six o'clock*. "And you go to the inn, Mr. A——, and see them off." "I shall, my Lord. I shall be there *punctually at six*." "*A quarter before six*, Mr. A——," returned Lord Nelson; "be there a quarter before six. To that *quarter of an hour* I owe everything in life."

HABITS AND MANNERS OF BISHOP BLOMFIELD.

The diligence displayed by Bishop Blomfield in his public business was observable also in all the work which he did in private. He rose in summer at six, in winter at half-past, and the time before breakfast was occupied by the study of Scripture, or with writing sermons and letters. The hours for prayers, for meals, and for everything in the household with which he had to do were regulated with the same punctuality as his business. The brief interval between prayers and breakfast would be seized for work. His letters accompanied him to the table, except when guests were in the house; for to them, in spite of his unceasing occupations, he never failed to show the attention of a kind and courteous host. His sermons, of which he wrote more than many parochial clergymen, were often commenced on the previous

Sunday, taken up again in the middle of unfinished sentences, during any spare minutes he could command, and completed long before the time of their delivery. A diligent student, his knowledge seemed to be arranged in his mind much as his letters were arranged on his shelves; in a moment he could lay his hand on a particular letter, though received years before; and in the same way he could in an instant draw from the store-house of his memory the knowledge which the occasion required, even though he might not have read anything on the subject for many years.

The society of literary men gave the Bishop peculiar pleasure, and this privilege he had enjoyed to some extent from the time when he won his university honours. On his promotion to the See of London he had greater opportunities of meeting the best men of the time. During his days of health and strength, the house at Fulham was filled with agreeable society; and such men as Sir James Mackintosh, Wordsworth, Rogers, the Bishop of Oxford, Sir David Dundas, Sir Henry Holland, and many others who might be named, gave no little charm to his table. At these times the Bishop entered with a keen relish into the delights of social intercourse, and contributed more than his share to the general enjoyment, by the animation, the humour, and the learning of his conversation. It was in the company of men such as the Chevalier Bunsen, Dr. Whewell, Macaulay, Hallam, and others of the same calibre, that the variety and exactness of Bishop Blomfield's knowledge were more fully shown. It was only in the intercourse of such men that he sustained a continuous conversation, the contact of equal minds seeming necessary to draw forth his latent powers and hidden stores. In his social intercourse with other minds he seemed to find relaxation in talk, which, while it did not tax his mind, was always instructive and agreeable, and often entertaining, for Bishop Blomfield was gifted with no ordinary flow of genuine humour. This gift, so dangerous when unchecked, was tempered in him as became a bishop, by charity and sobriety. His wit, as was natural in one whose early studies had been philological, was often *verbal*, and he was a great lover of puns. He excelled in relating anecdotes, and was second to none in the way in which he would tell, a good story—so pointed and epigrammatic, the very look and tone contributing to the effect, and all natural and without an effort, the outpourings of a genial nature, when, without offence, reserve could be laid aside.

While the Bishop's genial temperament found pleasure in innocent mirth, in his views of what was innocent he was guided by a high, and what some might think an over strict standard. He wrote to Lord Lowther, then Lord Chamberlain, requesting that the new pleasure grounds in St. James' Park might be closed during the hours of morning service, on Sundays. When invited to dinner on a Sunday by William IV., soon after his accession, he declined, stating that he never dined out on that day; and later in life he always opposed the opening of the Chrystal Palace, or any places of amusement on Sundays. He regarded with great caution the pleasures of the world; so that, without a tinge of puritanism in his temperament, he was careful in the amusements which he allowed in his own household. A playing card was never, with his knowledge, allowed in his house; he had an objection to public theatres, without any prejudice against the drama itself; and whilst he thought dancing an innocent and healthy pastime for the young, he disliked balls on account of the unwholesome excitement too often inseparable from them. He considered shooting unsuitable to the profession of a clergyman, and hunting as utterly inconsistent with that seriousness and quietness of demeanour and conduct, the want of which must weaken, if it does not destroy the effect of a clergyman's preaching.

There was in Bishop Blomfield's disposition a natural fondness for the young, which formed a link between himself and them. During his holidays, or when he had more leisure than usual, he would take part in his children's

I

recreations, and sometimes entertain them by composing amusing or descriptive verses. He had a gift of versification and even a poetic vein, which, however, he had scarcely any time to indulge.

But the Bishop's chief recreations were music and gardening. In both he took especial delight. His knowledge of music had been acquired in early years; and even in later life he would occasionally accompany his children. He had a cultivated and refined taste, and an ear so sensitive that the slightest discord, which would escape general observation, seemed to cause him acute pain. His acquaintance with the works of the best musicians was extensive, and he took every opportunity which did not interfere with more important engagements, of hearing the best performers, especially instrumentalists.

Gardening, however, was the Bishop's chief amusement. Early in life he had acquired a knowledge of botany, and he found in the palace gardens a soil in which he could employ and enlarge that knowledge. He introduced the latest improvements into the gardens, and planted it with new and choice trees. He seemed to know each tree and shrub, and to regard them with a kind affection; and when guests were with him it was his amusement to introduce them to the names and qualities of the rarer specimens. He took a lively interest in the Horticultural Society, and often attended the meetings at Chiswick Gardens, where he was seen examining each fruit and flower with close and delighted attention.

HUMANITY OF NELSON.

As soon as the Danish captains had hauled down their colours at the battle of Copenhagen, boats were sent from the English fleet to get possession of the prizes, but in defiance of all the rules of war, these boats were fired on by the batteries on shore, and even by the ships themselves that had struck, though the island batteries could only reach our boats by firing through those ships, thus, of course, adding to the loss which they had already sustained. Nelson was angry at this breach of the usual laws of battle, and shocked at the needless havoc which was being thus caused by it. In his view, the moment that the Danes on board the captured ships had become his prisoners, he had become their protector; and acting on this idea, and feeling that he had now attained so decisive a superiority in the battle that he could afford to be the first to propose its suspension, he retired to the stern gallery, and, while the enemy's bullets were still dealing death around him, wrote a letter to the Crown Prince. "He was authorized," it said, "to spare Denmark when she ceased to resist; but if the firing on his boats was continued, he must burn his prizes, without having the power of saving the brave men who defended them. The brave Danes," he added, "were his brothers, and should never be the enemies of the English." When the letter was finished, he sent to his cabin for wax with which to seal it. He was offered a wafer. "No," said he, "this is not a time to appear hurried or informal." The man who had been sent for the wax was killed on his way to the cabin; he ordered another messenger to be sent on the same errand, and having carefully sealed the letter, he sent Captain Sir Frederick Thesiger, a young officer who was serving on this occasion as a volunteer, to convey it, under a flag of truce, to the Crown Prince.

HONOURS PAID TO ARTHUR YOUNG.

In no country were the merits of Arthur Young better estimated than in France; but there was scarcely a city on the continents either of Europe or America that did not pay some tribute to his talents. The Economical and Agricultural Societies established at Berne, Zurich, Manheim, Celle, Florence, Milan, Copenhagen, Brussels, New York, Philadelphia, and Vienna all sent him their diplomas. The Society of Arts adjudged him the honorary gold medal; the Salford Agricultural Society presented him with a medal, inscribed, "For his services to the public," and he was complimented by the Board of Agriculture, with a gold medal for "long and faithful services in agriculture." George III. made him a present of a Spanish Merino ram; Count Rostopchin, the celebrated governor of Moscow, presented him with a snuff-box, turned by himself out of a block of oak, richly studded with diamonds, and bearing a motto in the Russian language which signifies, "From a pupil to his master;" and the Empress Catherine presented him, through the hands of her ambassador, with a magnificent gold snuff-box, together with two rich ermine cloaks, designed as gifts to his wife and daughter. In addition to these honours, his agricultural writings have appeared in almost every language in Europe. In France they were translated and published in 20 vols. by express order of the French Directory, and in Russia by command of the Empress Catherine.

CRABBE'S COURAGE.

Although so gentle and amiable in disposition, Crabbe seemed on all occasions to be insensible to physical danger.

Soon after he came into possession of the property at Parham, he detected his bailiff in some connection with smugglers, and charged him with the fact. The man flew into a violent passion, grasped a knife, and exclaimed, with an inflamed countenance, "No man shall call me a rogue!" Crabbe smiled at his rage, and said in a quiet tone, "Now, Robert, you are too much for me; put down your knife, and then we can talk on equal terms." The man hesitating, Crabbe, lifting his voice, added, "Get out of the house, you scoundrel!" and he was obeyed.

He was invariably bold and uncompromising in the midst of opposition and reproach. During the violence of a contested election at Trowbridge, he was twice assailed by a mob of his parishioners, with hisses and the most virulent abuse. He replied to their formidable menaces, by "rating them roundly." When the chaise drove up to his door on the day of election, to take him to the poll, a riotous and tumultuous assemblage besieged his house to deter him from going. The mob threatened to destroy the chaise, and tear him to pieces, if he attempted to set out. In the face of them he came out calmly, told them they might kill him if they chose; but whilst alive, nothing should prevent his giving a vote at the election according to his promise and principles; and he set off, undisturbed and unhurt, to vote.

POPULARITY OF CHIEF JUSTICE HOLT.

Of all the Judges in the annals of English History, Sir John Holt has gained the highest reputation, merely by the exercise of judicial functions. He was not a statesman, like Clarendon; he was not a philosopher, like Bacon; he was not an orator, like Mansfield; yet he fills nearly as great a space in the eye of posterity; and some enthusiastic lovers of jurisprudence regard him with higher veneration than any English judge who preceded or has followed him. The respect in which his conduct and abilities were held during his life, was on one occasion very strongly manifested. When William III. ascended the throne, both himself and his ministers were laudably anxious to elevate to the Bench the most learned and upright men that could be found in the profession of the law, the corruption and incompetency of the judges having been one of the chief grounds on which the nation had resolved upon a change of dynasty. Great deliberation was necessary for this purpose. After many consultations, to avoid all favouritism, the following plan was adopted, that every privy councillor should bring a list of the twelve persons whom he deemed the fittest to be the twelve judges, and that the individuals who had the greatest number of suffrages should be appointed. It is a curious fact that howsoever the lists of the different privy councillors varied, they all agreed in first presenting the name of Sir John Holt, such was his reputation for law—such satisfaction had he given in dispensing justice when Recorder of London, and in such respect was he held for his consistent career in public life. Sir John was made Chief Justice of the King's Bench. The King willingly ratified this choice, and when the appointment was announced in the *London Gazette*, it was hailed with joy by the whole nation.

WISDOM AND HUMANITY OF JUDGE HOLT.

Chief Justice Holt was the first to lay down the doctrine that the *status* of slavery cannot exist in England, and that as soon as a slave breathes the air of England he is free. The subject was brought before him on two occasions, and on both occasions he contended boldly for the rights of man. He said, at the second trial, " By the common-law, no man could have property in another man, except in special cases, as in a villain, or a captive taken in war; but in England there is no such thing as a slave, and a human being was never a chattel, to be sold for a price, and when wrongfully seized, to have a value put upon him in damages by a jury, like an ox or an ass."

He showed considerable boldness in construing the statute requiring persons to attend their parish churches. " Parishes," he said, " were instituted for the ease and benefit of the people, and not of the parson; that they might have a place certain to repair to when they thought convenient, and a parson from whom they had a right to receive instructions ; " and he held that a person was not subject to a penalty if he attended any other church than that of his own parish.

He put an end to the practice which had hitherto prevailed of giving evidence against a prisoner of prior misconduct. Thus, on the trial before him, of Harrison, for the murder of Dr. Clench, the counsel for the prosecution calling a witness to prove some felonious design of the prisoner three years before, the Judge indignantly exclaimed, " Hold, hold ! what are you doing now? Are you going to arraign his whole life ? How can he defend himself from charges of which he has no notice ? And how many issues are to be raised to perplex me and the jury ? Away! away! that ought not to be; that is nothing to this matter."

He likewise put an end to the revolting practice of trying prisoners in fetters. Hearing a clanking when Cranburne, charged with being implicated in the "Assasination plot," was brought to the bar to be arraigned, he said, without any complaint being made to him, " I should like to know why the prisoner is brought in ironed. If fetters were necessary for his safe custody before, there is no danger of escape or rescue here. Let them be instantly knocked off; when prisoners are tried, they should stand at their ease."

A still more important improvement in criminal trials on his suggestion was introduced, by Parliament passing an Act which for the first time allowed witnesses called for the prisoner to be examined upon oath.

THE "GREAT SEAL" REFUSED.

When William III. took the Great Seal from Lord Somers, who refused voluntarily to resign it, the King, considering that Chief Justice Holt was by far the fittest man to take possession of it, sent for him to Hampton Court, and showing him the " bauble," offered immediately to deliver it into his hand, with the title of Lord Chancellor, a peerage being to follow. The royal astonishment no doubt was great, when Holt pronounced these memorable words: " I feel highly honoured by your Majesty's gracious offer, but all the time I was at the bar, I never had more than one cause in chancery, and *that* I lost, so that I cannot think myself qualified for so great a trust." The King in vain attempted to shake his resolution ; all that Holt could be induced to promise at this interview was that, if there should be a necessity for putting the Great Seal into commission for a short time, he would act as one of the Lords Commissioners.

CHIEF JUSTICE HOLT'S BATTLE WITH THE CROWN.

While Chief Justice, Sir John Holt gained great popularity

by his contests with the two Houses of Parliament, for in each case he nobly asserted and vindicated his own independence. But in addition to his contests with these two branches of the legislature, he had also singularly enough to fight a battle with the Crown. The great sinecure office of Chief Clerk of the court of King's Bench, now compensated by a pension of £9,000 a year, falling vacant, Sir John Holt granted it to his brother Roland, and the question arose whether the patronage of it belonged to the Chief Justice or to the King? This came on to be decided at a trial at the bar before the three puisne judges and a jury. A chair was placed on the floor of the court for Lord Chief Justice Holt, on which he sat *uncovered* near his counsel. It was proved that the Chief Justices of the King's Bench had appointed to the office from the earliest times, till a patent was granted irregularly by Charles II. to his natural son, the Duke of Grafton, and there was a verdict against the King, which was confirmed on appeal to the House of Lords.

JOHN CONSTABLE AND SIR WILLIAM BEECHEY.

Sir William Beechey called upon Constable, and looking at one of his unfinished paintings, said, " Why, d——n it, Constable, what a d——n fine picture you are making ; but you look d——n ill, and you have got a d——n bad cold."

CONSTABLE'S NOTIONS OF THE REFORM BILL.

Writing to Leslie in 1831, Constable says, " What makes me dread this tremendous attack on the constitution of the country is, that the wisest and best of the Lords are seriously and firmly objecting to it, and it goes to give the Goverment into hands of the rabble and dregs of the people, and the devil's agents on earth, the agitators. Do you think that the Duke of Wellington, the Archbishop of Canterbury, and Copley, and Eldon, and Abbot, and all the wisest and best men we have would oppose it, if it were to do good to the country? I do not. No Whig Government ever can do good to this peculiar country."

LORD THURLOW AND THE DUCHESS.

The widowed Duchess of Rutland did not forget the poet Crabbe, the *protégé* of her lamented husband, and being kindly desirous of retaining him in her neighbourhood, she gave him a letter to Lord Chancellor Thurlow, earnestly requesting him to exchange the two small livings Mr. Crabbe held in Dorsetshire, for two of superior value in the vale of Belvoir. Crabbe proceeded to London, but was not very courteously received by Lord Thurlow. " No," he growled, " by G—d I will not do this for any man in England." But he did it, nevertheless, for a woman in England. The good Duchess, on arriving in town, waited on him personally to renew her request, and he yielded. Crabbe, having passed the necessary examination at Lambeth, received a dispensation from the Archbishop, and became rector of Muston, in Leicestershire, and the neighbouring parish of Allington, in Lincolnshire.

MUSIC AND ARCHBISHOP WHATELY.

Although full of poetic appreciation and power, Dr. Whately, like Samuel Johnson, had no ear for music, and his biographer expresses a doubt whether the Archbishop could at once distinguish the "Dead March in Saul" from "St. Patrick's Day." He once sent for a popular composer, who was a citizen of Dublin, and expressed a desire that he should furnish a chant within a given time. The task was executed to the almost enthusiastic satisfaction of the composer, whose equanimity was much disturbed by the Archbishop insisting that some sacred poetry, in the authorship of which he had an interest, should be set to the identical music supplied. In vain the composer endeavoured to explain that the Archbishop's lines fell short by several feet of the measure of the melody; but Dr. Whately pushed the objections aside and peremptorily desired that they should go in unaltered. The chant, with all its imperfections on its head, was subsequently often sung throughout the churches of the city, thus illustrating the virtue of canonical obedience, and at the same time showing that the Archbishop knew more about his mitre than his metre. Dr. Whately, however, although innocent of music, respected it as a great science, just as he respected trigonometry, of which he knew almost nothing; and when, in 1848, Jenny Lind, with her red coat and drum, took Dublin by storm, the Archbishop showed the daughter of the regiment considerable attention, and invited her to his house.

CONSTABLE AND ITALIAN MUSIC.

A mind like Constable's, united to a nervous temperament so sensitive, could not be indifferent to music. In his youth he was a good flute player, but he laid the instrument aside, as he found that painting required his whole attention. He preferred simplicity and expression to an ostentatious display of art, and once at a musical party, during a trio in Italian with which his ears were stunned, and which was only fit for the vast area of the opera house, he whispered to Leslie, "I dare say it is very fine, for it is very disagreeable; but if those people were to make such a noise before your door or mine we should send for the police to take them away."

CRABBE'S WRETCHED CONDITION IN LONDON.

In his "Journal," May 16th, 1780, the poet thus writes: "Oh, my dear Mira, how you distress me; you inquire into my affairs, and love not to be denied—yet you must. To what purpose should I tell you the particulars of my gloomy situation: that I have parted with my money, sold my *wardrobe*, pawned my watch, am in debt to my landlord, and finally at some loss how to eat a week longer? Yet you say, 'Tell me all.' Ah, my dear Sally, do not desire it; you must not yet be told these things. Appearance is what distresses

me—I *must* have dress, and therefore am horribly fearful I
shall accompany fashion with fasting; but a fortnight more
will tell me of a certainty."

FUNERAL OF CHIEF JUSTICE HOLT.

Lord Chief Justice Holt died at his house in Bedford Row,
London, on the 5th of March, 1710. The interment was
ordered to take place at Redgrave, in Suffolk, and not only
all the heads of the law, with the barristers and students, but
the principal nobility and gentry in London, of all shades of
political opinions, attended the funeral procession several
miles from the metropolis. When the hearse approached the
neighbourhood of Redgrave, it was met by an immense assemblage from the surrounding country. Redgrave Hall,
formerly the residence of Lord Keeper Bacon, and where he
had entertained Queen Elizabeth, had been purchased from
the family of the Bacons by Chief Justice Holt, and there he
spent his vacations as a private gentleman, mixing familiarly
with all ranks, and particularly with the more humble. In
consequence, all the inhabitants of Redgrave and its adjoining parishes now congregated to do honour to him whose
face they were to see no more, but whose virtues they were
to talk of to their children's children. They cared little about
his political conduct, but they had heard and they believed
that he was the greatest judge that had appeared on the
earth since the time of Daniel; and they knew that he was
condescending, kind-hearted, and charitable. It is said that
as the body was lowered into the grave prepared for it in the
chancel of the church at Redgrave, not a dry eye was to be
seen, and the rustic lamentations there uttered eloquently
bespoke his praise.

There is now to be admired a magnificent monument of
white marble, which his brother erected over his grave at a
cost of £1,500, representing him in his judicial robes under a
canopy of state, seated between emblematical figures of
JUSTICE and MERCY.

"COKE UPON LITTLETON."

The great work of Sir Edward Coke is his commentary on Littleton, which in itself may be said to contain the whole common law of England as it then existed. Notwithstanding its want of method and its quaintness, the author writes from such a full mind, and with such a mastery over his subject, and with such unbroken spirit, that Lord Campbell says every law student who has made or who is ever likely to make any proficiency, must peruse him with delight. This work was the valuable fruit of his leisure, after he had been tyrannically turned out of office, and the result of many years' labour.

CHIEF JUSTICE HOLT'S DOMESTIC BLISS.

Sir John Holt married Anne, the daughter of Sir John Crossley, a lady of strict virtue, but a shrew, and they lived together on the worst possible terms. She fell into ill health, and he was in high hopes of getting rid of her. To plague her husband, she insisted on consulting a physician with whom he had a personal quarrel, and who for this reason is said to have taken peculiar pains in curing her. She certainly survived him several years, and Dr. Arbuthnot, afterwards writing to Swift an account of his attendance on Gay the poet, said, "I took the same pleasure in saving him as Radcliffe did in saving my Lord Chief Justice Holt's wife, whom he attended out of spite to her husband, who wished her dead." Holt established against the Crown his right to appoint the chief clerk of his court, but the nomination of footmen in his family rested entirely with his wife. Nevertheless he left her by his will a jointure of £700 a year.

ST. DUNSTAN'S CLOCK.

The old church of St. Dunstan, in the West Fleet Street, had a large gilt dial overhanging the street, and above it two figures of savages, life size, carved in wood, and standing beneath a pediment, each having in his right hand a club, with which he struck the quarters upon a suspended bell, moving his head at the same time. To see the men strike was to a certain class of persons, very attractive, and opposite St. Dunstan's was considered a famous field for pickpockets, who took advantage of the gaping crowd. Among those who were struck by the oddity of the figures was the Marquis of Hertford, who, when a child, and a good child, was taken by his nurse to see the giants of St. Dunstan as a reward; and he used to say when he grew up to be a man he would buy those giants. Many a child of rich parents may have said the same, but in the present case the Marquis kept his word. When the old church of St. Dunstan was taken down, in 1830, Lord Hertford attended the second sale of the materials, and purchased the clock, bells, and figures for £300, and he had them placed at the entrance to the grounds of his villa in the Regent's Park, thence called St. Dunstan's Villa, and there the figures do duty to the present day.

A PAINTER'S EYE.

Gainsborough was once examined as a witness on a trial respecting the originality of a picture, and a counsellor endeavoured to puzzle him by saying, "I observe you lay great stress on a 'painter's eye,' what do you mean by that expression?" "A painter's eye," answered Gainsborough, "is to him what a lawyer's tongue is to you."

CRABBE'S DREAMS.

Lockhart, speaking of Crabbe, when he was visiting Sir Walter Scott, says, "I recollect that he used to have a lamp and writing materials placed by his bedside every night, and when Lady Scott told him she wondered the day was not enough for authorship, he answered, 'Dear lady, I should have lost many a good hit had I not set down at once things that occurred to me in my dreams.'"

YOUTHFUL EXPLOIT OF THE YOXFORD POET.

Poets are proverbially of a romantic disposition, and a wild freak of James Bird, the Yoxford poet, in his boyish days, attests his impetuosity of temperament, his ardent love of adventure, his unconquerable desire for knowledge, and the rainbow hue in which his young imagination loved to dwell. He had heard the merits of Kemble, the great London actor, described in the village, and his curiosity and fancy were powerfully excited. Closely treasuring in his own mind all that he had heard, in the course of a short time he collected a few shillings, and without apprising his parents of his intention, he started for the metropolis. His purpose was to witness and judge for himself one of those glorious exhibitions which had been sketched in all their vivid hues on his imagination. He achieved his object: he beheld the greatest of the great "strut his hour upon the stage," and was gratified, delighted, enchanted. Throughout his life recollections of that night never failed. But the pageant o'er, he had to return. And how stood his purse? Empty—all but empty; one solitary sixpence alone remaining. He started for home—had journeyed far, was hungry, thirsty, weary, and footsore, and was yet many miles from his father's happy hearth. A wretched roadside ale-house met his eye. The temptation was not to be withstood. He entered, called for a penny roll and cheese, and half-a-pint of ale, to recruit his wasted energies. After demolishing his frugal fare he tendered his sixpence, which, on receiving, the hostess pronounced a bad one, and in the spirit of another Zantippe commenced a strain of fierce and voluble abuse. At length, the poor boy, after a long endurance of the lady's vituperative display, entered into a compromise by leaving in pledge some portion of his wearing apparel! In his graphic relation of this anecdote in after life, it would be difficult to say whether humour or pathos predominated.

James Bird was extremely witty, and would delight a

company with his clever improvisations. His play upon words and merry puns brought Sydney Smith or Douglas Jerrold to memory. In the last letter that he ever wrote we find the following :—

> Have pity, dearest friends, on me,
>   And be not cross and *scoffy*,
> Though I've a good supply of TEA,
>   Alas! I've much more COUGH I (coffee.)

BISHOP BLOMFIELD AND THE DUKE OF CLARENCE.

Bishop Blomfield's acquaintance with the Duke of Clarence, afterwards William IV., had the following singular commencement. The Bishop addressed a letter to the Countess of Dysart, at Ham House, requesting permission to see that ancient mansion. The Countess, hospitable as she generally was, at first declined, saying, "I never saw any Bishop here in my brother's time." Afterwards, however, she relented, and as the most agreeable arrangement to all parties, desired Sir George Sinclair, who had married her granddaughter, to fix a day for the Bishop to dine there, adding that he might invite the Duke of Clarence and a large party to meet him. Sir George was not aware that the Duke had taken great offence at the Bishop for his recent speech and vote on Catholic emancipation. Observing that they took no notice of each other, he presented the Bishop to the Duke, who immediately addressed him in a voice loud enough to be heard by all the company: "I had lately the pleasure of seeing the Bishop of ——— along with me in the lobby of the House of Lords, but I had not the pleasure of seeing the Bishop of London." The Bishop courteously replied, "It is with regret that I ever vote on a different side from your Royal Highness." The Duke resumed, "I was the more surprised, and I consider you the more in the wrong, because I thought I had reason to expect the reverse." "Whether I was actually in the wrong or not," replied the Bishop, "my conscience told me that I was in the right." The Duke was about to continue, when dinner was fortunately announced. At table the Bishop drew him into conversation, and so completely conciliated his good opinion that some days after he said to Sir George Sinclair, "I like the Bishop far better than I expected, and I do not care how soon I have him to meet me again." He felt that he had gone too far, and asked, "How did the Bishop look when I told him my mind?" "I did not see," replied Sir George, "for my eyes were fixed on the ground." "Did any one else observe how he looked?" "No, I believe their eyes were turned in the same direction."

CLARKSON'S PERSEVERANCE.

A curious instance of Clarkson's sleuth-hound perseverance may be mentioned. The abettors of slavery, in the course of their defence of the system, maintained that only such negroes as were captured in battle were sold as slaves, and if not so sold then they were reserved for a still more frightful doom in their own country. Clarkson knew of the slave hunts conducted by the slave traders, but had no witnesses to prove it. Where was one to be found? Accidentally a gentleman whom he met on one of his journeys informed him of a young sailor in whose company he had been in about a year before, who had been actually engaged in one of such slave hunting expeditions. The gentleman did not know his name, and could but indefinitely describe his person. He did not know where he was, further than that he belonged to a ship of war in ordinary, but at what port he could not tell. With this mere glimmering of information Clarkson determined to produce this man as a witness. He visited, personally, all the sea-port towns where ships in ordinary lay, boarded and examined every ship without success, until he came to the very last port, and found the young man, his prize, in the very *last* ship that remained to be visited. The young man proved to be one of his most valuable and effective witnesses.

GAINSBOROUGH'S FORGERY.

Gainsborough, when a lad, was never so well pleased as when he could obtain a holiday, and set off with his pencil and sketch book on a long summer day's ramble through the rich hanging woods which skirted his native town. An expected treat of the kind having been refused him, Thomas, determined not to be disappointed, presented to his uncle, who was master of the Grammar School, the usual strip of paper, "Give Tom a holiday," in which his father's hand-writing was so closely imitated, that not the slightest suspicion of the forgery ever entered the mind of the master. Gainsborough accordingly set off on his rustic excursion, animated by that feeling of trembling hope which makes playing the truant, like other forbidden pleasures, such an exciting treat. He returned in the evening, his paper filled with woodland scenery: there were sketches of oaks and elms of majestic growth, clumps of trees and winding glades, sunny nooks and running water, that plainly indicated his love of the art. But alas! something had occurred during his absence which caused an inquiry to be instituted, and "Tom" was returned "absent without leave." Although he had copied his father's autograph so cleverly, the trick was found out, and the old gentleman, having a most mercantile dread of the fatal facility of imitating a signature, involuntarily exclaimed, "Tom will one day be hanged." When, however, he was informed how the truant school-boy had employed his stolen hours, and his son's multifarious sketches were laid before him, he changed his mind, and with a father's pride declared, "Tom will be a genius."

MAJOR MOOR AND HIS PET SNAKE.

Major Moor went out to India very young, and he says in his " Oriental Fragments:" "When I was an idle boy I caught a very young snake, not longer than my pen, and kept it some

K

time in a bottle, feeding it on flies and crumbs of bread. It thrived, and I removed him into a larger bottle, as more suited to his size. I was accustomed to take him out occasionally, and seeing what the Sampuris did, I amused my snake and myself, and sometimes a neighbour, by whistling or fluting to the dancing of my pet, as the erect, graceful, stately attitude and motion of this species of snake is usually called. I am all along speaking of the *cobra capella*, or hooded snake. I know of no other species apparently moved by music. I had deemed it expedient pretty early to extract or break his fangs with forceps, and my companion got on so well that he could at last of himself get out of a gallon bottle. He was then placed in a suitable jar, but as he grew he would occasionally get out, and a calling neighbour might, perhaps, find him on the sofa with or without me. I fancied that the creature knew me, and of a cold morning I have found him in my bed; and I became attached to him. My servant—I then had but one, a Mussulman—also liked him. He was, however, unpopular with my neighbours, and I found that I got laughed at, or worse, for such an apparent affectation of singularity. In consequence of this I resolved to part with my messmate, who had grown to an inconvenient size—perhaps a yard long, or nearly. At length I carried him to a rocky, sunny place, two or three miles off, and for ever quitted my singular companion."

CRABBE'S CHARITABLE DISPOSITION.

The charitable nature of the poet Crabbe caused him to be frequently imposed upon by fictitious tales of woe, which when he discovered, he merely said, "God forgive them. I do."

Whilst living at Trowbridge, his income amounted to about £800 per annumn, but he was a mild man in the matter of tithes. When told of many defaulters, his usual reply was: "Let it be; probably they cannot afford to pay so well as I can afford to want it. Let it be."

His voice failed him during his latter years, and he was imperfectly heard in the church. During this period he met a poor old woman in the streets whom he had for some time missed from the church, and asked her if she had been ill. "Lord bless you, sir, no," was the answer; "but it's of no use going to your church, for I cannot hear you." "Very well, my good old friend," said the pastor; "you do right in going where you can hear;" and he slipped a half-crown into her hand, and went away.

Though he was warmly attached to the Established Church, he was very liberal in his conduct to Dissenters, and that at a time when such conduct was not general. He held that

> "A man's opinion was his own, his due
> And just possession, whether false or true."

Of charity in the broadest sense of the term he evidently had a just perception, as he thus wrote to a friend :—
"Thousands, and tens of thousands of sincere and earnest believers in the gospel of our Lord, and in the general contents of the Scriptures, seeking its meaning with veneration and prayer agree, I cannot doubt, in essential, but differ in many points, and in some which unwise and uncharitable persons deem of much importance, nay, think that there is no salvation without them. Look at the good—good comparatively speaking, just, pure, pious—the patient and suffering amongst recorded characters ; and were not they of different opinions in many articles of their faith ? and can we suppose their heavenly Father will select from this number a few, a very few, and that for their assent to certain tenets, which causes, independent of any merits of their own, in all probability led them to embrace ? "

DR. WHATELY'S LOVE OF PHRENOLOGY.

Archbishop Whately devoted a large share of the time spent at the Board meetings of the Irish National Educational Society to scrutinizing, generally with a supercilious

expression, the phrenological developement of his colleagues
around. In the science of craniology Dr. Whately was a
devout believer. His comments and conclusions, seldom complimentary to those whom he examined, were for the most
part—happily for their peace of mind—confined to his own
cranium; but Provost Sadlier's head, which was peculiarly
flat at the top, happened to be directly under Dr. Whately's
eye at one of the meetings; this afforded too tempting an
opportunity to miss making a joke. "Have you heard of the
new phrenological test, gentlemen?" inquired the Archbishop, glancing significantly at the Provost; "take a handful of peas, drop them on the head of the patient; the
amount of the man's dishonesty will depend on the number
which may remain there. If a large number remain, tell the
butler to lock up the plate."

HABITS OF THE POET CRABBE.

During the latter years of his life, Crabbe worked chiefly
at night, after the family had all retired, and he had
generally by his side a glass of very weak spirits and water,
or negus. Whilst he stayed with Sir Walter Scott, in
Edinburgh, it was observed that he had a lamp and writing
materials placed by his bedside every night, and when Lady
Scott told him she wondered the day was not enough for
authorship, he answered, "Dear lady, I should have lost
many a good hit had I not set down at once things that occurred to me in my dreams." His note-book was at this
period of his life ever with him in his walks, and he would
every now and then lay down his geological hammer to
insert a new or amended couplet. Fossils were to him as
attractive in his age as weeds and flowers had been in his
youth. He would take long rambles among the quarries,
and spend hours on hours hammer in hand.

To children he was ever the emblem of kindness. No
word or look of harshness ever drove them from his side, and
although he preferred being alone in his geological rambles,

seldom inviting either of his sons to accompany him, yet
many a boy or girl out of a friend's family have been allowed
to attend him on an excursion, and mimic his labours with a
tiny hammer. He was peculiarly fond of the society and
correspondence of females ; nearly all his most intimate
friends were ladies. Men in general appeared to him too stern,
unyielding, reserved, and worldly ; and he ever found relief
in the gentleness, the tenderness, and the unselfishness of
woman. The critics of his last publication bestowed some
good-natured raillery on the increased tenderness of his love
scenes ; and some incidents in the later period of his own life
afforded his friends fair matter for a little innocent jesting ;
but none that knew him ever regarded him with less respect
on account of this pardonable weakness. Moore stayed a
few days with him in 1824, at the seat of the Marquis of
Bath, and he observes, " Among Crabbe's many amiable attributes, a due appreciation of the charms of female society
was not the least conspicuous. There was, indeed, in his
manner to women a sweetness bordering rather too much
upon what the French call *douccreaux*, and I remember
hearing Miss ———, a lady known as the writer of some of
the happiest *j'eau d'esprit* of our day, say once of him, in
allusion to this excessive courtesy, ' The cake is no doubt very
good, but there is too much sugar to cut through in getting
at it.' "

To his proper ministerial duties he was zealous, and he
would put off a meditated journey rather than leave a poor
parishioner who required his services. When he visited the
metropolis, after his reputation was established, his society
was courted, and he became a guest in the most distinguished
circles ; yet, on his return home he resumed, the next morning,
his visits among his parishioners, his cares of parish business,
and attended to his books and papers as if nothing extra had
occurred. His thorough and genuine simplicity was as
conspicuous in the pulpit as elsewhere. " I must have
some money, gentlemen," he would say, in stepping from

the pulpit. This was his notice of tithe day. Once or twice, finding it grow dark, he abruptly shut his sermon, saying, "Upon my word I cannot see; I must give you the rest when we meet again." Or he would enter a pew near the window, and standing on the seat, finish his sermon, standing, with the most admirable indifference to the remarks of his congregation.

In his young days he was particular as to his appearance and dress; but he for many years indulged largely in snuff-taking, and this habit somewhat interfered, as he grew old, with the effects of his remarkable attention to personal cleanliness and neatness of dress. The love of order, however, does not seem to have been very strongly developed, for his library was a scene of unparalleled confusion, windows rattling, paint in great request, books in every direction but the right. His granddaughter, whilst she was staying with him at Trowbridge, thought on one occasion she should surprise and please her grandpapa by putting every book in perfect order, making the best bound the most prominent. But on his return, thanking her for her good intention, he replaced every volume in its former state, "For," said he, "my dear, grandpapa understands his own confusion better than your order and neatness."

ONE OF THE FIRST MEN OF THE AGE.

Dr. Whately, whilst in Ireland, was very fond of familiarly gossiping with the head teachers of the model schools; but he was not always very sparing of their feelings, if the opportunity for a joke came in their way. Addressing a talented professor one day, he said, quite abruptly, "Mr. ———, *you are one of the first men of the age.*" "Really, your Grace," replied the flattered Professor, bowing lowly, "you are too kind, too complimentary. You over estimate the value of my services, and of my little publications, which owe their chief merit to the liberal use I make in them of your Grace's eminent works—" "I assert, sir, as a fact, that you are," replied the Archbishop, "*one of the first men of the age;*" but while the elated gentleman was bowing his thanks, the heartless primatial punster added : "I understand you were born January, 1801," and turning his back, walked off, unmindful of the height to which he first raised, and from which he so unceremoniously hurled the professor.

GAINSBOROUGH AND THE ALDERMAN.

Amongst the sitters that came to Gainsborough was a gentleman, whom Thicknesse calls an alderman and Allan Cunningham a lord, but whose importance, whether derived from a corporation or a peerage, was very apparent in his erect mien, his richly laced coat, and his well-powdered wig. Placing himself in an advantageous situation as to light, he began to arrange his dress and dictate his attitude in a manner so ludicrously elaborate that Gainsborough muttered, " This will never do." His excellency, having at length satisfactorily adjusted his person, exclaimed, " Now, sir, I desire you not to overlook the dimple in my chin." " Confound the dimple in your chin," said Gainsborough ; " I shall neither paint the one nor the other;" and he refused to proceed with the picture.

THE DUKE OF HAMILTON.

The late Duke of Hamilton was a keen sportsman, and in all the manly exercises had few equals. His Grace was partial to pugilism, and was also one of the best cricketers of his day. There was a mark in Lord's old cricket ground, at Marylebone, which was called "the Duke's stroke ; " it was of an unusual length, measuring from the wicket to where the ball fell one hundred and thirty-two yards, a greater distance than a ball was almost ever struck, except by his Grace.

Another of the Duke's amusements which he practised to get an appetite for breakfast, was to take a wherry at Westminster Bridge, and to give a waterman a guinea to row against him to Chelsea, where, should the waterman arrive first (which was seldom the case), he had an additional reward for his dexterity.

CHARITABLE DISPOSITION OF DR. WHATELY.

The power of Archbishop Whately's intellect is well-known, but the munificence of his charity is comparatively unknown. His generous disbursements are all the more remarkable from the ardour with which he always inculcated principles of economy. One of the copy heads supplied by him to the children of the National Schools is, " A penny saved is a penny gained." Dr. Whately's charity is also the more striking from the pertinacity with which he always laboured to disprove the merit of " good works."

A clergyman who made a touching appeal to his generosity was unhesitatingly accommodated with a loan of £400. He deserted the Archbishop's *levées*, and was not seen at the palace, or heard of for many years after. One day Dr. Whately's study door opened noiselessly, and the borrower stood before him, presenting an aspect half suggestive of Haydon's figure of " Lazarus," and half of the " Prodigal Son's Return." " Halloa ! " exclaimed the Archbishop starting up to kill the fatted calf; " what in the name of wonder became of you so long ? " " I did not like to present myself before your Grace," replied the clergyman, who was a man of high literary attainments and of higher principle, " until I found myself in a position to return the sum which you so generously lent me ; " saying which, he advanced to the study table and deposited upon it a pile of bank notes. "Tut, tut ! " said the Archbishop, taking the arm of his visitor, "put up your money; and now come down with me to luncheon."

A ripe scholar and gentleman died in Dublin, leaving his family almost destitute. Dr. Whately having been made acquainted with the circumstance, aided them by the munificent relief of £1000. A classical teacher was threatened by a legal execution. Mr. N——, on his behalf, represented his painful situation to the Archbishop, who, having been informed that £250 would make him a comparatively free and happy man, filled a cheque for that amount, and thus averted the catastrophe.

At a meeting of the Irish Zoological Society, when a subscription among the members was on foot, Dr. —— suggested that Archbishop Whately's name should be put down for at least £50. "He has not got it," interposed Sir Philip Crampton; "no one knows him better than I do; he gives away every farthing of his income, and so privately is it bestowed, that the recipients themselves are the only witnesses of his bounty.

Dr. Whately's generosity to the needy was not impulsive, but well regulated.

In the warmth of argument at a dinner party at Dr. Lloyd's, the following remark was drawn from him : "I have been Archbishop of Dublin for —— years. I have given away upwards of £50,000 in charity. I have doubtless frequently erred, but there is one thing with which I cannot reproach myself—I never relieved a beggar in the streets. I take care so to administer relief as not to encourage vice, or its mother, idleness."

To the poor of the district in which he resided, Dr. Whately and his wife were steady friends. Every poor woman, irrespective of her creed, had her weekly pension and bag of coal. When he gave away considerable sums of money to relieve deserving persons in temporary difficulties, he has sometimes been known to get them to sign a document promising to repay the amount whenever able, not to himself, but to persons circumstanced like those who had benefited by his bounty.

From the first year of his episcopate to the last, he dispensed, for the most part secretly, in charity, almost incredible sums ; and he was thus an example to the rich men in his diocese for plainness of living, and ready distribution of what God had given.

" HENSLOW A COMMON INFORMER."

At the election for members of Parliament for the town of Cambridge, in 1835, the candidates were the Right Hon. Thomas Spring Rice, Professor Pryme, Esq., and Sir J. L. Knight Bruce. The contest between Mr. Pryme (Liberal) and Sir J. L. Knight Bruce (Conservative) being very severe, bribery was resorted to, and the Reformers being made acquainted with some glaring cases, resolved to prosecute some of the most unscrupulous of the Tory partisans. A plaintiff was necessary. Tradesmen did not like to occupy so prominent a position, and the fear of vituperation made middle-class men shrink from the performance of a public duty. The committee appointed looked around them for a man who had the moral courage to bear odium in a good cause. Professor Henslow was suggested, and he did not hesitate one moment when applied to, and became the nominal prosecutor. The abuse and persecution which he had to sustain in consequence of this proceeding is well known in Cambridge, and has been often spoken of. Not only was the cry raised of "Henslow, common informer," whenever he appeared in the streets, but the same obnoxious words were written on the walls in such large and enduring characters that for a quarter of a century after the transaction they were distinctly visible in some places. They were seen and smilingly pointed out to a friend by the Professor himself, within twelve months of his decease. His services were, however, deeply appreciated at the time, for he received handsome testimonials, one from the town of Cambridge, another from the town committee appointed for the suppression of corruption, and a third from a committee of noblemen and gentlemen.

SIR CHRISTOPHER HATTON.

Sir Christopher Hatton, Lord Chancellor of England, but chiefly famed for his handsome person, his taste in dress, and his skill in dancing, resided at one time in Hatton Court,

Ipswich. He is said to have danced himself into the good graces of Queen Elizabeth. When young, he frequented the theatres, and studied dancing under the best masters. His abilities and agreeable manners caused him to be enrolled among a small company of gentlemen who performed masques at court. He thus had an opportunity of exhibiting his accomplishments before the Queen, and the tender heart of Elizabeth being at once touched by his athletic frame, manly beauty, and graceful air, she openly expressed her high admiration of his dancing. An offer was instantly made by her to admit him of the band of Gentlemen Pensioners. He expressed great willingness to renounce his prospects in the profession of the law, but informed her that he had incurred debts which were beginning to be troublesome to him. She advanced him money to pay them off, at the same time *(more suo)* taking a bond and statute merchant to repay her when he should be of ability. He was at first only a Gentleman Pensioner, or private in the body guard, but being henceforth the reigning favourite, his promotion was rapid. He was successively made a Gentleman of the Queen's Privy Chambers, Captain of the band of Gentlemen Pensioners, Vice-Chamberlain, and a member of the Privy Council; at last receiving the honour of knighthood, which was then considered as great a distinction as a peerage is now.

He annually presented the Queen with a New-year's gift, such as " a jewel of pizands of gold, adorned with rubies and diamonds, and flowers set with rubies, with one pearl pendant, and another at the top." In return he received a present of silver guilt plate ; and it was remarked that, while the portion of other courtiers never exceeded two hundred ounces, and was seldom more than fifty, he never fell short of four hundred.

Such marks of fondness gave rise to malicious whispers about the court, and among the vulgar the Queen was openly charged with lavishing her favours on the Vice-Chamberlain, and his letters to her Majesty justify the suspicion. Like most royal favourites he was ultimately neglected, and all contemporary accounts agree that the Queen's neglect and cruelty had such an effect upon his spirits that he died of a broken heart. In Trinity term, 1591, it was publicly observed that he had lost his gaiety and good looks. He did not rally during the Long Vacation, and when Michaelmas term came round he was confined to his bed. His sad condition being related to Elizabeth, all her former fondness for him revived, and she herself hurried to his house in Ely Place, with cordial broths, in the hope of restoring him. These she warmed and offered him with her own hand, while he lay in bed—adding many soothing expressions, and bidding him *live for her sake.* "But," he said, "all will not do; no pulleys will draw up a heart once cast down, though a Queen herself should set her hand thereunto."

He died on the 21st of November, in the 52nd year of his age, and had a most splendid funeral provided for him. The Queen, to divert her grief, did all that laid in her power to honour his memory. On the 16th of December, his remains were interred in St. Paul's Cathedral, more than three hundred Lords of the Council, nobles and Knights, attending by her order, and her band of Gentlemen Pensioners, which he had commanded, guarding the procession. A sumptuous monument was raised to him, which perished in the fire of London.

BERNARD BARTON'S LOVE OF HUMOUR.

Bernard Barton was very fond of humour, and an innocent joke was ever to him a source of pleasure. Writing to Miss Emma Knight, who was away from home, staying with her aunt who was "out of sorts," he says, "Would it do her any good to come and keep a stall at the Ipswich Bazaar? The sight of a drab bonnet presiding at one of the stalls would insure custom, I dare say, and I could write her some verses to sell ; only she must give me timely notice."

On one occasion he addressed a letter as under—

"JOHN MAJOR, BOOKSELLER AND PRINTER,
Who lives in summer as in winter,
In short, the whole year round complete,
At *Number* 50, in *Fleet Street*,
In London's famed and crowded city;
If not found there, the more's the pity."

In due time a reply came which bore the following—

"To *Bernard Barton*, far-famed writer,
Poetical and prose inditer,
Who makes a noise where'er be true folk,
Yet finds *repose* at *Woodbridge, Suffolk;*
If not just now about those parts,
Inquire in all good people's hearts."

DR. ROWLAND TAYLOR AND BISHOP BONNER.

Fox, the Martyrologist, says that after Dr. Taylor was condemned, he was bestowed in the Clinke till it was towards night, and then he was removed to the Counter near the Poultry. On the 4th February, Bonner, Bishop of London, came to the Counter to degrade him, first wishing him to return to the Church of Rome, and promising him to sue for his pardon. Whereunto Taylor answered, "I would you and your followers would turn to Christ; as for me I will not turn to Antichrist." "Well," quoth the Bishop, "I am come to degrade you, wherefore put on these vestures." "No," quoth Dr. Taylor, "I will not." "Will thou not?" said the Bishop, "I shall make thee, ere I go." Quoth Dr. Taylor, "You shall not, by the grace of God." Then Bonner caused another to put them on his back, and when thus arrayed, Taylor, walking up and down, said, "How say you, my Lord, am I not a goodly fool? How say my masters, if I were in Cheap should I not have boys enough to laugh at these apish toys and toying trumpery?" The Bishop proceeded with certain ceremonies till at the last, when according to the form he should have struck Taylor on the breast with his crosier, the Bishop's chaplain said, "My Lord, strike him not, for he will sure strike thee again," Taylor favoured the

chaplain's suspicion. "The cause," said he, "is Christ's, and
I were no good Christian if I would not fight in my Master's
quarrel." It appears that "the Bishop laid his curse upon
him, but struck him not," and after all was over, when he got
upstairs, he told Master Bradford (for both lay in one chamber) "that he had made the Bishop of London afraid," for
saith he, laughingly, "His Chaplain gave him counsel not to
strike with his crosier staff, for that I would strike again ; and
by my oath," said he, rubbing his hands, "I made him
believe I would do so, indeed."

THE YEOMANRY CAVALRY CORPS.

To the ever active intelligence of Arthur Young, we believe
the credit is due of suggesting the establishment of Yeomanry
Cavalry Corps; but Sir Thomas Gooch, Bart., of Benacre Hall,
Suffolk, was the first person who proposed to Government the
raising of Yeomanry Cavalry Corps in each district or hundred, which soon after took place pretty generally throughout Great Britain and Ireland. Sir Thomas made this pro-
posal in December, 1792, through Sir John Rous, to the
Right Hon. William Pitt, at that time Chancellor of the
Exchequer. Sir John Rous took the command of the first
troop of Loyal Suffolk Yeomanry Cavalry, in which Sir
Thomas was first lieutenant. Sir Thomas also raised a corps
of Volunteer Infantry, consisting of three companies.

SELF-DENIAL OF AN EAST ANGLIAN KING.

Of the youthful Oswald, an East Anglian King, who,
during the nine years of his reign, laboured to illustrate his
religion by a Christian life, and to benefit his time by a
consistent display of Christian graces, it is related that
during an Easter festival, a silver dish was filled with the
choicest danties, and presented for his refreshment. The
blessing was about to be pronounced, when the attendant who
had the office of relieving the poor informed his royal master
that the street was crowded with persons craving alms. The

sight of the prepared delicacies silently reproached the conscience of the sensitive monarch. Nor were the misgivings felt in vain, which suggested that perhaps it was his own self-indulgence which occasioned the visitation of his people's sufferings. Acting upon the impression that a king should not feed luxuriously whilst his subjects were starving with hunger, he declined, somewhat like David with the water at the well of Bethlehem, the offered refreshment which touched him with self-conviction. So, without tasting the dish, he ordered it to be distributed among the needy supplicants. It can be no matter of wonder that the benignant influence of Christianity should be diffused through East Anglia, under the mild and exemplary sway of a spirit so lowly and self-denying.

UNEXPECTED BIRTH OF SIR EDWARD COKE.

Edward Coke, the future Lord Chief Justice, was born on the 1st of February, 1551-2. He came into the world unexpectedly, at the parlour fireside, before his mother could be carried up to her bed; and from the extraordinary energy which he then displayed, high expectations were entertained of his future greatness. This infantine exploit he was fond of narrating in his old age.

SIR EDWARD COKE'S SECOND MARRIAGE.

Sir Edward Coke, during the life of his first wife, often resided at Huntingfield Hall, an estate he had acquired with his wife; but in 1598 he had the misfortune to lose her. She died on the 27th of June, and was buried in Huntingfield church on the 24th of July, "The delay being necessary," says Lord Campbell, "for the pomp with which her obsequies were celebrated."

From ambition and love of wealth, probably, rather than from thrift—

> " The funeral bak'd meats
> Did coldly furnish forth the marriage tables."

There was then at Court a beautiful young widow, only twenty years of age, left with an immense fortune, and without children, highly connected, and celebrated for wit as well as for birth, riches, and beauty. This was the Lady Hatton; she had been married to the nephew and heir of Lord Chancellor Hatton, and her first husband died in 1597. Coke immediately cast a longing eye on the widow's great possessions, and resolving to declare himself her suitor, he took the first opportunity to open his scheme to Lady Hatton's father and uncle. They, looking to his great wealth and high position, said they would not oppose it. What means were employed to win the lady's consent is unknown, but as he never appears to have won her affections, the probability is that she succumbed to the importunities of her relations. But though she consented to become his wife, she resolutely refused to be paraded in the face of the Church as the bride of the old wrinkled Attorney-General, who was bordering on fifty—an age that appeared to her like Methuselah; and she would only consent to a clandestine marriage by a priest, in a private house, in the presence of two or three witnesses. But here a great difficulty presented itself, for Archbishop Whitgift had just thundered from Lambeth an anathema against irregular marriages; and it was an awkward thing for the first law officer of the crown, celebrated for his judicial knowledge, and always professing a profound reverence for ecclesiastical authority, to set at defiance the spiritual head of the Church, and to run the risk of being debarred from the sacrament, forfeiting his property, and be liable to perpetual imprisonment. However, Coke determined to run all risks rather than lose the prize within his reach, and on the 24th November, 1598, in the evening, in a private house, without license or banns, he was married to Lady Hatton, in the presence of her father, who gave her away.

Proceedings were instituted by the Archbishop against Coke, the bride, the Lord Burleigh, and Henry Bathwell, the rector of Okeover, who had performed the ceremony ; but Mr. Attorney-General made a most humble submission, and in consequence there was passed a dispensation under the Archiepiscopal Seal, absolving all the defendants from the penalties they had incurred.

SIR EDWARD COKE'S DISLIKE OF DOCTORS.

Till he met with an accident by falling from his horse, Sir Edward Coke refused " all dealings with doctors." When turned of eighty, and his strength declining rapidly, a vigorous attempt was made to induce him to take medical advice, and a friend of his sent two or three doctors to regulate his health. But he told them that he had never taken physic since he was born, and would not now begin, and that he had now upon him a disease which all the drugs of Asia, the gold of Africa, and all the doctors of Europe could not cure—old age. He therefore thanked them and dismissed them nobly, with a reward of twenty pieces to each man.

THE KING OF THE BELGIANS AND ARCHBISHOP WHATELY.

Archbishop Whately was an odd man in many ways. He did not like people to ask him to dinner for the purpose of making a lion of him during feeding time ; those who ventured to do so often got an ominous dash of his great mane in their face. If he thought that people tried to make him a buffoon, no bust of Socrates could appear more grave. Clumsily try to draw him out, and he at once shut up. And hereby hangs a tale.

The King of the Belgians, having heard an animated description of Dr. Whately's conversational powers, which he was anxious to test, favoured him, when passing through Belgium, with an invitation to dinner at Laeken. The Archbishop, to the surprise of every one, and to the special disappointment of the King, maintained throughout the evening a complete impassiveness. Pegs were dropped, but the Prelate

L

folded himself in reserve, and refused to hang his usually
ready wit upon them. It was time to say something, and
Dr. Whately, when about to take leave, said, "Your Majesty
has done infinite mischief to all the kingdoms of the earth!"
Leopold smiled a ghastly smile, while some officious listeners
with, as they themselves thought, much tact, made an attempt
to turn the conversation. "My reason," said the Archbishop,
"for saying that your Majesty has done infinite mischief to
all the kingdoms of the earth is, because you have taught
your people the blessings of an elective monarchy."

GAINSBOROUGH AND REYNOLDS.

Between Gainsborough and Reynolds a very jealous feeling
existed for many years, but these illustrious rivals, nevertheless, fully admitted each other's excellence. "D—n him,
how various he is!" exclaimed Gainsborough, as he passed
before the pictures of Reynolds in one of the exhibitions.
"I cannot think how he produces his effects," said Reynolds,
while examining a portrait by Gainsborough. These were
greater praises, considering from whom they came, than
volumes of encomium from ordinary critics.

BISHOP BLOMFIELD AND THE REFORM BILL.

In the storm of popular indignation which followed the
rejection of the Reform Bill, when the Whig press declared
with one voice that the doom of the episcopal bench was
sealed, Bishop Blomfield did not escape entirely unnoticed.
He had purposely absented himself from the House of Lords
on that memorable occasion, when at half-past six o'clock, on
the morning of the 8th of October, the bill was thrown out
by a majority of forty-one, of whom twenty-one were bishops.
"The Times" said: "The Bishop of London did not vote
against the bill; but then he did not vote for it, and the
nation will not be served by halves." The parishioners of St.
Anne's, Soho, seeing it announced that Bishop Blomfield was
to preach in their church on October 23rd, signified to the

rector their intention of walking out in a body when the Bishop should appear in the pulpit. "Such a proof," said "The Times," "of public antipathy towards the entire order is without example in modern history, and is worth a whole library of comments." The Bishop, accordingly, thought it prudent not to fulfil his engagement.

LORD THURLOW AT WARREN HASTING'S TRIAL.

On one occasion, during the progress of the trial of Warren Hastings, Mr. Fox, struck by the solemnity of Lord Thurlow's appearance, said to the Speaker, "I wonder whether any man ever was so wise as Thurlow looks." Lord Brougham describes Fox's remark with a difference : "It was more solemn and imposing than almost any other person in public life, so much that it proved dishonest, since no man could be so wise as he *looked*." " Nor," says Lord Brougham, " did Thurlow neglect any of the external circumstances, how trifling soever, by which attention and deference could be secured on the part of his audience. Not only were the periods well rounded, and the connecting matter or continuing phrases well flung in, but the tongue was so hung as to make the sonorous voice peal through the hall, and appear to convey things which it would be awful to examine, too near and perilous to question. Nay, to the more trivial circumstances of his place, when addressing the House of Lords, he scrupulously attended. He rose slowly from his seat, he left the woolsack with deliberation ; but he went not to the nearest place, like ordinary Chancellors, the sons of mortal men ; he drew back a pace or two, and standing as it were askance, and partly behind the huge ball he had quitted for a season, he began to pour out, first in a growl, and then in a clearer and louder roll, the matter which he had to deliver, and which for the most part consisted in some positive assertions, some personal vituperations, some sarcasms at classes, some sentences pronounced upon individuals as if they were standing before him for judgment, some vague, mysterious threats of things purposely not expressed, and abundant protestations of conscience and duty in which they who keep the consciences of kings are apt to indulge."

BISHOP BLOMFIELD'S OPINION OF ROWLAND HILL.

Dr. Blomfield confessed that he had never heard but one good preacher, and that was Rowland Hill. Dr. Maltby accompanied Dr. Blomfield, and greatly admired the discourse; but when Mr. Hill floundered in attempting two pieces of Greek criticism, the two future Bishops sat and winked at each other.

A BISHOP AT BOWLS.

Strype says of Bishop Aylmer, that he was diligent, conscientious, and exact in the discharge of his duties, and careful in the ordination of ministers; yet he ordained his hall porter as a minister, and justified it on the ground of the small stipend of the place where he was appointed to preach. Daily service was regularly performed in the Bishop's palace, and his whole household, consisting of about four score persons, had to attend. Yet the Bishop was so fond of bowling as a recreation, that he not only resorted to it at every leisure opportunity, but regularly amused himself at this practice on Sundays, after evening prayer. His eagerness to get at his enjoyment, and his occasional vulgarity of expression, exposed him to the censure of many. Martin Marprelate says, " that he would spare him for that time, because it may be he was at his bowls ; and it was a pity to trouble him, lest he swore."

WHATELY'S CONVERSATIONAL POWERS.

In the unrestrained ease of the social circle, Dr. Whately was a very different character to what he was as a public legislator. In the first he was in the morning gown, slippers, and easy chair; as the public orator, he was strait-laced by Calvinistic influences around, and pinched by the tight, silver buckled shoes with which he tried to pick his steps among the traps that were set for him. In the pleasant talk of social intercourse he was a Goliath; put him on his legs, and his muscles became unstrung, and the contrast between Dr. Whately in homely society and Dr. Whately on the bench of bishops was thus very striking.

His conversation was as finished as Macaulay's studied sentences, and his marvellous power of impromptu quotation and illustration as ready, rich, and happy. He was never heard, either in abstruse discussion or in casual converse, to correct, or improve, or explain his words: all dropped from him as clear and as rightly placed as in his printed books. His mirth was enlivening, his raillery searching. Startling comparisons were warmed by genial humour, and made more attractive by flashes of keen and sparkling wit. The sharpness of the wit, however, was sometimes painful to bear, but he does not seem to have had a notion of the stinging vigour of his words, and he thus often inflicted pain without the slightest idea that he had done so. He delighted in the oddities of thought, in queer, quaint distinctions; and if an object had by any possibility some strange or distorted side, he would be sure to draw it in that light for the amusement of the company. His fund of anecdotes, alike from ancient lore and "modern instances," was inexhaustible and always ready at command; and though he could relate them with the raciest piquancy and point, he never told one for the anecdote's sake—always to mark some fallacy, or illustrate a moral truth.

That he was somewhat of a monopolist in conversation may be thus proved. During the latter years of his life he consented to fill the honorary office of Vice-President of the Royal Irish Academy, and in that capacity used sometimes to saunter into the Academy during an evening meeting, attended by three or four of his favourite chaplains; but he always took up a position in a room different from that in which the meeting was being held, and started an opposition

entertainment in the shape of a *conversazoine*, if such it could
be called, when the Archbishop talked the whole time himself. This marvellous flow of talk began about seven, and
generally lasted until after eleven o'clock.

CRABBE AND THE CONJUROR.

Whilst Crabbe was an apprentice to the surgeon at
Wickham-Brook, he was often employed in the drudgery of
the farm which his master occupied, was made the bed-
fellow and companion of the plough boy, and carried out
the medicines on foot to the patients in the neighbouring
villages. On day, as he mixed with the herd of lads at the
public-house, to see the exhibition of a conjuror, the magician,
having worked many wonders, changed a white ball to a
black, exclaiming, " *Quique olim albus erat nunc est contrarius
albo*; and I suppose none of you can tell me what that
means?" "Yes, I can," said George. "The d——l you
can," replied he of the magic wand, eyeing his garb; "I
suppose you picked up *your* Latin in a turnip field?" Not
daunted by the laughter that followed, Crabbe gave the
interpretation, and received from the seer a condescending
compliment.

LORD THURLOW AND GEORGE III.

Lord Thurlow over estimated his personal influence with the
King in treating Mr. Pitt with *hauteur*; and Lord North
foretold that, whenever Pitt said to the King, "Sire, the
Great Seal must be in other hands," the King would take
the Seal from Lord Thurlow, and never think anything more
about him. It turned out exactly as Lord North had said;
the King took the Great Seal from Lord Thurlow, and never
concerned himself about him afterwards. This mortified
Thurlow severely, and he is known to have said, "No man
has a right to treat another in the way in which the King
has treated me; we cannot meet again in the same room."
He now became so incensed with Mr. Pitt and his ministry

as to accuse them of having imposed upon the King in advising a measure for the encouragement of the growth of timber in the New Forest.

After the Cabinet to which Lord Thurlow belonged was broken up, and he was made a Baron and laid on the shelf, in the hope of regaining his ascendancy he took an uncomfortable villa, which had only the recommendation of being in the vicinity of Windsor Castle, and there for three years he was to be seen dancing attendance upon royalty, unnoticed and neglected by the King, who, when he heard of his late Chancellor's death, after an illness of a few hours, having cautiously inquired of the messenger if he were really dead, coldly observed, " Then he has not left a worse man behind him," " though the phrase which the king actually used was," says Lord Brougham, " less decorous and more unfeeling than the above."

CHANTREY AND CONSTABLE.

Leslie, speaking of " Hadleigh Castle," a picture of Constable's that was exhibited in 1829, says, " I witnessed an amusing scene before this picture at the Academy, on one of the varnishing days. Chantrey told Constable its foreground was too cold, and taking his pallette from him he passed a strong glazing of asphaltum all over that part of the picture, and while this was going on, Constable, who stood behind him in some degree of alarm, said to me, " There goes all my dew." He held in great respect Chantrey's judgment in most matters, but this did not prevent his carefully taking from the picture all that the great sculptor had done for it.

REVERENCE FOR IMAGES.

Stephen Gardiner, Bishop of Winchester, wrote to Bishop Ridley, remonstrating against what he considered the excesses of Ridley's friends. Gardiner humorously remarks, " After all, there is not much real superstition connected with images.

Men knelt before the silver crucifix; but the churchwarden who took it home from church was not afraid, like a reasonable man, to drink a pot of ale while the precious thing was under his gown."

SIR CHRISTOPHER HATTON'S LOVE OF DANCING.

Even while holding the Great Seal, Sir Christopher Hatton's highest delight continued to be in dancing, and as often as he had an opportunity he abandoned himself to this amusement. Attending the marriage of his nephew and heir with a judge's daughter, he was decked according to the custom of the age in his official robes, and it is recorded that when the music struck up, he doffed them, threw them down on the floor, and saying, "Lie there, Mr. Chancellor!" danced the measures at the nuptial festivity.

LYING ON BOTH SIDES.

When presiding in the Court of Chancery, Sir Christopher Hatton disarmed his censurers by courtesy and good humour, and he occasionally ventured on a joke. At one time, when there was a case before him respecting the boundaries of an estate, a plan being produced, the counsel on one part said, "We lie on this side, my Lord;" and the counsel on the other part said, "And we lie on this side, my Lord." Whereupon the Lord Chancellor Hatton stood up, and said, "If you lie on both sides, whom will you have me believe?"

SIR GERARD VANNECK'S ELECTION.

When Sir Gerard Vanneck was on his canvass for Suffolk, in 1790, his sister was very active in endeavouring to secure all the interest she could. A *freeholder* who had long admired Sir Gerard's very fine breed of greyhounds, was much solicited on this occasion, and he is said to have replied to the fair hand who requested his vote, somewhat bluntly but specifically, " *That if Miss Vanneck would give him a leap of her famous Dun, he was her man.*" His wishes to mend the breed of his greyhounds was, of course, complied with, and the vote was secured.

CONSTABLE'S OPINION OF HIS ART.

After Constable's death the following scrap was found among his papers, in his own hand-writing :—" My art flatters nobody by *imitation;* it courts nobody by *smoothness;* it tickles nobody by *petiteness;* it is without *fal de lal* or *fiddle de dee.* How then can I hope to be popular ? "

HABITS OF DR. WHATELY.

Whilst residing at Stillorgan, Archbishop Whately had a complete set of garden untensils, with which he used to work constantly, and often stripped himself to his shirt sleeves during the operation. He was attached to horticulture— especially fond of grafting, and his demesne at Redesdale contained a thousand standard specimens of the art, straight from his Grace's own hands. When engaged in the operation of cutting down trees, or grafting, he wore an apron— a veritable Bishop's apron—which had been worn out in episcopal service, or, at least, had become too shabby to wear in ordinary. He was in the habit of making two daily circuits of his demesne, attended by a ponderous walking-stick with a steel blade at the end, whereby he served both his own health and that of the trees and vegetation around, by looping off decayed branches, pruning unwhole-some redundancies of foliage, or in annihilating with the strong sweep of a dragoon, the indomitably propagative weeds which in irregular squares nodded defiance at him.

The Archbishop's tastes were extremely simple and unosten-tatious, unlike his predecessor, Dr. Magee, who loved display, and united the ambition of a Wolsey with the religious intolerance of a Knox. Dr. Whately hated parade or pomp.

The gilded decorations in the palace at Stephen's Green, which cost Dr. Magee so large a sum of money, were particularly obnoxious to Dr. Whately, and he had no sooner crossed the threshold of his new dwelling, than he threatened to have them all white-washed, and the walls of the palace dining-room came almost literally under this description. There was no state or elegance in his equipages, or manner of living; both were plain and much below what was consistent with his rank and position.

GEORGE IV. AND SIR CHARLES BUNBURY.

Sir Charles Bunbury, Bart., was one of the Stewards, and for many years one of the most influential members of the Jockey Club. George IV., whilst Prince of Wales, solicited Sir Charles's help in one of the awkward turf subjects. One of the Prince of Wales' horses (Escape) had lost a race which he was expected to win, and had won when he was expected to lose. The sporting world raised a furious clamour, which was re-echoed in the newspapers and the clubs of London. Imputations of foul play were cast very generally on the Prince's jockey (Chifney), and there were even found persons so audaciously disposed as to throw dirt at his Royal Highness himself. *Hinc illæ lachrymæ.* The Prince in consequence thus writes:—

"DEAR BUNBURY,

"I found on my arrival in London so many infamous and rascally lies fabricated, relative to the affair that happened at Newmarket, by republican scribblers, and studiously circulated through the country, that I judge it absolutely necessary that these calumnies should be contradicted in the most authentic manner. After having consulted with several of my friends, I leave what is passed, and the mode of contradiction, to be discussed between you and my friend Sheridan, who has been so good as to undertake the arrangement of this unpleasant business for me, and which is of more consequence than you can imagine.

"I am, dear Bunbury," etc., etc.

HABITS AND MANNERS OF DR. HYDE WOLLASTON.

William Hyde Wollaston, M.D., a name inseparably connected with chemical science, a man who, it is said, by the discovery of the malleability of platinum, realized £30,000, resided for some years at Bury St. Edmund's. He was the third son of the Rev. Francis Wollaston, F.R.S., rector of Chislehurst, in Kent. He seems to have been nursed in the lap of science, for his father's sister was the wife of the celebrated Dr. Heberden; his father was distinguished for astronomical pursuits, and his elder brother became Jacksonian Professor at Cambridge. William was educated at the Charter House, and afterwards went to Caius College, Cambridge, where he became a fellow, and received the degree of M.D. Upon quitting Alma Mater, he began his career at Huntingdon, but soon removed to Bury St. Edmunds', a town in which an uncle of his, Dr. Charlton Wollaston, had been well known as an eminent physician, and where some connections of the same name were still residing. Here his skill and kind manner soon won for him a reputation, and the friendship of some of the best and most intelligent residents of Bury and its neighbourhood. One of these friends, the kind-hearted Rev. Henry Hasted, read a paper before the members of the Bury and West Suffolk Archæological Institute, containing recollections of his friend Dr. Wollaston; and to that article we are indebted for the "reminiscences" which we now give.

Dr. Wollaston was fond of botany, and soon knew the habits of every rare plant in the neighbourhood of Bury St. Edmund's. Nothing escaped his eye. When crossing a heath at a smart trot, he suddenly pulled up, and exclaimed, "There's the *Linum radiola*," a plant well known, but so minute that his companion, when alighted from his horse and looking close to the ground, could scarcely at first descry it. He told a friend that he had made it a rule when he first took seriously to the study of botany, never to pass a flower or any particular plant without repeating to himself its trivial and its botanical name. This exact observation was characteristic of the man; every notable spring, or mineral, or tree in the neighbourhood was known, experiments made on them in his little study, with a few small phials, tests, and watch-glasses; the time of leafing and flowering of plants, the notes and scales of birds, the habits of animals, the motion and velocity of the clouds and winds, were to him "sermons in stones, and *food* in everything;" and when the day was gone, the stars were looked at with an artificial horizon of quicksilver in a *saucer*.

Great was the variety of his pursuits. His knowledge was very general, and ready to be communicated; indeed, it was scarcely possible to be in Dr. Wollaston's company half-an-hour without learning something, without hearing some new fact or having some old one put in a new light, almost incidentally, without effort or design. There was a kindness in the manner of communicating it; but if any great error was asserted, with a certain look or a single question, he would convince the assertor that he was wrong. His presence was courted by all; even in female society, it was remarked, "We are always glad to have William Wollaston to join our circle, for he always suggests something or other about our work, or what happens to be before us, which we were not aware of before;" and amongst the young, those at least who had any mind or any desire to learn, he entered into all their views and cheerfulness, the "playmate, ere the teacher of their mind," or rather, the teacher, while he seemed to be their playmate.

Intimately acquainted with Sir Henry Bunbury, he used occasionally to visit the worthy Baronet at Barton or at Mildenhall, and he had always some new object of inquiry in his mind or some new discovery to communicate. One year, when a large party had assembled in the library, he pretended to be examining a book in a distant corner, and sounded an extremely acute note on his little pipe, and glanced round to observe who caught the sound and who were unconscious of it. At another time he entered the room, blowing before him a tissue woven by spiders. One year he set Sir Henry drawing the human face in all directions, and invited arguments on his theory as to the principle on which one may account for the eyes of a portrait following the spectator through his changes of position. He was always inquisitive as to the observations made by persons who had happened to see trees struck by lightning. His own conviction appeared to be that the shattering of the bark and wood was occasioned by the sudden conversion of the sap and moisture into explosive gas. Likewise, he was curious in his inquiries as to what had been observed when meteoric stones had fallen, or particularly whether any one had seen the moving body, and could say whether it was falling obliquely or perpendicularly. He was very fond of playing at billiards; but his principal amusement seemed to be in watching the effect of one ball upon another, and the various effects produced by striking with the cue above, or below, or one side of the centre of the ball. He was likewise fond of chess, and he played the game well; but if he met with an antagonist who was rather superior to him, it was pleasing to see how Wollaston would buckle himself to his work, and sit up half the night contending for victory with all the ardour of a young man. He had a singularly piercing eye, and his friends well remember how he seemed to look into one's mind whilst he waited for an answer to an inquiry on an any subject in which he felt an interest, and the brief, expressive "*good*" with which he greeted the explanation, if it was satisfactory to him.

His kindness and manner in a sick room were no less proverbial than his skill and judgment. He was reserved, and this was by some mistaken for indifference, not knowing the extreme sensitiveness of his temperament, or that under a coldness of manner there lay hid a great warmth of heart. Soon after he came to Bury he was called in to attend a case that was thought very serious. Immediately after seeing the patient, he was asked his opinion of his condition; he replied, "You must consider I am a young man. I see nothing to be alarmed at; but you cannot expect me to speak at once decidedly," and he burst into tears. He was right in the opinion which he afterwards gave, as well as in his treatment of the case, but the circumstance showed, even in early days, what he suffered when having a patient seriously ill under his care. His acute sympathy with suffering led afterwards to his giving up the medical profession.

As a *physician* he stood deservedly high, but his friends felt that he was calculated for a higher meridian than Bury St. Edmund's, that London was the proper place for him; and thither, more in compliance with their urgency than his own wish, in 1797 he removed. For observing or hearing of anything that was remarkable he was now at the fountain head, but he went on with his profession for a short time only. Trifling cases or imaginary ills he was not inclined to attend to; serious ones gave him pain, and in the year 1800 he gave up practising as a physician. He had previously given his friend Hasted reason to think that the practice of physic "was not calculated to make him happy," and on relinquishing it he said, "Upon the common calculation my life may last so many years, would you for any compensation submit to be flogged every day during that period? Then do forgive me if I decline that mental flagellation termed anxiety, compared with which the loss of thousands is a flea bite."

Released thus from professional ties he was more at leisure for science, and he accompanied two friends on a tour to the lakes. Geology, as a study, was at that time in its infancy, but with the forms, fashions, and contents of the hills he seemed already well acquainted. He could only take the outline of the districts, for neither himself nor his friend could draw well, and they lamented their inability. This led to one of his nice inventions. When one of his friends called on him a few months afterwards, in town, he found him with a minute, truncated, and half-silvered prism, fastened with sealing wax to a piece of wire. "Look," said he, "here is the very thing we wanted at the lakes;" and very soon came forth that elegant and very useful little instrument, the "Camera Lucida."

A similar accident produced another most serviceable instrument in chrystalography, the reflective goniometer, and in later days another still, *viz.*, the synoptic scale, for chemical equivalents and monetary calculations.

Electricity was, as may be expected, a frequent subject of his investigation, and when that modification of it, galvanism and the voltaic pile, was first announced, he wrote, "I cannot write without a few words upon the most curious discovery (as it appears to me), unless we except cow-pox, which has been made in our time (describing the voltaic pile). Nicholson and Carlisle have already made the apparatus, and in one week added some very important facts on the decomposition of water by it." He had a minute tube in his *pocket*, which, with a wire, connecting through a few drops of muriate acid the zinc and the silver, showed the whole principle, and first set Dr. Currie on the right scent.

He soon made chemical matters, more particularly platinum, his study, and the union of science with diligence produced a due result—the labours of the philosopher not quite leading to the philosopher's stone, but turning a great deal into gold, not only placing himself at ease, but enabling him to do most liberal acts. It is said that when a near connexion wished for and requested him to obtain by his solicitation some place under Government, he said that he had never applied for himself or any other, and never would sacrifice his independence by so doing; but as a better mode of assisting he sent him the enclosed (it was a cheque, it is said, for £6000). A short time before his death he gave to the Geological Society £1000, and to the Royal Society £2000, three per cent. reduced, the dividends arising therefrom to be applied in promoting or rewarding scientific researches; and when he could no longer live to benefit the

living by such deeds, he bequeathed to every member of his
family a very considerable sum.

At ease and at liberty now to walk in the paths of science,
he was ever pursuing them. His knowledge was universally
admitted, his opinion repeatedly asked, and so cautious and
sure was his judgment that those who were in the habit of
asking it frequently gave him the name of "The Pope."
When in the country he was not disinclined to country
amusements. He took to fishing and even to shooting
during the last twelve years of his life, and by watching and
following the habits of his prey, and his observations of the
different modes of rising or moving of birds when on wing,
he generally succeeded. Sir Humphrey Davy, speaking of
Dr. Wollaston, says "that he became a distinguished fly-
fisher, and that the amusement occupied many of his leisure
hours during the last few years of his life, and that he applied his pre-eminent acuteness, his science, and his philosophy, to aid the resources and exalt the pleasures of this
amusement. Whether detecting by certain remains that
hyænas had inhabited the Yorkshire caves, or the manner
in which silkworms devoured the leaves of mulberries;
whether finding that enamelled glass might be tickled to
pieces by a particle of flint, or a web from its tenuity float
in a room, there was some observation or reasoning peculiarly his own; and in the street or the study, in town or in
the country; whether angling for trout, or testing for elements; whether attending to the "crops of partridges, or the
outcropping of strata," there was the same readiness and
keenness of mind.

He was fond of music, and attended the ancient concerts,
and liked pictures, and could beat the automaton at a game
of chess. The latter years of his life were the happiest, as he
could indulge in any taste he wished. At Sir Henry
Bunbury's he sometimes met Lyall, Sedgwick, Horner, and
Mrs. Somerville, and on such occasions he entered heartily
into the enjoyments of social life.

When he found his health failing, he consulted a medical friend, describing the symptoms as if they were those of another person. From the reply of his friend, who little thought they related to himself, it appeared that there was mischief near the brain, affecting the eyesight, producing paralysis, and foreboding what must soon be the termination. Even then he ceased not to "labour in his vocation;" what he considered his work was still uppermost in his mind. For many days previous to his death, experiments were carried on under his direction in the room adjoining that in which he lay, and almost at the last he seemed desirous to show how far disease could proceed without utterly destroying consciousness. When some friends around his bed were doubting whether he still retained his mental faculties, he made signs, as was his custom when unable to speak, for a pencil and paper; having written a few columns of numbers, he summed them up, and *the sum was correct.* He soon after expired, December 28th, 1828.

II.

Superstitions, Old Ballads, Historical Notices, Curious Customs, Scarce Documents, etc.

Superstitions, Old Ballads, Historical Notices, Curious Customs, Scarce Documents, etc.

FOLK LORE OF SUFFOLK.

We may say without any disparagement that the county of Suffolk is a stronghold of superstition, and the inhabitants of many of the villages do their best to preserve the fast fading remnants of the old beliefs and customs of their ancestors. Even belief in witchcraft is not altogether vanished, though we do not now oblige the poor, ugly, and elderly dames to sink or swim in the parish duck pond.

As the inhabitants of our rural districts believe in many things not admitted into the creeds of the more intelligent inhabitants of our towns, we embrace this opportunity to string together some old adages and popular superstitions that prevail among our labouring classes, in order that the more intelligent may be made acquainted with the dense mass of crude ignorance that surrounds them.

First of all we will glance at the proverbs respecting the "weather." Prognostications of fair or foul weather are very general. The husbandmen in the rural districts believe that "a red west" is a sign of wind, and "a red east" is a sign of rain, or as some of the peasants give it, in rhyme—

> "Evening red, and morning grey,
> Send the traveller on his way;
> But evening grey, and morning red,
> Send the traveller wet to bed."

The appearance of the rainbow is always noted by the shepherd, for—

> "A rainbow at morning
> Is the shepherd's warning;
> But a rainbow at night
> Is the shepherd's delight."

"A *burr*," that is, a *halo*, "round the moon is a sign of rain," if it is large. The proverb is—

> "Far burr, near rain;
> Near burr, far rain."

In autumn—

> "A mackerel sky
> Is either very wet or very dry."

If the wind veers to the north and continues there in a *dry* season, there will be no rain while the wind remains northerly; on the contrary, if the wind veers to the north in a *wet* season, it will continue wet so long as the wind remains in the same quarter. In whatever point the wind stands when the sun crosses the line on the 21st of March, it will remain principally in that direction until the 21st of June.

When a robin sings at the bottom of a bush it betokens bad weather, but if he sings at the top of a bush it will be fair.

The flight of wild fowl in the winter is always regarded as the precursor of severe weather.

Another proverb is thus expressed—

> "March dry, good rye;
> April wet, good wheat."

When you see the grey " shepherd's flock " before eight o'clock in the morning, it will rain before night.

> " If it rains before seven,
> 'Twill cease before eleven."

The sun rising clear in the morning and going to bed again (as it is called) immediately, is a sure indication of a foul day. When the small clouds are seen scudding before larger ones, they are called " *water carts*," and rain is sure to follow.

> " When the wind's in the south,
> 'Tis in the rain's mouth ;
> When the wind's in the east,
> 'Tis neither good for man nor beast."

There is also a saying with reference to the new moon, that—

> " When early seen
> 'Tis seldom seen,"

on account of the rain-clouds which are said to follow its early appearance.

The new moon " lying on its back," with the horns of her crescent pointing upward, is believed to indicate a dry moon; and on the contrary, when the new moon appears with the horns of the crescent pointing downwards, or as it is locally expressed, " when it hangs dripping," it will be a wet moon.

When the new moon happens on a Saturday it is superstitiously believed to be a sign of unfavourable weather, thus—

> " A Saturday moon—
> If it comes once in seven years, comes too soon."

And if in addition the full moon falls on a Sunday, it is said—

> " Saturday new, Sunday full,
> Never was good, nor never *wool*."

There is also a saying that " the sun is always seen on a *Saturday*," and this is firmly believed by many of the country people, who maintain that the sun always peeps through the clouds on that day, if only for a minute, just (as it were) to show his face.

Many of the weather proverbs handed down to us from our forefathers, are doubtless the embodiment, in quaint and pithy phrases, of the result of their observation and experience. But it must be confessed that there are some sayings in common use that have neither "rhyme nor reason." Thus—"When a cat wipes her face over her ears, it is a sign of fine weather; and when a cat sits with her back towards the fire it is a sign of frost."

And again—

> " A fine Saturday, a fine Sunday ;
> A fine Sunday, a fine week."

This is simply absurd, for if true there would be continual sunshine.

The following are also common weather proverbs—

> " If the rainbow comes at night,
> The rain is gone, quite."

> " When it rains with the wind in the east,
> It rains for twenty-four hours at least."

> " May never goes out without a wheat ear."

> " The grass that grows in Janiveer
> Grows no more all the year."

> " Cut your thistles before St. John,
> You will have two instead of one."

St. John's day is June 24th.

> " First comes David, then comes Chad,
> Then comes Winnold, as if he were mad."

This alludes to the stormy weather which is common at the beginning of March. St David's day is the 1st of March, St. Chad's the 2nd, and St. Winnold's the 3rd.

A sudden and local motion of the air, no otherwise perceptible but by its whirling up the dust on a dry road in perfectly calm weather, somewhat in the manner of a water spout, is reckoned a sign of approaching rain, and called by us "Roger's blast."

POPULAR REMEDIES FOR COMPLAINTS.

Many villages in the rural districts of the county are able to boast of their professor of the healing art, in the person of an old woman, who "bless" and "charm" away different maladies, especially wounds from scalding or burning, and who pretends to the power of curing diseases by certain cabalistic signs. And at the present day, in spite of the "march of intellect," a belief in the efficacy of charms for the prevention and cure of various kinds of diseases prevails far more extensively than many persons would readily believe. Two preliminaries are given as necessary to be strictly observed, in order to ensure a perfect cure. First, that the person to be operated upon comes with a full and earnest belief that a cure will be effected; and secondly, that the phrases "please" and "thank you" do not occur during the transaction. The established formula consists in the charmer's crossing the part affected, and whispering over it certain mysterious words. There is a very prevalent notion that if once disclosed, these mysterious words immediately lose their virtue, and the air of mystery which is thus thrown over the proceedings of the operators have probably contributed in no slight degree to perpetuate the popular belief in them. In consequence of this secrecy, it is difficult to ascertain what words are employed, the possessors generally being proof against persuasion or bribery.

It must not be supposed that these ignorant people make a trade of their supposed art; on the contrary, it is believed that any offer of pecuniary remuneration would at once break the spell, and render the charm of no avail.

Quaint remedies are frequently associated with superstitious fancies. Here is one that unites great superstition with supposed medicinal properties. A clergyman calling at a cottage one day, saw a small loaf hanging up oddly in a corner of the house. He asked why it was placed there, and was told that it was a *Good Friday loaf*, a loaf baked on Good Friday; that it would never get mouldy, and that it was very serviceable against some diseases, the bloody flux being mentioned as an example. Some weeks afterwards, the clergyman called again with a friend at the same house, and drew his attention to the loaf, which was hanging in its accustomed corner. The owner of the house, full of zeal to do the honours of his establishment, endeavoured to take the loaf down gently, but failing in the attempt, he gave a violent pull, and the precious loaf, to his great dismay, was shivered into atoms. The old man collected the fragments and hung them up again in a paper bag, with all the more reverence on account of the good which the loaf, as he alleged, had done his son. The young man, having been seized with a slight attack of English cholera, in the summer, secretly "abscinded" and ate a piece of the loaf, and when his family expressed astonishment at his rapid recovery, he explained the mystery by declaring that he had eaten of the Good Friday loaf, and had been cured by it.

This great success induced the family to have another loaf baked on the following Good Friday, and it was ascertained from other persons that such loaves were far from being uncommon in the parish.

Cure for Epilepsy or Hysteria.—If a young woman has fits she applies to ten or a dozen unmarried men (if the sufferer be a man, he applies to as many maidens) and obtains from each of them a small piece of silver of any kind, as a piece of broken spoon, or ring, or brooch, or buckle, and even sometimes a small coin, and a penny (without telling them the purpose for which the pieces are wanted); the twelve pieces of silver are taken to a silversmith, or other worker in metal, who forms therefrom a ring, which is to be worn by the person afflicted on the fourth finger of the left hand. If any of the silver remains after the ring is made, the workman has it as his perquisite, and the twelve pennies also are intended as the wages for his work, and he must charge no more.

Cures for the Hooping Cough.—Procure a live flat-fish—a "little dab" will do; place it whilst alive on the bare chest of the patient, and keep it there till it is dead.

If several children are ill, take some of the hair of the eldest child, cut it into small pieces, and put them into some milk, and give the compound to the youngest child to drink, and so on throughout the family.

Or, let the patient eat a roasted mouse; or, let the patient drink some milk which a ferret has lapped; or, let the patient be dragged under a gooseberry bush or bramble, both ends of which are growing in the ground. It is also said that to pass the patient through a slit in the stem of a young ash tree is a certain cure.

Some persons procure hair from the cross on the back of a donkey, and having placed it in a bag, hang it round the necks of their invalid children. The presumed efficacy in this hair is connected no doubt with the fact that the ass is the animal which was ridden by Jesus, and with the superstition that the cross was imprinted on its back as a memorial of that event.

An instance is known of a woman who obtained a certain number of "hodmidods," or small snails. These were passed through the hands of the invalids and then suspended in the chimney on a string, in the belief that as they died the hooping-cough would leave the children. At Monk's Eleigh a live frog was hung up the chimney, in the belief that its death by such means would effect a cure.

Cures for the Ague.—The Ague is a disease that was once very prevalent in Suffolk, although it is now, in the majority of the parishes, seldom met with.

Miss Strickland, in her "Old Friends and New Acquaintances," thus mentions a superstition that existed in her own district of the county. "Go to the four cross-ways to-night, all alone, and just as the clock strikes twelve, turn yourself

about three times and drive a tenpenny nail into the ground
up to the head, and walk away from the place backwards
before the clock is done striking, and you'll miss the ague;
but the next person who passes over the nail will take it in
your stead."

The Rev. Hugh Pigot says that during his residence at
Hadleigh a few years ago, he, whilst suffering from ague, was
strongly urged to go to a stile—one of those that are placed
across foot-paths—and to drive a nail into that part over
which foot passengers travel in their journeys.

Miss Strickland thus speaks of another remedy for this
disease: "Many of the charms ignorantly used by the East
Anglian peasantry, as cures for the ague, are evidently relics
of the sacrificial rites offered to the powers of darkness by
the pagan Saxons and Danes. In one district of Suffolk
I have heard of the following superstitious practice. A
man who had been labouring under an obstinate ague
for several months purchased a new red earthen pan,
in which he put the parings of his finger and toe nails,
together with a lock of hair, and a small piece of raw
beef, which in order to render the charm effectual, he
considered it necessary to steal. He then tied a piece of
black silk over the pan and buried it in the centre of a wood,
in ground that had never before been broken, in the firm
belief that, as the meat decayed his fever would abate and
finally disappear." A grosser oblation to the evil spirit
would scarcely have been offered by one of the heathen
inhabitants of central Africa.

To swallow a spider or its web when placed in a small
piece of apple, is an acknowledged cure for the ague. Miss
Strickland heretically mentions an instance of its being tried
in vain; but its failure excited great astonishment: "As true
as I'm alive, he (the ague) neither minded pepper and gin
taken fasting on a Friday morning, nor black-bottle spiders
made into pills with fresh butter."

The patient should take a handful of salt and bury it in

the ground, and as the salt dissolves, the patient will recover from the ague. Or the patient should gather some teazles from the hedgerows, and carry them about his person.

There was formerly a man in Hadleigh who "charmed" away the ague by pronouncing, or rather muttering over each child a verse of Holy Scripture, taken, it was believed, from the Gospel of St. John.

To prevent swelling from a thorn :—

> "Christ was of a Virgin born,
> And crowned was with a crown of thorns ;
> He did neither swell nor rebel,
> And I hope this never will."

At the same time let the middle finger of the right hand keep in motion round the thorn, and at the end of the words, three times repeated, touch it every time with the tip of your finger, and with God's blessing you will find no further trouble.

To extract a thorn from the flesh :—

> "Jesus of a maid was born,
> He was pricked with nails and thorn ;
> Neither blains nor boils did fetch at the bone,
> No more shall this, by Christ our Lord. Amen.
> Lord bless what I have said. Amen
> So be it unto thee as I have said."

To stop bleeding from arteries cut or bruised.—Repeat these words three times, desiring the blessing of God—

> "Stand fast ; lie as Christ did
> When he was crucified upon the cross ;
> Blood, remain up in the veins,
> As Christ's did in all his pains !"

To cure bleeding at the nose.—Wear a skein of scarlet silk round the neck, tied with nine knots down the front. If the patient is a male, the silk should be put on and the knots tied by a female, and *vice versa*.

To cure tooth-ache.—Always dress and undress the left leg and foot before the right one.   Mr. Rayson, writing in "The East Anglian," says that he has known this habit adopted and continued through life.

The Rev. Hugh Pigot, late of Hadleigh, says: "There was one old woman, of very witch-like appearance, who was supposed to have great skill in curing burns.   She prepared a kind of ointment, and when a patient applied to her she placed some of it upon the part affected, then made the sign of the cross over it, and muttered certain mysterious words, which she would not disclose to any one."   After many inquiries with the view of ascertaining what were the words employed on those occasions, the reverend gentleman heard from a man the following curious formula, the words of which must be repeated three times.

> " There were two angels came from the north,
>   One brought fire, the other brought frost;
>   Come out fire, go in frost,
>   Father, Son, and Holy Ghost."

There are many variations of this charm, but in substance the above is correct.

There are many persons who profess to be able to cure warts, or "writs," as they are called, by passing the hand over them and muttering at the same time some mysterious word.   The operator takes care to ensure his credit against mishaps, for as a necessary condition of success, he must be told the *exact* number of warts which are worn by the applicant for a cure.   If, therefore, the remedy fails, he attributes the failure to his having been kept in ignorance of the real number of warts.

If persons have any scruple against consulting such accredited professors of the healing art, they may get rid of their warts in other ways.   Thus: let the patient *steal* (it must be stolen, or it will have no efficacy) a piece of beef and bury it in the ground, and then as the beef decays, the warts will gradually die away.   Or, go to an ash tree, which has its "keys," that is, husks with seeds upon it, cut the initial letter both of your christian and surname on the bark, count the exact number of your warts, and cut as many notches in addition to the letters as you have warts, and then as the bark grows up your warts will go away. Or, take the froth of new beer, apply it to your warts when no one sees you (for secrecy is absolutely necessary), do not wipe it away, but let it work off of itself, for three mornings, and your warts will disappear. Or, gather a green sloe, rub it on your warts, then throw it over your *left* shoulder, and you will soon be free from them.

To hang a flint with a hole in it over the head of your bed is a preservative against the night-mare.

Another remedy is, before you go to bed, place your shoes carefully by the bed side " coming and going," that is, with the heel of one pointing in the direction of the toe of the other, and then you will be sure to sleep quietly and well.

To cure, or rather to prevent cramp, take the small bone of a leg of mutton, and carry it always about with you in your pocket. Or, wear a ring made out of an old coffin handle on one of the fingers. The parish clerks have been known to preserve the old coffin handles found in churchyards for the purpose of making *cramp rings*.

To cure wens or fleshy excrescences.—Pass the hand of a dead body over the part affected, on three successive days. The Rev. Hugh Pigot has known this to be tried at Hadleigh.

OMENS AND SUPERSTITIONS CONNECTED WITH MARRIAGE AND MATRIMONY.

The following spell is said to be still used by some country maidens in Suffolk :—

> " A clover of two, if you put in your shoe,
> The next man you meet in field or lane
> Will be your husband, or one of the name."

To ascertain whether her pretended lovers really love her or not, the maiden takes an apple pip, and naming one of her followers, puts the pip in the fire. If it makes a noise in bursting, from the heat, it is a proof of love; but if it is consumed without a crack, she is fully satisfied that there is no real regard towards her in the person named.

The kitchen maid, when she shells green-peas, never omits, when she finds one having *nine* peas, to lay it on the lintel of the kitchen door; and the first male who enters it is infallibly to be her husband, or at least her sweetheart.

If two persons wish to marry, they must take the church key and place it over the sixth and seventh verses of the eighth chapter of the Song of Solomon.

"Set me a seal upon thine heart, as a seal upon thine arm; for love is strong as death; jealousy is cruel as the grave; the coals thereof are coals of fire, which hath a most vehement flame. Many waters cannot quench love, neither can the floods drown it; if a man would give all the substance of his house for love, it would utterly be contemned."

Over the words they must hold the church key, balancing it by the end; and if the wards of the key incline towards the verses, which by a skilful manipulation they can easily be made to do, it is a sign that the course of true love will run smooth.

But if, after all, doubts of the lady's fitness to be his wife take possession of the gentleman's mind, there is another chapter in the Holy Bible which, if consulted, will either confirm or scatter them. That chapter is the last in the Book of Proverbs. It contains thirty-one verses, corresponding with the number of days in the longest months. The hesitating lover must ascertain on what day of the month the birthday of the lady falls, and then compare with the verse which agrees with it in number. He will thus find out the kind of life which he will lead with her in the event of marriage; and if the verdict prove unfavourable, he will have an opportunity of avoiding a match which he has such strong reason to believe will not be a happy one.

Do not marry on Christmas day if two other couples are about to go through the sacred ceremony at the same time, for rest assured that if *three* couples marry on that day, at the same time, one of the party will certainly die during the ensuing year.

If a pregnant woman meets a hare, and turns it back, the child will have a hare lip; but if she allows it to pass her, no harm will happen to her.

DANCING IN A HOG'S TROUGH.

The practice of the elder sisters dancing in a hog's trough in consequence of the youngest sister marrying before them, is known in several parts of the county. The Rev. Hugh Pigot ascertained that the custom was known at Hadleigh. A lad from Great Whelnetham mentioned such a custom whilst giving evidence before the Justices at Bury St. Edmund's; and a correspondent of "The East Anglian" says that he knew of a case in the neighbourhood of Eye, where the hog's trough was danced to pieces. It is considered the most correct thing to dance in green stockings.

CUSTOM AT THE BIRTH OF A CHILD.

There is an extraordinary notion in regard to the birth of children. As soon as they are born they ought, it is said, to be carried UP stairs, or they will never *rise* to riches and distinction in their after life; and accordingly, if there are no attics for the nurse to climb up into, she will sometimes mount upon a chair or stool with the new-born baby in her arms.

A CHILD'S PRAYER.

A popular prayer that is taught to children by some parents is clearly a relic of Roman Catholic times, and has been handed down from a period anterior to the Reformation, for it is an appeal to particular saints for their intercession with Almighty God. The words are these—

N

> " Matthew, Mark, Luke, and John,
> Bless the bed I lie upon ;
> Four corners to my bed,
> Four angels at its head,
> One to watch, two to pray,
> And one to bear my soul away ;
> God within and God without,
> Sweet Jesus Christ all round about ;
> If I die before I wake,
> I pray to God my soul to take."

There is sometimes this ludicrous variation of the fourth line—

> " Four angels all aspread."

It is very singular that in spite of its objectionable tenets this prayer should have survived the great change in religious opinion which took place in the sixteenth century, and still remain in popular use.

VARIOUS OMENS, BELIEFS, AND SUPERSTITIONS.

There are some persons who will never kill a pig when the moon is "wasting," lest the pork should waste in the pot. On the other hand, the clergyman of a country town says, "I know a respectable old lady who always has her corns cut at that time, supposing that the amputation is both more easy and more effectual."

Amongst the Romans sneezing, under some circumstances, at least, was reckoned ominous of evil; but amongst Suffolk people, to sneeze three times before breakfast is a pledge that you will soon have a present made to you. The sneezing of a cat, however, is considered to be an evil omen; it is a sign that the family of the owner will all have colds.

It is usual in this county to communicate family secrets to the bees, such for instance as a birth or death. If neglected on such occasions, the bees are apt, it is said, to take offence, and to remove to other residences where they will be treated with more confidence. They are said to be so sensitive as to leave houses, the inmates of which indulge habitually in swearing.

It is regarded as a bad omen, if when you leave a house you replace the chair on which you have been sitting against the wall; the probability, if not the certainty in that case is that you will never visit that house again.

That certain days are more lucky and auspicious than others is a very prevalent belief in many nations. Some remains of this notion exist among us, in the rural parishes more especially. Friday is considered an unlucky day. Sunday, on the other hand, is regarded as an auspicious day; and if persons have been ill and have become convalescent, they almost always get up for the first time on Sundays.

All medicine should be taken "next the heart," which means, in the dialect of Suffolk, that the best time for taking medicine is to take it in the morning, fasting.

A lady who has married, but who has not by marriage changed her maiden name, is the best of all persons to administer medicine, since no remedy given by her will ever fail to cure.

Persons will take the Bible to bed with them on New Year's eve, and as soon as they awake after twelve o'clock, they open it at random in the dark, mark a verse with their thumb, or stick a pin through a verse, turn down a corner of the page, and replace the book under the pillow. That verse is supposed to be a prophecy of destiny (good or bad) during the coming year.

If a corpse is *supple* after death, it is a sign that there will be another death in that family before very long.

To break a looking-glass is exceedingly unlucky, and will bring death to yourself or an intimate friend.

A belief in the existence of "Pharisees," or "Fairies," prevails; they ride young horses about in the night, so that the grooms on going into the stables in the morning find the horses all of a foam. But a hag stone, with a hole through, tied to the key of the stable door, protects the horses.

Belief in death-tokens is very prevalent; three raps at a bed's head, and the howling of a dog in front of your house during the night, are warnings that the death of some member of the family is at hand.

Taking a sprig of blackthorn, when in blossom, into a house, is considered to presage death to some member of the family.

If you have your clothes mended upon your back, you will be ill spoken of.

> "If you sweep the house with blossomed broom in May,
> You're sure to sweep the head of the house away."

If you break two things, you will break a third. A lady saw one of her servants take up a coarse earthenware basin, and deliberately throw it down upon the brick floor. "What *did* you do that for?" asked the mistress. "Because, ma'am, I'd broke tew things," answered the servant; "so I thout the third 'd better be this here," pointing to the remains of the least valuable piece of pottery in the establishment, which had been sacrificed to glut the vengeance of the offended ceramic deities.

SINGULAR WILLS AND BEQUESTS.

Eccentricity in one of the most solemn affairs of life is not an unfrequent occurrence among Englishmen; and we have collected a few instances to show that some of the residents in Suffolk have not been free from the singularity of curious bequests, nor in charging their wills with a sting or a stab at some relative with whom they were displeased.

WHIMSICAL WILL OF MR. RUFFELL.

The following is the whimsical will left in rhyme by Mr. Ruffell, of Shimpling, Suffolk, who died on the 28th of December, 1821.

As this life must soon end, this old frame must decay,
And this soul to some far distant clime wing her way ;
Ere that time doth arrive, men of sense must agree,
Now I'm well, strong, and hearty, my age forty-three,
I make this my last will, for I think it quite time,
It conveys all I wish, though it is written in rhyme.
To employ an attorney I ne'er was inclined,
They are pests of society—sharks of mankind ;
To avoid that base tribe, my own will I now draw,
May I ever escape coming under their paw.
To Ezra Dalton, my nephew, I give all my land,
With my old Gothic cottage, that thereon doth stand,
Is in Shimpling great road, in which I now dwell,
It appears like a chapel, or hermit's old cell :
With my furniture, plate, and linen likewise,
With securities, monies, and what may arise,
It's my wish and desire he should enjoy these,
And pray let him take e'en my skin if he please.
To my loving, kind sister, I give and bequeath
For her tender regard when this world I shall leave,
If she choose to accept it, my rump bone may take,
And may tip it with silver, a whistle to make.
My brother-in-law is a strange-tempered dog,
Is as fierce as a lion, in manners a hog,
A petty tyrant at home—his frowns how they dread,
Two ideas at once never entered his head ;
So proud and so covetous—nay he's so mean—
And I hate to look at him, the fellow's so lean ;
He ne'er behaves well, and tho' I'm unwilling,
I therefore at once cut him off with a shilling.
My executors, too, should be men of good fame,
I appoint Edward Ruffles, of Cockfield, by name,
With his old easy chair, his short pipe and snuff,
What matter his whims, he is honest enough ;
With Samuel Seelie, of Alpheton Lion,—
I like his strong beer, and his word can rely on ;
And when death's iron hand strike that fatal blow,
And this shattered old frame in the dust shall lie low,
Without funeral pomp these remains be conveyed
Unto Brent Eleigh church, near my father be laid.
This, wrote with my own hand, there can be no appeal,
I shall therefore at once set my hand and my seal,
As this my last will, I to this shall agree
This eighteenth day of March, eighteen hundred and three.

LORD CHEDWORTH'S WILL.

The following abstract of the celebrated "will" of Lord Chedworth gives an accurate account of the legacies left by his Lordship. They are certainly such as might well excite great curiosity among the inhabitants of this district, and also induce his relatives to contest the validity of the document in a court of law. The contest took place in the Court of Chancery, and the validity of the will was established. W. Pierson, Esq., was solicitor for the executors, and a pair of silver salvers, an inkstand, and an office table were presented to him by Richard Wilson, Esq., in token of appreciation of his indefatigable exertions.

Richard Wilson Esq., of London and Bildeston, Suffolk   £40,000

> This gentleman was in 1806 elected M.P. for Ipswich. He was a solicitor, and being employed by Lord Chedworth, he discovered that his Lordship's steward had committed fraud to an enormous amount, as, through the negligence of his Lordship, he had not received any regular account of the rents for nearly twenty years. By an injunction of the Court of Chancery, Mr. Wilson succeeded in detaining upwards of £60,000 that had been invested in the steward's name in various public and private securities.

Thomas Penrice, Esq., Surgeon, Great Yarmouth   £20,000

George Penrice, Esq.   £6,000

> A natural son of the above.

To that illustrious statesman and true patriot, Charles James Fox   £3,000

To the Rev. Thomas Crompton, in token that I am in perfect amity with him   £1,000

> This gentleman had been a pupil of Dr. Clubbe, in Ipswich, and became an intimate friend of his Lordship. Subsequently his political principles became Conservative, and his Lordship, in consequence, declined to correspond

with him, yet left him a handsome legacy; and
Mr. Crompton, in acknowledgment, published
in defence of his Lordship, a volume of his
letters and criticisms.

To his good friend the Rev. William
Layton . . . £1,300
To his sister, Mary Ann Layton £1,300
To Mr. Barney, merchant, Ipswich £4,000

> A cheesemonger, on the Quay; an intelligent
> and convivial man, whom his Lordship visited
> to have a game of whist and a chat with Miss
> Barney.

To Miss Ashpole £600

> Mr. Barney's sister-in-law.

To my friend, William Deane, of Ewarton,
Gent. . . . £6,000

> This legacy was in the codicil, and with this
> sum, we believe, the living of *Hintlesham* was
> purchased.

To the Rev. W. Clerke, of Norton, Clerk £200
To S. Clerke and C. Clerke, his sisters, each £200
To W. Smith, Bury St. Edmund's . £200
To Dr. Thomson . . £200
To James Sayers, of Great Yarmouth,
Attorney . . . £600
To James Pulham, of Woodbridge, Attorney £600
To the Rev. W. Glover, of the city of
Norwich . . . £200
To his cousin, Alexander Wright, Esq. £10,000
To his cousin, Mary Daniel, widow £10,000

> She was the wife of a deceased artist at Bath.

To invest in trust for the maintenance of his
cousin, William Wright, Clerk . £4,000
To his revered uncle, Thomas White, Esq.,
Tattingstone . . £1,000
To John Powell, of the Theatre Royal, Drury
Lane . . . £1,300
To my servant, Avery Truman £500

To my servant, Mrs. Rose Cockerill   £600
To my servant, William Lannip   £950
To my late servant, William Clarke   £500
To my servant, Susan Day   .   £100
To Lucy Pratt, Ipswich   .   £200

> He left to all who should be in his house at
> the time of his decease, two years' wages and
> mourning.

To Miss Forsett, Ipswich   .   .   £6,000

> Her brother was a plumber in St. Clement's,
> Ipswich, a leader among the Whigs, and a very
> gentlemanly tradesman, whom Lord Chedworth
> jocosely called "the Squire."

To Charlotte Selby, Ipswich   .   £500

> Afterwards Mrs. Oliver Iron

In trust for the maintenance of an infant
    daughter of Mrs. Edgar, of London, for-
    merly Sarah Ann Selby, of Ipswich   £13,000
To Richard Edgar, Esq., the father of the
    infant   .   .   .   £500
To Lucy Mary, the wife of Frederick Edgar,
    Esq., late Lucy Selby   .   £500
To Mary Taylor, widow, formerly of the
    Theatre Royal, Norwich   .   £13,000
To Harriet Taylor, daughter of the said
    Mary Taylor   .   .   .   £4,000
To Fanny Valentine, spinster, sister of the
    said Mary Taylor   .   .   £3,000
In trust for the benefit of Mary, the wife of
    William Howard, of London, to be applied
    to her use, and not to be subject to her
    husband's debts   .   .   £13,000

> This lady was the daughter of Mr. Robert
> Roper, a respectable farmer at Lackford, Suffolk,
> and was apprenticed to Mrs. Clarke, milliner,
> Ipswich.

To William Howard   £3,000

> Husband of the above.

In trust, the interest for the use of Harriet, the wife of Walter Bedell, of London, formerly Harriet Bannister, spinster	£2,500

> A daughter of the late J. Bannister, of the Norwich Theatre. She was apprenticed to Mrs. Lever, milliner, Ipswich.

To Elizabeth Edmead, formerly of the Theatre Royal, Norwich . .	£1,300
To Mary Ann Kent, formerly of the Theatre Royal, Norwich . .	£600
To Lydia Hallum, spinster .	£3,200

> A daughter of Admiral Hallum, who resided in Carr street, Ipswich.

To Margaret Lyddon, of Middlesex, widow, formerly Margaret Rix, of Ipswich, spinster	£3,000

> A great favourite of his Lordship. Her husband was Clerk to the Collector of Excise.

To Dorothy Gooch, Orford, Suffolk, spinster	£6,000
To Matilda Dier, spinster .	£300
To her sister, Mrs. Walford	£300
To Mrs. Willett, of Ipswich .	£200
To Edward Seymour, late of the Theatre Royal, Norwich . . .	£1,300
To William Graves, an annuity of .	£60

> He was his Lordship's barber.

His Lordship's love of female society, and his lax moral principles, may be inferred from the legacies above enumerated. His friend Crompton had on several occasions urged him to marry, and had even ventured to recommend to him a lady of their acquaintance as peculiarly worthy of his attentions, but his Lordship did not feel disposed to embark in the undertaking. The Misses Selby (and Miss Sarah in particular), whose father kept the Griffin inn, Ipswich, were great cronies of his; and the wife of Richard Wilson, Esq., was also a special favourite with his Lordship. Before marriage she carried on business as a milliner, in Ipswich, and it was said that his Lordship proposed to make her his

wife, yet forgave her telling him that she *preferred* Mr.
Wilson. His green-room entertainments and his love of the
drama are also indicated by his legacies.

Lord Chedworth died October 29th, 1804. Richard
Wilson and Thomas Penrice were executors, the latter
gentleman being residuary legatee; and Samuel Fitch,
Postle Jackson, and Charles Batley, all of Ipswich, were
witnesses to this extraordinary will, which bequeathed in
legacies more than one hundred and ninety thousand pounds,
and the residuary legatee received nearly an equal amount!

THE THELLUSON WILL.

Peter Isaac Thelluson, Esq., of Broadsworth, in the county
of York, M.P. for Malmesbury, Wilts, was born in France,
of a Genevese family, and as a London merchant, trading
in Philpot lane, he acquired an enormous fortune. He died
at his seat at Plaistow, Kent, July 21st, 1797, and when his
will was opened its provisions excited in the public mind
mingled wonder, indignation, and alarm. To his dear wife,
Ann, and children he left £100,000, and the residue of his
fortune, his immense real and personal property, amounting
to upwards of £600,000, he committed to trustees to be
laid out in the purchase of estates, and the rents and profits
to accumulate and again invested, during the lives of his
three sons, and the lives of their sons, and when the sons
and grandsons were all dead, then the entire property was
to be transferred to his eldest great-grandson. Should no
heir exist, the accumulated property was to be conveyed to
the sinking fund for the reduction of the national debt.
Various calculations were made as to the probable result of
the accumulation. According to the lowest computation it
was reckoned that at the end of seventy years it would
amount to £19,000,000. Some estimated the result at far
higher figures, and saw in the fulfilment of the bequest
nothing short of a national disaster. The will was generally
stigmatized as unwise or absurd, and moreover, illegal. The

Thelluson family resolved to test its legality in the Court of Chancery, on the ground that although the *corpus* of the property might have been rendered inalienable for a period thus limited, the rents and profits could not thus be disposed of; and that it was contrary to public policy to allow such an accumulation, which might render the individual in whom the whole might centre dangerous to public liberty, and too powerful for a subject. Lord Chancellor Lough-borough, in 1799, pronounced the will valid, and on an appeal to the House of Lords his decision was unanimously affirmed. The will, though within the letter of the law, was certainly adverse to its spirit, and in 1800 an Act introduced by Lord Chancellor Loughborough was passed by Parliament, forbidding such accumulations in future for a longer period than twenty-one years.

How ridiculous now appears this wonderful scheme for the accumulation of millions. The son of Peter Isaac Thelluson, the first Baron Rendlesham, died September, 1808, at the age of 46, as he was taking his diversion of shooting at Rendlesham, where he fell from his horse and instantly expired, having enjoyed his title only two years and a half; and the last grandson of Thelluson died in 1856. A dispute then arose whether Thelluson's eldest great-grandchild, or the grandson of Thelluson's eldest son should inherit. The House of Lords decided on appeal, in 1859, that Charles S. Thelluson, the grandson of Thelluson's eldest son, was the heir. It is said that instead of the property swelling to a magnitude dangerous to public liberty, the Court of Chancery conveniently eat up nearly the whole of the annual rents and profits, and that little more than the original sum of £600,000 fell to the heir.

THE ECCENTRIC WILLIAM JENNENS.

Most persons in this district have heard of the eccentric Mr. William Jennens, of Acton Place, near Long Melford, although few are aware of the singular facts connected with this

extraordinary individual. He was born in 1702, and died on
the 19th of June, 1798. He was the son of Robert Jennens,
aide-de-camp to the great Duke of Marlborough, and was
grandson of Humphrey Jennens, an eminent iron master of
Birmingham. His godfather was King William III., and
amongst other valuables discovered in his house, was a magnificent silver ewer, a present from the monarch at his bap-
tism. He had been page to George I., and having inherited
a large paternal property, and during his long life remained a
bachelor of very penurious habits, his accumulations increased
even beyond his powers of computation. He was the last
annuitant of the exchequer tontine of £100, a share for which
he had received £3000 a year for a long period. He had
property in almost every public security, and such was his
neglect, that the dividends on most of his stocks had not
been received since the year 1788, nor the interest due on his
mortgages for a length of time. In his iron chest, after his
decease, there were found bank notes to the amount of
£19,000, and several thousand new guineas. He had always
£50,000 in his banker's hands, and had not drawn a draft for
the last fourteen years. A will was found in his coat pocket,
sealed, but not signed, which was owing, as his favourite
servant stated, to his master leaving his spectacles at home
when he went to his solicitor's for the purpose of duly
executing it, and afterwards neglecting to repair the
omission. By this testamentary instrument, in which John
Bacon, Esq., of the First Fruits office, was left residuary
legatee, the whole of the property was intended to be totally
alienated from the channels into which it afterwards fell.
The most material sufferers by this informality of Mr. Jennens'
will are the Hanmer family, of Bettisfield Park, Flintshire,
and Holbrook Hall, Suffolk. The heir-at-law to the real
estate of Mr. Jennens was William Augustus Curzon, a boy
of ten years old, and son of the late Honourable Penn
Asketon Curzon, and grandson to a first cousin of Mr.
Jennens'. His personal property devolved on his cousins,

William Lygon, M.P., and Mary, relict of William, Earl of
Andover, eldest son of the late Earl of Suffolk. Thus his
almost incalculable wealth descended to three individuals, all
of whom previously possessed immense fortunes. On the
29th of the month in which Mr. Jennens died, his remains
were deposited with great pomp in the family vault at Acton.
The following is said to be an accurate statement of his
property.

South Sea Stock	£30,000	Interest on ditto	£8,725
Ditto, new ditto	30,000	,,	7,650
Ditto, old ditto	40,000	,,	9,600
India Stock	24,000	,,	18,570
Consols 3 per cent.	50,000	,,	17,570
Ditto, ditto (his mother's)	10,000	,,	5,450
Bank Stock	35,000	,,	19,600
Five per cent. ditto	20,600	,,	17,250
Four per cent. ditto	24,000	,,	11,520
Reduced Annuities	50,000	,,	16.800
Long Annuities	22,000	,,	22,000
	£325,600		£154,735

Account at the Bank of England .	£57,719
Ditto, at Childs' . .	6,000
Ditto, at Hoare's .	17,800
Ditto, at Stephenson's . .	19,300
Ditto, at Gosling's . .	7,000
Due upon 400 Shares in the London Insurance Office	3,400
In the New River Concern . .	5,000
Interest due on Mortgage .	200,000
Stock . . .	325,600
Interest on ditto .	154,735
	£796,554

To which add money found in the house, personality,

to an immense amount, and a landed estate of £8000 per annum.

EXTRACTS FROM THE WILL OF JOHN CORNWALLIS, ESQ.

One of the ancestors of the Marquis Cornwallis—John Cornwallis, Esq., of Broome, in the County of Suffolk, who died in the reign of Henry VII., made a will which contained some very curious items.

Thus: "I bequeth to a priest to syng and pray for my soule, my fader's soule, my muder's soule, all my friends' soules, and all chrysten souls for iii yeares, xxiii mare sterling. . . I bequeth to the high altar in the church at Broom vi *s.* vii *d.* for my tithes forgotten and other dutyes neglected. .. I will bequeth that myn executors shall live at Lyng Hall theiras now I dwell, to him that shall be myn heyre these presis following :—First in the chapell my greate masse booke, a vestment of silke, one challice. In the hall, the table, formys, and all the brewying vessell and standards in the brewhouse and bakehouse; one hole plow, a cart, and v horses to go with all; a gilt goblet with a cover that was my fader's, and a gilt cuppe with a cover standing, a great potte of brasse, and a second pot of brasse, ii spits, a grete and a lesse. . . I bequeth to the church of Eye iiii combe whete, to the church of Oxen iiii combe whete, to the church of Diss iiii combe whete, to the church of Palgrave one combe whete, to the church at Yaxley one combe whete. . . I bequeth to the Abbot of Bury myn amballing nagge."

EXTRACT FROM THE WILL OF PHILIP THICKNESSE, GOVERNOR OF LANDGUARD FORT.

"I, Philip Thicknesse, formerly of London, but now of Bologne, in France, leave my right hand, to be cut off after my death, to my son, Lord Audley; and I desire it may be sent to him, in hopes such a sight may remind him of his duty to God, after having so long abandoned the duty he owed to a father who once affectionately loved him."

WITCHCRAFT IN SUFFOLK.

In the times immediately preceding the Great Rebellion, and during its early progress, when religious excitement fostered the most extravagant delusions, the Eastern Counties were notorious for the number of their witches; and in no district of this country did the belief so generally or so strongly prevail, and Suffolk was peculiarly remarkable for the number of victims. The jealousies engendered, the cruelties practised, and the executions that resulted from the credulity of the people at this era, almost exceed belief. Dr. Zachary Grey says, "that between three and four thousand persons suffered for witchcraft in England and Scotland, from the year 1640 to the restoration of Charles II., in 1645." Fifteen were condemned at Chelmsford, and hanged, and in the same and following year about forty were hanged at Bury St. Edmund's, and later still sixteen were executed at Great Yarmouth, for this imaginary crime. Men of that day could not endure misfortune with patience, or believe that the Deity had any connection with their adversities. Sickness and death, blight on corn, murrain among cattle, were in consequence attributed to certain lame, ugly, old, and cross-grained dames, who in some instances claimed the power their neighbours believed them to possess. Storms of thunder and lightning, wind and rain, were attributed to witches, and at the sound of thunder the cry was, " Ring the bells, fumigate the air, and burn the witches." Ignorant physicians set down all doubtful diseases to the agency of witches, and that they could fly in the air on a broom-stick, make horses throw their riders, dry up springs, kill with lightning, bring the ague, pass through key holes, go to sea in cockle shells, and plague the farmer's wife by preventing butter from coming, was very generally believed.

The learned and devout Richard Baxter speaks of the judicial proceedings and executions for witchcraft in the eastern counties with great satisfaction. He writes, " The hanging of a great number of witches in 1645 and 1646 is famously known." Among the rest an old *reading parson*, named Lowes, not far from Framlingham, was one that was hanged, who confessed that he had two imps.

The following cases, copied from rare tracts and scarce documents, will illustrate this dark phase of the social and religious history of the people of Suffolk.

> *A Tryal of Witches at the Assizes held at Bury St. Edmund's,*
> *for the County of Suffolk, on the tenth day of March,*
> *1664, before Sir Matthew Hale, Kt., then Lord Chief*
> *Baron of His Majesty's Court of Exchequer.*

The prisoners, Rose Cullender and Amy Duny, widow, belonging to Lowestoft, were severally indicted for bewitching Elizabeth and Ann Durent, Jane Booking, Susan Chandler, William Durent, and Elizabeth and Deborah Pacey.

The prisoners pleaded " *Not Guilty.*"

Three of the parties above named, viz., *Ann Durent, Susan Chandler, and Elizabeth Pacey* were brought to Bury, to the Assizes; but when they went to the Court to give instructions for the indictments, they all three fell into strange and violent fits, screaming out in a most sad manner, so that they could not give evidence. After their recovery from their fits, they were struck dumb, "so that none of them could speak, neither at that time, nor during the Assizes, until the conviction of the supposed witches."

William Durent, being an infant, his mother, *Dorothy Durent*, deposed, that having occasion to go from home, she desired Amy Duny, her neighbour, to look to her child during her absence, for which she promised to give her a penny; that on her return home, she was angry with Amy Duny for having given suck to the child, contrary to her command. Thereupon high words ensued, and the same night her son fell into strange fits, and continued so for

several weeks. That the deponent, being exceedingly
troubled at her child's distemper, did go to a certain person
named *Doctor Jacob*, who lived at *Yarmouth*, who had the
reputation in the country to help children that were bewitched, who advised her to hang up the child's blanket in
the chimney corner all day, and at night, when she put the
child to bed, to put it into the said blanket, and if she found
anything in it, she should not be afraid, but to throw it into
the fire. And this deponent did according to his directions,
and at night, when she took down the blanket with an intent
to put her child therein, there fell out of the same a great
toad which ran up and down the hearth ; and she, having
only a youth with her in the house, desired him to catch the
toad and throw it into the fire, which the youth did accordingly, and held it there with the tongs; and as soon as
it was in the fire, it made a great and terrible noise, and
after a space there was a flashing in the· fire like gunpowder, making a noise like the discharge of a pistol, and
thereupon the toad was no more seen nor heard. It was
asked by the Court, if that after the noise and flashing there
was not the substance of the toad to be seen to consume in
the fire ? And it was answered by the said *Dorothy Durant*,
that after the flashing and noise, there was no more seen
than if there had been none there. The next day there came
a young woman, a kinswoman of the said *Amy*, and a neighbour of this deponent, and told this deponent that her aunt
(meaning the said *Amy*) was in a most lamentable condition,
having her face all scorched with fire, and that she was
sitting alone in her house, in her smock, without any fire.
And thereupon this deponent went into the house of the said
Amy Duny to see her, and found her in the same condition
as was related to her, for her face, her legs, and thighs, which
this deponent saw, seemed very much scorched and burnt
with fire; at which this deponent seemed much to wonder,
and asked the said *Amy* how she came into that sad condition ? And the said *Amy* replied, she might thank her for

it, for that she (this deponent) was the cause thereof, but that she should live to see some of her children dead, and she upon crutches. And this deponent further saith, that after the burning of the said toad, her child recovered and was well again, and was living at the time of the Assizes. * * * * * The deponent further said, that not long after, she (this deponent) was taken with a lameness in both her leggs, from the knees downward, that she was fain to go upon crutches, and that she had no other use of them, but only to bear a little upon them till she did remove her crutches, and so continued till the time of the Assizes that the witch came to be tried, and was there upon her crutches.

The writer of the account of the trial says : "There was one thing very remarkable, that after she had gone upon crutches for upwards of three years, and went upon them at the time of the Assizes, in the court, when she gave her evidence, and upon the juries bringing in their verdict, by which the said *Amy Duny* was found guilty, to the great admiration of all persons, the said *Dorothy Durent* was restored to the use of her limbs, and went home without making use of her crutches."

Concerning *Elizabeth* and *Deborah Pacey*, the first of the age of eleven years, and the other of the age of nine years, or thereabouts, the evidence that was given was to this effect :—

Samuel Pacey, a merchant of Lowestoft (a man who carried himself with much soberness during the trial, from whom proceeded no words either of passion or malice, though his children were so greatly afflicted), sworn and examined, deposeth : That his younger daughter, *Deborah*, upon Thursday, the tenth of October last, was suddenly taken with a lameness in her legs, so that she could not stand, neither had she any strength in her limbs to support her, and so she continued until the seventeenth day of the same month, which day being sunshiny, the child desired to be carried on the *east* part of the house, to be set upon the bank which looketh upon the sea, and whilst she was sitting there *Amy Duny* came to this deponent's house to buy some herrings, but being denyed, she went away discontented, and presently returned again, and was denyed, and likewise the third time, and was denyed as at first, and at her last going away, she went away grumbling, but what was said was not perfectly understood. But at the very same instant of time, the said child was taken with most violent fits, feeling most extream pains in her stomach like the pricking of pins, and shreeking out in a most dreadful manner like unto a whelp, and not like unto a sensible creature.

Amy Duny had long had the reputation of being a witch and sorceress; many of her kindred and relations had been accused for witchcraft, and some of them condemned. The child would sometimes cry out in her fits that *Amy Duny* was the cause of her malady, and that her apparition frightened her, and sometimes, "*There stands* Amy Duny, *there* Rose Cullender."

The children's fits varied; sometimes they would be lame on one side of their bodies, sometimes on the other, sometimes a soreness over their whole bodies, so as they could endure none to touch them; at other times they would be restored to the perfect use of their limbs and deprived of their hearing, at other times of their sight, at other times of their speech, sometimes for the space of one day, sometimes for two; and once they were wholly deprived of their speech for eight days together, and then restored to their speech again. At other times they would fall into swouning, and upon the recovery to their speech they would cough extremely and bring up much flegme, and with the same crooked pins, and one time a two-penny nail with a very broad head, which pins (amounting to forty or more) together with the two-penny nail were produced in court, with the affirmation of the said deponent that he was present when the said nail was vomited up, and also most of the pins.

In this manner the said children continued with this

deponent for the space of two months, during which time, in their intervals, this deponent would cause them to read some chapter in the *New Testament*. Whereupon this deponent several times observed that they would read till they came to the name of Lord, or Jesus, or Christ, and then, before they could pronounce either of the said words, they would suddenly fall into their fits. But when they came to the name of Satan or Devil, they would clap their fingers upon the book, crying out, "*This bites, but makes me speak right well.*"

Mr. Pacey further said, that finding his children continued to be tormented, and seeing no hopes of amendment, he sent them to his sister, at Yarmouth, to see whether change of air would do any good; but the aunt's testimony was very similar to that of the father—pins being vomited up by both children, and a two-penny nail, with a broad head, by the younger one.

Concerning *Ann Durent*, one of the parties supposed to be bewitched, present in court, *Edmund Durent*, her father, sworn and examined, said, That the said *Rose Cullender*, about the latter end of November last, came into his house to buy some herrings of his wife, but being denied by her, the said Rose returned in a discontented manner, and upon the first of December after, his daughter *Ann Durent* was very sorely afflicted in her stomach, and felt great pain, like the pricking of pins, and then fell into swouning fitts, and after the recovery from her fitts, she declared *that she had seen the apparition of the said* Rose, *who threatened to torment her.* In this manner she continued from the first of *December* until this present time of tryal, having likewise vomited up divers pins (produced here in court). This maid was present in court, but could not speak to declare her knowledge, but fell into most violent fits when she was brought before *Rose Cullender*.

Concerning *Jane Bocking*, who was so weak she could not be brought to the Assizes, and also of *Susan Chandler*, present in court, the evidence was given by the mother of the former, and the father and the mother of the latter.

The evidence against the prisoners for bewitching these children being closed, Mr. Serjeant *Keeling*, who was present with Mr. Serjeant *Earl*, and Mr. Serjeant *Barnard*, expressed himself " much unsatisfied with it, and thought it not sufficient to convict the prisoners, for, admitting that the children were in truth bewitched, yet," said he, " it can never be applyed to the prisoners upon the imagination only of the parties afflicted. For if that might be allowed, no person whatever can be in safety, for perhaps they might fancy another person, who might altogether be innocent in such matters."

There was also *Dr. Brown*, of *Norwich*, a person of great knowledge, who after this evidence given, and upon view of the three persons in court, was desired to give his opinion, what he did conceive of them; and he was clearly of opinion that the persons were bewitched, and said that in *Denmark* there had been lately a great discovery of witches, who using the very same way of afflicting persons by conveying pins into them, and crooked, as these pins were, with needles and nails. And his opinion was " that the devil in such cases did work upon the bodies of men and women, upon a natural foundation (that is) to stir up and excite such humours super-abounding in their bodies to a great excess, whereby he did in an extraordinary manner afflict them with such distempers as their bodies were most subject to, as particularly appeared in these children ; for he conceived that these swouning fits were natural, and nothing else but that they call the mother, but only heightened to a great excess by the subtilty of the devil, co-operating with the malice of these which we term witches, at whose instance he doth these villanies."

Other evidence was offered against the prisoners in proof of their being witches, of which the substance was as follows :—

One *John Soam*, of *Leystoff*, yeoman, a sufficient person, deposed, " That not long since, in harvest time, he had three carts which brought home his harvest, and as they were going into the field to load, one of the carts wrenched the window of *Rose Cullender's* house, whereupon she came out in a great rage, and threatened this deponent for doing that wrong, and so they passed along into the fields and loaded all three carts. The other two carts returned safe home, and back again, twice loaded that day afterwards ; but as to this cart which touched *Rose Cullender's* house, after it was loaded, it was overturned twice or thrice that day, and after that they had loaded it again the second or third time, as they brought it through the gate which leadeth out of the field into the town, the cart stuck so fast in the gate's head, that they could not possibly get it through, but were enforced to cut down the post of the gate to make the cart pass through, although they could not perceive that the cart did on either side touch the gate-posts." And this deponent further saith, " That after they had got it through the gateway, they did with much difficulty get it home into the yard ; but for all that they could do they could not get the cart near unto the place where they should unload the corn, but were fain to unload it at a great distance from the place ; and when they began to unload, they found so much difficulty therein, it being so hard a labour, that they were tired that first came, and when others came to assist them, their noses burst forth a bleeding ; so they were fain to desist and leave it until the next morning, and then they unloaded it without any difficulty at all."

Robert Sherringham also deposed against *Rose Cullender*, " That about two years since, passing along the street with his cart and horses, the axletree of his cart touched her house, and broke down some part of it, at which she was very much displeased, threatening him that his horses should suffer for it ; and so it happened, for all those horses, four in number, died within a short time after. Since that time he hath had great losses by the sudden dying of his other cattle; so soon as his sows pigged, the pigs would leap and caper, and immediately fall down and die. Also, not long after, he was taken with a lameness in his limbs, that he could neither go nor stand for some days. After all this he was very much vexed with a great number of lice of an extraordinary bigness, and although he many times shifted himself, yet he was not anything the better, but would swarm again with them, so that in the conclusion he was forced to burn all his clothes, being two suits of apparel, and then was clean from them."

Ann Sandeswel deposed, "That about seven or eight years since, she having bought a certain number of geese, meeting with *Amy Duny*, she told her, ' *If she did not fetch her geese home they would all be destroyed,*' which in a few days after came to pass."

Afterwards the said *Amy* became tenant to this deponent's husband for a house, who told her, " *That if she looked not well to such a chimney in her house, that the same would fall;* " whereupon this deponent replied that it was a new one, but not minding much her words at that time, they parted. But in a short time the chimney fell down, according as the said *Amy* had said.

Also this deponent further said that her brother, being a fisherman, and using to go into the *Northern seas*, she desired him to send her a firkin of fish, which he did accordingly, and she having notice that the said firkin was brought into Leystoff road, she desired a boatman to bring it ashore with the other goods they were to bring, and she, going down to meet the boatman to receive her fish, desired the said *Amy* to go along with her to help her home with it. *Amy* replied, " *She would go when she had it.*" And thereupon this deponent went to the shore without her, and demanded of the boatmen the firkin; they told her " that they could not keep it in the boat from falling into the sea, and they thought it was gone to the divel, for they never saw the like before."

And being demanded by this deponent whether any other goods in the boat were likewise lost as well as hers, they answered, "*Not any.*"

The prisoners upon being asked what they had to say for themselves, replied, "Nothing material to anything that was proved against them." Whereupon the judge, in giving his directions to the jury, told them that he would not repeat the evidence unto them, lest by so doing he should wrong the evidence on the one side or on the other. Only this, acquainted them that they had two things to inquire after, *First*, whether or no these children were bewitched; *Secondly*, whether the prisoners at the bar were guilty of it.

That there were such creatures as *witches* he made no doubt at all; for—*First*, the Scriptures had affirmed so much. *Secondly*, the wisdom of all nations had provided laws against such persons, which is an argument of their confidence of such a crime; and such hath been the judgment of this kingdom, as appears by that Act of Parliament which hath provided punishments proportionable to the quality of the offence. And desired them strictly to observe their evidence; and desired the great God of heaven to direct their hearts in this weighty thing they had in hand, *for to condemn the innocent, and let the guilty go free, were both an abomination to the Lord.*

With this short direction the jury departed from the bar, and within the space of half an hour, returned and brought them in both "*Guilty,*" upon the several indictments, which were thirteen in number, whereupon they stood indicted.

This was upon Thursday, in the afternoon, March 13th, 1662.

The next morning the three children with their parents came to the Lord Chief Baron *Hales'* lodging, who all of them spake perfectly, and were as in good health as ever they were; only *Susan Chandler*, by reason of her very much affliction, did look very thin and wan. And their friends were asked, at what time they were restored thus to their speech and health? And Mr. *Pacy* did affirm that within less than half-an-hour after the *witches* were convicted, they were all of them restored, and slept well that night, feeling no pain; only *Susan Chandler* felt a pain like pricking of pins in her stomach.

After, they were all of them brought down to the Court, but *Ann Durent* was so fearful to behold them, that she desired she might not see them. The other two continued in the Court, and they affirmed, in the face of the country and before the *witches* themselves, what before hath been deposed by their friends and relations, the prisoners not much contradicting them. In conclusion, the Judge and all the Court were fully satisfied with the verdict, and therefore gave judgment against the *witches* that they should be hanged.

They were much urged to confess, but would not.

The next morning the Judges went to Cambridge, and no reprieve being granted, the prisoners were executed on the Monday following, the seventeenth of March; but they made no confession.

[The above is an abridgment of an account of the trial taken by a person attending the Court, and printed for William Shrewsbury, at the Bible, in Duck Lane, 1682.]

CONFESSION OF A WITCH AT IPSWICH.

In the year 1645, it appears that the town of Ipswich was the residence of a notorious witch, who practised her sorceries on the unsuspecting or unwary. This beldame rejoiced in the name of Mother Lakeland, and was in process of time duly arraigned and condemned as a dealer in enchantments. Ultimately, however, she made a confession of her sins and iniquities before she departed this life; and in an old tract entitled, "The Laws against Witches and Conjurations," the following relation of her believed iniquity is to be found :—

"*The Confession of Mother Lakeland, of Ipswich, who was arraigned and condemned for a witch, and suffered death by burning, at Ipswich, in Suffolk, on Tuesday, the 9th September, 1645.*

"The said Mother *Lakeland* hath been a Professor of Religion, a constant hearer of the Word for these many years, and yet a *Witch* (as she confessed) for the space of near twenty years. The *Devil* came to her first, between sleeping and waking, and spake to her in a hollow voice, telling her that if she would serve him she would want nothing. After often solicitation, she consented to him ; then he stroke his claw (as she confessed) into her hands, and with her blood wrote the covenants. *(Now the subtilty of Sathan is to be observed, in that he did not press her to deny God and Christ, as he useth to do to others ; because she was a professour, and might have lost all his hold by pressing her too far.)* Then he furnished her with three imps, two little dogs, and a mole (as she confessed), which she employed in her services. Her husband she bewitched (as she confessed), whereby he lay in great misery for a time, and at last dyed. Then she sent one of her dogs to *Mr. Lawrence*, in *Ipswich*, to torment him and take away his life ; she sent one of them also to his child, to torment it, and take away the life of it, which was done upon them both; and all this (as she confessed) was because he asked her for twelve shillings that she owed him, and for no other cause.

" She further confessed, that she sent her mole to a maid of one *Mrs. Jennings*, in *Ipswich*, to torment her and take away her life, which was done accordingly, and this for no other cause but for that the said maid would not lend her a needle that she desired to borrow of her, and was earnest with her for a shilling which she owed the said maid.

"Then, she further confessed, she sent one of her imps to one *Mr. Beale*, in *Ipswich*, who had formerly been a suitor to her grandchild; and because he would not have her, she sent and burnt a new ship, that had never been at sea, that he was to go master of; and sent also to torment him and take away his life; but he is yet living, but in very great misery, and it is vainly conceived by the doctors and chirurgeons that have him in hand that he consumes and rots, and that half of his body is rotten upon him as he is living.

"Severall other things she did, for all which she was by law condemned to die, and in particular to be burnt to death, because she was the death of her husband (as she confessed), which death she suffered accordingly.

"But since her death, there is one thing that is very remarkable, and to be taken notice of: That upon the very day that she was burned, a bunch of flesh, something after the form of a dog, that grew upon the thigh of the said *Mr. Beale*, ever since the time that she first sent her imp to him, being very hard, but could never be made to break by all the means that could be used, break of itself without any means using. And another sore that at the same time she sent her imp to him rose upon the side of his belly, in the form of a fistula, which ran and could not be braked for all the means that could be used, presently also began to heale, and that there is great hopes that he will suddenly recover again, for his sores heale apace, and he doth recover his strength. He was in this misery for the space of a yeare and a halfe, and was forced to go with his head and his knees together, his misery was so great."

This "Confession" is the latest, we believe, that is known from the lips of a Suffolk sorceress; but it is lamentable to think that the practice of "testing" for witchcraft, such as swimming harmless persons, under the pretence of deciding whether they were possessed or not, continued down to a much later period.

WITCHCRAFT AT BRANDESTON.

The following extract from the parish Register of *Brandeston*, near Wickham Market, records a very extraordinary transaction :—

"6, Maü, 1596, JOHN LOWES, Vicar."

"After he had been vicar here about fifty years, he was executed in the time of the Long Rebellion, at St. Edmund's, Bury, with sixty more, for being a wizard. *Hopkins*, his chief accuser, having kept the poor old man, then in his eightieth year, awake for several nights, till he was delirious, and then confessed a familiarity with the Devil, which had such weight with the jury and his judges, viz., Sergeants *Godcold*, old *Calamy*, and *Fairclough*, as to condemn him, in 1645, or the beginning of 1646."

It appears from a writer in the "Suffolk Literary Chronicle," that some years after this occurrence, Mr. Rivett, who resided at Brandeston Hall, was applied to for information respecting this case, and that gentleman in reply wrote :—"I have it from them who watched with him, that they kept him awake several nights together, and ran him backwards and forward about the room until he was out of breath ; then they rested him a little, and then they ran him again ; and this they did for several days and nights together, till he was quite weary of his life, and scarce sensible of what he said or did. They *swam* him at Framlingham, but that was no true rule to try him by, for they put in honest people at the same time, and they swam as well as he."

Mr. Lowes, it seems, on his trial maintained his innocence to the last. The treatment he experienced as above mentioned was after the trial, and whilst in a state of delirium they extorted from him the following very strange confession : "That two imps attended him ; that the one was always putting him upon doing mischief ; that once, being near the sea, and seeing a ship under sail, this mischievous imp requested to be sent to sink it; that he consented to the importunity, and saw it without any apparent cause immediately sink before him." The following curious anecdote of this divine is likewise stated:—That being precluded Christian burial from the nature of his offence, he composedly and in an audible voice read the service over himself, on his way to execution.

In the parish register of Monk's Eleigh, there is the following entry :—

"Dec. 19th, 1748. Alice, the wife of Thomas Green, labourer, was swam, malicious and evil people having raised an ill report of her being a witch."

CHARM AGAINST WITCHCRAFT.

On one of the bricks which are close to the threshold of the door of Stanningfield church, is a glazed tile on which is a figure of a horse shoe, for the purpose it is said, of preventing witches from entering the church. However, in spite of this celebrated horse shoe, placed where it now is for the protection of the parish, it does not seem to have produced the desired effect, as so late as the year 1795, an unfortunate witch was discovered in Stanningfield, and went through the usual sufferings in a pond close by the church.

In July, 1792, an old woman applied to the justice of Bury St. Edmund's for redress against the imputation of witchcraft; but as she was informed that no cognizance could be taken of her case, she returned to her parish with a full determination to pass the common ordeal, and which, as it was solicited on her part, was inflicted by her husband, his brother, and another man.

The belief in witchcraft still lingers in our county. The Rev. Hugh Pigot, writing in 1863, says:—"I met in a cottage in Hadleigh a woman from Whatfield, who proved to be a devout believer in witchcraft. She said, with a positive earnestness which convinced me that she was sincere in her error, that she knew of several instances of it, and of some families who were in possession of the secret. One case was that of a poor girl who had been ill for a long time, and whose sickness apparently excited the commiseration of an aged female, who came every day to inquire after her. At length it occurred to one of the family that the old lady who seemed to have such a strong sympathy with the sufferer must needs be a witch, and accordingly it was proposed that a horse shoe should be affixed to the sill of the outer door, in order to prevent her from entering the house."

SONGS AND BALLADS.

Songs and ballads are, we fear, the only form in which poetry will be for many years popularily recognized by the people. They convey ideas higher that those entertained by the masses, but still within the reach of their understanding. Such rude poetry has been in all countries the earliest record of heroic and tragic acts and curious events. In the early stages of civilization the minstrel was a popular character, and in England and Wales the man who sang a tribute to the dead over the corpse of a fallen warrior, who poured forth a song at a time of revelry, or related in striking or pathetic language the marvellous tale, the wild adventure, love's sentiment and passion, was protected and caressed, his skill thought half divine, and his person held inviolable. For him there was no need of sword or spear. He that sang to every heart was welcomed by every hand, and even amidst a hostile host and in an enemy's country no man was his foe, and his song or his harp was a shield to him. The favourite themes of the ballad writers were love, war, and revelry, and some specimens of each class have been selected for insertion. In modern ballad literature, Robert

Bloomfield is to Suffolk what Beranger is to the French, and Burns to the Scotch nation. The recital of his "Richard and Kate" and "The Horkey," always delight the Suffolk peasantry.

We commence with a selection from

THE SONG BOOK OF AN IPSWICH MINSTREL.

At the Congress of the British Archæological Association, held in Ipswich, August, 1864, Mr. Thomas Wright, F.S.A., read a paper "On the MS. Song Book of an Ipswich Minstrel of the Fifteenth Century." He said the late Mr. Fitch had some years ago a MS. of songs and carols, apparently of the age of Henry VI., and which probably constituted the stock in trade of a professed minstrel, who sang at festivals and merry-makings. This MS. book was found among the municipal records of the borough of Ipswich, and it being thought that it had no business there, it was taken away. Mr. Fitch gave it to him (Mr. Wright), but being convinced that Mr. Fitch did so in ignorance of its real worth, he insisted on returning it, and it was now in a private collection in the north of England.

A manuscript collection of songs of so early a date is very rare. The only one known to Mr. Wright of a similar character is a Sloane MS. in the British Museum. On a comparison of the contents of the two manuscripts, it was found that a few of the pieces in the Ipswich song book are also in the Sloane MS., but by much the larger number of the songs contained in the Ipswich song book, including some of the most interesting and curious, appear to be unique, and the others are much better and more complete copies than those previously known.

The "Song Book" gives a general view of the classes of poetry then popular, and contains good examples of how the minstrels catered for the public taste. Rather a large proportion of its contents consists of carols and religious songs, such as were sung at Christmas, or perhaps at some other of the great festivals of the Church. Another class of productions in which this MS. for its date is peculiarly rich, consists of drinking songs. The collection also contains a number of those satirical songs against the fair sex, which were so common in the middle ages, and in addition the song book contains a few short moral poems.

We select the following as illustrations of its contents :—

> Bryng us in good ale, and bryng us in good ale ;
> For our blyssyd lady sak, bryng us in good ale.

Bryng us in no browne bred, for that is mad of brane,
Nor bryng us in no whyt bred, for therin is no game ;
    But bryng us in good ale.
Bryng us in no befe, for ther is many bonys (bones) :
But bryng us in good ale, for that go'th downe at onys (once) ;
    And bryng us in good ale.
Bryng us in no bacon, for that is passyng fate,
But bryng us in good ale, and gyfe us i-nough of that ;
    But bryng us in good ale.
Bryng us in no mutton, for that is often lene,
Nor bryng us in no trypes, for thei be syldom clene ;
    But bryng us in good ale.
Bryng us no eggys, for ther ar many schelles,
But bryng us in good ale, and gyf us no(th)yng ellys ;
    But bryng us in good ale.
Bryng us in no butter, for therin ar many herys (hairs),
Nor bryng us in no pygge's flesch, for that wyl mak us borys ;
    But bryng us in good ale.
Bryng us in no podynges, for therin is al Gode's good,
Nor bryng us in no venesen, for that is not for owr blod ;
    But bryng us in good ale.
Bryng us in no capon's flesch, for that is ofte der,
Nor bryng us no dokes (duck's) flesch, for thei slober in the mer (mire) ;
    But bryng us in good ale.

This curious drinking-song was printed by Ritson ("Dissertations on Ancient Songs and Music," p. 34), from

MS., Harl, 541, fol. 214; but the above, under Mr. Wright's additional care, is a much better and more perfect copy.

II.

How, gossipe myn, gossipe myn,
When wyll ye go to the wyn ?

I WYLL you tell a full good sport,
How gossyps gather them on a sort,
Theyre syk bodes for to comfort
    When thei mett in a lane ore stret.

But I dare not, fore ther displeasaunce,
Tell off thes maters half the substaunce ;
But yet sumwhatt off ther governaunce,
    As far as I dare, I will declare.

Good gossipe myn, where have ye be ?
It is so long syth I yow see ;
Where is the best wyn ? tell yow me,
    Can yow ought tell full wele.

I know a drawght off mery-go-downe,
The best it is in all thys towne ;
But yet wold I not, fore my gowne,
    My husband it wyst, ye may me trust.

Call forth yowr gossips by-and-by :
Elynore, Jone, and Margery,
Margaret, Alis, and Cecely,
    Fore thei will come both all and sume.

And ich of them wyll somewhat bryng,
Gosse, pygge, ore capon's wyng,
Pastes off pigeons, ore sum other thyng,
    Fore a galon off wyn thei will not wryng.

Go befoore, be tweyn and tweyn,
Wysly, that ye be not seen ;
Fore I must home, and come ageyn,
    To witt i-wys where my husbond is.

P

A strype ore ij God myght send me,
If my husbond myght her se me ;
She that is aferd, lett her fle,
   Quod Alis than, I dred no man.

Now be we in tavern sett,
A drowght off the best lett hyme fett,
To bryng owr husbondes out off dett,
   Fore we will spend tyll God more send.

Ech of them brought forth ther dysch,
Sume brought flesh, and sume fysh,
Quod Margaret mek, now with a wysh,
   I wold Ann were here, she wold mak us chere.

How sey yow, gossips, is this wyne good ?
That it is, quod Elenore, by the rood,
It cherisheth the hart and comfort the blood ;
   Such jonckettes among shall mak us lyv long.

Anne, byd fill a pot of muscadell,
Fore off all wynes I love it well ;
Swete wynes kepe my body in hele,
   If I had off it nought I shuld tak gret thought.

How look ye, gossipe, at the bordes end ?
Not mery, gossip ?   God it amend.
All shal be well, elles God it defend ;
   Be mery and glad, and sitt not so sadde.

Wold God I had don aftur yowr counsell !
Fore my husbond is so fell,
He betyth me lyk the devill off hell ;
   And the more I cry, the lesse mercy.

Alys with a lowd voyce spak than ;
I-wis, she said, lytyll good he cane
That betyth ore stryketh ony woman,
   And specially his wyff ; God gyve him short lyve !

Margaret mek seid, so mot I thryffe,
I know no man that is alyffe
That gyve me ij strokes, but he shall have fyffe,
   I am not aferd, though I have no berd.

On cast down her shott, and went her wey;
Gossip, quod Elenore, what dyd she paye?
Not but a peny? lo, therefore I saie,
    She shal be no more off owr lore.

Such gestes we may have i-nowe,
That will not fore ther shott alow;
With whom cum she, gossipe? with yow?
    Nay, quod Jone, I come alone.

Now rekyn owr shott and go we hence,
What? cost it ich off us but iij pence?
Parde, thys is but a smale expence,
    Fore such a sort, and all but sport.

Torn down the street where ye cum owt,
And we will compasse rownd ahowt;
Gossip, quod Anne, what nedyth that dowt?
    Yowr husbondes be plesyd, when ye be reisyd.

What so ever ony man thynk,
Whe cum fore nowght but fore good drynk,
Now lett us go whom and wynk;
    Fore it may be sen where we have ben.

Thys is the thought that gossips tak,
Ons in the weke mery will thei mak,
And all small drynk they will forsak;
    But wyne off the best shall han no rest.

Sume be at the taverne ons in a weke;
And so be sume every daie cke;
Ore ellis thei will gron and mak them sek,
    Fore thynges usid will not be refusyd.

Who sey yow, woman, is it not soo?
Yes, suerly, and that ye wyll know;
And therefore lat us drynk all a row,
    And off owr syngyng mak a good endyng.

Now fyll the cupe and drynk to me,
And than shal we good felows be,
And off thys talkyng leve will we,
    And speak then good off women.

An imperfect copy of this very curious ballad was printed by Ritson ("Ancient Songs," p. 77), from a MS. in the Cottonian library. There are considerable variations between his copy and the above, and his begins at the seventh stanza of the ballad in the Ipswich Minstrel's Song Book.

III.

Off all creatures women be best,
Ejus contrarium verum est.

In every place ye may well se,
That women be trew as tyrtyll on tre ;
Not liberall in langag, but ever in secrete
And gret joy among them is fore to be.

The stedfastnesse off women wil never be don,
So gentyll, so curtes, thei be everichon
Mek as a lambe, styll as a stone ;
Crockyd ne crabbyd fynd ye none.

Men be more combres a thowsand fold,
And I mervill who thei dare be so bold,
Ageynst women fore to hold,
Seeing them so pacient, soft, and cold.

Fore tell a woman all your counsayle,
And she cane kepe it wonder weyll,
She had lever go qwyck to hell,
Than to hire neyboure she wold it tell.

Fore by women men be reconsyled,
Fore by women was never man begiled,
Fore by women was never man betraied,
Fore by women was never man bewreyed

Now sey well by women, ore elles be styll,
Fore they never displeasid man by ther will ;
To be angry ore wroth thei cannot skyll,
Fore I dare sey thynk no ill.

Trow ye that they lyst to smatter,
Or ageynst ther husbondes to clatter ?

Nay, thei had lever fast bred and water
Then fore to presse such a matter.

Thowe all the pacience in the world wer drownd
And nonne were left here on the grownd,
Ageyn in women it might be fownd,
Such vertu in them doth abownd.

To the taverne thei will not goo,
Nore to the ale howse never the moo,
Fore, God wott, thei hartes shulbe woo
To spend ther husbondes' money soo.

If here wer a woman ore a mayd,
That list for to go freshly arayd,
Ore with fyne kerchefs to go displaid,
Ye wold saie thei be proud, it is evil said.

IV.

Doll thi ale, doll, doll thi ale, dole,
Ale mak many a mane to have a doty poll.

Ale mak many a mane to styk at a brere ;
Ale mak many a mane to ly in the myere ;
And ale mak many a mane to slep by the fyere ;
    With doll.

Ale mak many a mane to stombyl at a stone ;
Ale mak many a mane to go dronken home ;
And ale mak many a mane to brek hys tone ;
    With doll.

Ale mak many a mane to draw hys knyfe ;
Ale mak many a mane to mak gret stryfe ;
And ale mak many a mane to bet hys wyf ;
    With doll.

Ale mak many a mane to wet hys chekes ;
Ale mak many a mane to ly in the stretes ;
And ale make many a mane to wet hys shetes ;
    With doll.

Ale mak many a mane to stomble at the blokkes ;
Ale mak many a mane to mak hys hed have knokkes ;
And ale mak many a mane to syt in the stokkes ;
　　　　With doll.

Ale mak many a mane to ryne over the falows ;
Ale mak many a mane to swere by God and alhalows ;
And ale mak many a mane to hang upon the galows ;
　　　　With doll.

THE PLEASANT HISTORY OF THE KING AND LORD BIGOD, OF BUNGAY.

Tune—" Dunwich Roses."

Hugh Bigod was the descendant of Roger Bigod, who, at the time of the Norman Survey, was in possession of one hundred and seventeen manors in this county. The family came over with William the Conqueror; and for their eminent services at the battle of Hastings, Roger was thus richly rewarded. His brother, Hugh Bigod, was created by King Stephen Earl of East Anglia, and in 1166 was advanced by Henry the Second to the title and dignity of Earl of Norfolk, and died attainted in 1177. He was succeeded by his son, Roger Bigod, who, though heir to the Earldom of Norfolk, and to the Stewardship of the royal household, was obliged to purchase both by the payment of one thousand marks, in consequence of the attainder of his father. In the time of King John, he joined the refractory barons, and was one of the most active amongst them in procuring for the people that great palladium of English liberty, MAGNA CHARTA. He, dying in 1220, was succeeded by his son Hugh, the subject of the following ballad.

The Castle of Bungay is conjectured to have been built by this powerful family. During the intestine commotions in the turbulent reign of Stephen, it was so strongly fortified by Hugh Bigod, and stood besides in such an advantageous situation, that he was accustomed to boast of it as impregnable ; and is reported by Holinshed to have made use of this expression :

" Were I in my Castle of Bungaye,
   Upon the water of Waveney,
  I would ne set a button by the King of Cocknaye."

The King has sent for Bigod bold,
   In Essex, whereat he lay,
But Lord Bigod laugh'd at his Poursuivant,
   And stoutly thus did say:
   " Were I in my Castle of Bungay,
   Upon the river of Waveney,
  I would ne care for the King of Cockney."

Hugh Bigod was Lord of Bungay tower,
   And a merry lord was he;
So away he rode on his berry-black steed,
   And sung with license and glee:
   " Were I in my Castle of Bungay,
   Upon the river of Waveney,
  I would ne care for the King of Cockney."

At Ipswich they laugh'd to see how he sped,
   And at Ufford they star'd, I wis;
But at merry Saxmundham they heard his song,
   And the song he sung was this:
   " Were I in my Castle of Bungay,
    Upon the river of Waveney,
  I would ne care for the King of Cockney."

The Baily he rode and the Baily he ran,
   To catch the gallant Lord Hugh,
But for every mile the Baily rode,
   The Earl he rode more than two;
   Says, " Were I in my Castle of Bungay,
   Upon the river of Waveney,
  I would ne care for the King of Cockney."

When the Baily had ridden to Bramfield oak,
   Sir Hugh was at Ilksall bower;
When the Baily had ridden to Halesworth cross,
   He was singing in Bungay tower—
   " Now that I am in my Castle of Bungay,
   Upon the river of Waveney,
  I will ne care for the King of Cockney."

When news was brought to London town,
　　How Sir Bigod did jest and sing,
" Say you to Lord Hew, of Norfolk,"
　　Said Henry, our English King,
　　" Though you be in your castle of Bungay,
　　Upon the river of Waveney,
I'll make you care for the King of Cockney."

King Henry he marshal'd his merry men all,
　　And through Suffolk they march'd with speed,
And they marched to Lord Bigod's castle wall,
　　And knock'd at his gate, I rede ;
　　" Sir Hugh of the castle of Bungay,
　　Upon the river of Waveney;
Come, doff your cap to the King of Cockney ! "

Sir Hughon Bigod, so stout and brave,
　　When he heard the King thus say,
He trembled and shook like a May-mawther,
　　And he wish'd himself away :
　　" Were I out of my castle of Bungay,
　　And beyond the river of Waveney,
I would ne care for the King of Cockney."

Sir Hugh took three score sacks of gold,
　　And flung them over the wall ;
Says, " Go your ways, in the Devil's name,
　　Yourself and your merry men all !
　　But leave me my castle of Bungay,
　　Upon the river of Waveney,
And I'll pay my shot to the King of Cockney."

THE SUFFOLK WONDER ;

*Or, a Relation of a Young Man, who, a month after his death,
appeared to his Sweetheart, and carried her on horseback
behind him for forty miles in two hours, and was never
seen after but in his grave.*

The following tale is taken from " A collection of Old Ballads. Corrected from the best and most antient copies extant.
With introductions historical, critical, or humorous. Illus-

trated with copper plates." London, 1723—5, 12 mo., 3 vols.
It is thought to bear a considerable resemblance to the
celebrated German ballad of Leonore, by Bürger.

A wonder stranger ne'er was known,
Than what I now shall treat upon ;
In *Suffolk* there did lately dwell
A farmer rich, and known full well.

He had a daughter fair and bright,
On whom he plac'd his whole delight ;
Her beauty was beyond compare,
She was both virtuous and fair.

There was a young man living by,
Who was so charmed with her eye,
That he could never be at rest,
He was by love so much possest.

He made address to her, and she
Did grant him love immediately ;
But when her father came to hear,
He parted her and her poor dear.

Forty miles distant was she sent,
Unto his brother's, with intent
That she should there so long remain,
Till she had chang'd her mind again.

Hereat this young man sadly griev'd,
But knew not how to be reliev'd ;
He sigh'd and sobb'd continually,
That his true love he could not see.

She by no means could to him send,
Who was her heart's espoused friend ;
He sigh'd, he griev'd, but all in vain,
For she confin'd must still remain.

He mourn'd so much that doctor's art,
Could give no ease unto his heart ;
Who was so strangely terrify'd,
That in short time for love he dy'd.

She that from him was sent away,
Knew nothing of his dying day,
But constant still she did remain,
And lov'd the dead, altho' in vain.

After he had in grave been laid
A month or more, unto this maid
He came in middle of the night,
Who joy'd to see her heart's delight.

Her father's horse, which well she knew,
Her mother's hood and safeguard too,
He brought with him, to testify
Her parents' order he came by.

Which when her uncle understood,
He hop'd it would be for her good,
And gave consent to her straightway,
That with him she should come away.

When she was got her love behind,
They pass'd as swift as any wind,
That in two hours, or little more,
He brought her to her father's door.

But as they did this great haste make,
He did complain his head did ache ;
Her handkerchief she then took out,
And ty'd the same his head about.

And unto him she thus did say,
Thou art as cold as any clay ;
When we come home a fire we'll have ;
But little dream'd he went to grave.

Soon were they at her father's door,
And after she ne'er saw him more ;
I'll set the horse up, then he said,
And there he left this harmless maid.

She knock'd, and straight a man he cry'd,
Who's there ? 'Tis I, she then reply'd :
Who wonder'd much her voice to hear,
And was possess'd with dread and fear.

Her father he did tell, and then
He star'd like an affrighted man ;
Down stairs he ran, and when he see her,
Cry'd out, my child, how cam'st thou here ?

Pray sir, did you not send for me
By such a messenger ? said she,
Which made his hair stare on his head,
As knowing well that he was dead.

Where is he ? then to her he said,
He's in the stable, quoth the maid ;
Go in, said he, and go to bed,
I'll see the horse well littered.

He star'd about, and there could he
No shape of any mankind see ;
But found his horse all on a sweat,
Which made him in a deadly fret.

His daughter he said nothing to,
Nor none else, tho' full well they knew
That he was dead a month before,
For fear of grieving her full sore.

Her father to the father went
Of the deceased, with full intent
To tell him what his daughter said,
So both came back unto this maid.

They ask'd her, and she still did say,
'Twas he that then brought her away ;
Which when they heard, they were amaz'd,
And on each other strangely gaz'd.

A handkerchief she said she ty'd
About his head ; and that they try'd,
The sexton they did speak unto,
That he the grave would then undo :

Affrighted, then they did behold
His body turning unto mould ;
And though he had a month been dead,
This handkerchief was 'bout his head.

This thing unto her then they told,
And the whole truth they did unfold ;
She was thereat so terrify'd,
And grieved, that she quickly dy'd.

Part not true love, you rich men then,
But if they be right honest men,
Your daughter's love, give them their way,
For force oft breeds their lives' decay.

THE SUFFOLK COMEDY.

IN THREE PARTS.

To the tune of "Phillis the Lovely."

The following old legendary ballad is printed from an unique copy that was in the possession of the late Mr. John Raw, of Ipswich.

PART I.

You young men and maidens of beauty most bright,
Give ear to my story of love and delight ;
I know that most people will of it approve,
It shows that some maidens are crafty in love.
It is an old saying we often do hear,
That maids go a courting when it is leap-year ;
A comical courtship this proves in the end,
Most people will smile ere my song's at an end.
Young Cupid he ranges about now and then,
And maidens are wounded as well as the men ;
For all must submit to his conquering bow,
As now by experience you soon all shall know.
A handsome young lady in London did dwell,
Whose parents were dead, it is known very well ;
She had the possession, all in her own hands,
Of great store of riches, and houses, and lands.
A gentleman out of the country did ride,
And at a great milliner's shop in Cheapside
He took up his lodgings, as I do declare,
When many a beautiful lady came there,
Fine gloves, and rich ribbons, and fans there to buy,
And such other nick-nacks as pleased their eye ;
The gentleman of them did take a full view,
And often would pass a fine compliment too.

This beautiful lady amongst all the rest,
She came to the milliner's shop, I protest,
And seeing this gentleman, she, for her part,
That instant was wounded by Cupid's sharp dart.
This honoured beautiful lady by birth,
Thought him the handsomest creature on earth ;
So sweet was his carriage, such eloquent ways,
In person so graceful, exceeding all praise.
When business was over, this man to be plain,
Took coach, and then rode back to Suffolk again ;
At which the young lady was grieved full sore,
For he was the person that she did adore.
The ardour of love was enkindled so great,
Her fond heart lay panting and fearfully beat ;
So deep was she wounded, she could no more rest,
The tortures of love so inflamed her breast.
Then said the young beautiful lady, I find
That now I am greatly perplex'd in my mind ;
In love I am deeply entangled, she cry'd,
Oh ! that I could be but that gentleman's bride !
Methinks how delighted I'd be with the choice,
I do like his temper, and likewise his voice ;
His courteous behaviour, in every degree,
So fine is, so sweet, and so pleasing to me.
I never shall rest till I find out his name,
And learn by some method from what place he came ;
But now if my passion to him I unfold,
I fear he would slight me, and call me too bold.
But rather than I will quite languish and die,
In a very short time I am resolved for to try ;
Perhaps I by policy then may contrive,
To gain him I fancy, my heart to revive.

PART II.

Soon after, this beautiful young lady gay
In man's fine apparel herself did array ;
And for this spruce gentleman inquiry made,
Because now to love him her heart was betray'd.
They told her from St. Edmund's, Bury, he came,
Which is in the county of Suffolk by name.
Disguised she rode down to Suffolk, we find,
In order to ease her poor troubled mind.

In the fair town of Bury, then, as it is told,
This damsel then sought for this gentleman bold,
And in a short time did find out where he dwelt,
But who can express now the passion she felt!
This lady then went to a tavern hard by,
But drest like a man that no one might espy
That she was a woman, thus in her disguise,
She sent for this gentleman, with a design
To come and take part in a bottle of wine;
And soon to the tavern this gentleman came,
To visit the stranger of honour and fame.
The lady was like a young man to behold,
And said, Sir, excuse me for being so bold;
Though I am a stranger no harm do I mean,
In fair London city your face I have seen.
The gentleman straightway replied in mirth,
You're not a person of breeding and birth;
Is not your intention, I ask, me to cheat?
Now what is your business, pray let me intreat.
Sir, I came from London (I hope no offence),
To you in great business, and ere I go hence,
The truth of the matter you too soon shall know;
This set him a sighing, when she talked so.
They called for a supper, and when it was o'er,
The gentleman said, Sir, I do you implore
To tell me your business, then in her disguise
She acted her part now both cunning and wise.
Sir, I have a sister, a lady by birth,
She is the most beautiful creature on earth;
And she is worth hundreds and thousands a year,
To tell you the truth she does love you most dear.
My sister lies languishing now for your sake,
And therefore compassion I hope you will take,
And slight not a captive, in love so confin'd,
Your answer, I hope, will be loving and kind.
The gentleman answered without more ado,
You question me hardly, but now tell me true,
If that your faces resemble alike,
Then I with your sister a bargain will strike.
Dear sir, she is like me in every part:
Why then I can love her with all my fond heart;
If there be no bubble nor trick in the case,
Your sister's kind proffer I mean to embrace.

She said, I must ride on to Cambridge with speed ;
But since you have answered so kindly indeed,
I will ride to London, before you get there,
And, sir, you shall find that all matters are fair.

PART III.

The gentleman then, between hope and despair,
His journey to London forthwith did repair ;
He found where this beautiful lady did dwell,
And of her good fame he was pleased right well.
The lady got home, as before she had said,
And he was admitted by her waiting-maid
To the young lady's presence, approaching the room
To pay her his visit he then did presume.
Dear honour'd lady, excuse me nor blame,
From Bury St. Edmund's, in Suffolk, I came,
I had the good fortune your brother to see,
Who told me you had a great value for me.
Sir, what do you mean ? I declare on my death,
I have not a brother alive on the earth !
This filled the gentleman with much discontent,
And he said, on a fool's errand then I am sent.
So taking his leave, on his going away,
This beautiful lady she caused him to stay ;
And then unto supper she did him invite,
The charms of her beauty his soul to delight.
Worthy sir, she exclaimed, right welcome you be,
But pray now relate the whole matter to me ;
What person it was made use of my name,
Because to affront you he was much to blame.
Dear sir, I am sorry and grieved in heart
That you should have had such affront on your part.
Then all the whole matter he soon did declare ;
The lady she smiled, for she could not forbear.
He had but small stomach to eat at the first,
Her kind entertainment made him to mistrust
That it was but some juggle, the matter to prove
He greeted the lady with proffers of love.
She said, I now fancy that you have red hair.
Dear madam, you wrong me, I solemnly swear ;
So his wig he pulled off, and then, throwing it down,
Cry'd, madam, behold now my hair it is dark brown !

The lady burst out into laughter, and said,
Your wig will just fit me, as I am a maid ;
She her head-dress pulled off, and his wig she put on,
Saying, Sir, do I look like a handsome young man ?
The gentleman's heart then began to rejoice,
Saying, that is the face and the sweeet pretty voice
Which I met with at Bury, therefore he not coy,
For now I am crowned with rapture and joy.
Why, sir, are you sure on it ; perhaps you mistake ?
No, madam, I do not, my oath I can take.
Then how do you like me, sir ? tell unto me.
Sweet honoured lady, right happy I be !
Then a lady excuse, sir, I beg and intreat,
For I'm a poor captive who lies at your feet ;
I now crave your pardon for being so rude
On such a kind gentleman thus to intrude.
'Tis true, sir, I want not for silver or gold :
I hope you'll excuse me for being so bold,
For love is a witchcraft, none can it withstand,
When little brisk Cupid gets the upper hand.
Dear lady, your love makes amends for it all,
And therefore in right happy splendor we shall
Be crowned with comfort, when we are both ty'd,
And I shall be bless'd with a beautiful bride.
At Bow-church, in London, then married they were,
Attended with gentlemen and ladies fair ;
They rode down to Bury, and as many say,
Great feastings there lasted for many a day.

THE POLITICK MAID OF SUFFOLK, OR THE LAWYER OUTWITTED.

The following curious old ballad is printed from a copy that was obligingly communicated to the Rev. James Ford (the Editor of the old " Suffolk Garland ") by a gentleman whose collections in ancient English literature stood unrivalled in this country.

Come all ye young men and maids,
   Both of high and low degree ;
Or you that love a merry jest,
   Give ear awhile to me.

I'd have you give attention
  To what I have to tell,
Then hear it out, I do not doubt
  'Twill please you wondrous well.
'Tis of a wealthy lawyer,
  That did in *Suffolk* dwell,
He kept a handsome house-keeper,
  Her name was called Nell ;
He kiss'd and pressed her o'er and o'er,
  As I to you may tell,
Till her apron grew too short before,
  Alas! Poor Nell!
It happen'd on a certain day,
  As talking they were led,
She wept, she wail'd, she wrung her hands,
  And thus to him she said :
My virgin rose you stole away,
  Oh wed me, sir, said she,
Or I, like other girls, may say,
  Ah ! woe is me !
He straight gave her a loving kiss,
  And without more delay,
He took her by the lily white hand,
  And thus to her did say :
I wish old Nick may fetch me straight,
  (A woeful tale to tell)
If ever I prove false to thee,
  My dearest Nell.
Then thus with joys and loving toys,
  They past away the time,
Till seven months were gone and past,
  (But two left out of nine)
When from her place he turn'd her quite,
  As I to you may tell,
All for the sake of a lady bright,
  Alas, poor Nell!
But when she found she was deceiv'd,
  She wept and tore her hair,
And cry'd, there's no belief in man,
  It plainly doth appear.
Oh ! how could he so cruel be,
  Thus to trepan my heart ;

Q

But I will be reveng'd on him,
  Before that we do part.
Now it happen'd to this lady bright,
  Who liv'd a mile from town,
That this young lawyer every night
  Would walk to her from home.
Forgetting of his former vows,
  As I to you may tell,
And longing for a richer spouse,
  He left poor Nell.
As Nell was sitting all alone,
  Lamenting sad one night,
A project came into her head,
  Which made her laugh outright.
Thought she, I'll make myself as black
  As any devil in hell,
And watch some night for his coming home,
  Sing, O brave Nell!
She to a chimney sweeper went,
  And there a bargain made,
For to have his sooty clothes,
  And furthermore she said,
If that my counsel you'll but take,
  A guinea I'll give to thee;
Then let your little sweeper boy
  But come along with me.
She having learned the lad his tale,
  Thus unto him did say,
If you do act your part aright,
  You half-a-crown I'll pay.
She gave him squibs of gunpowder,
  And all appear'd right well,
To frighten her master, the lawyer,
  Sing, O brave Nell!
And coming to a lonesome wood,
  In ambush they did lie,
The which adjoining to a road,
  That the lawyer must come by;
With a pair of ram's horns on her head,
  In a lonesome place stood she;
But as for black, the sweeper's boy,
  She plac'd him on a tree.

It was just about the hour of one,
  As for a truth we hear,
The lawyer he came trudging home
  From the courtship of his dear ;
And stepping o'er to shun the dirt,
  As I to you may tell,
She quickly caught him by the skirt,
  Sing, O brave Nell!
Then with a doleful, hollow voice,
  She unto him did say,
According to your wish I come,
  To fetch you hence away.
She said, you must along with me
  Down to my gloomy cell,
Except to-morrow by break of day,
  You wed poor Nell.
With that the chimney-sweeper's boy,
  Set fire unto the train,
Which flew and crack'd about his head,
  And made him roar amain.
Dear Mr. Devil, spare me now,
  And mind but what I tell,
And I to-morrow by break of day,
  Will wed poor Nell.
Well look you do, the Devil cry'd,
  Or mind what I say to thee ;
Dou you see that little devil,
  That sits on yonder tree ?
If ever you do break your vow,
  As sure as hell is hell,
That little devil shall fetch you,
  If you slight poor Nell.
The lawyer he went trembling home,
  In a most dreadful fright,
And early in the morning,
  As soon as it was light,
With trembling joints and staring eyes,
  With looks both wan and pale,
He came to her with humble voice—
  Good-morrow, dear Nell.
With kisses and embraces,
  She granted her consent ;

And having got a license,
    Unto the church they went ;
Where he made her his lawful wife,
    As for a truth I tell,
And now they live a happy life,
    Sing, O brave Nell !
She never told to friend or foe,
    The trick which she had played,
Until some months after,
    When she was brought to bed ;
She told it at a gossiping,
    Which pleased the wenches well,
He was glad, and laugh'd and said,
    'Twas well done Nell !

THE LAMENTATION OF BECKLES.

A proper newe Sonet, declaring the lamentation of Beckles, a Market Towne in Suffolke, whiche was in ye greate winde upon S. Andrewe's eve laste paste, moste pittyfullie burnt withe fire, to the losse bye estimacion of twentye thousande poundes and upwardes, and to ye nombre of fourscore dwellinge houses, 1586.

To WILSON'S TUNE, FINIS T. D.

At London: Imprinted by Robert Robinson, for Nicholas Colme, of Norwich, dwelling in S. Andrewe's Churchyard.

With sobbing sighes and tickling teares
    My state I doe lament,
Perceiving howe God's heavie wrath
    Against my sinnes is bent.
Let all men viewe my woefull fall,
    And rue my woefull case,
And learne herebye in speedye sort
    Repentance to embrace.

For late in SUFFOLK was I seene
    To be a statelye TOWNE,
Replenished with riches store,
    And had in greate renowne :

Yea, planted on a pleasant soyle,
  So faire as hart could wishe,
And had my *Markets* once a weeke
  Well stored with fleshe and fishe.

A faire freshe *River* running bye
  To profite me withall,
Who with a cristall cleered *Streame*
  About my bankes did fall ;
My *Fayres* in Somer welthelye
  For to increase my store,
My *Meadowes* green, and COMMONS greate,
  What could I wishe for more ?

Fourscore houses in *Beckles* Towne
  Were burned to ashes quite,
And that which most lamentes my hart,
  The *House of God* I saye,
The *Church* and *Temple* by this Fyre
  Is cleane consumed awaye.

The *Market Place* and *Houses* fayre
  That stood about the same,
Hath felt the force and violence
  Of this most fearefull flame ;
Soe that there is no christian man
  But in his hart would grieve,
To see the smarte I did sustayne
  Uppon *Saint Andrew's Eve*.

Wherefore, goode Christian people, nowe
  Take warninge by my fall,
Live not in stryfe and envious hate
  To breed eche other thrall ;
Seeke not your neighbor's lastinge Spoyle
  By greedie sute and lawe,
Live not in discorde and debate,
  Whiche doth destruction drawe.

A mutilated copy of this rare ballad was discovered some few years ago in the binding of an old Italian work, printed in 1584, in the library of the Royal Society. T. D. was Thomas Delony, the "ballotting silkweaver," of Norwich,

and probably the above was one of his earliest productions.
" Wilson's Tune," or " Wilson's Wilde," as it is sometimes
called, is preserved in William Ballet's Lute Book, a MS.
in Trinity College, Dublin. A later impression of this
" Sonet " may be found among the Bagford Ballads, in the
British Museum.

THE LAMENTATION OF BECKLES.

*A brief sonet declaring the Lamentation of Beckles, a market
towne in Suffolke, which was in the great winde, upon St.
Andrew's eve, pitifully burned with fire, to the value, by estimation, of twentie thousand pounds, and to the number of fourscore dwelling houses, besides a great number of other houses.*

1586. To the Tune of " Labandalashotte," Finis of D. Sterrie.

*At London: Imprinted by Robert Robinson, for Nicholas Colman, of
Norwich, dwelling in St. Andrewe's Churchyarde.*

(The tune of "Labandalashotte" is mentioned in the "Handful of Pleasant
Delights," 1584, but it has not been recovered.)

I.

My lovinge goode Neighbors that come to beholde
Mee sillie poore Beccles in cares manyfolde,
Such robbing, such steeling for more to the lesse,
Such dishonest dealing, in tyme of distresse,
That whoe so harde harted and worn out of grace,
But pittie may pierce him to thinke of mie case ?

II.

But O my goode Neighbors that see mine estate,
Be all one as Christians, nor lyve in debate,
With wrapping and trapping, each other enthrall,
With watching and pryeing at each other's fall ;
With houing and shoving and striving in lawe,
Of God nor his Gospell once standing in awe ;
Lyve not in hart burning, at God never wrest,
To Christ once be turning, not use him in jest ;
Lyve lovelye together, and not in discorde,
Let me be your mirrour to lyve in the Lord.

These two ballads on Beccles formed part of a collection
of seventy ballads that were sold in London, in 1864, in a
folio volume, at the sale of the late Mr. Daniell's library,
for the sum of seven hundred and fifty pounds.

A MERRY SONG ON THE DUKE'S LATE GLORIOUS SUCCESS OVER THE DUTCH.

Southwold bay, or as it was anciently abbreviated "Sole
bay," is celebrated as the scene of an obstinate and san-
guinary naval engagement, on the 28th May, 1672. In it
the fleets of England and France were combined on the one
hand, against the Dutch fleet on the other. The former, of
101 sail of men of war, besides fire ships and tenders,
carrying 6018 guns and 34,500 men. The latter, including
fire ships and tenders, mustered 168, of which 91 were men
of war. The commanders of the combined squadron were
JAMES Duke of York, COUNT D'ETREES, and EARL OF
SANDWICH. Against these were opposed on the side of
the Dutch, DE RUYTER, BLANKART, and VAN GHENT,
accompanied by Cornelius de Witt, as deputy from the
States.

The English and French lay upon the bay in a very
negligent posture. Sandwich warned his brother commanders of their danger, but was answered by His Royal
Highness with an imputation upon his courage. The event
proved how unjust were such suspicions, and how much the
allies were indebted for their safety to the caution of the
man who had been so groundlessly censured. Upon the
appearance of the enemy there was much trepidation, and
the combined forces had to cut away some of their cables
before their ships could be got into readiness. Sandwich
left room for his comrades to disengage themselves by
hastening out of the bay. This judicious and well timed
movement prevented the destruction of the combined fleet
by de Ruyter's fire ships—a result which seemed inevitable

from the false and crowded position in which the English commanders had placed themselves.

Having thus succeeded in disentangling his confederates, the despised Sandwich rushed into the battle, determined to conquer or die. By presenting himself at every post of danger he drew towards him the fiercest shocks and bravery of his opponents. The entire squadron of Van Ghent was thus encountered single handed. But the intrepidity of Sandwich proved more than a match for the Dutch Admiral, whom he slew with his own hand, sinking a man of war and three other of the enemy's vessels. At this moment of un-equalled success, his battered ship was grappled and fired. Of the thousand brave hands that formed his crew but a small portion remained. His officers were all cut down, and himself surrounded with flames. Still was he thundering in the midst of the enemy—being vainly solicited to provide for his own safety; and when his burning vessel could no longer afford him fighting room, he boldly flung himself into the sea, and exposed by his gallant conduct, even in death, the rashness of the censure which impugned his bravery.

In the meantime the Duke of York was hotly pressed by De Ruyter; and so fiercely and obstinately was the dispute maintained between them, that of thirty-two engagements in which his Royal Highness had been engaged, he declared this to be the sharpest and longest. His ship became dis-abled, himself overpowered by numbers, and the enemy so sanguine by reason of his seemingly hopeless condition, that had not Sir Joseph Jordan come to his aid, the Duke must have shared the fate of Sandwich. Twice during the heat of the battle he was obliged to desert the ships in which he fought, in consequence of the damage and loss of men which they successively suffered. Night at last brought this well contested engagement to a close, in which the loss on both sides was nearly equal. The English were declared the victors, but the victory gained was nearly as disastrous as a defeat. The French ships scarcely took any share in the action. It is supposed that they had received secret orders to stand aloof, and to spare their hands, that the Dutch and English might be weakened by mutual animosity.

A letter in the possession of W. P. Hunt, Esq., of Ipswich, whose collection of MSS. and illustrations relating to Suffolk is unequalled in this county, gives an account of the finding of the body of the Earl of Sandwich. It is from Lord Clifford to the Duke of Laudendale, and is dated, Whitehall, June 11, '72. Speaking of the battle and the Earl of Sandwich, Lord Clifford says,

"His body is brought into Harwich, and found strangely. One of our ketches beeing neer the Long Sand Head but two days since, saw him floate upon the sea in fifteen fathom water, and knew him by the star upon his coate, and so sent his boate and took him up. His George and blue ribon is brought to the king; there was also his gold watch in his pocket, and three dimond rings on his fingers."

The following ballad was composed in reference to the battle, but unfortunately pays attention to the doings of His " Royal " Highness, to the neglect of the brave Earl Sandwich.

Tune—" Suffolk Stiles."

One day, as I was sitting still
Upon the side of Dunwich hill,
And looking on the ocean,
    By chance I saw de Ruyter's fleet,
    With Royal James' squadron meet,
    In sooth it was a noble treat
To see that brave commotion.

I cannot stay to name the names
Of all the ships that fought with James,
Their number or their tonnage ;
    But this I say, the noble host
    Right gallantly did take its post,
    And cover'd all the hollow coast
From Walderswyck to Dunwich.

The French, who should have joined the Duke
Full far astern did lay and look,
Although their hulls were lighter ;
     But nobly faced the Duke of York,
     Tho' some may wink and some may talk,
     Right stoutly did his vessel stalk
To buffet with De Ruyter.

Well might you hear their guns, I guess,
From Sizewell-gap to Easton Ness,
The show was rare and sightly ;
     They battled without let or stay
     Until the evening of that day,
     'Twas then the Dutchmen ran away,
The Duke had beat them tightly.

Of all the battles gain'd at sea
This was the rarest victory
Since Philip's grand armada ;
     I will not name the rebel Blake—
     He fought for Horson Cromwell's sake,
     And yet was forced three days to take
To quell the Dutch bravado.

So now we've seen them take to flight,
This way and that, where'er they might,
To windward or to leeward ;
     Here's to King Charles, and here's to James,
     And here's to all the captains' names,
     And here's to all the Suffolk dames,
And here's the House of Stuart.

THE MELFORD DISASTER.

A NEW BALLAD, TO THE TUNE OF "TOM OF BEDLAM," 1794.

The circumstances which gave occasion to this ballad are the following. Three young ladies of Melford agreed to bathe in a river about half-a-mile distant from the town, there being no private accommodation for that purpose in the neighbourhood. An early hour, at which they would be the least liable to be discovered by strangers, was determined on;

and at four o'clock in the morning they proceeded to the appointed place. But as they walked through the town, they were unfortunately espied by a blacksmith. Curiosity prompted him to find out whither the fair ones were hastening, but he did not discover himself to them till they were in the river, when, perceiving him approach, they screamed out, and prudently sat down in the water. The modern Vulcan, dead to the distresses of these Venuses, determined to divert his uncouth fancy by carrying off their clothes, with which he did not return. In this pitiable situation they were obliged to remain for nearly an hour, when a poor woman passing that way, on hearing of the rude behaviour which they had experienced, and their consequent embarassment, procured them such necessary articles of apparel as enabled them to return home with decency.

All in the land of Suffolk,
At Melford, the unwary,
   On the side of a bank,
   Was play'd such a prank,
By a devil yclept *Vagary.*

To look about thee, Bury,
(Thy ladies are so charming)
   I'd have thee begin,
   For the Father of Sin
Gets a taste that's quite alarming.

On Melford's reputation
For scandal we did take it,
   When 'twas talk'd with disdain,
   Among the profane,
That the ladies there go naked.

'Twas early in the morning,
Just as the sun was peeping,
   Three daughters of Eve
   Got up, without leave,
To a farmer's pond to creep in.

Nor, look ye, were they Naiads,
Nor, mind ye, were they Graces;
 For the women of old,
 By Ovid we're told,
Wash'd nothing but their faces.

Long time in nature's buff suits,
Not much oppress'd with blusbes;
 Now in, and now out,
 They paddled about,
Like ducks among the rushes.

Nor did ye dream, ye Fair ones,
When taking such a frolic,
 That the sweet West wind,
 Tho' it blew so kind,
Could give a maid the cholic.

While thus, in sportive humour
They flounced about, God bless 'em !
 That villain, old Nick,
 Was playing a trick,
On purpose to distress 'em.

Three things as soft as pillows,
With stays and caps together ;
 This cunning old wag
 Put into his bag,
And flew away like a feather.

Cloaks, petticoats, and kerchiefs,
On Satan's back suspended :
 With stockings and shoes,
 And eke furbelows,
Clean out of sight he ascended.

I'd sing the sequel solemn,
Did modesty allow it ;
 But a dock-leaf vest
 Is but ill exprest
By painter or by poet.

Let Coventry no longer
For sights like these be reckon'd ;

For, Melford, thy fame
Has got thee the name
Of Coventry the Second.

TO THE AUTHOR OF THE MELFORD DISASTER.

When fair Godiva undertook
  Thro' Coventry to pass,
None in the town presumed to look,
  Except one silly ass.
Unable he the sight to bear,
  Was struck with much surprise,
(Better for him he'd not been there—
  The fool lost both his eyes.)

If this had been thy luckless fate,
  Alas! poor Melford Tom,
Thou would'st have cursed thy addle pate
  For wandering from home.
Good folk, if to New Coventry
  You e'en should chance to roam,
You'll know it well, each child can tell
  You who is peeping Tom.

THE HUMBLE ADDRESS OF GEORGE PARISH AND EDWARD BELL, ESQUIRES, BELLMEN OF THE BOROUGH OF IPSWICH, IN FULL POTS ASSEMBLED.

These lines are a burlesque on the following most obsequious Address which was presented by the Borough of Ipswich to His Majesty George III., on his providential escape from the knife of Peg Nicholson.

"To THE KING'S MOST EXCELLENT MAJESTY.
" *The humble address of the Bailiffs, Burgesses, and Commonalty of the Ancient Borough of Ipswich, in Great Court assembled.*

" We, YOUR MAJESTY's dutiful and loyal subjects, the Bailiffs, Burgesses, and Commonalty of the Ancient Borough of Ipswich, beg leave humbly to offer YOUR MAJESTY our sincere and hearty congratulations on YOUR MAJESTY's providential escape from the late desperate attempt made upon YOUR MAJESTY's sacred person, an attempt which at once endangered YOUR MAJESTY's life, and the happiness of all YOUR MAJESTY's subjects.

"Fully sensible of the innumerable blessings we enjoy under YOUR MAJESTY's mild government, we fervently pray that YOUR MAJESTY's most valuable life may be preserved many years, and that YOUR MAJESTY may long reign over a free, happy, and loyal people.

"Given under our Common Seal, the 18th of August, 1786."

The BELLMEN OF IPSWICH, *unwilling to be outdone in loyalty to* HIS MAJESTY, *have composed an address equally as full of* MAJESTY *as that presented by their worthy Masters to* HIS MAJESTY, *of which the following is an exact copy.*

> To his *Majesty* most excellent,
> With humble duty we present,
> In lines replete with *Majesty*
> As lights upon the starry sky,
> *Your Majesty* to congratulate
> In being sav'd from th' attack of late—
> Th' attack against *your royal* life,
> By woman's hand and blunted knife.
> How could she dare to lift on high
> Her hand to stab *your Majesty?*
> That wicked hand, with rage so fierce,
> *Your Majesty's* kind heart to pierce!
> 'Twas happy for *your Majesty*
> That Providence was standing by,
> Or else, perhaps, *your Majesty*
> Might have received a blow so sly
> As would have killed *your Majesty.*
> What sorrow would the land o'erspread
> T' have heard *your Majesty* was dead!
> Your subjects would have wept full sore
> T' have seen *your Majesty* no more.
> Our thanks unfeign'd we send on high,
> To Him who sav'd *your Majesty,*
> And hope that he will hear our cry,
> And long preserve *your Majesty.*
>
> Given under *our* own great seal,
> The *lanthorn, staff,* and *midnight-bell.*

THE MONDAY NIGHTS' CLUB AT IPSWICH.

BY DR. CLUBBE.

The Monday Nights' Club, long celebrated for its social and convivial meetings among the people of Ipswich, was established in the year 1725, and consisted of an unlimited number of members. They met alternately at each other's houses on every Monday evening, and although there were many *wig* members amongst them, yet in politics they were all most decided *Tories*. The club ceased to exist in the year 1812. The following song, which was sung at their annual dinner, was written by Dr. Clubbe, a gentleman who practised for many years in Ipswich both as a surgeon and a physician. He was the eldest son of the Rev. John Clubbe, rector of Whatfield, and vicar of Debenham, and probably inherited much of that humorous and cheerful disposition for which he was celebrated.

In the year twenty-five, as by oral tradition,
    A set of choice spirits, enlivened by wine,
Agreed 'mong themselves, in a special commission,
    To erect a new banquet at Bacchus's shrine.

All rosy, good-humoured, and full of invention,
    By some proper name the new meeting to dub,
They agreed, one and all, not a voice in dissension,
    It's name shou'd be called, THE MONDAY NIGHTS' CLUB.

Prefix'd thus its name, time and place they selected,
    When and where they should hold their nocturnal carouses,
And one night in each week they by vote then directed,
    The club should be held at each other's own houses.

To secure its existence came next in discussion,
    For clubs, if not fostered, fall into decay :
They decreed all its members, in future succession,
    In *Religion* and *Party* shou'd think the same way.

In *Party*, the Tories shou'd first be admitted,
    And of them only those who reside in the town ;

In *Religion*, *Church Priests* shou'd alone be permitted,
    And *both* as the true and staunch friends of the crown.

A wag then exclaimed, My good friends, you're aware,
    Mere *Religion* or *Party* can't keep it from sinking;
We must make out a bill of some good wholesome fare,
    For no club can exist without eating and drinking.

Let its fare be quite simple—bread, butter, and cheese:
    Hot suppers inflame and distemper the brain,
Nice stomachs may then eat, or not, as they please,
    And sup and re-sup o'er again and again.

Let its liquors be port, punch, porter, and ale;
    In wine, says the proverb, there's truth and no care;
Each member may then in libations regale,
    And toast that first blessing of heaven, the Fair.

The fumes of *Tabac* sooth the ennui of thinking,
    Give a truce to the mind to reflect on its lass;
Long tubes are, of course, an appendage to drinking,
    For a whiff now and then adds new zest to the glass.

Well pleased with their banquet, now fully completed,
    They arose and took each a full bumper in hand,
Live for ever our club! with three cheers, they repeated;
    Be it envied by all other clubs in the land.

THE LOYALTY OF WOODBRIDGE.

BY WILLIAM STYGALL.

Friday, July the 8th, 1814, being the day appointed for the grand festival in commemoration of the return of peace, the ringing of bells, the martial music of fife and drum, and the thunder of artillery greeted the arrival of the morning in the town of Woodbridge. All was noise, and glee, and jollity; and that the amusements might not be alloyed by the dull occupations of business, the shops were closed at twelve o'clock. At that hour, also, on the firing of a cannon, the presidents, vice-presidents, and dinner company, sporting their true blue cockades and streamers, assembled in the Crown Meadow.

At half-past twelve another piece of ordnance gave the joyous intimation that the cooks were all busily employed in taking up and dishing the respective courses. In another half hour the dinner was on the table, and as soon as the whole had been properly arranged, a bugle sounded, the company arose, and the president invoked a blessing on the feast. Due time having been allowed for the destruction of beef and pudding, a second bugle sounded, the tables were cleared, thanks were returned, and as the first loyal toast, " the King," was given with three times three, from fifteen hundred voices at once, the air resounded with " the King," and the succeeding toasts made the very welkin shake. After the above the whole company adjourned to the " Olympic Course."

> " And there another feast began."

To describe particularly the numerous sports which awaited the spectators, would be *impossible :* they consisted of a Jerusalem pony race, a jumping match in sacks, foot races, grinning matches through horse collars, jingling matches, etc., etc. To crown the solemnities of the day, a grand bon fire was lighted, in which the effigy of Bonaparte was mercilessly consigned to the flames ; a brilliant display of fireworks succeeded, and closed this festival.

The loyal men of Suffolk to Woodbridge they did go,
On the eighth of July, to see a gallant show ;
For there were such doings as ne'er were known before,
And if you live a hundred years you'll see the like no more.

Fifteen hundred of the inhabitants din'd in the Market Place,
Off plum-pudding and roast beef, in remembrance of this peace ;
Men, women, and their children, all eat there very hearty,
And after dinner made a fire for to burn Bonaparte.

When the gentlemen had din'd the bells were set a ringing,
They had pipes and tobacco, and much jovial singing,
Then a toast they all drank, it was a noble thing,
The gallant " *Duke of Wellington,*" and sung " *God save the King.*"

R

When Bonaparte was in flames, how the fire blaz'd!
The gentlemen laugh'd very much, they were so greatly pleas'd;
The ladies at the windows stood, and lifted up the sashes,
And clapp'd their hands and all cried out, "*Burn the rogue to ashes!*"

But who can now repeat all the sports of that day,
The mirth and the fun, with which the time was pass'd away?
So full was the town, with people great and small,
That of all the sights in England surely *Woodbridge* beat them all."

RICHARD AND KATE; OR, FAIR DAY.

A SUFFOLK BALLAD, BY ROBERT BLOOMFIELD.

" Come, Goody, stop your humdrum wheel,
　　Sweep up your orts, and get your hat;
　　Old joys revived once more I feel:
　　'Tis Fair-day;—aye, and more than that.

" Have you forgot, Kate, prithee say,
　　How many seasons here we've tarried?
　　'Tis forty years, this very day,
　　Since you and I, old girl, were married!

"Look out; the sun shines warm and bright,
　　The stiles are low, the paths all dry;
　　I know you cut your corns last night:
　　Come, be as free from care as I.

" For I'm resolved once more to see
　　That place where we so often met;
　　Though few have had more cares than we,
　　We've none just now to make us fret."

　　Kate scorn'd to damp the generous flame
　　That warmed her aged partner's breast;
　　Yet, ere determination came,
　　She thus some trifling doubts express'd:

" Night will come on, when seated snug,
　　And you've, perhaps, begun some tale,
　　Can you then leave your dear stone mug—
　　Leave all the folks, and all the ale?"

" Aye, Kate, I wool ;—because I know,
　　Though time has been we both could run,
　　Such days are gone and over now ;—
　　I only mean to see the fun."

She straight slipped off the wall and band,*
　　And laid aside her lucks and twitches ;*
　　And to the hutch she reach'd her hand,
　　And gave him out his Sunday breeches.

His mattock he behind the door
　　And hedging gloves again replaced,
　　And look'd across the yellow moor,
　　And urged his tott'ring spouse to haste.

The day was up, the air serene,
　　The firmament without a cloud ;
　　The bee humm'd o'er the level green,
　　Where knots of trembling cowslips bow'd.

And Richard thus, with heart elate,
　　As past things rush'd across his mind,
　　Over his shoulder talk'd to Kate,
　　Who, snug tuckt up, walk'd slow behind.

" When once a giggling mawther you,
　　And I a red-faced, chubby boy,
　　Sly tricks you play'd me, not a few,
　　For mischief was your greatest joy.

" Once, passing by this very tree,
　　A gotch of milk I'd been to fill,
　　You shoulder'd me, then laugh'd to see,
　　Me and my gotch spin down the hill."

" 'Tis true," she said, " but here behold,
　　And marvel at the course of Time,
　　Though you and I are both grown old,
　　This tree is only in its prime ! "

" Well, Goody, don't stand preaching now ;
　　Folks don't preach sermons at a fair !
　　We've rear'd ten boys and girls, you know,
　　And I'll be bound they'll all be there."

' Terms used in Spinning.

Now friendly nods and smiles had they,
From many a kind, fair-going face;
And many a pinch Kate gave away,
While Richard kept his usual pace.

At length arrived amongst the throng,
Grand-children, bawling, hemm'd them round,
And dragged them by the skirts along,
Where gingerbread bestrew'd the ground.

And soon the aged couple spied
Their lusty sons and daughters dear;—
When Richard thus exulting cried:
"Didn't I tell you they'd be here?"

The cordial greetings of the soul
Were visible in every face,
Affection, void of all control,
Govern'd with a resistless grace.

'Twas good to see the honest strife
Which should contribute most to please,
And hear the long recounted life
Of infant tricks, and happy days.

But now, as at some nobler places,
Amongst the leaders 'twas decreed
Time to begin the Dickey Races,
More famed for laughter than for speed.

Richard look'd on with wondrous glee,
And praised the lad who chanced to win;
" Kate, wa'n't I such a one as he?
As like him, ay, as pin to pin.

" Full fifty years have passed away
Since I rode this same ground about;
Lord! I was lively as the day,
I won the high-lows out and out!

" I'm surely growing young again,
I feel myself so kedge and plump;
From head to foot I've not one pain;
Nay, hang me if I cou'dn't jump!"

Thus spoke the ale in Richard's pate,
A very little made him mellow ;
But still he loved his faithful Kate,
Who whisper'd thus, " My good old fellow,

" Remember what you promised me,
And see, the sun is getting low ;
The children want an hour, you see,
To talk a bit before we go."

Like youthful lover most complying,
He turn'd and chuck'd her by the chin,
Then all across the green grass hieing
Right merry faces all akin.

Their farewell quart, beneath a tree
That droop'd its branches from above ;
Awaked the pure felicity
That waits upon parental love.

Kate viewed her blooming daughters round,
And sons, who shook her withered hand ;
Her features spoke what joy she found,
But utterance had made a stand.

The children toppled on the green,
And bowled their fairings down the hill ;
Richard with pride beheld the scene,
Nor could he for his life sit still.

A father's uncheck'd feelings gave
A tenderness to all he said,
" My boys, how proud I am to have
My name thus round the country spread.

" Through all my days I've labour'd hard,
And could of pains and crosses tell ;
But this is labour's great reward,
To meet ye thus, and see ye well.

" My good old Partner, when at home,
Sometimes with wishes mingles tears ;
Goody, says I, let what wool come
We've nothing for them but our pray'rs.

May you be all as old as I,
And see your sons to manhood grow ;
And many a time before you die,
Be just as pleased as I am now."

Then (raising still his mug and voice),
" An old man's weakness don't despise !
I love you well, my girls and boys ;
God bless you all ! "—so said his eyes—

For as he spoke a big round drop
Fell bounding on his ample sleeve,
A witness which he could not stop,
A witness which all hearts believe.

Thou, Filial Piety, wert there,
And round the ring, benignly bright,
Dwelt in the luscious, half shed tear,
And in the parting word—Good night.

With thankful hearts and strengthen'd love,
The poor old Pair, supremely blest,
Saw the sun sink behind the grove,
And gain'd once more their lowly rest.

THE HORKEY.

A PROVINCIAL BALLAD, BY ROBERT BLOOMFIELD.

What gossips prattled in the sun,
    Who talk'd him fairly down,
Up, memory ! tell ; 'tis Suffolk fun,
    And lingo of their own.

Ah ! *Judie Twitchet !* * though thou'rt dead
    With thee the tale begins ;
For still seems thrumming in my head
    The rattling of thy pins.

Thou Queen of knitters ! for a ball
    Of worsted was thy pride ;

---

* Judie Twitchet was a real person, who lived many years with my mother's
cousin, Bannock, at Honnington.

With dangling stockings great and small,
    Aud world of clack beside !

We did so laugh ; the moon shone bright,
    More fun you never knew ;
'Twas farmer Cheerum's *Horkey night*,
    And I, and Grace, and Sue—

But bring a stool, sit round about,
    And boys, be quiet, pray,
And let me tell my story out,
    'Twas *sitch* a merry day!

The butcher whistled at the door,
    And brought a load of meat ;
Boys rubb'd their hands and cried, " There's more ! "
    Dogs wagg'd their tails to see't.

Ou went the boilers till the *hake* *
    Had much ado to bear 'em ;
The magpie talk'd for talking sake ;
    Birds sung ;—but who could hear 'em ?

Creak went the jack ; the cats were *scared*,
    We had not time to heed 'em ;
The *owd hins* cackled in the yard,
    For we forgot to feed 'em.

Yet 'twas not I, as I may say,
    Because as how d'ye see,
I only help'd there for the day—
    They cou'dn't lay't to me.

Now Mrs. Cheerum's best lace cap
    Was mounted on her head ;
Guests at the door began to rap,
    And now the cloth was spread.

Then clatter went the earthen plates,
    " Mind, Judie," was the cry ;
I could have *cop't* them at their pates,
    " Trenchers for me," said I.

       * A sliding pot hook.

That look so clean upon the ledge,
  And never mind a fall ;
Nor never turn a sharp knife's edge,
  But fashion rules us all.

Home came the jovial *Horkey load*,
  Last of the whole year's crop ;
And Grace among the green boughs rode,
  Right plump upon the top.

This way and that the waggon reel'd,
  And never queen rode higher ;
Her cheeks were colour'd in the field,
  And ours before the fire.

The laughing harvest folks, and John
  Came in and look'd askew,
'Twas my red face that set them on,
  And then they leer'd at Sue.

And Farmer Cheerum went, good man,
  And broach'd the *Horkey beer ;*
And *sitch a mort** of folks began
  To eat up our good cheer.

Says he, "Thank God for what's before us,
  That thus we meet agen,"
The mingling voices, like a chorus,
  Join'd cheerfully, "Amen."

Welcome and plenty, there they found 'em,
  The ribs of beef grew light,
And puddings—till the boys got round 'em,
  And then they vanish'd quite !

Now all the guests, with Farmer Crouder,
  Began to prate of corn ;
And we found out they talk'd the louder,
  The oftener pass'd the horn.

Out came the nuts ; we set a cracking ;
  The ale came round our way ;
By gom, we women fell a clacking,
  As loud again as they.

                    * Such a number.

John, sung "Old Benbow" loud and strong,
　　And I "The Constant Swain,"
"Cheer up, my Lads," was Simon's song,
　　"We'll conquer them again."

Now twelve o'clock was drawing nigh,
　　And all in merry cue,
I knock'd the cask, "Oh, ho!" said I,
　　", We've almost conquer'd you."

*My Lord** begg'd round, and held his hat—
　　Says Farmer Gruff, says he,
"There's many a Lord, Sam, I know that,
　　Has begg'd as well as thee."

Bump in his hat the shillings tumbled
　　All round among the folks;
"Laugh if you wool," said Sam, and mumbled,
　　"You pay for all your jokes."

Joint-stock you know among the men,
　　To drink at their own charges,
So up they got full drive, and then
　　Went out to *halloo largess*.

And sure enough the noise they made!!—
　　But let me mind my tale;
We follow'd them, we worn't afraid,
　　We'd all been drinking ale.

As they stood hallooing back to hack,
　　We lightly as a feather,
Went sideling round, and in a crack,
　　Had pinn'd their coats together.

'Twas near upon 't as light as noon;
　　'*A largess*' on the hill,
They shouted to the full round moon,
　　I think I hear 'em still!

But when they found the trick, my stars!
　　They well knew who to blame;
Our giggles turned to ha, ha, ha's,
　　And *arter* us they came.

　　　　* The leader of the reapers.

Grace by the tumbril made a squat,
    Then ran as Sam came by,
They said she could not run for fat;
    I *know* she did not try.

Sue, round the *neat-house** squalling ran,
    Where Simon scarcely dare;
He stopt—for he's a fearful man—
    " *By gom*, there's *suffen* † there ! "

And off set John, with all his might,
    To chase me down the yard,
Till I was nearly *gran'd* ‡ outright,
    He hugged so woundy hard.

Still they kept up the race and laugh,
    And round the house we flew ;
But, hark ye ! the best fun by half,
    Was Simon *arter* Sue.

She cared not, dark nor light, not she,
    So, near the dairy door
She pass'd a clean white hog, you see,
    They'd *kilt* the day before.

High on the *spirket* § there it hung,—
    " Now, Susie, what can save ye ? "
Round the cold pig his arms he flung,
    And cried, " Ah ! here I have ye ! "

The farmers heard what Simon said,
    And what a noise ! good lack !
Some almost laughed themselves to *dead*,
    And others clapt his back.

We all at once began to tell
    What fun we had abroad,
But Simon stood our jeers right well—
    He fell asleep and snored.

Then in his button-hole, upright,
    Did Farmer Crouder put

---

* Cow-house.   † Something there.   ‡ Strangled.
§ An iron hook.

A slip of paper, twisted tight,
   And held the candle *to 't.*

It smoked, and smoked, beneath his nose,
   The harmless blaze crept higher,
Till with a vengeance up he rose,
   "Grace, Judie, Sue; fire! fire!"

The clock struck one—some talk'd of parting,
   Some said it was a sin,
And *hitch'd* their chairs—but those for starting
   Now let the moonlight in.

Owd women, loitering for the *nonce**
   Stood praising the fine weather;
The menfolk took the hint at once
   To kiss them altogether.

And out ran every soul beside,
   A *shanny-pated* † crew;
Owd folks could neither run nor hide,
   So some *ketch'd* one, some *tew.*

They *skriggled* ‡ and began to scold,
   But laughing got the master;
Some *quackling* § cried, "Let go your hold!"
   The farmers held the faster.

All innocent, that I'll be sworn,
   There worn't a bit of sorrow;
And women, if their gowns *are* torn,
   Can mend them on the morrow.

Our shadows helter skelter danced
   About the moonlight ground;
The wondering sheep, as on we pranced,
   Got up and gazed around:

And well they might—till Farmer Cheerum
   Now with a hearty glee
Bade all, Good morn, as he came near 'em,
   And then to bed went he.

Then off we strolled, this way and that,
   With many voices ringing,

---

* For the purpose.   † Giddy—thoughtless.   ‡ To struggle quick.
   § Choking.

And echo answered us right pat,
  As home we rambled singing.

For when we laugh'd, it laugh'd again,
  And to our own doors followed ;
" Yo, ho ! " we cried, " Yo, ho ! " so plain,
  The misty meadows halloo'd.

That's all my tale, and all the fun ;
  Come, turn your wheels about,
My worsted, see !—that's nicely done,
  Just held my story out !

Poor Jude !—Thus Time knits or spins
  The worsted from Life's ball ;
Death stopped thy tales, and stopped thy pins,
  And so he'll serve us all.

THE GLORIOUS FIGHT OFF BOSTON LIGHTHOUSE, ON THE 1ST OF JUNE, 1813.

THE CHESAPEAKE PRIZE TO THE SHANNON. [*]

At Boston, one day,
  As the Chesapeake lay,
The Captain and crew thus began on :
  " See that ship out at sea !
  She our prize soon shall be,
'Tis the tight little frigate the Shannon ;
  How I long to be drubbing the Shannon ;
  We shall make a prize of the Shannon ;
  Oh ! 'twill be a good joke
  To take Commodore Broke,
  And add to our navy the Shannon."

Then he made a great bluster,
  Calling all hands to muster,
And said, " Now boys, stand firm to your cannon ;
  Let us get under way,
  Without further delay,
And capture the insolent Shannon.
  We soon shall bear down on the Shannon,
  The Chesapeake's prize to the Shannon,

* See " A Naval Duel," page 42.

Within two hours' space
We'll return to this place,
And bring into the harbour the Shannon."

Now alongside they range,
And broadsides they exchange ;
But the Yankees soon flinch from their cannon,
When captain and crew,
Without further to do,
Are attack'd, sword in hand, from the Shannon,
By the tight little tars of the Shannon ;
The brave Commodore of the Shannon,
Fir'd a friendly salute
Just to end the dispute,
And the Chesapeake struck to the Shannon.

Let America know
The respect she should show
To our National flag and our cannon,
And let her take heed,
That the Thames and the Tweed,
Give us tars just as brave as the Shannon.
Here's to Commodore Broke, of the Shannon,
To the sons of the Thames, Tweed, and Shannon ;
May the olive of peace
Soon bid enmity cease,
From the Chesapeake's shore to the Shannon.

IMPROMPTU.

" The bold *Chesapeake*
Came ont on a freak,
And swore she'd soon silence our cannon,
While the Yankees, in port,
Stood to laugh at the sport,
And see her tow in the brave *Shannon*.

" Quite sure of the game
As from harbour they came,
A dinner and wine they bespoke ;
But for *meat* they got *balls*
From our staunch wooden walls,
So the dinner *engagement* was *Broke*."

THE LAMENTATION OF STEPHEN SPINK, THE BRANDESTON POST-BOY.

These lines were written by the Rev. William Clubbe, who was in 1769 instituted to the vicarage of Brandeston. He was the second son of the Rev. John Clubbe, vicar of Debenham, and like his father possessed of a rich fund of natural humour.

"To the charitable and the uncharitable, to Christians, Jews, Turks, Infidels, and Heretics, Stephen Spink, post-boy, of Brandeston, begs leave to state a loss he has lately sustained in the nearest relation he had in the world—his only ass.

"Too modest to dwell upon any merits of his own, he begs leave to solicit your charity for those of the deceased animal.

"Of Christians, then, he is bold to ask because an ass once carried the Divine Author of their religion ; of Jews, because he comes the nearest to them of any brute in the creation in their obstinacy ; of Turks, because he is the parent of their favourite mule ; and of Infidels and Heretics because of his resemblance to them in stupidity.

"With the truly charitable he is sensible no arguments are wanted, and that with the uncharitable none will prevail. For the first, there-fore, as in duty bound, he will ever pray; to the latter, however unbecoming the mouth of a petitioner, he begs leave to say they may kiss the mark of Stephen Spink.

"Good people all, attend, I pray,
  And listen to my ditty,
For what poor *Stephen* has to say
  Will soon excite your pity.

"Both *lame* and *blind* he could not pass,
  A snail, so slow was he,
Till, mounted on his dapper *ass*,
  He flew like *Mercury*.

"Oft has he gone, when sent express,
  For newspaper or letter,
Within six hours, and sometimes less,
  Four miles and rather better.

"Such was the speed with which he went
  That he was call'd by most,

Who by his bag their letters sent,
The *Brand'ston flying post.*

" But see him now, poor fallen man,
On foot and forced to crawl,
As crooked and no faster than
A snail upon the wall.

" You, who have legs to walk upon,
Two, legs and want no more,
Pity the wretch that has but *one,*
And set him upon *four.*

" Then on his *ass* will *Stephen* ride
And wish for nothing higher ;
Nor envy the *equestrian* pride
Of *vicar* or of *squire.*

" So shall your humble post-boy thrive,
So blithe his hours shall pass,
That none in *Brand'ston town* shall live
Like *Stephen* and his *ass.*"

DICK DELVER, THE PRACTICAL PHILOSOPHER.

A SUFFOLK BALLAD, FROM REAL LIFE. BY THE REV. JOHN BLACK.

The Rev. John Black, the writer of these lines, was for
many years a resident in Woodbridge, and died there, August
30th, 1813, in the 59th year of his age. He was licensed
to the perpetual curacy of Butley, in 1789, and that of
Ramsholt, in 1807. Among the Fitch MSS. in the Ipswich
Museum, is the following receipt from this reverend gentleman, which shows the miserable stipend that he received as
perpetual curate of Butley :

"Received, March 25th, 1803, of Peter Isaac Thelluson, Esq , by the
hand of Mr. Thomas Abblitt, the sum of eight pounds, being half a year's
stipend due to me at the date hereof as curate of Butley.

"JOHN BLACK."

Though divines of contentment may preach,
And the learn'd of philosophy prate,

How few wisdom's temple can reach,
  How few are content with their state !
A philosopher lately I've seen,
  In his lowly condition content,
Unrack'd with the gout or the spleen,
  In a jacket oft patch'd, and yet rent.
Thus, the green pliant willow that bends
  To the blasts o'er the valley that sweep,
While the proud mountain oak that contends,
  Is rent from the side of the steep.
No time had Dick Delver to play,
  In youth he no playthings did lack :
Lonely watch'd he the *grunters* all day,
  As they *rooted* the *stubble* for *shack*.
Dick Delver, poor fellow, fell lame,
  A keen frosty night nipt his toes ;
To the fire he unthinkingly came,
  And lost them, while sunk in a doze.
A poor-house Dick Delver receiv'd,
  For what could the poor fellow do ?
Not long for his toes Dicky griev'd,
  But begun a young widow to woo.
For idleness, wise men remark,
  Is the parent of mischief and love ;
The widow grew pleas'd with her spark,
  And consented his helpmate to prove.
Her husband had *fall'n* 'mongst the slain,
  And left her *whole months* to bemoan ;
Untouch'd could a fond heart remain,
  When Dick for the loss could atone ?
They wedded :—their time gaily pass'd,
  No taxes or debts spoil'd their rest,
Each sun rose as bright as the last,—
  But what mortal can always be blest?
Dick Delver no widow had wed,
  Her husband, tho' down, was not slain ;
Like a hero he valiantly bled,
  And return'd his own deary to claim.
Dick Delver the charmer resign'd,
  Whom no longer he dared to retain,
And journey'd, like folks more refin'd
  To search for a doxy again.

To London Dick Delver now hied,
    Laid seize to a shoe blacking dame ;
The lady of blacking complied,
    And united they quickly became.
Of relations the lady could boast,
    And doubtless of no mean degree,
Who liv'd where the rocks of the coast
    Are wash'd by the spray of the sea.
From ocean the lady had sprung,
    As Venus, they say, did of old,
And Neptune had giv'n her a tongue
    Like Juno, the goddess, to scold.
Dick Delver and spousy left town,
    A visit of frendship to pay ;
But scarcely a week had been down,
    When they were not permitted to stay ;
Then plac'd in an overseer's cart,
    To his settlement off they were sent ;
Mistress Delver was loth to depart,
    But Dicky was always content.
To the *sandlands** of *Suffolk*, with speed,
    The pair in the cart were convey'd,
Where *heath-nibbling black-faces* feed,
    And burrows by rabbits are made.
No rabbits or sheep could delight
    The soul of Dick Delver's dear spouse,
Who'd rather have seen porters fight,
    Than crones on the prickly whin browze.
Around her she gaz'd with surprise,
    When churches like stables she saw,
Where no lofty steeples † arise,
    The traveller's attention to draw.
" What a dull, dreary country," she said ;
    " These *sandlands* I cannot abide ; "
Then off in a tangent she sped,
    And Dick heard no more of his bride.
Dick Delver got married once more,
    Rear'd a cot by the side of the road ;

* The part of the *sandlands* here alluded to is that which is south of the line of Woodbridge and Orford, where a large extent of poor and even blowing sand is to be found.

† The churches of Eyke and Sutton are both without steeples.

S

Of dickies and donkies keeps four,
   And industry decks his abode.
For sand and for whin-roots he digs,
   And sells them as fast as he can,
Grows potatoes, keeps chickens and pigs ;
   Is not Dick now become a great man ?
Where a *bridge** the fair *Deben* bestrides,
   And his fountains first mingle with brine,
There Dick, in his hall now resides,
   With a cart-lodge and donkey-shed fine.
Four trees, on the north, screen his cot,
   A *church* † in the background you spy,
And gypsies, encamp'd near the spot,
   Oft hang out their tatters to dry.
The sedge blossoms yellow below,
   Blue hyacinths cover the hills ;
While the nightingale's love or his woe,
   The valley with melody fills.
If all like Dick Delver would toil,
   Were all like Dick Delver content,
Each brow would be bright with a smile,
   And none to a prison be sent.

THE FOUNDLING OF SHOREDITCH AND THE IXWORTH DOCTOR.

Come all ye Christian people, and listen to my tail ;
It is all about a doctor was travelling by the rail,
By the Heastern Counties Railway (vich the shares I don't desire),
From Ixworth town, in Suffolk, vich his name did not transpire.

A travelling from Bury this doctor was employed,
With a gentleman, a friend of his, vich his name was Captain Loyd;
And on reaching Mark Tey station, that is next beyond Colchest-
Er, a lady entered into them most elegantly dressed.

She entered into the carriage all with a tottering step,
And a pooty little baby upon her bussum slep ;
The gentleman received her with kindness and siwillaty,
Pitying this lady for her illness and debillaty.

She had a fust-class ticket, this lovely lady said,
Because it was so lonesome, she took a secknd instead ;

* Melford bridge, near Melton.   † Ufford church.

Better to travel by secknd class, than sit alone in the fust,
And the pooty little baby upon her breast she nust.

A seein of her crying, and shiverin, and pail,
To her spoke this surging, the Ero of my tail ;
Says ee, " You look unwell, ma'am, I'll elp you, if I can,
And you may tell your case to me, for I'm a meddicle man."

" Thank you, sir," the lady said, " I only look so pale
Because I ain't accustom'd to travelling on the Rale ;
I shall be better presnly, when I've ad some rest ; "
And that pooty little baby she squeezed it to her breast.

So in conversation the journey they beguiled,
Capting Loyd, and the medical man, and the lady and the child,
Till the warious stations along the line was passed ;
For even the Heastern Counties' trains must come in at last.

When at Shoreditch tumminus at length stopped the train,
This kind meddicle gentleman proposed his aid again.
" Thank you, sir," the lady said, " for your kyindness dear ;
My carriage and my osses is probbibly come here.

" Will you old this baby, please, vilst I step and see ? "
The doctor was a family man : " That I will," says he.
Then the little child she kist—kist it very gently,
Vich was sucking his little fist, sleeping innocently.

With a sigh from her art, as though she would have bust it,
Then she gave the Doctor the child—wery kind he nust it ;
Hup then the lady jumped hoff the bench she sate from,
Tumbled down the carridge steps, and ran along the platform.

Vile all the other passengers vent upon their vays,
The Capting and the Doctor sate there in a maze :
Some vent in a Homminibus, some vent in a Cabby ;
The Capting and the Doctor vaited vith the babby.

There they sate, looking queer, for an hour or more,
But their feller passinger neather on 'em sore ;
Never, never back again did that lady come,
To that pooty sleeping hinfint, a sucking of his thum !

What could this pore Doctor do, bein treated thus,
When the darling baby woke, cryin for its nuss ?

Off he drove to a female friend, vich she was both kind and mild,
And igsplained to her the circumstance of this year little child.

That kind lady took the child instantly in her lap
And made it very comfortable by giving it some pap;
And when she took its close off, what d'you think she found?
A couple of ten pun notes sewn up in its little gownd!

Also in its little close was a note, which did conwey,
That this little baby's parents lived in a handsome way:
And for its Headucation they reglarly would pay,
And sirtingly, like gentlefolks, would claim the child one day,
If the Christian people who'd charge of it would say,
Per advertisement in the *Times*, where the baby lay.

Pity of this baby many people took,
It had such pooty ways, and such a pooty look;
And there came a lady forrard (I wish that I could see
Any kind lady as would do as much for me.

And I wish with all my art, some night in *my* night-gownd,
I could find a note stitched for ten or twenty pound)—
There came a lady forrard, that most honorable did say
She'd adopt this little baby which her parents cast away.

While the Doctor pondered on this hoffer fair,
Comes a letter from Devonshire, from a party there,
Hordering the Doctor, at his Mar's desire,
To send the little Infant back to Devonshire.

Lost in apoplexity, this pore meddicle man,
Like a sensable gentleman, to the Justice ran;
Which his name was Mr. Hammill, a honourable beak,
That take his seat in Worship street four times a week.

" O Justice!" says the doctor, " instrugt me what to do,
" I have come up from the country, to throw myself on you;
" My patients have no doctor to tend them in their ills,
"(There they are in Suffolk, without their draffts and pills.)

" I have come up from the country to know how I'll dispose
" Of this pore little baby, and the twenty pun note, and the clothes;
" And I want to go back to Suffolk, dear Justice, if you please,
" And my patients wants their Doctor, and their Doctor wants his feez."

Up spoke Mr. Hammill, sittin at his desk,
" This year application does me much perplisk ;
" What I do advise you is, to leave this babby
" I' the parish where it was left by its mother shabby."

The Doctor from his Worship sadly did depart—
He might have left the baby, but he hadn't got the heart
To go for to leave that Hinnocent, has the laws allows,
To the tender mussies of the Union House.

Mother, who left this little one on a stranger's knee,
Think how cruel you have been, and how good was he!
Think, if you've been guilty, innocent was she ;
And do not take unkindly this little word of me,
Heaven be merciful to us all, sinners as we be.

SUFFOLK TEARS ;

OR, AN ELEGY ON THAT RENOWED KNIGHT SIR NATHANIEL BARNARDISTON.

The Barnardistons were settled at Kedington ever since the year 1500. They resided at the Hall, a fine old mansion in that parish, and produced many persons of distinguished eminence. During the civil commotions in the reign of Charles I., this family is remarkable for having given rise to the appellation of "Roundhead." "The London apprentices," says Rapin, " wore the hair of the head cut round ; and the Queen, observing out of a window Samuel Barnardiston among them, cried out, ' See, what a handsome *round head* is there !' " Hence originated this name.

Sir Nathaniel Barnardiston, the subject of the following "Acrostic Elegie," who died July 25, 1653, appears to have been a man of exemplary piety and virtue, and a firm friend to the liberties of his country.

He represented the county of Suffolk in several Parliaments, and was well known as a staunch friend of the Puritan cause. His death called forth a multitude of elegaic verses, which were published together in a volume bearing the following title, which is in itself an eulogy of no mean description : —

"Suffolk Tears; or, Elegies on that Renowned Knight Sir Nathaniel Barnardiston, a Gentleman eminent for Piety to God, love to the Churche, and fidelity to his Country, and therefore highly honoured by them all. He was five times chosen Knight of the Shire for the County of Suffolk, and once Burgess for Sudbury. In the discharge of which Trust he always approved Himself Faithful, as by his great sufferings for the Freedoms and Liberties of his Country abundantly appear. A Zealous Promoter of the Preaching of the Gospel, manifested by his great care in presenting Men, Able, Learned, and Pious to the places whereof he had the Patronage, and also by his large and extraordinary bounty towards the advancing of Religion and Learning, both at home and in Foreign Plantations among the Heathen."

"*Dignum laude virum Musa vetut Mori.*"

"*London : printed by R. I., for Thomas Newberry, at the Three Lions, in Cornhil, near the Royal Exchange,* 1653."

The volume is printed in a quarto of 70 pages, and in the "Bib. Anglo Poet, 1815," published by Longman and Co., is marked at the enormous price of twelve guineas!

The funeral offerings contained in this volume, whilst they show the estimation in which their deceased object was holden, are curious specimens of the elegaic poetry of that period; and the poetical address to Lady Jane Barnardiston, by the Rev. Samuel Fairclough, Jun., which we give, is a rare example of Puritan flattery.

AN ACROSTIC ELEGY.

BY SIR WILLIAM SPRING, BART., OF PAKENHAM.

S hall *such* friends dye, and my muse *idle* hee ?
I s't possible ? can such stupidity
R emaine in *me*, and I not *dead* with thee ?
N ature don't give, but lend its *life* to men,
A nd at its *pleasure* cals it *back* ageu.
T he *image* grav'd on man God's right doth shew,
H *is* image 'tis, let *Cæsar* have his *due*,
A nd in this *Microcosme* we plainly see
N o less than part of *God's Divinity*,
I n *smaller letters;* for the soul's a *sparke*
E ven of his *kindling*, and (though in the dark,
L odg'd in the *grave*, the body seems to be)
L ets *hope*, and we shall find *re-unity.*

B ody and *soul* shal joyn by heaven's great power
A s *once* they were *before* the parting *hour ,*
R ally the *Atomes* shal, and *then* each part,
N ot losing *ought* by *God's* Almighty Art,
A ttaine shal to its *just* and *proper* due,
R eturning to its *corps* its former *hue ;*
D escend then shal the *Soul*, and with a kisse
I ts *antient friend* awake to perfect *bliss.*
S o these *new married couple* joyfully
T o heaven *ascend*, and *match eternity ;*
O heavenly *Musick !* endless harmony !
N one can *desire* to live, that's fit to die.

AN OFFERTORY.

BY THE REV. SAMUEL FAIRCLOUGH, M. A.

Thrice *Noble Lady*, spare that melting bead,
Our sorrows want no jewel from your head ;
Still let those silver drops that lightly lye
Like little delug'd worlds within your eye,
Fixed abide in their own brightest sphear,
His *fame* wants not those *pendents* for her ear ;
Those falling stars rob heaven, we need not thence
Borrow our griefs or *tax you with expence.*
Behold how every Mourner brings his sheet
To wipe your eyes and weep himself ; 'tis meet
That this so public loss by th' Countries charge
Should mourned be : *Spare, Madam*, then ; this large
And thicker volume that is here annext
Is but our Comment on that public text.
Come, Argus Hieraclitus, lend your eyes
To pay on's tomb a liquid sacrifice ;
Lo ! all the grass that round about him lye
Hangs full of tears, *shed from* Dame Nature's *eye ;*
See how sad Philomele (that yonder sits,
And to the dancing twig her music fits)
Now mourns for him ; the silver brook runs on
Grumbling to leave those loved banks, whereon
A Mansion once he had, that's now set round
With *Cypress trees*, and with their branches crown'd
So dark, it seems *Night's Mantle* for to borrow,
And may be called *the gloomy den of sorrow.*

E'er *since* he di'd, the heavens their griefs to tell,
Daily in tears to earth's wet bosom fell ;
Not in an April storm, or those in *June*,
 Whose trembling Cadents *makes it rain in tune*,
But like a grave December day, or those
Who mourn in *Cicero's* stile, and weep in prose.
Madam, you see all Nature's wat'ry store
Attends this sable day—weep you no more.
Angels, that on *your eyes* with bottles wait
To catch your *falling tears*, do now retreat
With vessels, anon again they'l stoop
And lightly hover round the *mourning troop*,
Whilst I in silence do his *Shrine* adore ;
If worship doth offend, I then implore
And crave a favor, Madam, 'tis this one—
Adde to his memory no pictur'd stone,
Lost whilst within the church my vows I pay,
I to the image of this saint should pray.

EPITAPH ON JOHN ELWES, ESQ.,

THE MISER, WHO LIVED AT STOKE BY CLARE.

HERE, to man's honour, or to man's disgrace,
Lies a strong picture of the human race,
In ELWES' form—whose spirit, heart, and mind,
Virture and vice in firmest tints combin'd ;
Rough was the rock, but blended deep with ore,
And base the mass—that many a diamond bore :
Meaness to grandeur, folly join'd to sense,
And av'rice coupled with benevolence :
Whose lips ne'er broke a truth, nor hand a trust,
Were sometimes warmly kind—and always just :
With power to reach ambition's highest birth,
He sank a mortal—groveling to the earth ;
Lost in the lust of adding pelf to pelf,
Poor to the poor—still poorer to himself :
Whose wants, that nearly bent to all but stealth,
Ne'er in his country's plunder dug for wealth ;
Call'd by her voice—but call'd without expense,
His noble nature rous'd in her defence ;
And in the Senate, labouring in her cause,
The firmest guardian of the fairest laws

He stood ; and each instinctive taint above,
To every bribe preferr'd a people's love ;
Yet still with no stern patriotism fir'd,
Wrapt up in wealth, to wealth again retir'd ;
By Penury guarded from Pride's sickly train,
Living a length of days without a pain,
And adding to the millions never tried,
Lov'd—pitied—scorn'd—and honour'd—ELWES died !
Learn from this proof, that, in life's tempting scene,
Man is a compound of the great and mean ;
Discordant qualities together tied,
Virtues in him and vices are allied :
The sport of follies, or of crime the heir,
We all the mixtures of an ELWES share.
Pondering his faults—then ne'er his worth disown,
But in *his* nature recollect *thine own ;*
And think—for life and pardon where to trust,
Was GOD not MERCY, when his creatures dust ?

A RHYME OF ST. EDMUNDSBURY ABBEY SEVEN HUNDRED YEARS AGO.

Seven hundred years have passed away since powerful and great,
St. Edmundsbury Abbey stood, in proud monastic state :
A bold, stupendous building then, a rich and holy pile,
None other Abbey half so fam'd in Britain's sea-girt isle.

Then, at the sainted Edmund's shrine, were costliest offerings brought,
E'en crowned monarchs at its foot the Virgin's aid have sought ;
Here too have warlike nobles met ; here too was fram'd the deed
Those self-same nobles forc'd their king to sign at Runnymede.

Within those cloister'd walls there dwelt, in those long years ago,
A learned monk, who studied much the Abbey's weal or woe—
One Jocelin, of Brakèlond, who left a record rare,
A valued roll of great events, while he was dweller there.

He tells us how, under Abbot Hugh, such vast abuse accrues,
That Hugh himself ran into debt full heavy with the Jews,
And debt and interest increas'd to almost frightful sway ;
Small wonder, when at cent. per cent. 'twas usual rate to pay !

At length the vessels from that shrine, so sacred and so old,
And all its costly ornaments were ta'en and pledged for gold !

No punishment attended those who did th' unholy deed,
But Hugh himself at last was left to die in abject need.

Then came the Abbot Sampson, who of a different school,
Brought soon the Abbey's wide estate to discipline and rule ;
He clear'd it of its heavy debts, not that he niggard were,
For gen'rous he, although he us'd much diligence and care.

Sampson's inauguration was the wonder of the town,
For with the goodly Abbot did a thousand guests sit down,
And in the grand refectory, for ev'ry after year,
Each burgess would at Christmas-tide partake the Abbot's cheer.

Of Rougham and of Bradfield, the manors did he hold,
Their farm deficiencies made up with forty pounds of gold ;
And those old halls and buildings did he put in stout repair,
Where kites and crows, for many a year, the only tenants were.

And hereabout the land improv'd, and much to tillage brought,
Moreover, too, by his command, a strict account was sought,
Of hidages and foder corn, of hen-rents, and such dues,
For much the farmers would conceal, and much the Abbey lose.

Yet Abbott Sampson had a heart replete with grateful love,
As Elias, of Elmeswell, and the Risby Knights did prove ;
And kindness render'd to him once, was ne'er by him forgot,
For when but a poor cloister monk, much sorrow was his lot.

Once sent to Rome for Papal grant (a journey sore and long)
That Woolpit church for ever to the Abbey might belong ;
Himself and errand he conceal'd 'neath Scottish beggar's dress,
For those convulsed times compell'd much care and thoughtfulness.

But worldly troubles oft would break the calm of Abbot life,
Thus London's merchant citizens with Bury were at strife,
Because their carts from Yarmouth home, with usual fishy freight,
Had fifteen-pence been tax'd each, when at the northern gate.

Once, too, in Bury churchyard, on the holy natal day,
The servants of the Abbot, with burghers met to play
At wrestling match, and divers sports; but sad disputes arose,
And knives were drawn, and blood was shed, for words gave place to blows.

Full sorely was the Abbot grieved, he mourned his task in view,
For excommunication now was monk and layman's due ;

'Twas passed beneath the sacred roof, where each man was by name
Cast from the bosom of the Church, with sorrow and with shame.

Forth from the holy pile they went! Sad sight for Bury then,
Before St. Mary's door fell down a hundred cursed men,
And for the Church's mercy prayed, with feet and shoulders bare,
Regardless of the public eye, and winter's piercing air.

The Abbot wept! nor him alone—all Bury mourned that day,
And to the holy father did for absolution pray;
While he, rememb'ring penitence, in goodness quick resolved
To list to mercy's voice, and bade the guilty be absolved.

Thereon they all were smartly whipped (the burgess of the town)
And then absolved, and furthermore the Abbot did lay down
Severest threats and penalties, if ever from that day
In Bury churchyard shows or sports should dare to make their way.

    *   *   *   *   *   *

Thus was it in the olden time, seven hundred years ago;
Race after race hath passed away, the Abbey's self laid low,
But churches, tower, and gate yet stand, each in its beauty rare,
May heaven and good St. Edmund long these precious relics spare!

FRANCES E. P.

A DESCRIPTION OF CHRISTMAS HUSBANDLY FARE.
BY THOMAS TUSSER.

The "Christmas Husbandly Fare" is interesting as a genuine picture of the mode of living in this county in the sixteenth century. The different viands enumerated are still known by the names which they bear in the text, if we except "shred pies," which appear to be mince pies, as they are now called.

At Christmas, good husbands,* have corn on the ground,
In barn and in soller, worth many a pound;
With plenty of other things—cattle and sheep,
All sent them (no doubt on) good houses to keep.
At Christmas, the hardness of winter doth rage,
A griper of all things, and specially age:

---

* A contraction for good husbandmen.

Then lightly † poor people, the young with the old,
Be sorest oppresed with hunger and cold.
At Christmas, by labor is little to get,
That wanting, the poorest in danger are set ;
What season then better, of all the whole year,
Thy needy, poor neighbour to comfort and cheer ?
At this time, and that time, some make a great matter ;
Some help not, but hinder the poor with their clatter,
Take custom from feasting, what cometh then last ?
Where one hath a dinner, a hundred shall fast.
To dog in the manger, some liken I could,
That hay will eat none, nor let other that would.
Some scarce, in a year, give a dinner or two,
Nor well can abide any other to do.
Play thou the good fellow ! seek none to misdeem ;
Disdain not the honest, though merry they seem,
For oftentimes seen, no more very a knave
Than he that doth counterfeit most to be grave.
Good husband and huswife, now chiefly be glad,
Things handsome to have as they ought to be had.
They both do provide, against Christmas do come,
To welcome good neighbour, good cheer to have some.
Good bread, and good drink, a good fire in the hall,
Brawn, pudding, and souse, and good mustard withall :
Beef, mutton, and pork, shred pies of the best,
Pig, veal, goose, and capon, and turkey well drest ;
Cheese, apples, and nuts ; joly carols to hear,
As then in the country is counted good cheer.
What cost to good husband is any of this ?
Good household provision only it is.
Of other the like, I do leave out a many,
That costeth the husbandman never a penny.
At Christmas be merry, and thankful withall,
And feast thy poor neighbour, the great with the small ;
Yea, all the year long, to the poor let us give,
God's blessing to follow us while we do live.

EXTRAORDINARY SALE BY AUCTION.

At the commencement of the present century, there resided
in Ipswich an auctioneer who was very unsuccessful in

† An old form of expression. The author means that poor people, *of
course*, are sorely oppressed.

effecting sales; some wag, to whom this was known, prepared a hand-bill, of which the following is a copy, and this was circulated among our townsmen.

TO BE SOLD BY AUCTION,

BY PRIVATE CONTRACT,

AT A REPOSITORY NEAR THE POST OFFICE,

IPSWICH,

BY SIMON NEVERSELL,

ON SATURDAY, THE THIRTY-SECOND INSTANT.

₊ The Sale to begin precisely at five minutes past Ten o'clock in the Afternoon.

LOT.

1 A Copper Cart Saddle, a Leather Hand-saw, two Woolen Frying-pans, and a Glass Wheelbarrow.

2 Three pairs of Pease Straw Breeches, a China Quarter Cart, and two Glass Bedsteads with Copper Hangings.

3 Two Marble Bonnets, a Feather Cap, an Iron Gown, two Straw Petticoats, and three Glass Shoes.

4 Deal Coal Grate, with Paper Smoke Jack, a Mahogany Poker, China Tongs, Cotton Shovel, and a pair of Gauze Bellows.

5 Two Second-hand Coffins with Glass Nails, three Glass Coach-wheels with Cambric Tire, two Persian Saddles, and a Wooden Bridle.

6 A Leather Tea-kettle, an Iron Feather-bed, six pairs of Brass Boots, and a Steel Night-cap.

SUNDRIES.

Pewter Waistcoat, and three Flint Wigs. A Bell-metal Chaff-sieve, and Calimanco Hog-trough. A Buck's-skin Warming-pan, and a Pewter Looking-glass. A Japan Cleaving-beetle, and a Leather Mattock. Three Silk Hog-yokes, and a Pinchbeck Swill-tub. Four Sheep's-skin Milk Pails, and a Wheat-straw Trammel. A Lamb's-skin Grindstone, and a Horse-leather Hatchet. A pair of Pewter Pudding-bags, and a Canvass Gridiron. A Dimity Coal-scuttle, A Wooden Timber Chain, and a Brass Cart Rope.

₊ A FEW more articles, too NUMEROUS to mention.

PRINTED BY J. BUSH.

THE FARMERS' DAILY DIET.

BY THOMAS TUSSER.

Thomas Tusser here gives a highly interesting description of the farmers' mode of living in Suffolk in the Elizabethian age. Salt meat, and fish both fresh and salted, it is evident, were standing articles of diet. But few delicacies are enumerated, but everything is substantial and wholesome, though plain.

A plot set down for farmers' quiet,
As time required, to frame his diet,
With sometimes fish, and sometimes fast,
That household store may longer last.
Let Lent, well kept, offend not thee,
For March and April breeders be ;
Spend herring first, save salt fish last,
For salt fish is good when Lent is past ;
When Easter comes, who knows not then
That veal and bacon is the man ;*
And Martilmas beef† doth bear good tack
When country folks do dainties lack ;
When Macrell ceaseth from the seas,
John Baptist brings grass-beef and pease.
Fresh herring plenty, Michell‡ brings,
With fatted crones and such old things.
All Saints¶ do lay for pork and souse, §
For sprats and spurlings‖ for their house.
At Christmas play, and make good cheer,
For Christmas comes but once a year ;
Though some then do, as do they would,
Let thrifty do as do they should.
For causes good so many ways
Keep Embrings* well and fasting days,
What law commands we ought t' obey,
For Friday, Saturn, and Wednesday.

* That is, is proper to be used.
† Beef dried in the chimney, like bacon, and is so called because it was usual to kill the beef for this provision about the Feast of St. Martin, Nov. 1st.
‡ Michaelmas.   ¶ All Hallows tide.   § Pigs' ears, feet, rinds, etc.
‖ A small sea fish, probably smelts.   * The Ember days or weeks.

The land doth will, the sea doth wish,
Spare sometimes flesh and feed of fish ;
Where fish is scant, and fruit of trees,
Supply that want with butter and cheese.

SUFFOLK WORDS AND PHRASES.

The following very clever illustration of Suffolk words
was written by the late Rev. George Turner, of Kettleburgh,
and sent to the late Major Moor :—

K ——, *May* 22*nd*, 1814.

"Dear Frind,

"I was axed some stounds agou by Billy P., our sesser at
Mulladin, to make inquiration a' yeow if Master —— had pahd in
that money into the Bank. Billy P. he fare kinda unasy about it, and
when I see him at church to-day, he sah, timmy, says he, prah ha yeow
wrot ? so I kinda wif't him off, and I sah, says I, I heent hard from
Squire D—— as yet, but I dare sah I shall afore long, so prah write me
some lines an send me wahd witha the money is pahd a' noe. I don't
know what to make of our Mulladin folks, nut I ; but somehow or
another they're allus in dibles, an I'll be rot if I don't begin to think
some on 'em a'l tahn up scaly at last ; an as to that fulla——, he grow
so big and so purdy, that he want to be took down a peg ; an I am glad
to hare that yeow gint it em properly at Wickhum. I'm gooin to meet
the Mulladin folks a' Friday, to go a' bounden, so prah rite me wahd
afore thennum, an let me know if the money be pahd, that I may make
Billy P—— asy. How stammin cow'd 'tis now-a-days ; we heent
no feed no where, an the stock run bloren about for wittles, just as
if twa winter ; yeow may pend on't twool be a mortal bad season for
green geese, an we shant have no spring wahts afore soom fair. I clipt
my ship last Tuesday (list a me, I mean Wensday), an tha scringe up
their backs so nashunly I'm afeard they're wholly stryd ; but stru's God
'tis a strange cow'd time. I heent got no news to tell ya, only we're all
stammenly set up about that there corn bill : folks don't fare to like
no matters, on tha sah there was a nashun noise about it at Norrij last
Saturday was a fautnit. The mob thay got 3 efigis—a farmer, a squire,
an a milla ; an stru as you're alive, they hung um all on one jibbet—
so folks sah. Howsumever, we are quite enough here, case we fare to
think it for our good. If you see that there chap Harry, give my
sarvice to em.

"I remain, yar tru frind,

—— ——"

BURY FAIRS.

The following account of the Fairs held at St. Edmund's, Bury, is extracted from a *scarce* pamphlet, entitled, "AN HISTORICAL ACCOUNT OF STURBRIDGE, BURY, AND THE MOST FAMOUS FAIRS IN EUROPE AND AMERICA; INTERSPERSED WITH ANECDOTES CURIOUS AND ENTERTAINING; and Considerations upon the Origin, the Progress, and Decline of all the temporary Marts in this kingdom." Cambridge, 8vo.

"The Fair of Bury St. Edmund's, formerly one of the most resorted Marts in the kingdom, was instituted as early as the year 1272, in the latter part of Henry III.'s reign. This Monarch, returning from Norwich, where he had been to quell a great riot between the citizens and the Monks, passed through Bury in his way to London; there he paid his devotions to the shrine of St. Edmund; and at the requisition of Simon de Cutton, Abbat and Lord of Bury, he granted him a charter for a Fair, to be kept annually without the precints of the Monastery, three days before and three days after the Feast of St. Matthew, which has been since protracted to an uncertain length, for the advantage of the Traders and the diversion of the Company. By this charter the Abbat had the tolls of the Fair, and the sole government of it by his Steward, with the oversight of the Weights and Measures, and the licensing of all the Booths therein. The Townsmen, and all within a mile round the town were then subject to the Abbat; and the Alderman, at the entrance upon his office, swore before the Steward of the Abbey that he should maintain the peace of the Borough, and in nothing damage or hurt the Abbat or convent in any of their rights and privileges. King Henry III. gave to this Monastery special marks of his favour for having received one hundred and twenty marks of the Abbat and Monks towards the marriage of his sister, Isabella, with Frederic, Emperor of Germany.

"Bury was then the great Wool Staple in the East of England, and is still very considerable, employing the poor in combing and spinning. The *Wool Stalls*, in St. Andrew's Street, are very small in comparision of the spacious magazines, where all the Wool of the country was deposited. Some of the Flemings, brought hither by the Earl of Leicester, and several artificers, who came over with Queen Isabel, Consort of Edward II., established at Bury Woollen Manufactures.

"The tyranny of the Abbat, and the oppression of his Officers caused divers insurrections of the Townsmen. For one of them, headed by

Richard Drayton and Robert Foxton, the first of Edward III., 1327, they plundered the Church and the Abbey, and carried away their charters, one of which was that granted by Henry III. for St. Matthew's Fair. The insurgents extorted a charter from Richard de Draughton, Abbat of Bury, whom they kept prisoner with some of his Monks, till they had sealed a grant of the tolls and Government of this Fair to the guild of merchants and Alderman ; but this instrument, drawn up by commission, was declared void by the king's Manual Seal, and the Abbat restored to his privileges. This fair was since kept by prescription, and the Monks, taking advantage of the credulous superstition of the times, made a considerable collection in Vows, Masses, and Offerings to St. Edmund's shrine amongst his Votaries. The Abbat kept an open table whilst the Fair lasted, for noble guests, and persons of inferior rank were daily entertained in the Refectory with the Monks. There were different *Rows* assigned for the Manufacturers of Norwich, Ipswich, Colchester, the Londoners, and the Dutch ; the Jewellers, Silversmiths, Toymen, and Silk Mercers occupied all the Avenues to the Abbat's Palace. Minstrels, Juglers, and Mountebanks were commonly allowed to perform their feats of dexterity during the Fair, which brought together a great concourse of gentlemen and ladies from Suffolk, Norfolk, and Essex.

" Mary Tudor, Queen of France, relict of Louis XII., and sister of Henry VIII., who married afterwards Charles Brandon, Duke of Suffolk, went every year from her Manor of *Westhorp* to this Fair ; she had a magnificent Tent, with a splendid retinue and a band of music to attend, and to recreate the persons of distinction who came to pay her homage. The Duke, who was the most dexterous man of his age in tilting, engaged from all parts of the kingdom several armed Knights to these martial exercises, which made this Fair for some years frequented by many noble personages.

" John Melford, the last Abbat, surrendered the Abbey at the dissolution ; the Alderman received the Toll and assumed the Government of this Fair. King James I., in the sixth year of his reign, gave the reversion of the Fairs and Markets of Bury in Fee Farm to the Corporation.

" The *Market Cross* is converted into a Theatre, used only during this Fair by the Norwich Comedians. This Fair has considerably decreased for forty years past, and is now become rather a place of amusement than Temporary Mart, as most of the Merchandises now brought hither are chiefly articles of luxury and curiosity.

" John Lydgate, the famous poet, who was a Monk of St. Edmund's, wrote an elegant Latin Poem upon Bury Fair, in 1435.

" This Fair is held on a spacious PLAIN betwixt the magnificent *Gate* of the *Abbey* and the Town. It begins the 21st of September, and lasts

T

fourteen days. It is the rendezvous of the *Beau Monde* every afternoon, who conclude their evening by the Plays or Assemblies. This Fair consists chiefly of several *Rows* of Haberdashers, Milliners, Mercers, Silversmiths, and Toy Shops, which make a fine show.

"MIDSUMMER FAIR is of much more ancient date than Sturbridge. Fuller attributes its institution to children frequently playing on the very *spot* where it is kept to this day ; their parents or relations often accompanied them, to prevent any danger from the vicinity of the water, or to keep them off hurt and mischief. This *Field* being more and more resorted to in the summer season, booths were erected for the accomodation and entertainment of the company, and at last some pedlars began to sell their wares as early as the year 1106."

The Midsummer Fair is now quite extinct, but the grand Fair is still held on the Angel Hill, between the Abbey Gate and the town. It commences about the second week in October, and lasts three weeks, its great attractions being petty shows, roundabouts, gingerbread stalls, and toys. It is a perfect nuisance to the respectable inhabitants of the town.

A good idea of the importance of Bury Fair during the last century, may be gathered from the following advertisements from newspapers of a century ago, or thereabouts.

ADVERTISEMENTS IN CONNECTION WITH BURY FAIR.

TO THE LADIES.

BULL, HAIR DRESSER,

FROM NO. 2, EAGLE STREET, PICCADILLY, LONDON,

TAKES the Liberty of informing the Nobility and Gentry that he is at MR. MEAD's, Cabinet and Chair maker, in the Cook Row, Bury St. Edmund's, during the fair. LADIES who please to honour him with their commands, may depend upon having their hair dressed in the most fashionable taste, as it is now worn at the Courts of London and Paris. Great attention will be paid to render that part of the dress elegant and fashionable. He has a great variety of False Hair, to imitate Nature ; Bowes for the ladies, to fix on themselves, that never want dressing ; Tetes, Braids, Curls, Sheniongs, with or without long Hair ; ditto, with Curls, on a new construction. Coshasis, etc., to dress the hair upon.

He likewise intends being at Bath the Autumn season; to be heard of at Mr. Green's, facing York Houses.

₊ All orders sent to the above places punctually attended to.

Bury, November 21st, 1769.

This is to give notice to Gentlemen, Ladies, and others, THAT the famous MUFFIN MAKER, from London, is come to this Town, at the Spread Eagle, in the Butter Market, where Gentlemen, Ladies, aud others may be sure of as good Muffins and Crumpets as in London, and will continue selling the above during the whole season. All favours will be ever esteemed by their most humble servant,

SAMUEL SHED.

TO THE NOBILITY, GENTRY, ETC.,

WHO ARE ADMIRERS OF THE EXTRAORDINARY PRODUCTIONS OF NATURE.

TO BE SEEN

DURING BURY FAIR, AT THE BOTTOM OF THE ANGEL HILL,

MARIA TERESA,

THE AMAZING CORSICAN FAIRY,

who has had the honour of being shown three times before their Majesties. She is only 34 inches high, weighs but 26 lbs., and is allowed to be the finest display of Human Nature in Miniature that was ever shown in England.

To be seen from ten in the morning till nine at night. Gentlemen and Ladies, one shilling; servants, etc., sixpence.

The following is an account of some of the performances now exhibiting in the Theatre, BURY ST. EDMUND'S, by Mr. HERMAN BOAZ, the so celebrated German Artist.

He first produces a living Pidgeon to the company, which said Pidgeon he suspends by a garter hanging from the ceiling, and the shadow of the Pidgeon being reflected against the wall by means of a candle, Mr. Boaz then takes a sword with which he pierces the said shadow, at which instant blood will fly from the real Pidgeon; and in drawing the Sword across the Neck of the Shadow upon the wall, he will cut off the head of the real Pidgeon, which is at least six yards distant.

He shatters a large Pane of Glass into fragments, about the Breadth of a Shilling, the length he is not at all solicitous about, and eats them all very readily. He does the same with a Pound of Ten-penny Nails, or small Tenter hooks.

He gives any person leave with a sharp instrument (but first warmed) to strike at the naked Calf of his Leg with all his Force, and in less than three minutes the Wound heals, without a scar, and with the loss of about a Table spoonful of Blood.

He takes the Watch of any Gentleman in company, and by only stroking the Glass with the Ball of his Thumb, the watch shall stop as long as the Company shall think proper.

He takes a New Pack of Cards, with which he performs above two hundred Tricks, after which he eats the whole Pack in presence of the company, drinking a half pint of wine after it. He afterwards eats the Decanter, by way of Digestion.

N.B.—Mr. Boaz will continue to exhibit in Bury, every Evening during the next week, at seven o'clock; but as Methodists, and People of weak Minds in Town have imagined he deals with a Demon, or something supernatural, he here solemnly declares to such that their Notion is utterly false. He does not deny a Communication with ariel Beings, of which the Learned know well enough the middle Region of the Air is full, but this Communication he humbly conceives to be owing to his exemplary life.

DURING the present time of St. EDMUND BURY Fair, will be exhibited in a commodious BOOTH, on the ANGEL HILL, facing Cook Row, the capital collection of living WILD PRODUCTIONS, which were shown all last winter, facing Temple Bar, London, with several additions. The famous Lion Combatant, who in a few weeks is to encounter many Bull Dogs, being matched by two noble personages for a large sum of money: a young he Lion not above ten weeks old, so that the curious may now have an opportunity of that which will not present itself again in an Age, of taking a Lion in their arms, etc. The celebrated Oriental Tyger, which is as large as many heifers, and as beautiful as the Queen's Zebra. There is likewise a multiplicity of other extraordinary Phenomena.

In 1766 we find advertised:

" The ASSEMBLIES for the time of BURY FAIR, are fixed as follows :—

The First on Monday,	the 6th of October	
Second on Wednesday,	the 8th	,,
Third on Friday,	the 10th	,,
Fourth on Monday,	the 13th	,,
Fifth on Wednesday,	the 15th	,,

The particulars of the Assemblies will be advertised next week.

SAINT EDMUND'S OAK.

Lord Arthur Hervey, in his address to the members of "The Archæological Institute," on the occasion of their visit to Bury St. Edmund's, in 1854, said :

"I cannot help adverting to a most singular tradition, to which I confess I give implicit credence. At Hoxne, a few miles from hence, was an old oak tree, which had always been known as St. Edmund's Oak. The common tradition was (perhaps it had ceased to be the common *belief*) that it was the very identical oak to which King Edmund was tied, some thousand years ago, when he was shot at by the Danes. Some seven or eight years since, this venerable tree split from extreme old age, and in its very centre, which was then exposed to view, was found an old arrow-head. This remarkable fact, coupled with the previous tradition, makes me believe that this was the very oak tree to which St. Edmund was bound in the forest of Hoxne."

ROYAL VISITORS TO BURY ST. EDMUND'S.

Lord Arthur Hervey, in the address above mentioned, says :

"I could give you a goodly list of monarchs and other illustrious personages who came from the earliest times to pay their devotions at St. Edmund's shrine. But I must first call your attention to a remarkable circumstance. Though King Edmund, the Saxon patriot, died in defending his country against the Danes, yet some of the first kings who did honor to his shrine were themselves Danes and Normans. King Sweyn, having been rash enough to come and ravage St. Edmund's patrimony, came to an untimely end, and was said to have acknowledged on his death-bed that his sacriligious violence had been the cause of his death, through the intervention of King Edmund. In consequence, his son, King Canute, came to make his offerings at the grave of the offended saint, and to expiate his father's impiety, took off his crown and presented it at the shrine. King William the Conqueror did great honour to St. Edmund, and granted him many privileges. I fancy he came there in person, for it is said that he placed a *cultellum* on the shrine. Now it would be a curious speculation to inquire why Danes and Normans thus united in honouring an Anglo-Saxon saint; and it is a matter for philosophical inquiry whether it arose from policy, in order to conciliate their English subjects, or whether from a superstitious dread of St. Edmund's vengeance, and a desire to propitiate his favour; or whether we see in it a faint image of the blessed power of Christianity to unite the most discordant elements. For my own part, I would fain hope that there was at work in this something at least of the power of that religion which had before united in one holy fellowship Jews, Samaritans, and Gentiles; and which was now able to unite in the same bonds Normans, Danes, and Saxons. * * * *

"King Edward the Confessor often came to Bury, and was wont, when within a mile of the spot where his royal predecessor, St Edmund, lay, to take off his shoes and approach bare-foot. Here King Henry II. took the cross, and on that occasion Abbot Sampson was so inflamed with warlike ardour to take the cross, that it was almost impossible to restrain him from doing so. Nor could he be deterred from his purpose till the King absolutely forbad him, saying it was not safe for the peace of the counties, that the Abbot of St. Edmund and the Bishop of Norwich should both be absent at the same time. I may mention by the way, as a proof of the singular veneration felt for St. Edmund and his Abbey, that when all England was forced to contribute to the ransom of King Richard, and all the abbeys and monasteries were ransacked of their gold and silver vessels for that purpose, no one dared to touch the shrine of St. Edmund, and it remained inviolate till the Reformation. What became of it then is unknown. The painted case which belonged to Horace Walpole's collection, and was bought at Strawberry Hill sale, I believe, by the Duke of Sutherland, is pretty well ascertained not to have had anything to do with St. Edmund's shrine. Richard the Lion-hearted himself came to Bury twice. King John also came (no honour to us that he did), and did *not* earn golden opinions. The sarcastic Jocelin de Brakland complains of his great shabbiness: the only thing he offered to St. Edmund was a piece of silk, which he borrowed from the convent. On a subsequent occasion, however, he in some measure redeemed his character. King Henry III. held a Parliament here. Edward I. visited Bury thirteen times, and also held his Parliament here A. D. 1296. Here poor Edward II. came and shed over the place the sad hue of his sorrows and misfortunes: he probably came to St. Edmund's shrine to seek some solace from those heavy cares which weighed him down to the ground. He spent his Christmas here; but, doubtless, it was not a merry Christmas, for he knew that his faithless Queen Isabella was near at hand. In point of fact, she landed in Suffolk, and soon afterwards raised a large force at Bury and in the neighbourhood, with which she ultimately drove her unhappy husband from the throne. Richard II. and his Queen passed ten days here; and here Henry VI. held a Parliament. I will read to you, from Dugdale, a short and characteristic description of the manner in which the King passed the time from Christmas to St. George's day (April 23).

" ' Abbot Curteys made great preparations for the visit, and put the abbatial palace, which was at that time much out of repair, into complete readiness for the reception of his royal guest. The aldermen and burgesses of Bury, dressed in scarlet, accompanied by the commons of the town, who also wore a red livery, met the king, to the number of five hundred, upon Newmarket heath. The royal retinue before this extended a mile. They brought the King within the precincts of the monastery by the south gate. Here he was received by the whole convent, the Bishop of Norwich and the Abbot appearing in full pontificials, the Abbot sprinkling the King with holy water, and presenting a cross to his lips. Procession, with music, was next made to the high altar of the church, when the antiphon used in the service for St. Edmund ("Ave rex gentis Anglerum") was sung. After this the King paid his devotions at St. Edmund's shrine, and then passed to the Abbot's palace. He remained with the Abbot till the Epiphany, but afterwards removed to the prior's lodgings, where he stayed till the 23rd of January, the vicinity of the water and the vineyard which led into the open country, and gave facility to the sports of the field, rendering the situation particularly agreeable.'

"In connection with this visit of King Henry VI., I may refer to an interesting picture in Dugdale's Monasticon (the only one remaining) of St. Edmund's shrine, in which Henry VI. appears in the act of making his devotions before it."

ANNIVERSARIES OF BISHOP BLAIZE AND ST. CRISPIN.

During the last century Trade Guilds existed in many towns, those of the woolcombers being most numerous in this district. These "Guilds" were trading fraternities, established to exercise control over particular handicrafts, and were often benefited by monarchs and monarchs' favourites, at the expense of the public. On anniversary days they usually had a procession, a sort of open air recognition of their fraternity, in some places rivalling the Lord Mayor's show, in London. In "The East Anglian" we find the following account, taken from a MS. Common Place Book, of the celebration of St. Blaizes and St. Crispin's days at Bury St. Edmund's.

"February 3, 1777.

"This day, Monday, being the anniversary of Bishop Blaize, the same was observed in this town, in a manner far surpassing anything of the kind ever seen. The Cavalcade consisted of between 2 and 300 Woolcombers, upon Horses, in uniforms properly decorated, Bishop Blaize, Jason, Castor, and Pollux, a band of music, drums, colours, and everything necessary to render the procession suitable to the greatness of the Woollen manufactory. The following lines were spoken by the Orators:—

"With boundless Gratitude, Illustrious Blaize,
Again we celebrate and speak thy Praise;
Britons do still revere, and Fame proclaim
To wondering nations thy auspicious Name.
Thousands to thee, the Founder of our Art,
With thy Great Sire, their equal warmth impart;
With Breasts inflamed we now our Homage pay,
And sound thy worth on this thy Festal Day.
And thou, Great Jason, Prince in war renown'd,
To Greece with Drum and Silver Trumpet's sound
Dauntless drove forward with thy conquering sword,
Slaughtered the Guards that dare resist thy Word;
Colchis, amaz'd, beheld her soldiers slain,
And thou Possessor of Her greatest gain.
Defended still by our own Laws, we boast
Our Art the noblest formed on Albion's coast;
To Each, our Patron, now our thanks we pay,
And thus in Publick we our joy display;
While you assist, Commerce can never fail,
Nor other Pow'rs o'er Briton's Sons prevail.

"Oct. 31st, 1777.

"Last Saturday being the anniversary of St. Crispin, the Shoemakers made a grande Procession on Horseback, from the Southgate, thro' all the principal Streets, with Trumpets in front, and the rest of the band, joined with drums, fifes, etc., between the divisions, on which occasion there was more company in town than was ever remembered before. The Prince was mounted on a fine grey Horse and most magnificently habited. He was attended by his nobles, superbly dressed in green and white, and his guards in blue and white, which made a very good appearance. His noble and warlike Br. Crispianus appeared in a coat of Mail, attended by his troops, in two divisions, one in red and white, the other in purple and white. They all rode in half boots, made of morocco, in different colors adapted to their uniforms; their jackets and caps were extremely neat and in elegant taste, made all of leather. The principal characters in the procession were remarkably well chosen, and the pleasing effect of the fancy dresses had showed great judgment in the managers and far exceeded the warmest expectations of the beholders. The Prince, attended by his guard, with his torch bearers and a grand band of musick playing before him, went to the Play, and was received with every mark of Respect."

TOWN CRIERS' REGISTERS.

One of the documents relating to the town of Clare, in the custody of the Chief Steward of the Honor, is a register of things cried in its market. It extends nearly through a century, the first entry being dated in 1612 and the last in 1711. The quaint description of articles lost or found, the singular nature of the dresses worn by the individuals who " ran away," and the peculiar manner of spelling the names of persons, places, and things, cannot fail to interest our readers.

EXTRACTS FROM THE REGISTERS KEPT BY THE CRIERS OF CLARE, SUFFOLK.

1620. 16th June—Ther was criede in Clar m'kett, a flea bitten greye nagg with a white mane, taken up at Denston by the Lord of the manor of Denston, his bailiffe their as a straye.

1687. 25th Feb.—Ther was one Bassilley Lonely, Aboute 14 years of Age, Beeing An Apprentice to a Shoemaker in Melford, was openly cryed in Clare markett, with proviso, that if any man Could bring tidins to the Cryer he should be well paid for his paynes, and this was done by the order of the Bayliefs of the burrow.

1689. 31st May—Ther was Cried downe in Clare markett Catherine Frost, wife of Nathaniell Frost, of Hundon, in Suff., yeoman, by me, Edmund Warren, xr.

1692. 9th October—Cryed yr one browne blacke horse, About 14 hands high, with A starr on his foorehead and whight foot behinde, and A wall eye on the oft side, and the other eye is in his head, but he is allmost blinde of both, and two sadle spots on etch side of his back, taken or strayed oute of the pasture of Mr. John Brooke, minister of Greate Yeldom, in Essex, &c.

1692. 16th December—Cryed a broune Cow about 9 or 10 years ould, with crumpled horns, with a whight place between her foore leggs, and some whight upon her Throate, taken up Ahoute Could fayer day, last, by Mr. Waldgrave Sidy, of uper yeldham, Essex.

1693. 2nd December—Cryed att severall places in Clare, A hagg Saw of John ssollowes in Clare, it is ahout 4 foot long. Borrowed or stolen oute of his shop Aboute 3 or 4 months agoe.

1694. 21st December—Cryed in Clare Markett, a girle ahoute 14 years of age, of a middle statur, with a full red face, cloathed in sad cullored cloathes, who ran away from her master, Thomas Betts, a bricklayer of Stoke by Clare, upon the 28th day of Novemher last.

1696. 2nd October—Cryed in Clare markett, a ladd that rann away from Isaac Brounesmyth, in grigory parish, in Sudbury; he is ahoute 17 or 18 years ould, with afresh cullered light brounc heare, An ould black hatt and a fuschin frock, with an ould coate under it, with sad cullered briches and sad cullered stockens.

1701. 28th March—Cryed in Clare markett, one John Wade, the sonn of William Wade, of Clare, Glover, that non of the King's Subiocts should lend the said John Wade Anything upon his father's Account, nor pay him Any of his father's debts.

1701. 11th September—Cryed in Clare, one Thomas Sparrow, apprentice to one John Barnard, of Sudbury, who did run away from his master on the 23rd day of last August: he hath a ruddy complection and browne hair, with a scarr upon his forehead, with a sad cullered fuschin frock, and a pair of callimankoe briches and sad cullered stockens.

1704. 7th July—Cryed in Clare markett, one John Woods, Apprentice to John Snell, in Clare, who Ran Away from his master, the boy Ahoute 15 years of Age, with a lank Broune Thick head of hair, and A Round Plumpe palle vissage; he hath had the small pox; he had a light cullered Coate and Wescoate, and Britches of Sinniment Culler, and Gray Wollen Stockens and a black hatt.

1710. 2nd February—Cryed down in Clare Markett, one Sarah Wordeley, the wife of ould Mr. Wordeley, of Glemsford, in Suff. for westening and makeing Away her housband's Estate, and this I was ordered to doe by Roger Wordeley his sonn, who did promise me I should sustain no wrong for so doeing.

COCK FIGHTING IN SUFFOLK.

It is not known when the barbarous pastime of Cock-fighting was introduced into England, but it is supposed to have been brought here by the Romans. From the time of

Henry II. it seems to have been a popular amusement in this country, and the Cock Pit at Whitehall was erected by a crowned head, for the more magnificent celebration of the pastime.

The reproach incurred by this pastime in England is greatly aggravated by two sorts of fighting, called the "battle royal," and the "Welsh main." In the battle royal, an unlimited number of fowls are pitted, and when they have slaughtered one another for the diversion of the spectators, the single surviving bird is to be esteemed the victor, and carries away the prize.

The Welsh main consists, we will suppose, of sixteen pairs of cocks ; of these, the sixteen conquerors are pitted a second time, the eight conquerors are then pitted a third time, the four conquerors a fourth time, and lastly the two conquerors are pitted a fifth time ; so that thirty-one cocks are sure to be murdered for the sport and pleasure of men, who would have regarded it as a great affront to have been accused of either want of feeling or morality.

A century ago, the men of Suffolk appear to have been very fond of this kind of amusement. During the three days of the races at Ipswich, a main of cocks was fought each day at the "Cock and Pye" inn, between the gentlemen of Essex and Suffolk, or Norfolk and Suffolk. At Bury St. Edmund's, also, it was annually practised, for two days, at the "Three Tuns" inn. At the "White Horse," Stoke Ash, near Eye, the lovers of the sport used to assemble ; Suffolk and Norfolk each shewed twenty-one cocks on a side, and the fight was for two guineas a battle, and twenty guineas the odd battle. At the Royal Cock Pit, in Newmarket, on the 5th, 6th, and 7th of March, 1767, a main of cocks was fought for five guineas a battle, fifty guineas the odd battle, and four hundred guineas, bye. It is stated that on this occasion Mr. Burdett fought his cocks with his new-fashioned spurs. At Beccles the same pastime was regularly indulged in during the race week, the stakes on the odd battle being sometimes as high as fifty guineas, and it was so usual a part of the race entertainment that we find it inserted at the end of the advertisement of the races, in the same way as an ordinary is at the present day. The cock pit was sometimes at the "Falcon," sometimes at the "Angel," and at other times at the "White Swan."

PETTY SESSIONS FOR HIRING OF SERVANTS.

A century ago, it was customary once a year to hold what was called a "Petty Sessions" in each of the Hundreds of Suffolk, for the Hiring and Retaining of Servants. The male and female servants used to assemble every Michaelmas at a time and place fixed by the chief constable of the hundred, and the "Sessions" was generally held at some noted public-house in the district. Thus, for Plomesgate, it was held at the "Green Man," Tunstall; for Cosford, at the "Crown," Bildeston; for Blackbourn, at the "Boar," Walsham le Willows; for Blything, at Halesworth, sometimes at the "Tuns," and sometimes at the "Angel;" for Bosmere, at the "Crown," Coddenham, etc. Sometimes *two* were held in one year, as in 1765, Hundred of Stow, one was held at the "Shepherd and Dog," Onehouse, and another at the "White Horse," at Finborough; and in Hartismere, one at the "White Horse," Stoke, and another at the "Greyhound," Botesdale. But as the holding of two Sessions led to great inconveniences, the chief constable of each hundred was ordered and directed by the magistrates at the General Quarter Sessions, held at Beccles in the same year, 1765, that only one Petty Session for the Hiring and Retaining of Servants should be held in each Hundred.

Old Acts of Parliament had originated this custom by enacting that ploughmen and other laborers should be hired to serve for a full year, and not by the day. The servants open to engagements stood in a row at a particular spot, some of them exhibiting a straw in their mouths, to indicate their unengaged condition. A small sum of money given to each servant was supposed to legalize the contract. When the business of the day was over, amusement began. Dinner was provided at each of the public houses at which the Petty Sessions was held, the best rooms being laid out with tables and forms for the entertainment of the multitude. The announcement of the dinner always formed part of the advertisement, the stereotype phraseology being, " Where all persons will meet with a hearty welcome from their humble servant." The lads brought in the lasses when the amusement began, and it is acknowledged that coarseness, if not something worse, prevailed. Few persons will regret that this custom, a relic of feudalism, has long since passed away.

PUNISHMENT OF DEATH BY BURNING.

In the month of April, 1763, a woman was strangled and burnt to death on Rushmere Heath, near Ipswich, under sentence of the Judge of Assize, for the murder of her husband. The criminal law was at this period very severe and cruel, and this burning to death was one of the savage remains of Norman policy. Murder of a husband was petty treason, and the law prescribed that for this offence the criminal should be burnt alive. The Sheriff who did not execute the sentence of burning alive, was liable to a prosecution ; but, fortunately, men were too humane to carry the sentence into effect, and the practice was to strangle the victims by drawing away a stool from under their feet before the faggots were piled round the stake. The case at Rushmere Heath was that of Margery Beddingfield, for being an accomplice in the murder of her husband, John Beddingfield, of Sternfield, in Suffolk. A farm servant, Richard Ringe, her paramour and the actual murderer of John Beddingfield, was sentenced to be hanged at the same time and place.

The sentence upon Margery Beddingfield was that she should be " taken from hence to the place from whence you came, and from thence to the place of execution, on Saturday next, where you are to be burnt until you be dead, and the Lord have mercy on your soul!'"

SELLING A WIFE.

This odious custom was not unknown in the county of Suffolk; and as numerous instances may be cited as having occurred in various parts of England, foreigners cannot well be blamed for thinking wife-selling a publicly recognized national custom among us. Few persons of the present day have seen a husband offer his wife for sale, in a public street or market-place, with a halter round her neck; but the case has ofttimes occurred in this county. In 1787 we find the following announcement in print:—

> "A farmer of the parish of Stowupland sold his wife to a neighbour for five guineas, and being happy to think he had made a good bargain, presented her with a guinea to buy her a new gown; he then went to Stowmarket, and gave orders for the bells to be rung upon the occasion."

The above extract is made from the columns of the "Ipswich Journal," January 28th, 1787. It is given as news in the ordinary column, without any remark as to its being an unusual occurrence.

HOUR GLASSES IN PULPITS.

In Kedington church, near Clare, Suffolk, on the left side of the pulpit, is the stand for supporting the hour-glass, formerly used by ministers when preaching. It is a slender, turned pillar, rising about thirteen inches above the side of the pulpit, and surmounted by an iron ring, or rim, six inches in circumference.

These hour-glasses are relics of Puritanic times, and appear to have constituted, in those days, part of the furniture of the pulpit. In the accounts of the churchwardens of Mellis for 1629, appears, "Item, an houre glasse 9d. Item, the hour glasse frame, 8d." Though sermons at the present day seldom exceed three-quarters of an hour in delivery, the practice of long preaching in the olden times much prevailed, and the general poverty of the country and the scarcity of clocks and watches doubtless gave rise to the adoption of the hour-glass, for the measurement of a brief portion of our fleeting span. Dyos, in a sermon preached at St. Paul's Cross, in 1570, speaking of the walking and profane talking in the church at sermon time, also laments how they grudged the preacher his *customary hour*. So that an hour seems to have been the practice at the Reformation. That the practice was general, may be inferred from the fact that in the preface to the Bishop's *Bible*, printed by John Daye, in 1569, Arch-bishop Parker is represented with an hour-glass at his right hand. Hogarth, in his "Sleeping Congregation," has introduced an hour-glass on the left side of the preacher. It also figures in the engraving of the painting, by Wilkie, of John Knox preaching before Mary Queen of Scots. Butler, in his *Hudibras*, speaks of "gifted brethren preaching by a carnal *hour-glass*." In the days of Cromwell, on first getting into the pulpit and naming the text, the preacher turned up the glass; and if the sermon did not hold till the glass was empty, it was said by the congregation that the preacher was lazy; and if he continued to preach much longer, they would yawn and stretch, and thus signify to the preacher that they began to be weary of his discourse, and wanted to be dismissed. Congregations were not, however, always tired out by one hour's preaching. In the frontispiece of Dr. Young's book, entitled, "*England's Shame; or, a Relation of the Life and Death of Hugh Peters, London,* 1663," Peters is represented preaching, and holding an *hour-glass* in his left hand, in the act of saying, "I know you are good fellows, so let's have another *glass*." Macaulay also gives us a welcome illustration. Speaking in his History of England (vol. ii.) of Gilbert Burnet, Bishop of Salisbury, he says: "He was often interrupted by the deep hum of his audience; and when, after preaching out the hour-glass, which in those days was part of the furniture of the pulpit,

he held it in his hand, the congregation clamourously
encouraged him to go on till the sand had run off once
more."

At the top of the staircase leading to the Council Chamber
of the Town Hall, Ipswich, a venerable relic of ancient
customs has long hung up unused—we allude to the
" ducking stool," into which refractory Ipswich scolds of
former days were used to be fastened and dipped into the
water, to cool their angry passions.   It is in the form of a
strong-backed arm-chair, with a wrought iron rod, about an
inch in diameter, fastened to each arm in front, meeting in a
segment of a circle above ; there is also another iron rod,
affixed at the back, which curves over the head of the person
seated in the chair, and is connected with the others at the
top, to the centre of which is fastened an iron ring for the
purpose of slinging the machine into the river.   It is plain
and substantial, and has more the appearance of solidity
than antiquity in its construction.

When required for use, the chair was hung on a sort of
axle, on which it played freely, so as always to remain in the
horizontal position.   The scold being well fastened in her
chair, the two beams were placed as near to the centre as
possible, across a post on the water side, and being lifted up
behind, the chair of course dropped into the cold element.
The ducking was renewed according to the degree of
shrewishness possessed by the patient.   This funny mode
of punishing scolding women was often employed during the
sixteenth and seventeenth centuries, and Clarke, in his
History of Ipswich, says, that in the Chamberlain's books,
belonging to the Corporation of Ipswich, there are entries
for the payments of persons employed in using the ducking
stool, and that in the year 1597, three unfortunate females
underwent this opprobrious ceremony.   The fee for inflicting
this punishment was 1s. 6d.

HEART BURIAL AT HOLBROOK CHURCH.

Holbrook, a small village about six miles from Ipswich, on the banks of the Stour, possesses a church which in more than one respect is of considerable interest. The nave and chancel are of the early decorated style, and were probably built at the commencement of the fourteenth century, soon after Edward II. began to reign. On the north side of the chancel is, or rather was, the founder's tomb, coeval in style with the earliest part of the church. Close to the tomb, and raised three feet from the ground, is a small niche, about the size of an ordinary piscina, of undoubtedly the same period as the founder's tomb. The slab within it contains a small figure, so mutilated that it is almost impossible to say whether it had been a whole effigy, or only part of one, as at Narborough, in Norfolk. The general form of the head, and the pillow upon which it rests, are sufficiently clear, and there is enough of the left arm remaining to show that the hands either met in the usual attitude of prayer, or what is probable, owing to subsequent discoveries, that it held a metal or stone heart.

Upon removing the slab on which this effigy was carved, a solid stone was found, in the centre of which was sunk a circular hole, as sharp and as perfect in its outlines as the day the masons cut it, about five hundred and fifty years ago. This sinking measures six inches in diameter at the top, and tapers down to four inches and three-quarters at the bottom, the depth being six inches.

Inside this, and closely fitting to the sides, almost as if it had been cast in it, was a metal vase or jar, nearly perished by corrosion. It had a metal cover, with a knob, which being thicker and heavier than the rest, upon the decay of the lower part, sank down by its weight into the centre of the vase. Upon lifting it and removing the pieces of metal, the vase was found to be three-parts full of a chalk, lime,

U

and loamy substance, in which were interspersed several small pieces of charcoal, and other substances, the nature of which could not be satisfactorily discovered by analysis. There can be, however, but little doubt that the vase contained the remains of a defectively embalmed heart; or it may have been (considering the presence of charcoal) burnt previously to its interment.

ANGLO-SAXON BURIALS IN SUFFOLK.

Various Anglo-Saxon relics having been at different times discovered on the heath at West Stow, Suffolk, the attention of the Rev. E. R. Benyon, the proprietor of the heath, was in 1851 directed to the circumstances, and systematic excavations were in consequence made for the purpose of ascertaining whether more important remains could be found. The result of these labours demonstrated that the spot had been a burial place of the Anglo-Saxons. The site of the graves, the intervals of which varied from two or three feet to as many yards, which was the most general distance, were indicated by a dark streak in the gravel or sand. The skeletons, about 100 in number, were found lying with their heads to the South-west and their feet to the North-east, a position observable at other burial places of the same people. The bodies were interred just within the gravel, which is only fifteen or eighteen inches below the surface. With the skeletons were found urns, beads, brooches, spear-blades, etc.

Three modes of sepulture appear to have prevailed at West Stow-heath :—

　　1.　That of burning the body and placing the ashes in an urn.
　　2.　That of burying the body entire without a coffin or cist, but with the garments, weapons, and ornaments of the deceased.
　　3.　That of burial in coffins.

The two former seemed to have prevailed contemporaneously, but it would appear from the small number of urns containing ashes that the practice of burning the dead was on the decline.

The presence of Saxon urns in graves which contained skeletons may indicate the partial adoption of usages which custom had stamped as sacred, after those usages had become superseded by others of totally different character. Over what period of time the interments at Stow-heath extended it is not easy to determine, for history is almost silent as to the condition of our island from the third century to the conversion of the Saxons to Christianity; but it is probable that they extended from the fifth to the seventh centuries.

The *Urns*, five in number, discovered at Stow-heath, are all of unburnt earth, and of considerable substance; one of them, in form resembling those of Roman manufacture, was full of burnt ashes of bones and of wood. It was found in a round hole at the head of a grave, and had pieces of charcoal about it, but there was no charcoal or bones in any other part of the grave. It fell down with the loosened soil before it was seen, and became much broken, but the workmen carefully gathered up all the fragments, which being united, it was deposited in the Museum of the Suffolk Archæological Institute at Bury St. Edmund's. As such urns are but seldom met with in an entire state, it is probable that they may have sustained some injury during the ceremony of cremation, being manufactured on the spot and dried by the fire of the funeral pile.

Stone Coffin. A stone coffin was discovered, and this is believed to be the only one ever found in a Saxon burial place in this kingdom. It is hewn out of a solid block of Barnack or Northamptonshire stone, is five feet eight inches in length, and lidless. It was partially embedded in the gravel, and when found was only about fifteen inches under the surface. A few bones, of a small size, probably those of a youth or a female, with the half of a small bronze clasp, and one or two pieces of iron, were within it.

Bosses of Shields, a *Sword* three feet long and an inch and a half broad, *Spears*, an *Arrow-head* of iron, *Knives*, a pair of *Tweezers*, a *Hair-pin*, *Girdle-hanger*, *Buckles* of iron and bronze,

Brooches, a large number of *Beads*, and some *Coins* were also found with the remains of the dead.

INVIDIOUS DISTINCTION.

In the Registers of the parish of Mellis from 1783 to 1791, "An Account of Baptisms of those Children whose Parents were relieved by the Parish at the time they were born," was entered separately in the Register Book, and also during the same period was entered a separate "Account of Persons buried at Mellis at the Parish expense." The rector (Rev. Henry Creed), when he made the extract, remarked, "I know of no reason why this invidious distinction was made between rich and poor."

THE FORMATION OF THE EARLIEST CONGREGATION OF THE INDEPENDENTS IN SUFFOLK.

Several Christian Societies of Noncomformists were formed in Suffolk during the years 1652 and 1653, upon the model of those established at Yarmouth and Norwich. The inhabitants of Beccles took the lead. The church book opens with the following record :—

The 6th day of ye fifth month, com'only called July, 1652. "The names of such persons whoe have covenanted togither to walk in ye wayes of Christ according to Gospell Order, with an account of such matters as have occurred in ye Church att Beccles.

"In the day and yeare above written, these following p'sons joyned in covenant together under ye visible Regiment of Christ, according to ye Gospell, viz., Joh. Clarke, James King, jun., Robt. Otley, Edm. Nevill, Joh. Morse, Wm. Cutlove, Edm. Artis, Robt. Harne, Joh. Botswaine."

Although this mutual engagement was all that was essential to the formation of a Church of Christ, yet on an occasion so deeply interesting, and fraught with consequences so momentous, it was natural that the brethren elsewhere should be requested to add their approval, their counsel, and their prayers. In the Congregational Church

Book at Norwich, a letter is stated to have been received from the Christians at Beckles, by which they signified their intention to gather into church fellowship, "and desired the church would send messengers, to be there upon the 23rd of July, 1652." Daniel Bradford, James Gooding, and Samuel Clarke, were selected for this service.

The first of these three individuals had been "employed in the army," when the Yarmouth church was formed, and was afterwards a deacon at Norwich. The other two appear to have been among Mr. Bridge's companions in exile, and to have returned with him. Doubtless they were men whose zeal was chastened by experience and discretion, and whose piety had stood the test of time and persecution.

Within twelve months of the formation of the church twenty-one other persons had joined. The first of these was Mr. Joseph Cutlove, who appears to have been at the same time portreeve of the Corporation at Beccles, and to have had some influential friends among the members of the Long Parliament. Amongst the names is also that of "Humphrey Brewster," one of the truly honourable family to whom belonged the Hall and Manors of Wrentham, and who for many years greatly encouraged and supported the dissenting interest there; and "Francis Hayloveke," subsequently a deacon of the church.

During the above period there was no recognised pastor. But in the year 1653 occurs this memorandum :—

29 d., 5 m., com'only called July.　　　　A Pastor was chosen.

Who this was is rather uncertain; perhaps Mr. John Clarke.

He seems to have been a Minister in the Established Church, for in the parochial register under the years 1647 and 1648 are recorded the baptisms of two sons of "John Clarke, minister, and of Ann his wife." It is also observable that his name is the first enrolled on the list of members of the Independent Church. And among the individuals subsequently admitted was "Anna" his wife, which serves to identify him with the person mentioned in the parish register.

There is a curious jug, or pitcher, belonging to the ringers of Hadleigh. This "pitcher," as it is called, has two ears, and is circular in shape, swelling out in the middle, and being more contracted at the end. The material of which it is made is brown earthenware, glazed, and the following are the dimensions :—

	FEET.	INCHES.
Height	1	$3\frac{1}{2}$
Diameter at the base		$7\frac{1}{4}$
Diameter of the mouth, inside		4
Diameter of the mouth, outside		5
Circumference of the base	2	$4\frac{1}{2}$
Circumference of the middle at the largest part	3	$5\frac{1}{2}$
Circumference of the neck, including the spout		4
Depth of the neck		$2\frac{3}{4}$
Width across the handles	1	$2\frac{1}{4}$

The jug holds sixteen quarts, and bears this inscription, very rudely indented, apparently with a chisel, when the clay was soft, and running round the vessel without any regard to uniformity of size in the letters, or to straightness of line. The first word, *ME*, or perhaps *MEI*, is in italics; the rest of the letters are in Roman capitals.

"*ME* THOMAS WINDLE, ISAAC BVNN, IOHN MANN, ADAM SAGE, GEORG BOND, THOMAS GOLDSBOROVGH, ROBART SMITH, HENRY WEST."

These were, no doubt, the names of the eight ringers, as Hadleigh belfrey has eight bells, and below the names are these lines—

> "If yov love me dve not lend me,
> Evse me ofton and keep me clenly,
> Fill me fvll, or not at all,
> If it be strovng, and not with small."

Below all, in the front, is the word "Hadly;" underneath one handle is the date, 17, T. G. 15, and underneath the other, 17, R. O. 15. The letters T. G. and R. O. being, probably, the initials of the potters.

The jug is in the possession of Mr. Pettitt, of the "Eight Bells" inn, Angel street, who holds it for the ringers, of whom he is the leader. He has had it about twenty-seven years, having claimed it on the death of John Corder, the parish clerk, who had formerly the custody of it, and he believes that it has always belonged to the Hadleigh ringers. Mr. Pettitt says that it is still occasionally used by the ringers on the occurrence of any profitable wedding, and it has been introduced into the belfry. It is said to be filled every Christmas by mine host of the "Eight Bells," when the ringers assemble for a "frolic," with strong beer, which in Angel street goes by the name of "Old King William;" and any stranger going into the room is compelled to pay six-pence to arrest the natural effects of their potations, by keeping it "full," according to its own request.

At Hinderclay a ringers' pitcher is still preserved in the church tower, of form and size similar to the Hadleigh jug. It is thus inscribed—

" By Samuel Moss, this pitcher was given to the noble society of ringers at Hinderclay, in Suffolk, viz., Tho. Sturgeon, Ed. Loch, John Haw, Ric Ruddock, and Ralf Chapman, to which society he once belonged, and left in the year 1702.

> From London I was sent,
> As plainly doth appear ;
> It was with this intent,
> To be filled with strong beer.
> Pray remember the pitcher when empty."

At Clare there is also a "jug" of a similar kind, which belongs to the ringers of that place. It will hold more than seventeen quarts.

THE CASE OF MARGARET CUTTING, OF WICKHAM MARKET.

THE FOLLOWING IS TAKEN FROM THE "BRITISH SPY," AND THE
LETTER IS DATED JANUARY 10, 1742-3.

*An account of Margaret Cutting, a young woman, now living at
Wickam Market, in Suffolk, who speaks readily and intelligibly,
tho' she has lost her tongue.*

Mr. Boddington, Turkey Merchant, at Ipswich, first communicated
this extraordinary Fact, and his account was read before the Royal
Society, July 1, 1742, who thought it so remarkable as to desire a very
exact Enquiry to be made into the Truth of it, which was accordingly
made by Mr. Boddington, the Rev. Mr. Notcutt, and Mr. Hammond, a
skilful Anatomist, who, after the strictest Examination, attested the
following circumstances :—

"We have this April 9th, 1742, seen Margaret Cutting, who informed
us she was but twenty-four years old, that when she was but four years
of age a cancer appeared on the upper part of her tongue, which soon
eat its way quite to the root. Mr. Scotchmore, surgeon, at Saxmundham,
used the best means he could for her relief, but pronounced the case
incurable. One day, when he was injecting some medicine into her
mouth, her tongue dropped out, the girl immediately saying, to their
great surprise, '*Don't be frightened, mamma, it will grow again.*' In
a quarter of a year after she was quite cured. In examining her mouth
we found not the least appearance of any tongue remaining, nor any
Uvula; but we observed a fleshy excrescence under the left jaw,
extending itself almost to the place where the *uvula* should be, about
a finger broad. This did not appear until some years after the cure.
It is not moveable. The passage to the throat where the *uvula* should
be is circular, and will admit a small nutmeg. She performed the
swallowing of solids and liquids as well as we could. She discoursed as
well as other persons do, but with a little tone through the nose.
Letters and syllables she pronounced very articulately, and vowels
perfectly, as also those consonants that require most the help of the
tongue, d, l, t, r, n. She read to us in a book very distinctly, and sung
very prettily. What is still more wonderful, notwithstanding the loss
of this organ, she distinguishes all tastes very nicely. To this certificate
may be added the attestation of Mr. Dennis, tobacconist, in Aldersgate
Street, who has known her many years, and upon frequent inspections
had found the case before recited true. A letter from the young woman
herself to Mr. Dennis, owning the fact entirely, was also read. Some
few instances of the like nature have occurred, particularly one related

by Tulpices, of a man, himself examined, who having had his tongue cut out by the Turks, after three years could speak distinctly.

" N.B.—All the original papers are lodged with the Royal Society."

ROYAL TRAVELLING IN SUFFOLK IN 1736—7.

In January, 1736—7, His Majesty George II. had been a considerable time on his voyage from Helvœtsluys to England, occasioned by stormy and contrary winds, and had been also exposed to the most imminent danger. On the 14th of the month, the vessel appeared off Lowestoft, and when the royal barge approached the shore, a body of sailors belonging to the port, uniformly dressed in seamen's jackets, rejoicing that their King, after having escaped the perils of the ocean, was honouring their native town with a visit, waded into the sea, and meeting the barge took it on their shoulders, with the King, the Countess of Yarmouth, and all the attendant nobility in it, and carried it to the beach without suffering it to strike the ground.   His Majesty was met at the sea shore by John Jex, Esq., of that town, with his carriage, who conducted him to his house—Mr. Jex having the very high honour of being coachman.   The monarch landed about twelve at noon, and about two hours after set off for London.   Between six and seven o'clock in the evening, Mr. Carrington, one of the King's messengers, arrived at the post office in Ipswich with the agreeable news that His Majesty would be there that night, on which the bailiffs, portmen, etc., assembled in their formalities to receive him at St. Margaret's gate.   The whole town was immediately illuminated, and Christchurch, the house of Thomas Fonnereau, Esq., in particular, made a most splendid appearance.   His Majesty did not arrive till after the clock had struck eleven, having been nine hours on the journey from Lowestoft; and when the cortège appeared, the crowd was so great at the gate that the magistrates could not pay their duty to him there, but repaired to the White Horse, and attended him as he came out of his carriage.   He immediately went up stairs into the great dining-room, whither they were soon admitted with several of the clergy of the town, and all had the honour to kiss his hand. Mr. Bailiff Sparrow, finding that His Majesty was much fatigued, addressed him in a short speech, setting forth the joy the Corporation felt in paying their duty to him, after the many anxious thoughts they had had on account of the great danger that he had experienced. The King came in the same chaise from Lowestoft, but at Saxmundham he was accommodated with a set of Lord Strafford's horses, which brought him to Ipswich. The messenger, who was gone forward, left orders for a coach and chaise, with four horses each, to be hired at Ipswich, and as many dragoons as could be collected were to attend as an escort. His Majesty entered the coach a little before twelve, and passed through the town, attended by the joyful acclamations of a numerous crowd of people, and was pleased to take notice of the ladies, who shook their handkerchiefs at the windows in the Market-place, by waving his hat. When he reached Copdock, it was so dark that lights were deemed necessary. The officer that went in advance inquired of the landlady at the "White Elm" if she had any flambeaux, or could procure any. Being answered in the negative, he asked her if she had any LINKS. "Aye, that I have," said she ; "and some as good as His Majesty, God bless him! ever eat in all his life ; " and immediately produced some fine sausages! The King stopped at Isaac Spencer's, at the Swan Inn, Stratford St. Mary, where he laid himself down to rest for three or four hours, and about six o'clock took coach for London. A messenger had been sent from Woodbridge to Felixstow, who ferried over to Harwich, and ordered coaches to go to Stratford ready for the King. His Majesty went through Colchester without stopping, and arrived at St. James's Palace about two in the afternoon. What a striking contrast this mode of travelling presents to the present rapidity of royal conveyance!

HABITS OF A LADY IN THE LAST CENTURY.

A glance at the life of Lady Hanmer, Sir Thomas Hanmer's first wife, will give an insight into the expenses, and enable our readers to guess the habits of a lady of fashion a hundred and fifty years ago. Isabella, Duchess of Grafton, was the sole heiress of Henry Bennett, Earl of Arlington, one of the principal ministers of Charles II. In 1682, when only fifteen years of age, she was married to Henry Fitzroy, the second son of the Duchess of Cleveland, created at his birth Baron Sudbury, Viscount Ipswich, Earl of Euston, and Duke of Grafton. She had been betrothed ten years previously, when she was only five years of age, and the bridegroom nine. The venerable Evelyn was very partial to her. He says, " I was at the marriage of Lord Arlington's lovely daughter (a sweet child, if there ever was any) to the Duke of Grafton. The Archbishop of Canterbury officiated, the king and all the grandees of the Court being present . . . . . I confess," says Evelyn, " I would give my Lady Arlington little joy, and so I plainly told her; but she said the King would have it so, and there was no going back. Thus the sweetest, hopefulest, most beautiful child, and most virtuous, too, was sacrificed to a boy that had been rudely bred, without anything to encourage them but His Majesty's pleasure. I pray God the sweet child may find it to her advantage, who, if my augury deceive me not, will in a few years be such a paragon as were fit to make a wife to the greatest prince in Europe."

The death of her husband, who was slain during the siege of Cork, in 1690, left her a widow at the early age of twenty-two; and though the widowed Duchess was rich, one of the most celebrated beauties of the Court, and of irreproachable character, she did not marry again until 1698, when she gave her hand to the graceful and accomplished Thomas Hanmer, then a handsome youth of twenty-one. The private account book of the Duchess, from the year 1708, ten years after her second marriage, and when she was beginning to fall into the "sere and yellow leaf," is exceedingly interesting. Within the cover is written with child-like simplicity, "Isabella Grafton is my name." The spelling of her Grace affords us a very sorry example of the education of ladies of high birth in that age : "*Pade for four peaces of Turkey taby,*" is a specimen of the Duchess's orthography. It appears that the Duchess had £500 a-year allowed her as pin-money, a rare pittance for a woman of her rank and independent fortune. Operas and card parties appear to have been her principal amusements, but what more could be expected when the Duchess of Marlborough says that Queen Anne never read, and that cards entirely occupied her thoughts in her youth ; and Miss Strickland remarks that throughout a voluminous correspondence Her Majesty never makes a literary quotation or mentions a book as if she had actually read it. The Duchess was expensive in dress, and apt to lose money at play. The balances every quarter tell always heavily against her, and only once she enters a balance of two guineas in her favour. Such entries as the following occur, "Lost at cards this month £17 4s. Lost to Sir Thos. Hanmer (her husband) £7 10s. 6d." The theatres were the resort of all who pretended to taste, and the Duchess was a frequent visitor. The sums paid at the playhouses and operas are minutely entered, and no traces of hiring of boxes for a term are found. The entrance money was paid at the door, and in 1708 half a guinea (10s. 6d.) ; from 1709 to 1721 it was only 8s. The London season seems to have begun in November, and lasted to the end of June. Presents to the principal actors were regularly made. Mrs. Oldfield, who moved like a goddess among the stiff puppets of the scene, and used the tones of nature on the stage, and the gold-laced, highly powdered, scented, and diamonded Colley Cibber were among the recipients of one guinea. People of fashion seemed to have nursed their children by a contribution levied on their acquaintance at every christening. "To my Lady Hervey's

christening £10 15s." "To my Lady Rebecca Holland's
christening £10 15s." The expense of the sedan chair was
great—the entries are numerous and heavy : "To Ben, the
chair-man, £13." "Paid the chair-men £16 14s." Other
items will be interesting to modern ladies : "For half a yard
of black velvet 8s. 6d." "To Lady Jersey's woman for a
french gownde £20." "Paid to Lady Charlotte de Rouse for a
black-laced scarfe £16." "For a pair of black silk stockings
12s." "A pair of scarlet stockings 7s. 6d." "For three
dozen gloves £3 4s. 6d." "Lutestring for a pettycoat
£4 10s." "For altering of smock 18s." "For cutting
my hair £1 1s. 6d." "To a man for cleaning my teeth 10s."
"To the corn-cutter 10s. 6d." "For a black lace hood £3."
"Paid for a quart of brandy 1s. 3d." "To Mrs. Lilly for 2
pounds of green tea £2 8s." Occasionally there are such
entries as : "Given to the *Mob* 2s. 6d." "To a poor body 6d."
"To the poor people 8d." These, we presume, were her
Grace's charities. Her largesses were much more liberal :
"To the Duke of Grafton's cook £2 3s." "To a woman
who brought French fashions £1 1s. 6d." "Given to a
gentleman of my Lord Bolingbroke's £2 3s." In the literary
line the outlays are very small, but they are not for *trifling*
books : "Atterbury's Sermons 6s." "Nelson's Festivals and
Fasts 5s. 6d." "Cave's Primitive Christianity 6s." "For
Dr. Prideaux's Connexion of the Testaments 15s. ;" and
sometimes the "Flying Post" or the "Evening Post" at 1½d.
each. Six quires of paper, such as a duchess might use,
cost 3s. 10d. "Seven places for the Play at Bury 17s. 6d."
An advertisement in the "Courant" about her Grace's
lost watch-case 3s. 6d. As her Grace waxed in years the
nature of her expenditure varied. The cost of brandy and
Brazil snuff and the losses at cards increased, while operas and
plays ceased to be numbered among the Duchess's expenses.

The old age of cards, drinking, and snuff-taking form a
singular and painful contrast to the innocence of her childhood
and sweetness of her youth, as traced by the good Evelyn.

HABITS OF A COUNTRY SQUIRE IN SUFFOLK, 1790.

The following interesting description of the habits of a country squire and his wife during the latter part of the last century appears in the life of the poet Crabbe, by his son. He says, " On the third day we reached Parham, and I was introduced to a set of manners and customs of which there remains, perhaps, no counterpart in the present day. My great-uncle's establishment was that of the first-rate yeoman of that period—the yeoman that already began to be styled by courtesy an Esquire. Mr. Tovell might possess an estate of some eight hundred pounds per annum, a portion of which he himself cultivated. Educated at a mercantile school, he often said of himself, 'Jack will never make a gentleman;' yet he had a native dignity of mind and of manners which might have enabled him to pass muster in that character with any but very fastidious critics. His house was large; and the surrounding moat, the rookery, the ancient dovecot, and the well-stored fish-ponds, were such as might have suited a gentleman's seat of some consequence; but one side of the house immediately overlooked a farm-yard full of all sorts of domestic animals, and the scene of constant bustle and noise. On entering the house there was nothing at first sight to remind one of the farm—a spacious hall, paved with black and white marble; at one extremity a very handsome drawing-room, and at the other a fine old staircase of black oak, polished till it was as slippery as ice, and having a china clock and a barrel-organ on its landing places. But this drawing-room, a corresponding dining parlour, and a handsome sleeping apartment, were all *tabooed* ground, and made use of on great and solemn occasions only—such as rent days, and an occasional visit with which Mr. Tovell was honoured by a neighbouring peer. At all other times the family and their visitors lived in the old-fashioned kitchen, along with their servants. My great-uncle occupied an arm-chair, or in attacks of gout a couch on one side of a large open chimney. Mrs. Tovell sat at a small table, on which in the evening stood one small candle in an iron candlestick, plying her needle by the feeble glimmer, surrounded by her maids all busy at the same employment; but in winter a noble block of wood, sometimes the whole circumference of a pollard, threw its comfortable warmth and blaze over the apartment.

"At a very early hour in the morning the alarum called the maids, and their mistress also, and if the former were tardy, a louder alarum and more formidable was heard chiding the delay; not that scolding was peculiar to any occasion—it regularly ran on through all the day, like bells on harness, inspiriting the work whether it were done ill or well. After the important business of the dairy and a hasty breakfast, their respective employments were again resumed, that which the mistress took for her especial privilege being the scrubbing of the floors of the state apartments. A new servant, ignorant of her presumption, was found one morning on her knees hard at work on the floor of one of these preserves, and was thus addressed by her mistress, ' *You* wash such floors as these! Give me the brush this instant, and troop to the scullery and wash that, madam . . . . . As true as G—d's in heaven here comes Lord Rochford to call on Mr. Tovell; here, take my mantle (a blue woollen apron), and I'll go to the door.'

" If the sacred apartments had not been opened, the family dined in this wise :—the heads seated in the kitchen, at an old table ; the farm men standing in the adjoining scullery, door open ; the female servants at a side table, called *a bouter* ; with the principals at the table perchance some travelling rat catcher, or tinker, or farrier, or an occasional gardener in his shirt sleeves, his face probably streaming with perspiration.

" On ordinary days, when the dinner was over, the fire replenished, the kitchen sanded and lightly swept over in waves, mistress and maids, taking off their shoes, retired to their chambers for a nap of one hour to the minute. The dogs

and cats commenced their siesta by the fire, Mr. Tovell dozed
in his chair, and no noise was heard except the melancholy
and monotonous cooing of a turtle-dove, varied, however, by
the shrill treble of a canary. After the hour had expired, the
active part of the family were on the alert, the bottles (Mr.
Tovell's tea equipage) placed on the table, and as if by instinct some old acquaintance would glide in for the evening's
carousal, and then another, and another. If four or five arrived, the punch-bowl was taken down, and emptied and filled
again. But whoever came it was comparatively a dull
evening, unless two especial Knights Companions were of the
party; one was a jolly old farmer, with much of the person
and humour of Falstaff, a face as rosy as brandy could make
it, and an eye teeming with subdued merriment, for he had
that prime quality of a joker, superficial gravity; the other
was a relative of the family, a wealthy yeoman, middle-aged,
thin, and muscular. He was a bachelor, and famed for his
indiscriminate attachment to all who bore the name of
woman—young or aged, clean or dirty, a lady or a gipsy, it
mattered not to him—all were equally admired. He had
peopled the village green, and it was remarked that, whoever
was the mother, the children might be recognised in an instant to belong to him. Such was the strength of his constitution that though he seldom went to bed sober he retained
a clear eye and a stentorian voice to his eightieth year, and
coursed when he was ninety. He sometimes rendered the
colloquies over the bowl peculiarly piquant, and as soon as
his voice began to be elevated, one or two of the inmates, my
father for example, withdrew with Mrs. Tovell into her own
sanctum; but I, not being supposed capable of understanding
much of what might be said, was allowed to linger on the
skirts of the festive circle, and the servants being considered
much in the same point of view as the animals dozing on
the hearth, remained to have the full benefit of their wit,
neither producing the slightest restraint nor feeling it themselves."

SIR SIMONDS D'EWES' LOVE LETTER.

The famous antiquary and puritan, Sir Simonds D'Ewes, Bart., M.P. for Sudbury in the Long Parliament, has left us in his autobiography some curious details of his private life. He studied at Cambridge, and having been trained there for the law, he afterwards took up his abode at the Temple. His parsimonious father allowed him but a very niggardly stipend, and both at Cambridge and in the Temple, young D'Ewes, frugal as he was, often found himself short of cash. He commenced reporting law cases, but his delight was " in examining records and other exotic monuments of antiquity."

The attention of D'Ewes was not, however, confined to law and records. He was anxious for a monied wife, and to rich heiresses and family records he devoted himself with intense earnestness. It was his strongest passion to be thought a gentleman, and it was a sad grief to him that some of his family had been of humble occupation. "Seeing," he says, "that Divine Providence had blessed my father with a wife that was the heir of her father's estate, I did not doubt but he would in mercy vouchsafe to me the like happiness." After some unsuccessful attempts at matchmaking, his wish was gratified. A lady was discovered, not "a penniless lass wi' a long pedigree," but an heiress with something in hand and an ample estate in reversion. This lady was the only child of Sir William Clopton, of Kentwell Hall, Suffolk. To Mistress Anne Clopton, before she was *fourteen years of age*, D'Ewes was united in marriage, in October, 1626. It must have been a pitiable rather than an amusing spectacle, to see this precise and formal puritan, who did "firmly believe that I was elected from all eternity," joining hands at the altar to a mere child, for the sake of wedding himself to " pure blood," and a "sole heir." In his autobiography are the following lines :—

"*August the 31st.*—I sent my servant over to Clare with a diamond carcanet (necklace), to be presented to Mistress Clopton, and a letter

x

with it, which being the only lines I sent her during my wooing time, and but short, I have thought good to insert in this place.

"'FAIREST,

"'Blest is the heart and hand that sincerely sends these meaner lines, if another heart and eye graciously deign to pity the wound of the first and the numbness of the latter: and thus may this other poor inclosed carcanet, if not adorn the purer neck, yet be bidden in the private cabinet of her whose humble sweetness and sweet humility deserves the justest honour—the greatest thankfulness. Nature made stones, but opinion jewels ; this, without your milder acceptance and opinion, will prove neither stone nor jewels.   Do but enhappy him that sent it, in the ordinary use of it, who, though unworthy in himself, resolves to continue your humblest servant,

"'SIMONDS D'EWES.'"

ILLEGAL CARPENTERS THREATENED.

Some of our readers will doubtless be very much surprised on perusing the following advertisement, which appeared in the columns of the "Suffolk Chronicle," February 23, 1811, threatening to prosecute any journeyman carpenter working at his trade who had not served the full seven years' apprenticeship, or any master carpenter, or employer, who gave work to such a person.   The advertisement ran as follows :—

"A CAUTION

To Master and Journeymen Carpenters in the Borough of Ipswich, in the County of Suffolk.

"The numerous intrusions on the trade in direct violations of the ancient statutes of the Realm, to the injury of the trade and the public in general, has, by a late decision in the Court of King's Bench, before Lord Ellenborough, been proved by an action of debt under the following statute, to justify all proceedings against those who violate the same :—

Evan v. Hunter.

"By the statute in the fifth year of the reign of Elizabeth, cap. 4, sec. 31, It is enacted that it shall not be lawful for any person or persons to set up, occupy, or exercise the art, mystery, or occupation of a carpenter, except he shall have been brought up therein seven years at least as an apprentice in manner and form aforesaid ; nor set any person at work at the above trade except he shall have been apprenticed as aforesaid, upon pain that every person willingly offending shall forfeit and lose for every default *forty shillings* for every month.

" The defendant, a master carpenter, near Manchester Square, employed a person named Delastone in the above trade, and this was an action of debt to recover the penalties given by the above statute. Delastone not having served an apprenticeship, nor being under indenture at the time, the Jury, under his Lordship's direction, found a verdict for the plaintiff for £20, being ten months' penalty.

" The Trade are happy to say the above case has met the decided approbation of many respectable masters, who have given their great encouragement by discharging every illegal exerciser of the trade from their employ, and therefore hope that every master and journeyman in the Town and Borough of Ipswich will consider it their indispenable duty individually to persevere in maintaining that right so wisely provided by their ancestors.

" N.B.—Any person acting contrary to the above statute, will be proceeded against accordingly by the legal followers of the trade in the Borough of Ipswich."

Distressing as it is to think that such petty tyranny ever existed among working men, we cannot feel too thankful that such injustice has passed away, we trust, for ever.

INSCRIPTION ON THE FOUNDATION-STONE OF CARDINAL WOLSEY'S COLLEGE, AT IPSWICH.

In Ingram's " Memorials of Oxford," speaking of Oxford Cathedral, says, " In the outer division of the Chapter House, against the south wall, is the foundation-stone of Wolsey's College, at Ipswich, rescued from destruction by the Rev. Richard Canning, Rector of Harkstead and Freston, in Suffolk, who found it built into a wall, and bequeathed it to the Dean and Chapter in 1789. The inscription (at length) runs thus :—' Anno Christi, 1528, et Regni Henrici Octavi Regis Angliæ 20, mensis vero Junii 15 positum per Johannun Episcopum Lidensem.' This Bishop was John Holt, titular Bishop of Lydda, and probably a suffrangan of Lincoln."

This passage has excited some controversy, for Mr. Ingram

was the first to read the doubtful contraction lidem, Liden-sem, contrary to the received opinion of most antiquaries, that Lincoln is meant. The foundation-stone of Wolsey's College at Ipswich was laid in the year 1528; but according to Stubbs' "Registrum Sacrum Anglicanum," p. 147, John Holt was not appointed Suffrangen of Lydda until 1530. More-over, as Kirby (" Suffolk Traveller," edit. 1764, p. 48) further remarks, "John Longland, Bishop of Lincoln, did certainly lay the foundation-stone of Wolsey's College at Oxford, and preached a sermon from Prov. ix, 1. That stone was laid 20th March, 1525. As the stone of Wolsey's College at Ipswich was laid a little more than three years after that, it seems not improbable that the same person might be employed on a like occasion at Ipswich. For this reason (and because the word could not mean any other English bishop in that year) we suppose the last word on the inscrip-tion to stand for *Lincoln*. But as the stone would not admit of more letters, that word consists of five only, and is plainly abbreviated in two places, which abbreviations have rendered the meaning of it somewhat doubtful." The Editor of "Notes and Queries," says, " We are inclined to think there must be some defect in this part of the inscription, for Dr. Ingram has 'lidem'; whereas Gough (Camden's 'Britannica,' 11, 85) has 'Liôem'; and in the 'Beauties of England and Wales,' xiv, 253, it is spelt 'Linem.' "

GARDNER, THE HISTORIAN OF DUNWICH.

The remains of Thomas Gardner, the well-known and self-taught historian of Dunwich, are interred under the south wall of Southwold church. He was a *salt officer* of Southwold, that is, resident revenue officer, appointed as collector of duties at the Salt Works, Southwold; and having been twice married, there are three stones to mark the respective graves of himself and each of his wives, interred on either side of him. The inscriptions on the three stones partake of the quaintness and sobriety of the author's living style, and richly deserves to be commemorated in our pages. The stone on the south side records as follows :—

"TO THE MEMORY OF RACHEL, THE WIFE OF THOMAS GARDNER,
WHO DIED 9TH MARCH, 1729, AGED 35 YEARS.
AND RACHEL, THEIR DAUGHTER, WHO DIED APRIL 18TH, 1729,
AGED 12 YEARS.

" Virtue crowned during life
Both the daughter and the wife."

The stone on the north side is thus inscribed :—

" MARY, THE WIFE OF THOMAS GARDNER, DIED 3RD MAY, 1759,
AGED 67 YEARS.

" Honour ever did attend
Her just dealings to the end."

The middlemost stone of the three, which are as close one to the other as though they would indicate that the sleepers beneath them drew most lovingly together, and would not be separated even in death, bears this characteristic notice :—

"IN MEMORY OF THOMAS GARDNER, SALT OFFICER,
WHO DIED MARCH 30TH, 1769,
AGED 79 YEARS.

" Between HONOUR and VIRTUE here doth lie
The remains of old Antiquity."

CURIOUS INSCRIPTION IN BRAMFIELD CHURCH.

The following quaint and unique inscription appears on one of the tablets in the ancient church of Bramfield, a village about nine miles south of Southwold :—

Between the remains of her brother Edward
And of her husband Arthur,
Here lies the body of Bridgett Applewhaite,
Once Bridgett Nelson ;

After the fatigues of a married life,
Borne by her with incredible patience
For four years and three-quarters, bating three weeks,
And after the enjoyment of the glorious freedom
Of an easy and unblemisht widowhood
For four years and upwards,
She resolved to run the risk of a second marriage bed,
    But death forbad the banns ;
And having with an apoplectick dart,
(The same instrument with which he had formerly
    Despatched her mother),
Touched the most vital part of her brain.
She must have have fallen directly to the ground,
    (As one thunder strook),
If she had not been catch't and supported
    By her intended husband ;
    Of which invisible bruise,
After a struggle for above sixty hours
With that grand enemy to life,
(But the certain and merciful friend to helpless old age),
In terrible convulsions, plaintive groans, or stupefying sleep,
Without recovery of her speech or senses,
She died, on the 12th day of Sept , in the year of our Lord, 1737,
          And of her own age 44.

SALE OF ROBERT BLOOMFIELD'S EFFECTS.

The sale catalogue of the goods, books, MSS., and general effects of Robert Bloomfield is an interesting and rare document. We give a few extracts therefrom, as a mournful record of value to all who feel an interest in the author of "The Farmer's Boy."

His books, prints, drawings (215 lots), and furniture (105 lots), were sold in the humble house in which he died, at Shefford, Beds, on the 28th and 29th May, 1824. The far greater number of his books had been presented to him by his friends, viz., the Duke of Grafton (a very liberal contributor), Dr. Drake, James Montgomery, Samuel Rogers, Mrs. Barbauld, Richard Cumberland, Sir James Bland Burges, Capel Lofft, etc. His autograph manuscript of " The Farmer's Boy," elegantly bound, was sold for £14; of "Rural Tales," boards, £4; of "Wild Flowers," for £3 10s.; of "Banks of the Wye," for £3; of "May Day with the Muses" (imperfect) for 10s., and "Description of the Æolian Harp" (he was a maker of æolian harps) for 15s. His few well-executed drawings, by *himself* (view of his City Road cottage and garden, etc.) produced from 5s. to 18s. each. Among his furniture were "A handsome inkstand, presented to him by the celebrated Dr. Jenner" (in return for his sweet poem of "Good Tidings"), and the celebrated oak table which Mr. Bloomfield may be said to have rendered immortal by the beautiful and pathetic poem inscribed to it in his "Wild Flowers." The first was sold for £6 10s. and the second for £14. The original miniature of Bloomfield, an admirable likeness, by Edridge, from which the portrait of him was engraved that was prefixed to the first edition of his Poems, was in 1853 in the possession of the late George Daniel, Esq., of Canonbury, London.

GARRETT'S IRON WORKS,—1765 AND 1865.

There are but few existing large firms that have the means of comparing their position with what it was a century ago. The following advertisement, however, from the pages of the "Ipswich Journal," of 1765, will enable our readers, with the help of a few facts which we shall supply, to contrast the magnitude of the Leiston Works at the present day with the humble position of the great-grandfather of the present head of the firm, a century ago :—

"THIS IS TO INFORM THE PUBLICK,

"That whereas I, Richard Garret, of Woodbridge (late of Ufford), in the county of Suffolk, Blade-smith, have always stamped my Sickles and other Edge-tools with my name, R. GARRET, and have acquired, by using the best steel and great care in the workmanship, a large demand for my wares (especially Sickles and Hoes); but my name, R. Garret, has of late been counterfeited, and stamped on sale Sickles and Hoes by some bad person or persons in or near Sheffield, in Yorkshire, and been sold wholesale to several shops in Norwich, Yarmouth, Harleston, Diss, Beccles, Bungay, Halesworth, Lowestoft, and many other towns and country shops in the counties of Suffolk and Norfolk at Ten shillings a dozen at most, which Sickles and Hoes have been retailed for my make at Eighteen-pence each (the price mine are sold at) to Farmers and poor Laborers, when such sale Sickles and Hoes ought not to be sold for more than Fourteen-pence each, and profit sufficient for an honest man.

"Now for preventing such an imposition on the Public and prejudice to myself I have added a star to my former Mark on my Sickles and Hoes, &c., and am resolved the Law shall determine whether such Makers and Sellers have a right to act as above without being punished as cheats and counterfeits.

"R. GARRET."

Let us now glance at the origin, progress, and present condition of Leiston Iron Works.

The origin of Leiston Works is to be dated from 1778, in which year the son of the above-named Richard Garrett went from Woodbridge and commenced business at Leiston in the trade followed by his father, viz., "Sickle and Edge-tool Maker and Blade Smith." He employed a wheel worked by a single horse, to drive a grindstone, and had at most from eight to ten men. The business did not increase beyond this in his time.

He was succeeded by his son in 1805, who in his turn relinquished the works in favour of the present head of the firm in 1836, and died the year after. He, as well as his father and grandfather, excelled in the production of tools used in husbandry, though till the year 1806 the sickle was the chief instrument of their manufacture. At this period Mr. Garrett engaged in making a threshing machine, patented by Mr. John Ball, of Hetheringsett, near Norwich, the first of its kind that was usefully applied to threshing purposes in this country. This was considered a serious undertaking for one in Mr. Garrett's humble position, but as the speculation succeeded beyond the most sanguine expectations of the patentee, it brought both him and the manufacturer into great repute amongst the agriculturists of the Eastern counties of England.

With the advent, however, of the present Mr. Richard Garrett as head of the firm, the prosperous state of the Leiston Works may be said to commence. In him great self-possession and force of character are united, and intimately acquainted as he was with the manufacture of agricultural implements from his youth upwards, he, when the whole weight of the business rested on his shoulders, applied himself with great energy to carry out the various projects which he considered essential to the successful working of this industrial community. When, in the spring of 1836, the business was relinquished in his favour, about sixty men and eight or ten horses were employed; no steam power up to that period had been brought into use. Now the number of hands is from six hundred to seven hundred, besides which employment is found for five powerful steam engines, a steam hammer, and all sorts of appliances for working in iron and wood, boiler making, cast and malleable iron foundry, gas works, etc., etc. There is a tramway directly through the Works, which also places them in direct communication with the Railway. The space occupied by the shops, etc., is upwards of ten acres. Garrett & Sons have at the present time agents for their machinery in all the principal towns of Great Britain and Ireland, and depots in the leading cities and towns in Europe, India, and Australia. They have received from various societies twenty gold and sixty-eight silver medals, besides twelve hundred pounds in cash, and have been distinguished by the highest possible awards at each of the Great International Exhibitions, viz., London, 1861 and 1862; Dublin, 1853; Paris, 1855; London, 1862; Hamburg, 1863.

Entering the Works, the offices are on the left hand, and attached to them are a suite of private offices. The ninety feet shaft is a prominent object for miles round. The engine-house is formed by a set of three gigantic boilers made by the firm. The portable engine erecting shop is ninety feet by fifty feet, sufficiently large for nine engines, four or five a week being fitted. It contains a magnificent collection of planing, slotting, and boring machines, and some remarkably fine lathes. The manufacture of road locomotives is becoming an important branch of the business carried on by the firm; the steam ploughing and cultivating apparatus is also extensively manufactured. It is adapted for hilly as well as for flat land, and as many as forty or even fifty acres of land can be advantageously cultivated without any removal of the engine or windlass. From seven to ten acres per day can be broken up with an ordinary eight or ten horse portable engine, which is also available for threshing.

Adjoining the engine erecting shops, are the stores—marvellous in regard to quantities. Above this shop are galleries used for fitting.

The "testing shop" or "break house" is an important part of the Works, for here all the engines are examined by one of the firm. In the boiler-house there are usually one hundred boilers in stock, of from twenty-three to twenty-five horse power. The steam sawing mills are large and suitable, and the beautiful morticing and tenoning machines are particularly worthy of notice. There is also in this shop one large sawing frame with forty-eight saw blades, and marvellous as the statement may appear, it is a fact that by the aid of this machine the largest tree ever grown can be cut into boards in thirty seconds! It will cut the largest, roughest, or most crooked tree grown in England, as the grain runs.

The threshing machine was one of the first agricultural implements to which the attention of this firm was directed, and nearly two thousand machines have been made at the Leiston Works during the last sixteen years.

The iron foundry is a hundred and twenty-five feet by a hundred and twenty-five, there being three cupolas. Founding is either in casting any quantity of metal in the solid, or with a score (by means of which the metal is preserved of a determined thickness or substance) or in plain casting. In the smithy, which is a hundred and forty feet by eighty feet, there are eighty forges and two steam forges. Adjoining is one of the lathe shops, and above are large fitting shops. The inward and outward traffic of the Works ranges between 15,000 and 20,000 tons annually; that is, so much material of all sorts goes in in a rough state and comes out in a manufactured form.

Near the Works is a large building constructed at the sole cost of Mr. Richard Garrett, Sen., known as the Works' Hall. It is a Mechanics' Institute, Reading Room, and Lecture Hall, and also a depot for the Ninth Suffolk, or Leiston Works' Rifle Corps.

SOLEMN LEAGUE AND COVENANT.

At a meeting of the Society of Antiquaries, on the 11th of December, 1851, the Rev. R. B. Exton, of Cretingham, in Suffolk, exhibited an original roll containing the Solemn League and Covenant, as subscribed in that parish, on the 20th March, 1643. The signatures attached are those of "Ro Sayer" (vicar of Cretingham from 1634 to 1650), and forty-three of his parishioners, of whom seventeen only signed by marks.

MARRIAGES A CENTURY AGO.

A curious feature connected with Marriage in the middle of the last century—the publishing of the dower of the lady in the announcement of the marriage, is shown by the following extract taken from the Fitch MSS. in the Ipswich Museum. It relates to the daughter of Dr. Messenger Monsey, an eccentric physician, who resided at Bury St. Edmund's. The date is December, 1753.

"Yesterday was married at Lee church, in Kent, Mr. William Alexander, an eminent merchant, to Miss Monsey, daughter of Dr. Monsey, a lady of £6000 fortune."

CURIOUS INSCRIPTIONS.

The following inscription was found in the kitchen of Gippeswyk Hall, Ipswich. Supposed date, the beginning of the sixteenth century. It is still preserved.

He. that.
seteth. do
wn. to. mete.
and. leteth.
grace. pas.
Sēteth. do
wn. leik. a
n. oxe. and
ryseth. leik.
a. nase.

[He that sitteth down to meat, and letteth grace pass, sitteth down like an ox, and riseth like an ass.]

A short time since, there was at the "King's Head," at Stutton, the following poetical invitation to weary travellers:

"Good people, stop, and pray walk in,
Here's foreign brandy, rum, and gin;
And, what is more, good purl and ale,
Are both sold here by old Nat Dale."

Over the door of a chandler's shop at Drinkstone, in August, 1776, as recorded by the newspapers of that date, there was a sign-board with the following inscription:—

" Hear Liss one woo Cuers a Goos,
Gud. Dare. Bako sole Hare."

The information the village scribe wished to convey is contained in these words:—" Here lives one who cures agues. Good beer. Tobacco sold here."

It was formerly the practice to inscribe knives with mottoes. There was, in the collection of the late Mr. Mills, of Norwich, a knife with a brass handle, of the period of Charles II., and which was found at Woodbridge, on which the following distich was inscribed :—

> " He that doth a good knife lack,
> Buy me, I am steel unto the back."

It was with our forefathers a common practice to inscribe church bells with mottoes, sacred and otherwise. The following is on a bell at Clare, in the church of St. Peter and St. Paul :—

> " While thus we join in cheerful sound,
> Let love and loyalty abound.
>
> " Mears, London, fecit, 1779."

On the tenor bell at Kersey church is this inscription :—

> " Samuel Sampson, churchwarden, I say,
> Caused me to be made by Colchester Grayc.
> " 1638."

POSIES ON RINGS.

Some old rings with inscriptions, called " Posies," have been found in various parts of Suffolk.

Upon one found in Ixworth church :—

> " God alone made vs two one."

Upon one found near Woodbridge :—

> " If in my love thou constant bee,
> My heart shall never part from thee."

Upon a small but massive lady's ring found at Hundon:—

> " I like my choyse."

Upon one found at Westleton :—

> " Love Virtue."

Upon one found at Dunwich :—

> " Let Virtue be
> A guide to thee."

THE SMALLEST PULPIT IN SUFFOLK.

The pulpit in Stoke-by-Clare church, is probably the *smallest* in the county of Suffolk. It is octangular, and its interior diameter only 20½ inches. It is handsomely decorated with well designed tracery work, carved in oak, of which material the pulpit also is formed. The whole is in excellent condition.

III.

--

Selections from Suffolk Poets, Bards, and Rhymers.

III.

Selections from Suffolk Poets, Bards, and Rhymers.

EPISODE OF ROSIPHELE.

BY JOHN GOWER.

JOHN GOWER is supposed to have been born some time about the year 1325, and to have consequently been a few years older than Chaucer. He was a gentleman possessing a considerable amount of land in the county of Suffolk. He wrote a poetical work in three parts, the last part of which was a grave dissertation on the Morals and Metaphysics of Love ; and the solemn sententiousness of this work caused Chaucer to denominate its author " The Moral Gower."

Rosiphele, Princess of Armenia, a lady of surpassing beauty, but insensible to the power of love, is represented by the poet as reduced to an obedience to Cupid by a vision which befell her on a May-day ramble. The opening of this episode is as follows :—

> When come was the month of May,
> She would walk upon a day,
> And that was ere the sun arist,
> Of women but a few, it wist ;*

> * Few of her women knew of it.

Y

And forth she went privily,
Unto a park was fast by,
All soft walk, and on the grass,
Till she came there the land was,
Through which ran a great river,
It thought her fair ; and said, here
I will abide under the shaw,*
And bade her women to withdraw ;
And there she stood alone still,
To think what was in her will.
She saw the sweet flowers spring,
She heard glad fowls sing,
She saw beasts in their kind :
The buck, the doe, the hart, the hind,
The males go with the female ;
And so began there a quarrel
Between love and her own heart,
Fro which she could not astart.
And as she cast her eye about,
She saw clad in one suit, a rout
Of ladies, where they comen ride
Along under the woode side,
On fair ambuland horse they set,
That were all white, fair, and great ;
And everich one ride on side,
The saddles were of such a pride ;
So rich saw she never none,
With pearls and gold so well begone,
In kirtles and in copes rich,
They were clothed all alich,
Departed even of white and blue,
With all lusts that she knew.
They were embroidered over all :
Their bodies weren long and small,
The beauty of their fair face
There may be none earthly thing deface :
Crowns on their heads they bare,
As each of them a queen were ;
That all the gold of Crœsus' hall
The least coronal of all

* A grove.

Might not have bought, after the worth ;
Thus comen they ridand forth.

In the rear of this splendid troop of ladies, the princess
beheld one mounted on a miserable steed, wretchedly adorned
in everything excepting the bridle.　On questioning this
straggler why she was so unlike her companions, the visionary
lady replied that the latter were receiving the bright
reward of having loved faithfully, and that she herself was
suffering punishment for cruelty to her admirers.　The
reason that the bridle alone resembled those of her companions was, that for the last fortnight she had been sincerely
in love, and a change for the better was in consequence
beginning to show itself in her accoutrements.　The parting
words of the dame are—

Now have ye heard mine answer ;
To God, madam, I you betake,
And warneth all for my sake,
Of love that they be not idle,
And bid them think of my bridle.

It is scarcely necessary to remark that the hard heart
of the Princess of Armenia is duly impressed by this lesson.

THE LONDON LYCKPENNY.

BY JOHN LYDGATE.

John Lydgate, the chief immediate follower of Chaucer
and Gower, is supposed to have been born at Lydgate, in
Suffolk.　He was a monk of Bury St. Edmund's, and his
poetical compositions range over a variety of styles.　"His
muse," says Warton, "was of universal access ; and he was
not only the poet of the monastery, but of the world in
general."　The principal works of this versatile writer are
entitled, "The History of Thebes," "The Fall of Princes,"
and "The Destruction of Troy."　He at one time kept a
school in the monastery for the instruction of young persons

in the art of versification. A poem of his, called "The London Lyckpenny," is curious for the particulars it gives respecting the city of London in the early part of the fifteenth century. The poet has come to town in search of legal redress for some wrong, and visits in succession the King's Bench, the Court of Common Pleas, the Court of Chancery, and Westminster Hall.

> Within the hall, neither rich, nor yet poor
>   Would do for me aught, although I should die ;
> Which seeing, I gat me out of the door,
>   Where Flemings began on me for to cry,
>   "Master, what will you copen* or buy ?
> Fine felt hats ? or spectacles to read ?
> Lay down your silver, and here you may speed."
>
> Then to Westminster gate I presently went,
>   When the sun was at high prime,
> Cooks, to me, they took good intent,†
>   And proffered me bread, with ale, and wine,
>   Ribs of beef, both fat and full fine ;
> A fair cloth they gan for to spread,
> But, wanting money, I might not be sped.
>
> Then unto London I did me hie,
>   Of all the land it beareth the price :
> "Hot peascods !" one began to cry,
>   "Strawberry ripe, and cherries in the rise !" ‡
>   One bade me come near and buy some spice ;
> Pepper, and saffron they gan me beed ; §
> But for lack of money, I might not speed.
>
> Then to the Cheap I gan me drawn,
>   Where much people I saw for to stand ;
> One offered me velvet, silk, and lawn,
>   Another he taketh me by the hand,
>   "Here is Paris thread, the finest in the land !"
> I never was used to such things indeed,
> And, wanting money, I might not speed.

* *Koopen* (Flemish) is to buy.   † Took notice—paid attention.
        ‡ On the twig.   § Offer.

Then went I forth by London stone,*
  Throughout all Canwick street :
Drapers much cloth me offered anon ;
  Then comes me one cried, "Hot sheep's feet;"
  One cried mackerel, rushes green, another, gan greet,†
One bade me buy a hood to cover my head ;
But, for want of money, I might not be sped.

Then I hied me unto East Cheap,
  One cries ribs a beef, and many a pie ;
Pewter pots they clattered on a heap ;
  There was harp, pipe, and minstrelsy :
  Yea by cock ! nay by cock ! some began cry ;
Some sung of Jenkin and Julian for their meed ;
But, for lack of money, I might not speed.

Then unto Cornhill anon I yode,
  Where was much stolen gear among ;
I saw where hung mine owne hood,
  That I had lost among the throng.
  To buy my own hood I thought it wrong :
I knew it well, as I did my creed ;
But, for lack of money, I could not speed.

The taverner took me by the sleeve,
  "Sir," saith he, "will you our wine essay ?"
I answered, "that can not much me grieve,
  A penny can do no more than it may ;"
  I drank a pint, and for it did pay ;
Yet, sore a hungered, from thence I yede,
And, wanting money, I could not speed, etc.

A PRAISE OF HIS LOVE,

WHEREIN HE REPROVETH THEM THAT COMPARE THEIR LADIES WITH HIS.

BY THE EARL OF SURREY.

Henry Howard, Earl of Surrey, 1516—1546, known as the
first writer of English blank verse, is supposed to have been

---

* A fragment of London stone is still preserved in Cannon street, formerly
called Canwick or Candlewick street.   † Cry.

born in the year 1516 or 1517; but whether at Framlingham, at Tendring Hall, Suffolk, or at Kenninghall in Norfolk, is uncertain. He was beheaded on Tower Hill, January 21st, 1546—7, and his body was interred in the church of All Hallows, Barking Tower Street, and after the lapse of nearly seventy years it was removed to Framlingham by his second son, who erected a stately monument to his memory. The influence which Surrey influenced over English poetry was very great. He is said to have been the first English poet who understood and exemplified the art of translation. He is among the earliest of our love poets: his language is often happy, and never superfluous.

Give place, ye lovers, here before
That spent your boasts and brags in vain:
My lady's beauty passeth more
The best of yours, I dare well sayen,
Than doth the sun the candle light,
Or brightest day the darkest night.

And thereto hath a troth as just
As had Penylope the Fair;
For what she saith, ye may it trust,
As it by writing sealed were:
And virtues hath she many mo'
Than I with pen have skill to show.

I could rehearse, if that I would,
The whole effect of Nature's plaint,
When she had lost the perfect mould,
The like to whom she could not paint;
With wringing hands, how she did cry,
And what she said I know it, aye.

I know she swore with raging mind,
Her kingdom only set apart,
There was no loss by law of kind
That could have gone so near her heart;
And this was chiefly all her pain;
" She could not make the like again."

Sith Nature thus gave her the praise,
To be the chiefest work she wrought ;
In faith, methink, some better ways
On your behalf might well be sought,
Than to compare, as ye have done,
To match the candle with the sun.

AN EPITAPH ON CLERE, SURREY'S FAITHFUL FRIEND AND FOLLOWER.*

Norfolk sprung thee, Lambeth holds thee dead ;
Clere, of the Count of Cleremont, thou hight
Within the womb of Ormond's race thou bred,
And saw'st thy cousin crowned in thy sight.
Shelton for love, Surrey for lord, thou chase ; †
(Aye, me ! whilst life did last that league was tender),
Tracing whose steps thou sawest Kelsal blaze,
Landrecy burnt, and battered Boulogne render. ‡
At Montreuil gates, hopeless of all recure,
Thine Earl, half dead, gave in thy hand his will ;
Which cause did thee this pining death procure
Ere summers four times seven thou couldst fulfil.

---

* Thomas Clere, whose family, of Clere-mont, in Normandy, came into England with the Conqueror, was the youngest son of Sir Robert Clere, of Ormesby, in Norfolk, and Alice, daughter of Sir William Boleyn, by Margaret, daughter and co-heir of the Earl of Ormond. Hence the allusions in the Epitaph to his being sprung from Norfolk, having been born at Ormesby ; to the Count of Cleremont, from whom he derived his name ; and to his cousin, Anne Boleyn, at whose coronation he is here stated to have been present. The Shelton, whom he is stated to have chosen for love, was one of the daughters of Sir John Shelton, of Shelton, in Norfolk ; but there is no evidence of his having been married to her. He was a follower and friend of Surrey, and attended him as his page. Surrey was greatly attached to him, and amongst other proofs of his friendship, made over to him all his rights in the Manor of Wyndham, which he had received by grant from the King. Clere died on the 14th of April, 1545, and was buried at Lambeth, in a chapel belonging to the Howard family, where the above verses were engraved on a tablet, placed on a wall near the tomb.

† Did choose.

‡ These lines allude to the expeditions to Kelsal, in Scotland; Landrecy, in the Netherlands ; and Boulogne, in France ; at which Clere was present in his attendance on Surrey.

Ah! Clere ! if love had booted care or cost,
   Heaven had not won, nor earth so timely lost. *

ON THE DEATH OF SIR THOMAS WYATT.

Wyatt resteth here, that quick could never rest ;
   Whose heavenly gifts increased by disdain ;
And virtue sank the deeper iu his breast,
   Such profit he by envy could obtain.

A head, where wisdom mysteries did frame ;
   Whose hammers beat still in that lively brain
As on a stithe,† where that same work of fame
   Was daily wrought, to turn to Britain's gain.

A visage stern and mild, where both did grow
   Vice to contemn, in virtue to rejoice :
Amid great storms, whom grace assured so
   To live upright, and smile at fortune's choice.

A hand, that taught what might be said in rhyme,
   That reft Chaucer the glory of his wit,
A mark, the which (unperfected for time)
   Some may approach, but never none shall hit.

A tongue, that served in foreign realms his King ;
   Whose courteous talk to virtue did inflame
Each noble heart; a worthy guide to bring
   Our English youth by travail unto fame.

An eye, whose judgment none affect ‡ could blind,
   Friends to allure, and foes to reconcile ;
Whose piercing look did represent a mind
   With virtue fraught, reposed § void of guile.

  * These lines explain their own story. Clere, in a moment of peril, when he was protecting his wounded friend at one of the gates at Montreuil, received a wound, from the consequences of which he lingered several months, and ultimately died.

  † A blacksmith's anvil. The shed or shop containing the anvil was called a *stithy*, now *smithy*.

  ‡ Sometimes printed *effect*—affection, passion.

  § In the sense of calmly fixed—resolved.

A heart, where dread was never so imprest
    To hide the thought that might the truth advance ;
In neither fortune loft,* nor yet represt
    To swell in wealth, or yield unto mischance.

A valiant corpse,† where force and beauty met:
    Happy, alas ! too happy, but for foes,
Lived, and ran the race that nature set
    Of manhood's shape, where she the mould did lose.

But to the heavens that simple soul is fled,
    Which left, with such as covet Christ to know,
Witness of faith, that never shall be dead ;
    Sent for our health, but not received so.

Thus for our guilt this jewel have we lost ;
The earth his bones, the heavens possess his ghost.

GOOD ALE.

BY JOHN STILL, D.D., BISHOP OF BATH AND WELLS.

John Still, 1543—1607, was born at Grantham, in Lincoln-shire. Having been sent to Christ's College, Cambridge, he was elected to a Fellowship there in 1560. He became famous as a preacher, and was appointed Lady Margaret Professor of Divinity, in 1570 ; Chaplain to Archbishop Parker, and Rector of Hadleigh, in 1571 ; Master of Trinity College, in 1577 ; and Bishop of Bath and Wells, in 1592. He was the author of a " Ryght Pythy, Pleasaunt, and Merie Comedie, intytuld, Gammer Gurton's Needle. London, 1595," the second act of which opens with the following " drinking song," which is valuable for its vein of simplicity and humour, and for its being the first drinking ballad of any merit in our language. Original copies of this play are very rare. One sold at the Duke of Roxburgh's sale, in 1812, for £8 8s. ; another copy sold, in 1825, for £10 ; and one at the sale of Mr. Daniel's collection, in 1864, for £64 !

    * Lofty—prosperous.   † Body.

I cannot eat but little meat,
   My stomach is not good ;
But sure I think that I can drink
   With him that wears a hood.
Though I go bare, take ye no care,
   I am nothing a colde ;
I stuffe my skin so full within
   Of joly good ale and old.

      Back and side, go bare, go bare,
        Booth foot and hand go colde ;
      But belly, God send thee good ale i'noughe,
        Whether it be new or old.

I love no rost, but a nut-browne toste,
   And a crab laid in the fire ;
A little bread shall do me stead,
   Moche bread I not desire.
No frost, no snow, no winde, I trow,
   Can hurte me if I wolde :
I am so wrapt and throwly lapt
   Of joly good ale and old.

      Back and side go bare, etc.

And Tib, my wife, that as her life,
   Loveth well good ale to seeke,
Full ofte drinks shee, till ye may see
   The tears run downe her cheeke ;
Then dooth she trowle to me her bowle,
   E'en as a mault worm sholde ;
And saith, " Sweet heart, I tooke my part
   Of this joly good ale and old."

      Back and side go bare, etc.

Now let them drink, till they nod and winke,
   E'en as good fellows should do ;
They shall not misse to have the blisse
   Good ale dooth bringe men to ;
And all good sowles that have scoured bowles,
   Or have them lustely trolde,
God save the lives of them and their wives,
 , Whether they be young or old.

      Back and side go bare, etc.

BALLAD UPON A WEDDING.

BY SIR JOHN SUCKLING.

Sir John Suckling [1608—1642], born at Twickenham, baptised there February 10th, 1608—9; resided at Barsham, Suffolk; was M.P. in the Long Parliament; became a staunch adherent of Charles I., and fled to France on the discovery of a plot, in which he joined, to rescue Strafford from the Tower. He died at Paris, it is said, by suicide, in the thirty-fourth year of his age. His "Ballad on a Wedding" is equal to the pictures of Chaucer.

I tell thee, Dick, where I have been,
Where I the rarest things have seen ;
   Oh, things without compare !
Such sights again cannot be found
In any place on English ground,
   Be it at wake or fair.

At Charing Cross, hard by the way
Where we (thou know'st) do sell our hay,
   There is a house with stairs ;
And there did I see coming down
Such folk as are not in our town,
   Vorty at least, in pairs.

Amongst the rest, one pest'lent fine,
(His beard no bigger, though, than thine),
   Walk'd on before the rest ;
Our landlord looks like nothing to him :
The King, God bless him ! 'twould undo him,
   Should he go still so drest.

    *   *   *   *

But wot you what? the youth was going
To make an end of all his wooing ;
   The parson for him staid ;
Yet by his leave, for all his haste,
He did not so much wish all past,
   Perchance, as did the maid.

The maid, and thereby hangs a tale,
For such a maid no Whitsun ale *
    Could ever yet produce ;
No grape that's kindly ripe could be
So round, so plump, so soft as she,
    Nor half so full of juice.

Her finger was so small, the ring
Would not stay on which they did bring,
    It was too wide a peck:
And, to say truth (for out it must),
It look'd like the great collar (just)
    About our young colt's neck.

Her feet beneath her petticoat
Like little mice stole in and out,
    As if they fear'd the light.
But oh ! she dances such a way !
No sun upon an Easter day†
    Is half so fine a sight.

     *   *   *   *

Her cheeks so rare a white was on,
No daisy makes comparison ;
    Who sees them is undone,
For streaks of red were mingled there,
Such as are on a Cath'rine pear,
    The side that's next the sun.

Her lips were red, and one was thin,
Compar'd to that was next her chin,
    Some bee had stung it newly ;
But, Dick, her eyes so guard her face,
I durst no more upon them gaze
    Than on the sun in July.

   * Whitsun ales were festive assemblies of the people of whole parishes at Whit-Sunday.
   † This allusion to Easter-day is founded upon a beautiful old superstition of the English peasantry that the sun dances upon that morning.

Her mouth so small, when she does speak,
Thou'dst swear her teeth her words did break,
 That they might passage get ;
But she so handled still the matter,
They came as good as ours, or better,
 And are not spent a whit.

  •   ‘   ’   *

Passion, oh me ! how I run on !
There's that that would be thought upon,
 I trow, besides the bride :
The bus'ness of the kitchen's grate,
For it is fit that men should eat ;
 Nor was it there denied.

Just in the nick, the cook knock'd thrice,
And all the waiters in a trice
 His summons did obey :
Each serving man, with dish in hand,
March'd boldly up, like our train'd-band,
 Presented, and away.

When all the meat was on the table,
What man of knife, or teeth, was able
 To stay to be entreated ?
And this the very reason was,
Before the parson could say grace,
 The company were seated.

Now hats fly off, and youths carouse ;
Healths first go round, and then the house,
 The bride's came thick and thick ;
And when 'twas nam'd another's health,
Perhaps he made it her's by stealth,
 And who could help it, Dick ?

O' th' sudden, up they rise, and dance ;
Then sit again, and sigh, and glance ;
 Then dance again, and kiss.
Thus sev'ral ways the time did pass,
Till ev'ry woman wish'd her place,
 And ev'ry man wish'd his.

By this time all were stol'n aside
To counsel and undress the bride :
    But that he must not know ;
But yet 'twas thought he guess'd her mind,
And did not mean to stay behind
    Above an hour or so.

LINES TO THE MISSES HARLAND.

BY THE REV. WILLIAM BROOME.

The Rev. William Broome, died 1745. He was a native
of Cheshire, was educated on the foundation at Eton, and
afterwards sent to St. John's College, Cambridge, by the
contributions of his friends. In 1713, he was presented by
Lord Cornwallis to the rectory of Stuston, Suffolk, where he
married a wealthy widow. In 1720, he was presented by his
Lordship, to whom he was chaplain, to the rectory of Oakley,
and in 1728, he was presented by the Crown to the rectory
of Pulham, in Norfolk, and in the same year to the vicarage
of Eye. He died at Bath, November the 16th, 1745, and
was interred in the Abbey Church. Though it cannot be
said that he was a great poet, yet he cannot be thought a
mean one whom Pope chose for an associate in translating
the "Odyssey" of Homer. Pope's enemies attacked him in
a way that gave great praise to Broome, as the following
lines of Henley will show :—

"Pope came off clean with Homer ; but they say
    Broome went before, and kindly *swept the way.*"

Broome's share in the work was the translation of eight
books : the 2nd, 6th, 8th, 11th, 12th, 16th, 18th, and 23rd,
together with all the notes. He did not consider himself
liberally treated by Pope, and the disappointed labourer
charged his master with avarice. Pope, in consequence, with

that petty spite which was his strongest characteristic, abused Broome in the " Dunciad," and in the " Bathos."

On hearing Miss Harland (afterwards Lady Gage, of Hengrave), sing, and her sister and herself play on different musical instruments, the following lines were written, at Sproughton, near Ipswich, in 1737, at the seat of Captain, afterwards Admiral Harland, and the ladies were aunts to the late Sir Robert Harland, Bart. of Orwell Park.

> Strange stories of old by poets are told,
>   Of the pow'r of sweet Orpheus's lyre,
> And how that Amphion, if them we rely on,'
>   The bare stones could with motion inspire.
>
> Such hyperboles strained, which may credit have gain'd,
>   I could ne'er be induc'd to believe ;
> But a truth I'll proclaim of two ladies' fair fame,
>   And in that none whatever deceive.
>
> If Miss *Harland* sings, while on tuneful strings,
>   She herself and Miss *Edith* both play ;
> The two here first named, how much so e'er famed,
>   Never charmed hearers more than will they.

REFLECTIONS ON MY OWN SITUATION.

WRITTEN IN T—T-NGST-NE HOUSE OF INDUSTRY, FEBRUARY, 1802,

BY MRS. ANN CANDLER.

Anne Candler [1740—1814], born at Yoxford, November 18th, 1740. Her father was in business as a glover, at Yoxford. In her twenty-second year she married a worthless man belonging to the village of Sproughton, who, a year after her marriage, enlisted into the Guards, and after enduring many privations, she became an inmate of Tattingstone Workhouse, and was there secluded from the world for nearly twenty years. Here she frequently indulged the poetic faculty, and her case and her abilities being made known to Mrs. Elizabeth Cobbold, that lady generously

came forward to help her. Ann Candler's poems were
collected, and under the favourable auspices of Mrs.
Cobbold, published in a small volume. By this means a
sum of money was raised, which enabled her to leave
the workhouse, and hire lodgings for herself. She first
lived at Copdock, and afterwards at Holton, near Stratford
St. Mary, where she died, on the 15th September, 1814,
aged seventy-four.

How many years are past and gone,
   How alter'd I appear,
How many strange events have known,
   Since first I entered here!

Within these dreary walls confin'd,
   A lone recluse I live,
And, with the dregs of human kind,
   A niggard alms receive.

Uncultivated, void of sense,
   Unsocial, insincere;
Their rude behaviour gives offence,
   Their language wounds the ear.

Disgusting objects swarm around,
   Throughout confusions reign;
Where feuds and discontent abound,
   Remonstrance proves in vain.

No sympathising friend I find,
   Unknown is friendship here:
Not one to soothe or calm the mind,
   When overwhelmed with care.

Peace, peace, my heart, thy duty calls,
   With cautious steps proceed;
Beyond these melancholy walls,
   I've found a friend indeed.

I gaze on numbers in distress,
   Compare their state with mine;
Can I reflect, and not confess
   A Providence divine?

And I might bend beneath the rod,
    And equal want deplore,
But that a good and gracious God
    Is pleased to give me more.

My gen'rous friends, with feeling heart,
    Remove the pond'rous weight,
And those impending ills avert
    Which want and woes create.

Yet what am I, that I should be
    Thus honor'd and carest?
And why such favours heaped on me,
    And with such friendship blest?

Absorb'd in thought, I often sate
    Within my lonely cell,
And mark'd the strange mysterious fate
    That seem'd to guide me still.

When keenest sorrow urg'd her claim,
    When evils threaten'd dread,
Some unexpected blessing came,
    And rais'd my drooping head.

In youth strange fairy tales I've read,
    Of magic skill and pow'r,
And mortals in their sleep convey'd
    To some enchanted tower.

In this obscure and lone retreat,
    Conceal'd from vulgar eyes,
Two rival genii us'd to meet,
    And counterplots devise.

The evil genius, prone to ill,
    Mischievous schemes invents;
Pursues the fated mortal still,
    And ev'ry woe augments.

Insulted with indignant scorn,
    Aw'd by tyrannic sway;
A prey to grief each rising morn,
    And cheerless all the day.

z

But fate and fortune in their scenes
  A pleasing change decree :
The friendly genius intervenes,
  And sets the captive free.

Content and freedom thus regain'd,
  Depriv'd of both before ;
So great the blessing, when obtain'd,
  What can he wish for more ?

The tales these eastern writers feign,
  Like facts to me appear ;
The fabled sufferings they contain
  I find no fiction here.

And since, in these romantic lays,
  My miseries combine,
To bless my lengthen'd wane of days,
  Their bright reverse be mine.

Look down, O God! in me behold
  How helpless mortals are,
Nor leave me friendless, poor, and old,
  But guide me with thy care.

A FARMER'S WIFE IN OLD TIMES.

BY ROBERT BLOOMFIELD.

Robert Bloomfield [1766-1823], a natve of Honington, in Suffolk, was the youngest son of a tailor, who died before Robert was a year old, leaving a widow with six children. At the age of eleven Robert went as " Farmer's Boy " to Mr. Austin, a farmer at Sapiston; but his mother being unable to provide with him clothes, he was after a short time placed in charge of his elder brother George, in London, to learn the art of shoemaking. A knowledge of reading and writing was all that he had acquired in the country, but being furnished with a few books in London, he as he verged towards manhood, improved his education, and whilst working with six or seven men in a garret, he composed, mentally, his poem of "The Farmer's Boy," and a great portion of it was composed, arranged and re-arranged without committing a line to paper. The poem was rejected by several publishers, and ultimately issued through the exertions of Capel Lofft, Esq., who generously aided the poor poet. Its success was so great that 20,000 copies were sold in three years, and editions were published in German, French, and Italian. He published several more volumes of poetry, but unfortunately died in poverty in the fifty-seventh year of his age, at Shefford, in Bedfordshire.

> Forth comes the maid, and like the morning smiles,
> The Mistress, too, and follow'd close by Giles ;
> A friendly tripod forms their humble seat,
> With pails bright scour'd and delicately sweet ;
> Where shadowing elms obstruct the morning ray,
> Begins the work, begins the simple lay ;
> The full charged udder yields its willing streams,
> While Mary sings some lover's amorous dreams ;
> And crouching Giles, beneath a neighbouring tree,
> Tugs o'er his pail and chants with equal glee ;
> Whose hat with tatter'd brim, of nap so bare,
> From the cow's side purloins a coat of hair,
> A mottled ensign of his harmless trade,
> An unambitious, peaceable cockade.
> As unambitious, too, that cheerful aid
> The mistress yields besides her rosy maid !
> With joy she views her plenteous reeking store,
> And bears a brimmer to the dairy door.

SUFFOLK CHEESE.

> Unrival'd stands thy country cheese, O Giles !
> Whose very name alone engenders smiles ;
> Whose fame abroad by every tongue is spoke,
> The well-known butt of many a flinty joke,
> That pass like current coin the nation through ;
> And ah ! Experience proves the satire true.
> Provision's grave, thou ever craving mart,
> Dependent, huge metropolis ! where Art
> Her poring thousands stows in breathless rooms,

Mid'st pois'nous smokes and steams and rattling looms;
Where grandeur revels in unbounded stores,
Restraint, a slighted stranger at their doors ;
Thou, like a whirlpool, drain'st the countries round,
Till London market, London price resound
Through every town, round every passing load,
And dairy produce throngs the Eastern road.
Delicious veal and butter every hour
From Essex lowlands, and the banks of Stour,
And further far, where numerous herds repose,
From Orwell's brink, from Waveny or Ouse.
Hence, Suffolk dairy-wives run mad for cream,
And leave their milk with nothing but its name—
Its name derision and reproach pursue ;
And strangers tell of " three times skimm'd sky blue."
To cheese converted, what can be its boast ?
What but the common virtues of a post !
If drought o'ertake it faster than the knife,
Most fair it bids for stubborn length of life ;
And like the oaken shelf whereon 'tis laid,
Mocks the weak efforts of the bending blade ;
Or in the hog-trough rests in perfect spite,
Too big to swallow, and too hard to bite.
Inglorous victory ! Ye Cheshire meads,
Or Severn's flow'ry dales, where plenty treads,
Were your rich milk to suffer wrongs like these,
Farewell your pride ! farewell, renown'd cheese !
The skimmer dread, whose ravages alone,
Thus turn the mead's sweet nectar into stone.

HARVEST HOME.

Now e'er sweet Summer bids its long adieu,
And winds blow keen where late the blossom grew ;
The bustling day and jovial night must come,
The long accustom'd feast of Harvest Home.
No blood-stain'd victory, in story bright,
Can give the philosophic mind delight ;
No triumph please, while rage and death destroy,
Reflection sickens at the monstrous joy.
And where the joy, if rightly understood,
Like cheerful praise for universal good ?
The soul, nor cheek, nor doubtful anguish knows,

But free and pure the grateful current flows.
Behold the sound oak table's massy frame,
Bestride the kitchen floor ! the careful dame
And generous host invite their friends around,
For all that clear'd the crop or tilled the ground,
Are guests by right of custom ; old and young,
And many a neighbouring yeoman join the throng,
With artizans, that lent their dext'rous aid,
When o'er each field the flaming sunbeams played.

Yet plenty reigns, and from her boundless hoard,
Though not one jelly trembles on the board,
Supplies the feast with all that sense can crave,
With all that made our great forefathers brave:
Ere the cloy'd palate countless flavours tried,
And cooks had Nature's judgment set aside.
With thanks to Heaven, and tales of rustic lore,
The mansion echoes when the banquet's o'er ;
A wider circle spreads, and smiles abound,
As quick the frothing horn performs its round ;
Care's mortal foe, that sprightly joys imparts,
To cheer the frame and elevate their hearts ;
Here, fresh and brown, the hazel's produce lies,
In tempting heaps, and peals of laughter rise ;
And crackling music, with the frequent song,
Unheeded, bear the midnight hour along.

Here once a year Distinction low'rs its crest,
The master, servant, and the merry guest
Are equal all ; and round the happy ring
The reaper's eyes exulting glances fling,
And warm'd with gratitude, he quits his place,
With sunburnt hands and ale enliven'd face,
Refills the jug, his honor'd post to tend,
To save at once the master and the friend ;
Proud thus to meet his smiles, to share his tale,
His nuts, his conversation, and his ale.

Such were the days—of days long past I sing,
When Pride gave place to Mirth without a sting ;
Ere tyrant custom's strength sufficient bore,
To violate the feelings of the poor.

AN ELEGY ON THE ENCLOSURE OF HONINGTON GREEN.

BY NATHANIEL BLOOMFIELD.

Nathaniel Bloomfield was a brother of the author of " The Farmer's Boy," and was born at Honington. The spot which is the subject of the following ballad was less than half-an acre in extent; but it was an ornament to the village, and to the Bloomfields, whose cottage was close by, every circumstance gave it peculiar endearment. Capel Lofft said, that as a poetical effusion, this elegy had the tone, simplicity, sweetness, and pleasing melancholy of the ballad.

Nathaniel had the honour of a lash from Byron, thus :—

> " If Phœbus smiled on you,
> Bloomfield! why not on brother Nathan too ?
> Him too the Mania, not the Muse, has seized ;
> Not inspiration, but a mind diseased :
> And now no boor can seek his last abode,
> No common be enclosed, without an ode."

> The proud City's gay wealthy train,
>   Who nought but refinements adore,
> May wonder to hear me complain
>   That Honington Green is no more ;
> But if to the Church you e'er went,
>   If you knew what the village has been,
> You will sympathise, while I lament
>   The Enclosure of Honington Green.

> That no more upon Honington Green
>   Dwells the Matron whom most I revere,
> If, by pert observation unseen,
>   I e'en could indulge a fond tear ;
> Ere her bright morn of life was o'ercast,
>   When my senses first woke to the scene,
> Some short happy hours she had past
>   On the margin of Honington Green.

> Her parents with plenty were blest,
>   And num'rous her children, and young ;

Youth's blossoms her cheek yet possest,
  And melody woke when she sung,
A Widow so youthful to leave
  (Early clos'd the blest days he had seen),
My Father was laid in his grave,
  In the Churchyard on Honington Green.

I faintly remember the Man
  Who died when I was but a child ;
But far as my young mind could scan,
  His manners were gentle and mild ;
He won infant ears with his lore,
  Nor let young ideas run wild,
Tho' his hand the severe rod of pow'r
  Never sway'd o'er a trembling child.

Not anxiously careful for pelf,
  Melancholic and thoughtful, his mind
Look'd inward, and dwelt on itself,
  Still pensive, pathetic, and kind ;
Yet oft in despondency drown'd,
  He from friends and from converse would fly,
In weeping a luxury found,
  And reliev'd others' woes with a sigh.

In solitude long would he stay,
  And long lock'd in silence his tongue ;
Then he humm'd an elegaic lay,
  Or a psalm penitential he sung.
But if with his friends he regal'd,
  His mirth, as his griefs knew no bounds ;
In no Tale of Mark Sargent he fail'd,
  Nor in all Robin Hood's Derry downs.

Thro' the poor Widow's long lonely years
  Her Father supported us all ;
Yet sure she was loaded with cares,
  Being left with six children so small.
Meagre want never lifted her latch,
  Her cottage was still tight and clean,
And the casement beneath its low thatch
  Commanded a view o'er the Green.

O'er the Green, where so often she blest
　　The return of a husband or son,
Coming happily home to their rest,
　　At night, when their labor was done :
Where so oft in her earlier years
　　She with transport maternal has seen
(While plying her housewifely cares)
　　Her children all safe on the Green.

The Green was our pride through the year,
　　For in spring, when the wild flow'rets blew,
Tho' many rich pastures were near,
　　Where cowslips and daffodils grew ;
And tho' such gallant flow'rs were our choice,
　　It was bliss interrupted by fear—
The fear of their Owner's dread voice,
　　Harshly bawling, " You've no business here ! "

While the Green, tho' but daisies its boast,
　　Was free as the flow'rs to the bee,
In all seasons the Green we lov'd most,
　　Because on the Green we were free.
'Twas the prospect that first met my eyes,
　　And memory still blesses the scene,
For early my heart learnt to prize
　　The freedom of Honington Green.

No peasant had pin'd at his lot,
　　Tho' new fences the lone heath enclose ;
For, alas ! the blest days are forgot,
　　When poor men had their sheep and their cows.
Still had Labour been blest with Content,
　　Still Competence happy had been,
Nor Indigence utter'd a plaint,
　　Had Avarice spar'd but the Green.

Not Avarice itself could be mov'd
　　By desire of a morsel so small :
It could not be lucre he lov'd,
　　But to rob the poor folk of their all.
He in wantonness ope'd his wide jaws,
　　As a Shark may disport with the Fry,
Or a Lion, when licking his paws,
　　May wantonly snap at a Fly.

Could there live such an envious man,
  Who endur'd not the halcyon scene,
When the infantine peasantry ran
  And roll'd on the daisy-deck'd Green ?
Ah ! sure 'twas Envy's despite,
  Lest Indigence tasted of bliss,
That sternly decreed they've no right
  To innocent pleasure like this.

Tho' the youth of to-day must deplore
  The rough mounds that now sadden the scene,
The vain stretch of Misanthropy's power,
  The enclosure of Honington Green ;
Yet when not a green turf is left free,
  When not one odd nook is left wild,
Will the children of Honington be
  Less blest than when I was a child ?

No !—childhood shall find the scene fair,
  Then here let me cease my complaint ;
Still shall health be inhal'd with the air,
  Which at Honington cannot be taint ;
And tho' Age may still talk of the Green,
  Of the Heath and free Commons of yore,
Youth shall joy in the new-fangled scene,
  And boast of *that* change we deplore.

Dear to me was the wild, thorny hill,
  And dear the brown heath's sober scene :
And youth shall find happiness still,
  Tho' he roves not on common or green :
Tho' the pressure of wealth's lordly hand
  Shall give emulation no scope,
And tho' all the appropriate land
  Shall leave Indigence nothing to hope.

So happily flexile man's make,
  So pliantly docile his mind,
Surrounding impressions we take,
  And bliss in each circumstance find ;
The youths of a more polish'd age
  Shall not wish these rude commons to see ;
To the bird that's inur'd to the cage,
  It would not be bliss to be free.

THE POPPY AND THE CORN—A FABLE.

BY MISS E. KNIPE, AFTERWARDS MRS. ELIZABETH COBBOLD.

Mrs. Elizabeth Cobbold [1767—1824] was born in London, and was the daughter of Mr. Robert Knipe, of Liverpool. In 1790 she was married to William Clarke, Esq., a portman of the Borough of Ipswich, a gentleman twice her own age, and became a widow within six months of her marriage. It was not long, however, before she a second time entered the conjugal state. John Cobbold, Esq., of the Cliff Brewery, Ipswich, a widower with fourteen children, was the second husband. Well acquainted as she was with music, botany, conchology, and general literature, and possessing artistic powers of no mean order, as well as the power of addressing a public audience, this alliance placed her at once in a position congenial to her tastes and feelings, and she became the leader in literary circles, the friend of artists, and the patron of innocent amusements. For more than twenty years she shone pre-eminently in the circle in which she moved, and the mansions of Cliff and Holywells were hospitably opened to all who belonged to the literary or artistic craft. Some of her poems were published immediately after her decease, but the following poem, penned when she was Miss Knipe, is from the valuable collection of W. P. Hunt, Esq., and has not, we believe, been previously published :—

'Twas on a sultry summer's day,
Where Phœbus shot his fiercest ray,
And drank the liquid gems of morn,
Amid a field of waving corn
A proud, conceited Poppy grew,
And gloried in her vermil hue.
Now here, now there, her head inclin'd,
And wanton'd with the passing wind ;
Play'd off a thousand flirting airs,
And scorn'd the humble Barley Ears,
Unless when, by the breath of heaven,

Against her stem reluctant driven,
Their deeper red inflam'd her breast,
And thus her neighbours she addrest :
" Vile miscreants, hence ! and learn to know
What duty 'tis to me you owe.
Obey with reverential awe
Your sov'reign, I, by nature's law ;
'Tis she who bids me higher tower :
Yield, then, to conscious Beauty's power!
Do not my charms attract the eye ?
My graceful form ? my vermil dye ?
The gaudy tulip, or the rose,
Not half such splendour can disclose.
View, then, my brighter glory's blaze,
And at an awful distance gaze."
With virtuous warmth the Corn reply'd :
" Vain, gaudy thing ! elate with pride,
What use have all thy boasted charms ?
Can they protect, or ward from harms ?
Weak is thy conscious beauty's pow'r ;
The spoiler comes in fatal hour,
And tears thee from thy native bed—
Then, fading, droops thy languid head ;
No longer charming to his eye,
He throws thee unregarded by,—
In a loathsome dunghill doom'd to die.
A widely diff'rent fate attends
Thy scorn'd, thy now neglected Friends.
For us e'en man bestows his cares,
For us the kindly soil prepares,
Protects our growth with fond concern,
And builds for us the spacious barn ;
Matur'd, we then enrich his hoard,
And grace the homely, plenteous board.
With joyful gratitude 'tis ours
To bless his gay, convivial hours.
The solid pleasures we bestow
Thy vanity can never know."

This moral truth through life we find :
Virtue alone can bless mankind ;
Without it, what is beauty's power ?
A toy—the gewgaw of an hour.

TO SHAKSPEARE.

BY CAPEL LOFFT.

Capel Lofft [1751—1824] was born in London, educated at Eton and Cambridge, and in 1775 was called to the bar. He, however, had but little practice, and after he succeeded to his uncle's property at Stanton, in Suffolk, he was much better known as a politician than as a barrister. He was a leader among the Reform party at county meetings. He had a great love of literature, and through him Bloomfield's "Farmer's Boy" was introduced to the public.

> Thy name, O Homer! thine, great Shakspeare, writ
> In *starry* characters!—Shakspeare, whose eye
> With eagle intuition, pierc'd the maze
> Of moral nature, gave to airy being
> A local habitation and a name;
> The unresisted master of the heart,
> Whether in terror cloth'd, he shake our souls,
> Strike dumb the guilty, and appal the free,
> Shew Vice her proper feature, and present
> All-lovely Virtue in her heavenly form;
> Or time the melting chords of sympathy,
> And wake, with magic touch, the tender sense
> To sweet vibrations of unutter'd joy;
> Or with creative energy, call forth
> Ideal characters and worlds his own.
>
> *Endosia*, Book iv.

Kirke White, having published a few sonnets in the "Monthly Mirror," in the composition of which he had not observed the rules of that peculiar kind of poetry, Capel Lofft addressed to the youthful author the following elegant admonition, which Kirke White gracefully acknowledged in a sonnet, in which the hints of his kind patron were adopted.

> Ye, whose aspirings court the muse of lays,
>   "Severest of those orders which belong

Distinct and separate to Delphic song,"
Why shun the sonnet's undulating maze ?
And why its name, boast of Petrarchian days,
　　Assume, its rules disowned ? whom from the throng
The muse selects, their ear the charm obeys
　　Of its full harmony ;—they fear to wrong
The SONNET, by adorning with a name
　　Of that distinguished import, lays, though sweet,
　　Yet not in magic texture taught to meet
Of that so varied and peculiar frame.
O, think! to vindicate its genuine praise
Those it beseems, whose lyre a favoring impulse sways.

PIOUS FRIENDSHIP.

BY MRS. BARBAULD.

Mrs. Barbauld [1743—1825] was born at the village of Kibworth Harcourt, in Leicestershire. She was the eldest child and only daughter of the Rev. John Aikin, LL.D., a dissenting minister, who was master of an excellent academy. She gave early indications of uncommon powers of mind, and in 1773 she was persuaded to publish a volume of miscellaneous poems, which was so well received that four editions were issued within the year. In 1774 she was married to the Rev. Rochemont Barbauld, a dissenting minister, who had charge of the Unitarian congregation at Palgrave, in Suffolk. The newly married pair opened a school, and Mrs. Barbauld's literary fame, and her devotion to the duties of instruction, soon secured celebrity and success to the Palgrave academy. Her "Early Lessons for Children," and "Hymns in Prose," have proved invaluable manuals for the young. She died at Stoke Newington, in the eighty-second year of her age.

How blest the sacred tie that binds
In union sweet according minds !
How swift the heavenly course they run,
Whose hearts, whose faith, whose hopes are one !

To each the soul of each how dear!
What jealous love, what holy fear!
How doth the generous flame within
Refine from earth and cleanse from sin!

Their streaming tears together flow
For human guilt and mortal woe;
Their ardent prayers together rise
Like mingling flames in sacrifice.

Together both they seek the place
Where God reveals his awful face;
How high, how strong, their raptures swell,
There's none but kindred souls can tell.

Nor shall the glowing flame expire
When nature droops her sickening fire:
Then shall they meet in realms above,
A heaven of joy, because of love.

THE SUN FLOWER.

BY LORD THURLOW.

Edward Hovell, the second Baron Thurlow [1781-1829], was the eldest son of Thomas Thurlow, Bishop of Durham, the brother of Lord Chancellor Thurlow. He was born 10th of June, 1781, and succeeded to the dignity of Baron Thurlow, of Thurlow, September, 1806, by virtue of a special limitation in the patent of creation. On the 13th November, 1813, he married Mary Catherine Bolton, the daughter of Mr. James Bolton, and many years on the Covent Garden stage, and noted for having made her *debut* in the character of *Polly Peachum*, by whom he had three sons. He assumed the name of Hovell, pursuant to royal sign manual, dated July 8th, 1814; and died 3rd. June, 1829. He published several volumes of poems.

Behold, my dear, this lofty flower,
That now the golden sun receives;

No other deity has power,
    But only Phœbus, on her leaves ;
As he in radiant glory burns,
From east to west her visage turns.

The dial tells no tale more true,
    Than she his journal on her leaves,
When morn first gives him to her view,
    Or night, that her of him bereaves,
A dismal interregnum bids,
Her weeping eyes to close their lids.

Forsaken of his light, she pines
    The cold, the dreary night away,
Till in the east the crimson signs
    Betoken the great God of day ;
Then, lifting up her drooping face,
She sheds around a golden grace.

O Nature, in all parts divine !
    What moral sweets her leaves disclose,
Then in my verse her truth shall shine,
    And be immortal, as the rose,
Anacreon's plant ; arise, thou flower,
That hast fidelity thy dower !

Apollo, on whose beams you gaze,
    Has filled my breast with golden light;
And circled me with sacred rays,
    To be a poet in his sight :
Then thus I give the crown to thee,
Whose impress is fidelity.

ALDBOROUGH A CENTURY AGO.

BY GEORGE CRABBE.

George Crabbe [1754-1832], whom Byron describes as "Nature's sternest painter, yet the best," was born at Aldborough, where his father was Collector of duties on Salt, the same as Gardner, the Historian, was at Dunwich. Crabbe was apprenticed to a surgeon, which profession the author for a time adopted. Meeting with but little success, and having

become enamoured of authorship, he determined to seek his
fortune in London, where a short time starvation stared him
in the face.   He made unsuccessful applications for relief to
Lord North, Lord Shelburne, and Lord Chancellor Thurlow,
but was ultimately rescued by Edmund Burke, to whom he
most pathetically made known his destitute condition.   By
the assistance of Burke, Crabbe was enable to prepare himself
for holy orders, and was ordained priest in 1782.   He was a
curate at Aldborough, then chaplain to the Duke of Rutland,
and died rector of Trowbridge, in Wiltshire.   Crabbe's poem
of "The Library," was published in 1781, and his "Tales of
the Hall," his last publication, in 1819.   For these Tales
and the copyright of his previous works, Mr. Murray gave
the poet the sum of *three thousand pounds.*

> Lo!   where the heath, with withering brake grown o'er,
> Lends the light turf that warms the neighbouring poor;
> From thence a length of burning sand appears,
> Where the thin harvest waves its withered ears;
> Rank weeds, that every art and care defy,
> Reign o'er the land, and rob the blighted rye;
> There thistles stretch their prickly arms afar,
> And to the ragged infant threaten war.
> There poppies, nodding, mock the hope of toil,
> There the blue bugloss paints the sterile soil;
> Hardy and high above the slender sheaf,
> The slimy mallow waves her silky leaf;
> O'er the young shoot the charlock throws a shade,
> And clasping tares cling round the sickly blade;
> With mingled tints the rocky coasts abound,
> And a sad splendour vainly shines around.
>
> So looks the nymph whom wretched arts adorn,
> Betrayed by man, then left for man to scorn;
> Whose cheek in vain assumes the mimic rose,
> While her sad eyes the troubled breast disclose;
> Whose outward splendour is but folly's dress,
> Exposing most, when most it gilds distress.
>
> Here, joyless roam a wild amphibious race,
> With sullen woe displayed in every face;

Who far from civil arts and social fly,
And scowl at strangers with suspicious eye.

Here, too, the lawless merchant of the main,
Draws from his plough the intoxicated swain;
Want only claimed the labour of the day,
But vice now steals his nightly rest away.

Where are the swains, who, daily labor done,
With rural games played down the setting sun;
Who struck with matchless force the bounding ball,
Or made the pond'rous quoit obliquely fall;
While some huge Ajax, terrible and strong
Engaged some artful stripling of the throng,
And fell beneath him, foiled, while far around
Hoarse triumph rose, and rocks returned the sound?
Where now are these? Beneath yon cliff they stand,
To show the freighted pinnace where to land;
To load the ready steed with guilty haste,
To fly in terror o'er the pathless waste,
Or, when detected in their straggling course,
To foil their foes by cunning or by force;
Or yielding part (which equal knaves demand)
To gain a lawless passport through the land.

Here, wandering long 'amid these frowning fields,
I sought the simple life that Nature yields;
Rapine and wrong, and fear usurped her place
And a bold, artful, surly, savage race,
Who, only skilled to take the finny tribe,
The yearly dinner, or septennial bribe,
Wait on the shore, and as the waves run high,
On the tossed vessel bend their eager eye,
Which to their coast direct its venturous way,
Theirs or the ocean's miserable prey.

As on their neighbouring beach yon swallow stand,
And wait for favouring winds to leave the land;
While still for flight the ready wing is spread,
So waited I the favouring hour and fled,
Fled from the shores where guilt and famine reign,
And cried, ah! hapless they who still remain!—
Who still remain to hear the ocean roar,

A A

Whose greedy waves devour the lessening shore.
Till some fierce tide, with more imperious sway,
Sweeps the low hut and all it holds away ;
When the sad tenant weeps from door to door,
And begs a poor protection from the poor !

THE AUTHOR RECTOR.*

" Then came the *Author-rector* : his delight
  Was all in books, to read them, or to write :
  Women and men he strove alike to shun,
  And hurried homeward when his tasks were done :
  Courteous enough, but careless what he said,
  For points of learning he reserved his head,
  And when addressing either poor or rich
  He knew no better than his cassock which ;
  He like an osier was of pliant kind
  Erect by nature, but to bend inclined,
  Not like a creeper, falling to the ground,
  Or meanly catching on the neighbours round :—
  Careless was he of surplice, hood, and band,
  And kindly took them as they came to hand ;
  Nor, like the doctor, wore a world of hat,
  As if he sought for dignity in that;
  He talk'd, he gave, but not with cautious rules,
  Nor turned from gipsies, vagabonds, or fools ;
  It was his nature, but they thought it whim,
  And so our beaux and beauties turned from him."

THE VILLAGE.

WRITTEN UPON THE ROOKERY HILL, AT YOXFORD.

BY JAMES BIRD.

James Bird [1788—1839], the Yoxford poet, as he was
familiarly called, was born at Earl Stonham, and was
apprenticed to a miller; and about 1814 embarked in business as a miller at Yoxford, where he continued to reside
until his death.   In 1816 he married Emma, the daughter of

---

* " The Author-rector," says his son, " is in all points the similitude of
Mr. Crabbe himself, except in the subject of his lucubrations."

Mr. Hardacre, bookseller, of Hadleigh; and, relinquishing the "Mills," he commenced business as a bookseller and druggist. In 1819 he published "The Vale of Slaughden," an historical poem; and this was followed by many others. His good social disposition, and strong literary tastes, endeared him to a large circle of acquaintances; but his constitution, ever delicate, was undermined by pulmonary disease; and he died on the 26th March, 1839.

'Tis night—the weary world is still
    Forgotten and alone;
I muse, upon the wooded hill,
    Beneath the summer moon,
That seems as though she smiled more bright,
While listening to the bird of night!

Beside me sweeps the spreading glade;
    Around me spring the flowers;
And far below, amid the shade
    Of happy green wood bowers,
All bright beneath the spangled skies,
My loved and lovely village lies.

There many a high aspiring dome
    And lowly cot is seen;
There many a glad and peaceful home,
    Where pride nor care has been—
Where hearts are undisturbed by strife,
Unruffled on the sea of life.

And yet, perchance, of all who now
    Rest there, enchained by sleep,
Some wretch may wake with throbbing brow,
    And eyes unclosed, to weep:
Whose heart within its blighted core,
May feel the glow of hope no more!

Oh! in a spot so fair as this,
    Which Nature's heavenly hand
Has painted for her bower of bliss,
    Her Eden of the land;
In this fair spot life's stream should glide,
One sweet, unchanged, unbroken tide.

Dear, peaceful village! though from thee
    My thoughts are wont to roam
To distant scenes o'er earth and sea,
    Thou only art my home;
In thee alone my treasure lies—
My all of joy beneath the skies!

Here, here alone, I feel the spell,
    All earthly spells above;
Oh! here my friends, my children dwell,
    Here smiles my own true love!
Vain world! I would not change this spot
For all thou hast and I have not.

Now sleep, the beauteous landscape fades
    Beneath the waning moon;
And I forsake these lovely glades
    To seek my home alone;
Still, still the scene shows fair and bright—
Thou Village of my heart! Good night!

WOMAN'S TONGUE.

Sweet woman's tongue! I love to hear its chime
That drowns the heavier iron tongue of time!
Rich in its tones, and varied in its power,
Its accents falling like an April shower
Upon the snowdrops of man's heart, to cheer,
Warm, soften, cherish, animate, endear!

RURAL VIEW OF SUFFOLK.

Health smiles around thy richly wooded dales,
Luxuriant uplands, and refreshing vales;
Thy fields are like a fairy garden, wide,
Where art and nature are so close allied,
Their happy union has subdued the wild:
Their home is here, and beauty is their child!
Fair district! where I drew my natal breath,
Awoke to life, and hope to sleep in death—
Where I have seen, and loved to see, green nooks,
Have heard, and joyed to hear, thy murmuring brooks—
Where I beheld, and gladdened to behold,
Lime, elm, ash, beech, and towering oaks of old—

Where I have felt sink in my heart the beams
Of the bright sun, that glowed on hills and streams ;
Fain would I hope, in honour of my theme,
This dream of loveliness no fictious dream !

WOMAN'S HEART.

That hallowed sphere, a woman's heart, contains
Empires of feeling, and the rich domains
Where love, disporting in his sunniest hours,
Breathes his sweet incense o'er ambrosial flowers ;
A woman's heart !—that gem, divinely set
In native gold—that peerless amulet,
Which, firmly linked to love's electric chain,
Connects the worlds of transport and of pain !

THE SITE OF DUNWICH.

Where the lone cliff uprears its rugged head,
Where frowns the ruin o'er the silent dead,
Where sweeps the billow on the lonely shore,
Where once the mighty lived, but live no more ;
Where proudly frowned the convent's massy wall,
Where rose the gothic tower, the stately hall,
Where bards proclaimed, and warriors shared the feast,
Where ruled the baron, and where knelt the priest,—
There stood the city in its pride—'tis gone !
Mocked at by crumbling pile, and mouldering stone,
And shapeless masses which the reckless power
Of time hath hurled from ruined arch and tower !
O'er the lone spot, where shrines and pillared halls
Once gorgeous shone, the clammy lizard crawls ;
O'er the lone spot, where yawned the guarded fosse,
Creeps the wild bramble, and the spreading moss :
Oh ! time hath bowed that lordly city's brow,
In which the mighty dwelt—where dwell they *now ?*

WOMAN'S FAITH.

Oh ! loved and loveliest of creation's forms,
Devoted woman !—when distracting storms
Tumultuous sweep o'er man's ambitious breast,

Thy love can charm his troubled soul to rest,
And, like a sun-beam on the tempest's gloom,
Shed light and beauty o'er his darkest doom !
While man, still varying with the varying hour,
Flits, like the restless bee, from flower to flower,
Thy faith remains—upon thy breast alone
Eternal love hath fixed his certain throne !
Thou art man's changeless comforter—his all—
His hope—his heaven—although his earliest fall !
Oh ! when thy fair, but rash and erring hand,
In Eden dared to break the dread command,
Then Adam, doubtless, from that fatal tree,
Deemed ruin welcome, since it came by thee !

TO THE SWALLOW.

BY MRS. FORD.

Lœtitia Jermyn [1788—1848] second daughter of Mr.
George Jermyn, at an early age evinced a taste for poetry
and general literature, and her graceful writings appeared in
many periodicals of the day. She was born at Ipswich,
October 8, 1788, and was married in 1830 to the Rev. James
Ford, Fellow of Trinity College, Oxon, and vicar of Navestock, whose topographical and antiquarian researches she
materially aided during an engagement of twenty years, and
to whose well-stored mind he constantly referred in all his
literary pursuits. Possessing unusual conversational powers
and sparkling wit, combined with a lively manner and great
personal attractions, she was an ornament to the society in
which she moved. Her love of nature led her to the study of
Entomology. She published, in 1827, the "Butterfly Collector's Vade-Mecum," dedicated to the Rev. William Kirby.
She was a good botanist, and a knowledge of conchology
also ranked among her many attainments. She died
at the Vicarage, Navestock, after a short illness, July 15,
1848.

" The swallow is one of my favourite birds."—SALMONIA.

Oh, swift-wing'd bird of sunny skies
And gentle zephyrs, how I prize,
Lov'd, vagrant swallow, thy return
From thy far distant long sojourn!
Thou rival of the nightingale,
That sweetly throngs the dewy vale,
Pours her rich melody along,
And trills her softly plaintive song;
As she mine ear, thou gladd'st mine eye,
In graceful curves now sweeping by;
Now lightly skimming o'er the pool,
Shaded by alders, dank and cool,
Now dashing with quick flash away,
Like some bright meteor, now at play
In the warm sunbeams gaily glancing,
The beauty of each scene enhancing.
Oh, harbinger of summer hours,
Of balmy airs, and fragrant flow'rs;
Oh, joyous prophet of the year,
To me thou ever shall be dear.
'Midst nature's loveliest forms, thy life,
Oh, happy bird, midst pleasures rife,
With mingled sweets of hue and scent,
Beneath the azure vault is spent.
To thee stern winter is unknown;
Thou then to other climes art flown.
When autumn dons her russet hue,
To England's meads thou bid'st adieu,
And to Italia's regions bright,
And orange groves directs thy flight,
Delighted there at will to roam,
Or make new myrtle bow'rs thy home;
Or, travelling on to farther lands,
'Midst Afric's palms and burning sands,
Pursuing still with untir'd wing
And instinct true, thy wandering,
Where'er thou art, whate'er the clime,
Beauteous, though transient, is thy time,
Like the ephemera—thy prey—

Whose life is scarce one joyous day ;
How, taught of heaven thy course to bend,
And, at appointed seasons, wend
From shore to shore, from year to year,
Thou sacred bird, com'st duly here—
Com'st with bright summer in thy train,
To charm and welcome us again.

THE SKYLARK.

" Of all birds I should like to be a lark."—WASHINGTON IRVING.

Of all the joyous birds that fly
Through the mild blue of summer's sky,
None like the lark so charms my sight,
None seems so happy, free, and light !
He revels in morn's earliest prime,
Luxuriates in day's brightest time ;
In the year's blythest season, too,
He comes his pleasures to renew.
From the fresh meads, and opening flowers,
All fragrant with the dewy showers,
Sated with sweets, from earth he springs,
His upward flight to heaven he wings ;
Soaring aloft to greet on high
The morning stars with melody.
Hark to that note, so loud and clear,
How it comes trilling on the ear !
Now like a stream, the gushing song,
Note over note, it flows along ;
Never tiring, never palling,
In soft, delicious cadence falling.
Oh ! who for operas would care,
Or concerts, that can freely share,
As through the verdant field he strays,
The music of the lark's sweet lays ?
Oft, as I mark his vocal rise,
I wish, like him, to mount the skies ;
And think, while listening to his glee,
" I of all birds a lark would be ! "

TO A VERY YOUNG HOUSEWIFE.

BY BERNARD BARTON.

Bernard Barton [1784-1849], the Quaker Poet, was born in London. His father and mother were members of the Society of Friends. After an apprenticeship at Halstead, in Essex, he in 1806 entered into partnership with Mr. Jesup, of Woodbridge, as a corn and coal merchant, and the year after married the sister of his partner ; but she died twelve months after marriage in giving birth to a daughter, who became a solace to her father until his death. In 1810 he accepted an engagement as clerk in the bank of Messrs. Alexanders and Co., in which office he remained until the day of his death. He published many volumes of poems, but the title of one of them would most aptly describe the whole —" Household Verses." They did not win for him a lofty niche in the Temple of Fame, but they made for him a home in many hearts. In 1846, Sir Robert Peel recommended the " Quaker Poet " to the Queen, as a fit subject for an annual pension of £100, and Bernard Barton gratefully accepted the boon. He died February 19th, 1849.

To write a book of Household song
　Without one verse to thee,
Whom I have known and loved so long,
　Were all unworthy me.

Have I not seen thy needle plied
　With as much ready glee
As if it were thy greatest pride
　A sempstress famed to be ?

Have I not ate pies, puddings, tarts,
　And bread thy hands had kneaded,
All excellent—as if those arts
　Were all that thou hast heeded ?

Have I not seen thy cheerful smile
    And heard thy voice as gay
As if such household the while
    To thee were sport and play.

Yet can thy pencil copy well
    Landscape, or flowers, or face;
And thou canst waken music's spell
    With simple, natural grace

Thus variously to play thy part,
    Before thy teens are spent,
Honours far more thy head and heart
    Than mere accomplishment.

So wear the wreath thou well has won,
    And be it understood,
I framed it nor in idle fun
    For girlish womanhood;

But in it may a lesson lurk,
    Worth teaching now-a-days,
That girls may do all household work
    Nor lose a poet's praise.

WINTER EVENING DITTY, FOR A LITTLE GIRL. *

'Tis dark and cold abroad, my love, but warm and bright within,
So ransack o'er thy treasured store, and evening's sports begin;
The playthings, what an endless list! thy dolls, both great and small;
Empty thy Lilliputian hoard, and let us see them all.

---

* This and the preceding poem to "A Very Young Housewife," referred to
Miss Emma Knight, the daughter of a long-tried and much esteemed friend
of the Poet. This dear child he petted almost as much as his own, presents
being a favourite mode of manifesting his esteem, and when she grew to
womanhood he frequently employed her in making fair manuscript copies of
his verses, as he ofttimes had applications for more copies than he could find
time to make. His letters to her were generally addressed to "Dear Puck,"
or "My dear Puck." In 1833, writing to her on her birth-day, he says,
" As thou art now grown so great a girl [she was then fourteen years old] as
to be likely to go out to tea now and then with dear mamma, it has occurred

There's not a king who wears a crown, nor miser hoarding pelf,
More absolute and rich than thou, my little sportive elf;
Those dolls thy docile subjects are, that footstool is thy throne,
Aud all the wealth which mammon boasts is worthless to thy own.

Or must it be a living thing to please thy fancy now,
There's puss, although she looks so grave, as fond of play as thou ;
Who patiently submits to sports which common cats would tire,
Contented, if she can but keep her post beside the fire.

She quietly consents to be in baby garments drest,
Or, in thy little cradle rock'd, as quietly will rest ;
I know not which most happy seems, when mirthful is your air,
Nor could I find a puck, or puss, with either to compare.

But if a graver mood be thine—with needle and with thread—
When sport grows dull, e'en give it o'er, and play at work instead ;
Yet much I doubt, though sage thy look, and busy as a bee,
Whether that fit of sempstresship will long suppress thy glee.

But hark ! I hear the curfew-bell—thy little eyes grow dim ;
Put by thy work, dolls, toys, and all, and say thy evening hymn :
'Tis said ! now bid us all farewell ; kiss dear mamma—and then
Sweet sleep and pleasant dreams be thine till morning dawn again.

to me whether a little portable workbox, just large enough to carry a pretty piece of work, and a few needful implements with them at such times, might not be the fittest trifle I could think of to mark my affectionate interest in thy returned birthday." In a letter of a later date, accompanying a present of a piece for a gown : "It is not, however, by any such slight and perishable memorials that I could wish thee to estimate my affectionate interest in thy welfare. That, my dear friend, bears date before gowns formed part of thy wardrobe, and will I hope and trust outlast the wear and tear of the present and many more."

Of the latter poem, he wrote to Mrs. Knight soon after he had penned it : "A piece which I have written since thy leaving home is a grand favourite of mine for its delectable childishness. I defy Wordsworth to go beyond it in its tone of nursery simplicity. It is a 'Winter Evening's Ditty,' about little Puck, her dolls and her playthings, and puss in the cradle, and her notability and sempstresship, and her evening hymn, etc. They said at first I dared not *print* it, but I most assuredly will, for I am more inclined to be proud of it than of anything I ever wrote."

TO THE MEMORY OF ROBERT BLOOMFIELD.

Thou should'st not to the grave descend
　Unmourned, unhonor'd and unsung;
Could harp of mine record thy end,
　For thee that rude harp should be strung,
And plaintive notes as ever rung
　Should all its simple strings employ,
Lamenting unto old and young
　The bard who sung the Farmer's Boy.

The *Harvest Home's* rejoicing cup
　Should pause when that sad note was heard,
The *Widow* turn her *Hour glass* up,
　With tenderest feelings newly stirr'd;
And many a pity-waken'd word,
　And sighs that speak when language fails,
Should prove thy simple strains preferr'd
　To prouder poets' lofty tales.

Circling the *Old Oak Table* round,
　Whose moral worth thy measure owns,
Heroes and heroines yet are found,
　Like *Abner and the Widow Jones;*
There *Gilbert Meldrum's* sterner tones
　In virtue's cause are bold and free,
And ev'n the patient sufferer's moans
　In pain and sorrow plead for thee.

Nor thus beneath the straw-roof'd cot
　Alone, should thoughts of thee pervade,
Hearts which confess thee, unforgot,
　On heathy hill, in grassy glade;
In many a spot by thee array'd
　With hues of thought, with fancy's gleam,
Thy memory lives—in Euston's shade,
　By Barnham Water's shadeless stream.

And long may guileless hearts preserve
　Thy memory, and its tablets be;
While nature's healthy power shall nerve
　The arm of labour toiling free:

While childhood's innocence and glee,
   With green old age enjoyment share,
Richards and Kates shall tell of thee,
   Walters and Janes thy name declare.

How wise, how noble was thy choice,
   To be the bard of simple swains,
In all their pleasures to rejoice,
   And soothe with sympathy their pains ;
To sing with feeling in thy strains
   The simple subjects they discuss,
And be, though free from classic chains,
   Our own more chaste Theocritus !

THE VALLEY OF FERN. *

There is a lone valley, few charms can it number
   Compared with the lovely glens north of the Tweed ;
No mountains enclose it, where morning mists slumber,
   And it never has echoed the shepherd's soft reed :
No streamlet of crystal, its rocky banks laving,
   Flows through it, delighting the ear and the eye,

* Bernard Barton, writing to Mrs. Knight, in 1826, says, " I have received this morning a letter from Capel Lofft, from which I extract the following, thinking that however extravagant it may be as applied to the poetry of the ' Valley of Fern,' it will please you to find the tribute paid to our favourite spot has excited some attention.

" ' We have read with pleasure your verses on Felixstow, but with peculiar delight that calm, and soothing, and soul-elevating poem, " The Valley of Fern." I cannot but wish to know to what particular spot your muse attaches this pure spirit of immortality. I wish to give to this airy being a local habitation and a name—pure, touching, sublime—this is poetry.' "

We can fortunately give this lonely spot a local habitation. In reply to a question, Mrs. Knight thus wrote me, a few years prior to her decease : " ' The Valley of Fern ' is a beautiful little wild, sequestered spot, lying on the left of the high-road leading to Melton, and behind what is called Leeks hill, never noticed, I dare say, until the Poet immortalized it. I well remember going through it, for the first time, one summer day, with him and my two sisters, and enjoying its romantic stillness. The next day he brought in the first part of the poem and read it to us, when we suggested a few verbal alterations, which he readily responded to, and from that day it was an adopted pet with us. I think this was in 1816 or 1817. We trio of

On its side no proud forests, their foliage waving,
  Meet the gales of the autumn or summer wind's sigh.
Yet by me it is prized, and full dearly I love it,
  And oft my steps thither I pensively turn ;
It has silence within, heaven's proud arch above it,
  And my fancy has named it the Valley of Fern.

Oh deep the repose which its calm recess giveth,
  And no music can equal its silence to me ;
When broken 'tis only to prove something liveth,
  By the note of the sky-lark or hum of the bee.
On its sides the green fern to the breeze gently bending,
  With a few stunted trees, meet the wandering eye ;
Or the furze and the broom their bright blossoms extending,
  With the braken's soft verdure delightfully vie ;
These are all it can boast, yet, when fancy is dreaming,
  Her visions, which poets can only discern,
Come crowding around, in unearthly light beaming,
  And invest with bright beauty the Valley of Fern.

Sweet valley, in seasons of grief and dejection,
  I have sought in thy bosom a shelter from care,
And have found in my musings a bond of connexion
  With thy landscape so peaceful and all that was there :
In the verdure that soothed, in the flowers that brighten'd,
  In the blackbird's soft note, in the hum of the bee,
I found something that lulled and insensibly lighten'd,
  And felt grateful and tranquil while gazing on thee.
Yes, moments there are when mute nature is willing
  To teach, would proud man but be humble and learn,
When her sights and her sounds on the heart-strings are thrilling,
  And this I have felt in the Valley of Fern.

For the bright chain of being, though widely extended,
  Unites all its parts in one beautiful whole,
In which grandeur and grace are enchantingly blended,
  Of which God is the centre, the light, and the soul.

sisters were very frequently his companions in rural walks, at which time I
was engaged to my gentle and gifted cousin, James Knight.

  "B. B. very frequently allowed us to exercise a censorship on minor points
in his poems, professing himself no disciple of Lindley Murray, while my
sisters had been thoroughly trained into the observance of his rules. In after
years, we mostly read over his proof sheets as they came from the publishers."

And holy the hope is, and sweet the sensation,
　Which this feeling of union in solitude brings;
It gives silence a voice, and to calm contemplation,
　Unseals the pure fountain whence happiness springs.
Then Nature, most loved in her loneliest recesses,
　Unveils her fair features, and softens her stern,
And spreads, like that Being who bounteously blesses,
　For her votary a feast in the Valley of Fern.

And at times in its confines companionless straying,
　Pure thoughts, born in stillness, have pass'd through my mind;
And the spirit within, their blest impulse obeying,
　Has soar'd from this world on the wings of the wind.
The pure sky above, and the still scene around me,
　To the eye which survey'd them no clear image brought;
But my soul seemed entranced in the vision which bound me,
　As by magical spell, to the beings of thought.
And to Him, their dread Author, the fountain of feelings,
　I have bow'd while my heart seem'd within me to burn,
And my spirit contrited, for mercy appealing,
　Has call'd on His name in the Valley of Fern.

Farewell, lovely valley; when earth's silent bosom
　Shall hold him who loves thee, thy beauties may live,
And thy turf's em'rald tints, and thy broom's yellow blossom,
　Unto loiterers like him soothing pleasures may give.
As brightly may morning, thy graces investing
　With life and with light, wake thy inmates from sleep;
And as softly the moon, in still loveliness resting,
　To gaze on its charms, thy lone landscape may steep.
Then should friend of the Bard who hath paid with his praises
　The pleasure thou'st yielded e'er seek thy sojourn,
Should one tear for his sake fill the eye while it gazes,
　It may fall unreproved in the Valley of Fern.

THE DYING CHILD.

" *What should it know of death?* "—WORDSWORTH.

BY GEORGE WILLIAM FULCHER.

George William Fulcher [1795-1855] was for many years
a bookseller at Sudbury, and the author of " The Village
Paupers," in addition to many miscellaneous poems, one of

which, "The Dying Child," the world will not willingly
let die. He was the author of "The Life of Gainsborough,"
and of several pamphlets. Of the "Sudbury Pocket
Book," which he started in the year 1825, he was for
many years the editor. As one of the guardians of the
Sudbury Union, as well as a magistrate of the Borough, Mr.
Fulcher was highly respected, and on more than one occasion
was elected as mayor of the town in which he so long resided.
He died suddenly of disease of the heart, on June 19th,
1855.

Come closer, closer, dear mamma,
    My heart is filled with fears,
My eyes are dark, I hear your sobs,
    But cannot see your tears.

I feel your warm breath on my lips
    That are so icy cold ;
Come closer, closer, dear mamma,
    Give me your hand to hold.

I quite forget my little hymn—
    "How doth the busy bee,"
Which every day I used to say
    When sitting on your knee.

Nor can I recollect my prayers,
    And, dear mamma, you know
That the great God will angry be,
    If I forget *them* too.

And dear papa, when he comes home,
    Oh, will he not be vex'd ?
"Give us this day our daily bread"—
    What is it that comes next ?

"Thine is the kingdom and the power ; "
    I cannot think of more :
It comes and goes away so quick,
    It never did before.

Hush, darling ! you are going to
   The bright and blessed sky,
Where all God's holy children go
   To live with him on high.

But will he love me, dear mamma,
   As tenderly as you ?
And will my own papa, one day,
   Come and live with me too ?

But you must first lay me to sleep
   Where grandpapa is laid ;
Is not the churchyard cold and dark,
   And shan't I feel afraid ?

And will you every evening come
   And say my pretty prayer
Over poor Lucy's little grave,
   And see that no one's there ?

And promise me whene'er you die
   That they your grave shall make
The next to mine, that I may be
   Close to you when I wake.

Nay, do not leave me, dear mamma,
   Your watch beside me keep,
My heart feels cold—the room's all dark,
   Now lay me down to sleep.

And should I sleep to wake no more,
   Dear, dear mamma, good bye ;
Poor nurse is kind, but oh, do *you*
   Be with me when I die !

THE STEPMOTHER.

" She saw me weep, and asked in high disdain
  If tears would bring my mother back again ? "

Well, I will try and love her then,
   But do not ask me yet ;
You know my own dear dead mamma
   I never must forget.

Don't you remember, dear papa,
  The night before she died,
You carried me into her room?
  How bitterly I cried!

Her thin white fingers on my head
  So earnestly she laid,
And her sunk eyes gleamed fearfully,—
  I felt almost afraid;—

You lifted me upon the bed
  To kiss her pale, cold cheek,
And something rattled in her throat,
  I scarce could hear her speak;

But she did whisper—"When I'm gone
  For ever from your sight,
And others have forgotten me,
  Don't *you* forget me quite."

And often in my dreams I feel
  Her hand upon my head,
And see her sunken eyes as plain
  As if she were not dead.

I hear her feeble, well-known voice
  Amidst the silent night,
Repeat her dying words again—
  "Don't *you* forget me quite."

It sometimes wakes me, and I think
  I'll run into her room,
And then I weep to recollect
  She's sleeping in the tomb.

I miss her in our garden walks,
  At morn and ev'ning prayer,
At church, at play, at home, abroad,—
  I miss her everywhere:—

But most of all I miss her when
  The pleasant daylight's fled,
And strangers draw the curtains round
  My lonely little bed!

For no one comes to kiss me now,
  Nor bid poor Anne, " Good night,"
Nor hear me say my pretty hymn—
  I shall forget it quite!

They tell me *this* mamma is rich,
  And beautiful, and fine,
But will she love you, dear papa,
  More tenderly than mine ?

And will she, when the fever comes
  With its bewildering pain,
Watch night by night your restless couch
  Till you are well again?

When first she sung your fav'rite song—
  " Come to the sunset tree,"
Which my poor mother used to sing
  With me upon her knee,

I saw you turn your head away,
  I saw your eyes were wet ;
'Midst all our glittering company
  You do not quite forgot !

But must you never wear again
  The ring poor mother gave ?
Will it be long before the grass
  Is green upon her grave ?

He turn'd him from that gentle child,
  His eyes with tears were dim,
At thought of the undying love
  Her mother bore to him.

He met his gay, his beauteous bride,
  With spirits low and weak,
And miss'd the kind, consoling words
  The dead was wont to speak.

Long years roll'd on, but hope's gay flowers
  Blossom'd for him in vain ;
The freshness of life's morning hours
  Never returned again.

THE OUTLAW'S WIFE TO HER HUSBAND.

BY LUCY EMILY PRATT.

Mrs. Pratt, of Sudbury (formerly Lucy Emily Fulcher), was born April 27th, 1825. She was the eldest daughter of Mr. G. W. Fulcher, the editor of the " Sudbury Pocket Book," and was, during her maiden and married life, a frequent contributor to that periodical. She was married to Mr. Henry Spooner Pratt, in 1848, and died January 2nd, 1851

" Urge me no more, I could not bear
 Thee to go forth alone ;
Thou wert indeed an exile there,
 A hopeless, friendless one.

" I will go with thee ; I have weighed
 The dangers that betide,
And I am sure my safest place
 Is by my husband's side.

" And there are other lands as bright,
 And other skies as fair,
Where yet thou mayest dwell in peace,
 Although an *outlaw* there.

" Outlaw ! I had not thought to hear
 That linked with *thy* name ;
Yet, dearest, it can never be
 To thee the brand of shame.

" There is no crime upon thy head,
 No guilt upon thy brow ;
I still may honour while I love :
 Then could I leave thee now ?

" My kindred, friends, what could they be
 When thou wert gone, to me ?
I quit my native land—but oh !
 My *home* is aye with thee."

THE OLD FOUNDRY.

BY MRS. BIDDELL.

The furnace fires are out, the lathes are still,
  The engine puffs its fiery breath no more ;
No longer now is heard the groaning mill,
  No busy feet are tramping on the floor.

Some threescore years ago, an anxious man
  Beside that furnace took his earnest stand,
Marking the fiery flood, when first it ran,
  Flaming and sparkling o'er the sabled sand,

From its hot prison to its destined mould ;
  And from his bosom burst the father's prayer,
That he might prosper, and his sons behold,
  And share the fortunes which he founded there.

His was a hopeful spirit—he had felt
  The bitter pangs of unrequited care ;
Like his own metal, though his heart might melt,
  'Twas but a brighter, better form to wear.

He lived to prove how industry may tread
  A height proud indolence may never claim ;
His sons have prospered, as their father sped,
  And far and wide resounds that father's name.

For sixty years those furnace fires were glowing ;
  The old man sleeps—his children's children now
Set on another spot their engines going,
  A cloudy coronet on Orwell's brow.

Yet ere those fires were quenched, the iron tower,
  Begirt by dusky forms, or pensive band,
Saw its last stream the ancient furnace pour,
  And the *last ploughshare* glittered in the sand.

Silent and sad, they saw the metal gleam,
  The " melting mood " their simple hearts confessed,
Some tear-drops hallowed that last parting stream,
  And transient sorrow touched his rugged breast.

OLD FOUNDRY! I have known thee long and well,
  And childhood's memories haunt thy blacken'd walls,
Hark to the sound! it is thy passing bell:
  How many a thought its iron tongue recalls

Of thee and thine; thy curfew notes have pealed,
  Thy fires are out, and silence reigns alone,
Where busy hundreds thy dark chambers filled,
  And giant engines gave a stirring tone.

Change ere the scene—where Orwell's waters glide,
  Bright with the fires, surrounding banks display,
While sail and steamer crowd the flowing tide,
  Rich with materials brought and borne away.

There thy successor boldly rears its head;
  Long may it flourish, and its memory be
As dear to kindred hearts, when years are fled,
  As thine, OLD FOUNDRY, ever will to me.

June 14th, 1849.

ARCHBISHOP SANCROFT. ON HIS RETIREMENT TO HIS PATRIMONIAL FARM, AT FRESSINGFIELD, IN SUFFOLK.

BY THE REV. JOHN MITFORD.

The Rev. John Mitford [1781—1859] was born August 13th, 1781. His father, John Mitford, Esq., was descended from the "Mitfords," of Mitford Castle, and was formerly a commander in the service of the East India Company. His son, John, after being educated at Tunbridge by the well-known Dr. Vicesimus Knox, was entered at Oriel College, Oxford, where he had for his tutor the celebrated Dr. Copleston, and for his intimate associate the still more celebrated Reginald Heber. In 1810, he was appointed to the vicarage of Benhall, and at a later period he became rector of Stratford St. Andrew, and of Weston. For many years he was editor of the "Gentleman's Magazine, and he edited and published a number of volumes relating to the poets and poetry of England. He was intimately acquainted with the

Greek and Roman classics, as well as with Italian, French, and German literature, and he had at his decease a finer collection of Elizabethian books than any other collector in the district. He died at Benhall, April 27th, 1859.

And such was he, whom time could never wrong
(His name would sanctify the weakest song),
Who left high Lambeth's venerable towers
For his small heritage and humble bowers,
Conscience and faith his guide. And what if now,
Taking the mitre from his aged brow,
(Crowds round his knees, and many a furrow'd cheek,
And glistening eye, that seemed indeed to speak
Better than language, seeing him depart,
In the meek sorrows of a silent heart:
Soft, gentle deeds, blossoms of love, that hung
Ever around him—could they want a tongue?
Tears, too, from childhood, and the words that call
'Father and friend,' were heard alike from all.)
Gently he passed beside them, with a mien
Temper'd with hope and fortitude serene.
Nor deem him unattended with a train
Of more sublime emotions, free from pain
Of doubt or fear—like an unclouded day
Upon the golden hills in endless ray,
A well-spring in his heart without decay ;
As one who knew that God a home had made
For those he cherished, in the humble shade.
Now, with his staff, on his paternal ground,
Amid his orchard trees he may be found,
An old man late returned, where he was seen
Sporting, a child, upon the village green—
How many a changeful year had passed between,
Blanching his scattered hair, yet leaving there
A heart kept young by piety and prayer ;
That to the inquiring friend could meekly tell :
" Be not for me afflicted—it is well,
For in my great integrity* I fell ;
'Twas in my great integrity I made
The choice that sends me to my native shade."

* The words Sancroft addressed to his chaplain on his death-bed.

THE SOLDIER'S BRIDE TO HER HUSBAND AFTER HIS ESCAPE FROM IMMINENT DANGER.

BY ELIZA ACTON.

Eliza Acton was the eldest daughter of a Mr. Acton who was for many years managing clerk in the firm of Trotman, Halliday, Studd & Co., of St. Peter's, Ipswich, and being an ingenious man, and an active, attentive servant, the firm was induced to give him a share in the business. Miss Acton's poems were published in 1826, and the first edition (of 500) sold very readily, and a second was issued in the following year. She left Ipswich, and resided for some time in France, and on her return to England she went to live at Hampstead. Whilst residing there, she turned her attention to a different subject to poetry. She prepared a "Cookery Book," which was published by the Messrs. Longman, as "Miss Acton's Cookery Book," and it having become the best book in the trade, it was doubtless to her much more remunerative than poetry. Coming from the pen of so practical a person as the author of the "Cookery Book," these poems have a peculiar interest.

I tremble at thy peril past!
 It shakes me, like some fearful dream,
In horror's mould of madness cast,
 To chill the warm heart's living stream.

I shudder but to view that fate,
 Which would have rent my soul's last tie
To earth, and left me desolate,
 Beyond all thought of agony.

Spar'd is the blow which would have left
 Within the world no breathing thing
So utterly of hope bereft,
 So crush'd by loneliest suffering,

As she, who warmly grateful now,
  Pours her best orisons to Heaven,
For life to one beloved as thou,
  In danger saved, in mercy given.

Oh! when the battle's rage is round,
  Amidst the fearful strife, for thee
May that protecting aid be found,
  Which now restores thee safe to me!

FORGIVE THEE!—YES.

Forgive thee!—yes—when ev'ry cord
  Which binds my soul to earth is broken ;
When scarce I hear the whisper'd word,
  By gentlest tongues around me spoken.

Forgive thee!—yes—thy once-lov'd name
  Shall mingle with my faltering breath,
When, fainter still, this languid frame
  Shall bend before the touch of death.

Forgive thee!—yes—when, paler still,
  This cold and fading brow shall be,
And o'er my head the latest chill
  Comes on of mortal agony.

Forgive thee!—yes—but rest awhile,
  'Till mem'ry of the past hath perish'd :
'Till from my mind that voice, that smile,
  Have passed as though they ne'er were cherished.

Come, when each hope is rais'd to heav'n,
  Which wither'd in the world's cold shade ;
And thou, e'en thou, shalt be forgiven
  The wretchedness which thou hast made.

SONNETS TO A YOUNG MOURNER WIDOWED ERE WEDDED.

BY THE REV. R. B. EXTON.

The Rev. Richard Brudenell Exton [1780—1863], born
in the parish of St. Peter's, Marlborough, Wilts, March 17th,

1780, instituted to the rectory of Athelington, in 1822, and to the vicarage of Cretingham, in 1827. Was domestic chaplain to George Earl of Clarendon, and a Justice of the Peace for the County of Suffolk He was the author of "Centenary of Sonnets," "Sixty Lectures on the Psalms," "Blank Verse Sermon," etc., etc. Died August 23rd, 1863.

Dear one, be comforted! dream o'er again,
Since life is all a dream, the blissful past;
That time thy gentle spirit, wont to taste,
Unaw'd, the promise neither false nor vain,
Soft whisper'd to thine ear by guileless love,
And Hope, his fair attendant, as they wove
The rainbow chaplet for thy virgin brow,
Ere call'd to breathe the fond, eternal vow.
Yes—court again the bright illusive scene,
'Till, as the glow of youth serenely fades,
Thy chasten'd vision shall descry (between
The twilight dim, and evanescent shades,
Here measuring our moments) that the birth
Of aught to cherish, is not—cannot be of earth.

But though the sunny morn its brief career,
Hath closed amid the tempest's fatal strife,
Sweeping from off the cheerful ways of life
Him whose young love did all its scenes endear,
The first, last, sole desire of thine eyes;
Time's vagrant pinion shall not wrap for aye
In shadowy terrors thine appointed day,
Nor from the smile of yon cerulean skies
Veil thine imploring glance. The stricken flow'r
Bends her meek head; anon, ere yet the storm
Hath ceased upon her humble couch to lower,
In timid faith she lifts her bruised form,
And, prescient of the joy his presence brings,
Awaits the sun's return with healing in his wings.

Thus shall there dawn for thee a cloudless morrow,
And in the brightness of its rising beam,
No more to haunt thee, be absorb'd the theme,
Too dearly nurs'd, of unavailing sorrow.

Spirits like thine, endued (but to be made
Perfect through suffering) with the passive love
Of sweet humility, at length shall soar
Where death's dread power never did invade :
And there to realize, beyond the reach
Of thought, faith, feeling, to the mortal given,
More than the sage's pen on earth can teach,
All that inspires the seraph's song in heaven :
For love with immortality doth reign,
And to its portals bright shall Hope thy feet sustain.

PRAISE TO THE HEROES.

BY WILLIAM JOHNSON FOX.

William Johnson Fox [1786—1864] was born at Wrentham, near Beccles, but his parents soon after removed to
Norwich, and at the age of twelve he became a weaver boy.
At fourteen, the loom was exchanged for the banker's desk,
and after remaining six years at the bank, he entered
Homerton Academy, as a student, under Dr. Pye Smith, and
in due time issued forth as a minister among the Calvinistic
Independents. In a few years, however, he found his
theological opinions so much at variance with his position,
that he honestly resigned his charge, and he then entered the
Unitarian body as a minister. Ultimately he became one of
the most finished orators of his age, and eminent as a
philosophical teacher, rather than as a Christian minister.
He was one of the most influential speakers in the Anti-Corn
Law movement, and he was elected M.P. for the Borough of
Oldham, without his having asked for a vote or spent a
shilling in obtaining one.

Praise to the heroes
  Who struck for the right,
When freedom and truth
  Were defended in fight:

Of blood-shedding hirelings
    The deeds are abhorred,
But the patriot smites
    With the sword of the Lord.

Praise to the martyrs
    Who died for the right,
Nor ever bowed down
    At the bidding of might :
Their ashes were cast
    All abroad to the wind,
But more widely the blessings
    They won for mankind.

Praise to the sages,
    The teachers of right,
Whose voice in the darkness,
    Said, " Let there be light."
The sophist may gain
    The renown of an hour,
But wisdom is glory,
    While knowledge is power.

Heroes, martyrs, and sages,
    True prophets of right !
They foresaw and they made
    Man's futurity bright ;
Their fame would ascend,
    Though the world sunk in flames :
Be their spirit on all
    Who sing praise to their names !

STABAT MATER.

Jews were wrought to cruel madness,
Christians fled in fear and sadness :
    Mary stood the cross beside.

At its foot her foot she planted,
By the dreadful scene undaunted,
    Till the gentle Sufferer died.

Poets oft have sung her story,
Painters decked her brow with glory,
   Priests her name have deified :

But no worship, song, or glory,
Touches like that simple story—
   Mary stood the cross beside.

And when under fierce oppression,
Goodness suffers like transgression,
   Christ again is crucified ;

But if love be there, true-hearted,
By no grief or terror parted,
   Mary stands the cross beside.

TO PRISCILLA WAKEFIELD.

ANON.

It is not fit that thou should'st leave
   Life's busy scene and varied throng ;
Until the Muse a wreath shall weave
   Around thy name, of deathless song.

Thou wert the first a path to spy,
   Untrod before, through learning's maze,
Science and art to simplify,
   And render plain to childhood's gaze.

Thy " Leisure Hours " allured us o'er,
   From tales of ghosts and giants strange ;
Thy " Anecdotes " enchanted more
   Than all the tales of fairy range.

Numbers have trod thy useful course,
   And justly won the meed of praise ;
But still to thee we trace the source
   Of learning, wove 'mid pleasure's ways.

When last I saw thee, time had laid
   His withering hand upon thy form ;
But yet within the mind still played,
   Bright as the lightning 'mid the storm.

As to the oak the ivy clings,
  Shedding spring's brightness all around,
And o'er its leafless age now flings
  That shelter which in youth it found:

Oh, thus our harps of *thee* shall breathe,
  Who taught us wisdom's worth to know,
And grateful memory fondly wreathe
  The fadeless ivy for thy brow.

THE GOLDEN BEE.

BY MISS MATILDA BETHAM EDWARDS.

PART I.

Laden with precious merchandise, the growth of Chinese soil,
And costly work of Chinese hands, the patient wealth of toil,
Over the wave with outspread sails, like white-winged bird at sea,
Swiftly, gaily, homeward bound, sped on the Golden Bee.

Stored with such peachy-textured silks as shimmer in the sun,
With countless rainbow-tinted gleams, and never keep to one—
Silks to burnish Beauty's self with a new resplendent ray—
Silks an English queen might wear on her coronation day.

She had chests of fragrant tea-leaves to make social household boards,
Or to be the one sweet luxury of widows' scanty hoards;
With grotesque and dainty ivories, carved by coarse-grained hands,
For idle money-spenders in rich European lands.

Cloudless the sky, fresh blew the breeze; the Captain's heart was light,
As on the deck he lingered late, and watched the coming night;
If sweet the journey homewards from an unpropitious sail,
'Tis sweeter still where Fortune smiles, in port, and sea, and gale.

Blithe was the Captain's gallant heart, for things had prospered well,
Soon should he reach his home on shore, with much good news to tell;
Good news for his Parsee merchants, and for the fair young wife,
Whose sweet affection made the joy and beauty of his life.

Soon should he kiss his bonnie boy, and hold him on his knee,
Awhile he'd listen, eager-eyed, to stories of the sea;
Soon should he kiss his latest-born, and then the Captain smiled—
Smiled, father-like to think of *her*, his little unseen child.

A tear ran down his sun-burnt cheek, a mild joy lit his eye,
So sweet were thoughts of love and home, so near they seemed to lie ;
Whilst, through his great rough heart diffused such pure and soft
    delight,
Which, like an even song of praise, went up to heaven's height.

One by one, upon the waves, twinkled every rising star,
And Dian trailed her golden hair over the deep afar ;
Whilst lonely o'er the vastness of that solitary sea,
Glided, as on feathered feet, the good ship, Golden Bee.

Hark ! what terrific cry was that of horror and affright,
Which broke like some tempestuous sound the stillness of the night,
Rousing the crew from rest and sleep to tremble with dismay,
Waking the Captain's sunny dreams of harbour far away ?

Oh, Captain, wake ! 'tis but a dream—the harbour is not won,
Thou dost not clasp thy Mary's hand, or kiss thy little son !
Thy baby sweetly sleeps on shore, that shore is far from thee ;
Oh, Captain, wake ! for none but God can save thy Golden Bee.

" Fire ! " 'twas an awful sound to hear on solitary seas,
With double danger in the breath of every fresh'ning breeze ;
An awful sight it was to see, the vessel all alight,
As if a blazing meteor dropped into the darksome night.

Foremost and calm, amid his crew, the Captain gave command,
Nor backward, in a moment's need, to help with skilful hand ;
Awhile the courage in his voice, and firmness on his brow,
Imparted strength and hope to hearts which ne'er had drooped till now.

Three days, three nights the vessel burned ; oh, Heavens! 'twas strange
    to be
'Mid fire unquenchable, with all the waters of the sea !
But neither skill nor strength availed : the fatal breezes blew
Death and destruction, fiery-winged, threatened the gallant crew.

And all was lost—those gorgeous silks would sweep no palace now,
Those ivory fans would never feign a breeze to beauty's brow ;
The aromatic leaf could soothe no weary student's brain,
Or freshen lips in fever heats upon the bed of pain.

"Get out the boat!" with firm, quick voice, the short command was
    said,
And no man spoke, but straight and swift the order was obeyed;
Then, one by one, the crew stepped forth, but all looked back with tears,
Upon the bonnie Golden Bee, their home of many years.

But first the Captain snatched from flame, and pressed within his breast
A relic of departed days, of all his heart loved best :
A little Prayer-book, well-worn now, a gift in early life,
Sweet token from his early love, ere yet he called her wife.

And, quick as falls a lightning shaft, when thunder is behind,
A thousand recollected joys flashed o'er his troubled mind ;
Of happy, happy courtship days, and later still, more sweet,
The tranquil joys of married life, the sound of baby feet.

Amid a death-like silentness of breeze, and sky, and sea,
Beneath a burning noon-day sun, they left the Golden Bee ;
And when they saw the blackened wreck totter amid the foam,
Each sailor breathed a prayer to God, and thought of wife and home.

Then out upon a lonely sea, six hundred miles from land,
The solitary boat sailed forth with that courageous band ;
Sailed forth as drifts a withered leaf upon the surging tide,
With only hope to be their strength, and only God as guide.

No white sail specked the arid sky, no cloud or shadow came
To cool that blue abyss of air, which seemed to be aflame ;
No breeze sprung up to aid their oars, no friendly ray of light,
Of moon, or star, shone out to guide their dreary path at night.

Oh, God! it was a fearful thing to float and drift away
Upon so wild a wilderness, day after weary day,
With meagre store of food and drink, which, ere two days had rolled,
They measured out as never yet a miser did his gold.

" Oh, Captain!" cried a sailor boy, "I ran away to sea,
And well I know my mother's heart has sorely grieved for me ;
Will some one take my parting love ?—I shall not reach the shore ! "
And then he smiled a saintly smile, nor smiled, nor spoke no more.

Then tenderly, with bare brown hands, his comrades did prepare
An humble shroud, and wrap'd him in with more than woman's care ;
And all stood up, and bared their heads, awhile the Captain read
The Church of England's requiem over its ransomed dead.

The red sun dipp'd into the sea; and lit the west afar,
The crimson clouds paled one by one, beneath the evening star ;
A calm of even-tide enwrapp'd both breeze, and sky, and wave,
When in God's great cathedral vault the sailor found a grave.

They wept no more—but, silent, stood and watched the placid deep,
Thinking with wistful hearts of him who slept such blessed sleep ;
And one, a gaunt and giant man, sent forth a bitter cry,
And clenched his hand, and shrieked aloud, "Oh, master, let us die !"

Oh, let us die ! The words rang forth through the sweet summer air,
As if a mad and tortured soul breathed out its last wild prayer.
They sounded far athwart the sea, and up into the sky,
Till even silence seemed to make the echo, "Let us die !"

Then rose the Captain, sternly sad, and where the sun had set
He waved one hand, and cried, in tones which could command them yet—
"Oh, comrades ! will you see *His* works, and doubt that He can still
Save, e'en in the eleventh hour, if such should be his will?

"Oh, whilst there's life, despair not ! Have we mothers, children,
    wives ?
Does not *their* memory give us all the strength of double lives?
Mind ye not how the widow's cruse, though wasted, filled again ?
We've yet the widow's God o'erhead, and yet a little grain.

"Oh ! tender wives, who live for us, our hearts consent to take
A little hope, a little faith, for your beloved sake :
Oh, children of our dearest love ! oh, pleasant home ashore !
Our souls can brave a thousand deaths to call ye ours once more ! "

PART II.

Where palaces of merchant kings in marble splendour rise,
And gleam beneath the burning blue of fair Calcutta's skies—
Where orange groves and myrtle bowers weigh down the sultry air,
The Captain's fair young wife abode, and watched his coming there.

c c

She never heard the billows roar, or saw a ship at sea,
Without a thought of those who steered the bonnie Golden Bee ;
She never kissed her babes at night, or woke at dawn of day,
Without a prayer that God would speed her sailor on his way.

One night rose up a fierce monsoon, and with a sudden roar,
Startled the waves from twilight rest, and dashed against the shore,
Where all night long they shrieked and wailed, and sobbing sunk to
  sleep,
As dying groans of shipwrecked men fade on the silent deep.

The Captain's babes serenely slept, and through the tempest smiled,
As sweet forget-me-nots bloom fair amid an Alpine wild ;
The mother, weeping, clasped her hands, and, pacing to and fro,
Prayed, with a white-faced misery, in murmurs faint and low :—

" Oh ! husband, art thou safe ashore, or shipwrecked on the sea,
And do the wild waves bring from far thy drowning voice to me ?
Oh ! father of my sleeping babes, 'tis hard that thou must bear
Dangers unspeakable, which I, thy own wife, may not share !

" Oh, God ! who, mid ten thousand worlds, has fixed thy glorious seat,
And cares for every human heart that worships at thy feet,
Pity my happy, helpless babes—*my* watchful agony,
And guide my husband's precious life in safety back to me."

Days glided by, and brought the time when every ship might be
That one for which her soul was sick of wistfulness to see ;
Days grew to weeks, and still she watched, and hoped, and prayed .the
  same,
For the Golden Bee's safe advent, which never, never came.

Then rose a morn, when hope grew faint within her patient heart,
When every sudden voice or step would make her pale and start
With some deep, undefined fear, that brought no words or tears,
But worked upon her maiden cheeks the furrowed grief of years.

Ah me ! the sailor's lot was hard, to drift upon the waves,
Which yawned beneath the tempest's breath, and showed a thousand
  graves,
With scarce a hope of seeing wife or children any more—
But oh ! the woman's part was worse—to wait, and weep ashore !

She held her children to her heart, and prayed without a word
(Ofttimes the heart's unspoken prayer by Heaven is soonest heard) ;
Aud if they heedless played or slept, the passion of her grief
Would spend itself in wailing tears, which brought her no relief.

Then, as a soft and tranquil day follows a night of rain,
And drooping flowers will feel the sun, and ope their leaves again :
For sweetest sake of feeble babes, no helper by save One,
She learned to lead a widowed life, and say, " Thy will be done."

One night the moon escaped from clouds, and with a pale light gleamed
Over the sea, which felt the glow, and murmured as it dreamed ;
Her bright boy cradled at her feet, her baby on her breast,
She sung her evening cradle song, and hushed the pair to rest.

And with the heaven's tranquil light upon her golden hair,
The mother's love within her eyes—eyes that were still so fair ;
She looked like some Madonna, of antique Italian art,
Such as breathe the whole religion of the painter's pious heart.

Awhile the elder child still drowsed, and, like a dove in June,
Cooed from his little downy nest unto his mother's tune,
A ship that bore a foreign flag rode calmly with the tide,
And dropp'd its anchor in the port, by the fair city's side.

Before the mother's voice had ceased its chanting fond and sweet,
A distant footstep echoed through the silence of the street ;
And when the boy's blue, dreamy eyes sought for her face no more,
A shadow flecked the window panes, and paused without the door—

A shadow of a human form, but oh, so white and wan !
As if the strong vitality of manhood must be gone ;
Then came a low-breathed, tender voice, it only murmured, " Wife ! "
And heart to heart the two were clasped, called back to new, glad life.

For hours they hardly spoke a word, but, shedding blessed tears,
Poured out their prayers of thankfulness to One who always hears ;
Those tears fell on their sleeping babes. O, children, ye receive
Such pure baptismal rite as Church or Priesthood ne'er can give.

GENIUS.

BY REV. GOODWIN BARMBY.

Among the leaves spread of a strawberry bed
  Was a living and delicate tomb,
Which, under the rich fruit so fragrant and red,
  Hung in web of a frail insect loom ;
And a spirit was there in that sepulchre fair,
  And had panted within itself long,
Like the frail, shrouded soul of some genius rare,
  Or like bard who would live in sweet song.

The bright sun it shone the rich red fruit upon,
  And lit up with a beam that thin tomb,
And the stir of a life—faintly coming—then gone,
  And now seeking for light in the gloom ;
And then, with a gentle pulse, rising in power,
  Throbbed forth in that sepulchre dim,
Like the soul of a Genius, waiting its hour
  When the sunshine was beaming for him.

The sun it rose high, and its warmth floated nigh
  The frail tomb in the strawberry leaves,
And the tomb was a cradle for infancy's sigh,
  And a cot with a thaw in the eaves ;
And an emerald eye, and a rich feathered thigh,
  And a soft, dim-hued winglet appeared,
Like young bard, or young song-thrush preparing to fly,
  Ere the pinions of flight had been reared.

The sun threw a flush o'er a burning rose bush,
  And all idly the chrysalis hung,
For the gallant New-Born, breathing love for the blush
  Of the rose, into giddy flight sprung ;
And so fondly he flew on the soft breeze that blew,
  That he reached with delight the loved flower :
As the soul of a bard a rich poem would view,
  And by flight should grow conscious of power.

And upon the sweet flower he enchanted the hour,
  And basked in her smile, and the sun,

And his bright wings displayed, with their rare-coloured dower,
  And the soft-feathered down they had on ;
The panting wings rich with red velvet were drest,
  And dark bars, and white rings, and light plumes,
And enraptured he lay in his black, glossy vest,
  Like a genius whom glory illumes.

But a cloud hid the sun, and a storm shower came on,
  And the rain-drops destroyed its bright dyes,
And its velvet was crape, and its scarlet was dun,
  And the tears dimmed its emerald eyes ;
And its young breath was faint, and unheard was its plaint,
  And it died on the breast of the rose,
Like a genius too fair, at once martyr and saint,
  And whose glories have death for their close.

THE HAND OF FRIENDSHIP.

Give me the hand that is warm, kind, and ready ;
Give me the clasp that is calm, true, and steady ;
Give me the hand that will never deceive me,—
Give me its grasp, that my soul may believe thee !
  Soft is the palm of the delicate woman,
  Hard is the hand of the rough, sturdy yeoman :
  Soft palm or hard hand, it mattereth never,
  Give me the grasp that is friendly for ever !

Give me the hand with the grasp of a brother ;
Give me the hand that has harmed not another ;
Give me the hand that has never forsworn it,—
Give me its grasp, that my love may adorn it !
  Lovely the palm of the fair, blue-veined maiden,
  Horny the hand of the workman o'erladen :
  Soft palm or hard hand, it mattereth never,
  Give me the grasp that is friendly for ever !

EYES OF BROWN.

Eyes of blue may sweetly pierce,
Eyes of black are quick and fierce ;
But the eyes whose power I own,
Are my lady's eyes of brown.

When in motion, liquid light,—
Softly dark and darkly bright,—
Like a stream o'er red-mossed stone,
Gleams in amber 'mid their brown.

When at rest their shades are deep,
As if meaning great they keep;
As a tarn on mountain high
Seems that it would hold the sky.

Dark as any tarn are they,
When lit from the gates of day;
Clearer brims its cup, and fills
Up the grand hush of the hills.

Like twin mountain tarns, her eyes,
Solitary sanctities,
Musing 'mid ways seldom trod,
Up amid the hills of God.

Yet so large,— so soft their orbs,
All the heaven she absorbs,
From their fringes shines again
In the path God walks with men.

Oh, to look up to those eyes
Well might make the sceptic wise!
And might teach him how the light
Gleameth through the darkest night.

Simpler cares to them belong,
Not less worthy, though, of song:
Glance of kindness in distress,
Look of love, to soothe and bless,

All the care to watch and ward,
All the womanly regard,—
All the upturned gaze of prayer,
In those eyes of brown are there.

Let the blue eyes sweetly pierce,
Let the black ones sparkle fierce;
But the eyes whose power I own
Are my lady's eyes of brown!

THE FARMERS' CLUB.

BY MR. ROBERT HUGHMAN.

RECITED BY THE AUTHOR TO THE MEMBERS OF THE YOXFORD FARMERS' CLUB, AT THEIR
ANNUAL MEETING IN OR ABOUT THE YEAR 1845, BUT NOT PREVIOUSLY PUBLISHED.

"Ipse dies agitat festos : fususque per herbam
Ignis ubi in medio et socii cratera coronant."
Very. Georgicon, C. 527.

The Farmers' Club, its rise and progress, all
Belonging to its fate, except its fall
(That day by some foreboded long ago,
May its fair genius far avert as now !)
Its full-moon gatherings, and though last, not least,
The crowning glories of its annual feast
Deserve a song : who shall a song refuse ?
Farmers were always favourites with the muse ;
The subject is divine, although the style
In which 'tis handled may provoke a smile :
Smile on ! I love to see you once a year,
But mind the Attic caution—" Strike, but hear ! "*
"Happy the man," the Mantuan minstrel sings,
"Who knows the causes of material things : " †
Happy the club, forsaking folly's shoals,
Which studies principles instead of rules,
Which Nature makes its universal law,
And from her source alone will maxims draw.
Her book is ever open, read and think !
At the unsullied fount of wisdom drink !
Those tainted streams, coloured by human art,
Pervert the judgment and pollute the heart.
Nor is this all false theorists will do,
They shame your sense, and pick your pockets, too ;
The first offence may be in silence past,
But where's the farmer can forgive the last ?
With rules on reason built I wage no strife,
They are the ready change of rural life ;
Reduced in bulk, and ready for the hand,
They pass like current money through the land.

* Themistocles to Eurybiades (vide Plutarch).
† Felix qui potuit cognoscere causas.

No—rules like these you cannot prize too well,
They are the very pith of principle.
Wheat is the best supply for future store,
Bread suits the wants and purpose of the hour ;
Of principles the same's as truly said,
They are the wheat, and rules the daily bread.
About your grain you little caution need,
I know you all on finest households feed ;
You sift your flour before your loaves are made,
Yet swallow rules with principles unweighed.
Consistent husbandmen ! although ye laugh,
Such rules may choke you—they are only chaff !
   Allen ! to thee the Farmers' Club belongs,
Its sage discussions and its social songs.
To Allen Ransome we award their claim,
Their "local habitation and their name."
   Ashbocking was the Reuben of thy strength,
Yoxford thy Joseph to succeed at length :
Upon the first the sire benignant smiled,
But yet the younger was the favourite child.
Then, year by year, thy sons on every hand,
In patriarchal numbers filled the land ;
Weak, strong, and wise, in different degree,
Like members of a human family.
   Ashbocking, like a wayward, first-born child,
By promise pamper'd, by indulgence spoiled,
Engross'd its father's undivided care,
And bloom'd a season in its native air ;
But when, transplanted from its genial bed,
The gas of Ipswich glittered round its head,
With civic honours when they would instal
The rustic beauty in the Temperance Hall ;
When gownsmen, townsmen, chymists, artizans,
On her fair bosom laid licentious hands,
The scientific synod quailed the dame,
And made her faithless to her maiden fame ;
Like an exotic flower, she pined away,
And briefly blended with her kindred clay.
Her members mourned her fate in "forty-three,"
And drank to her immortal memory.
   Woodbridge full soon resigned its infant breath,
Chilled by the breeze that blew from Kesgrave Heath.
   Then Harleston like a river rolled along,

Awhile united and by union strong—
The rock of politics asunder tore,
The tide that ran harmonious just before—
Two angry streams now vex the fruitful plain,
In mutual murmurs at each other's gain.
Health to that half who dare express their thought,
And use the freedom which their fathers bought !
Health to that better half, who raised the hand
To question politics that cramped the land !
What ! cast your brains and purses in the earth,
Nor scan the laws that make or mar its worth ?
Thus Harleston a divided city shews,
" Part with the Apostles hold, and part wi' the Jews."

 Then Wrentham, after many a social year
Of monthly converse, and of annual cheer,
Fell a sad victim to some sudden fate,
In the full bloom and manhood of its state.
About its case the doctors couldn't agree,
Some knew, but durst not tell its malady :
The heart was sound enough, while others said,
Some hinted inflammation in the head ;
Or head, or tail, the effects were just the same :
Something was wrong, and dissolution came.
Yet still each member's disembodied sprite
Will haunt the " Eagle " on the wonted night,
Will dance around the door, pale, grey, or blue,
Hankering for joys they in the body knew ;
Glide through the key-hole of the well-known room,
Their favourite glass and former seat resume,
Ring for the waiter in the usual way,
When hostess comes and finds the de'il to pay.

 Thus four have fallen through influence malign,
Cold, fever, apoplexy, and decline !
And yet lament not, Allen, they are gone,
Thou still canst number many a thrifty son :
Apples may hang too thick upon the tree,
Some fall, and leave the rest to ripen free ;
The strongest still are those that longest last,
As the best fruit survives the sternest blast.
All things decline at length, and so must we,
Not Farmers' Clubs can an exception be :

Our Farmers' Club may die —its members *must*,
Chairman and treasurer are but kindred dust ;
E'en your poor Secretary's busy head
Shall soon repose, and all his cares be fled ;
Time, ruthless time shall soon arrest his quill,
Numb be his guiding hand, his prompting brain be still !
Another shall your monthly notes record,
And your minutes, at the annual board.
Another Chairman other times shall see,
Another Cross, control the treasury ;
Another race of farmers here shall sit,
And canvass every word we said or writ :
Perhaps on some sound resolution pause,
Or give some freeborn sentiment applause ;
In the dim records left behind us see
The dawn of free inquiry doomed to be
The dayspring of the lights of husbandry.
Earth's inmost powers shall they then explore,
Free from the trammels which their fathers wore ;
O'er the rich meadows spread the thick manure,
In lessened game and lengthened lease secure.
The strong Guano range in triple row,
Till merchants want another Ichaboe ;
No embryo thistle, million-blown in seed
Shall on the vitals of their furrows feed,
But war untired be waged with every weed.
   The sister arts shall lend their social aid,
Swell the full ear, and urge the exuberant blade ;
The stringent clause that cramped the generous plan,
And put the soil's improvement under ban,
And drew a curse from many a starving man,
Before a wise generation's eye
Back to the shades of feudal night shall fly,
Nor stain the parchment with its odious dye.
Tenants and lords shall social compacts draw,
With half the skin and less than half the law ;
The farmers' children to the fourth agree,
Shall heir at will their father's husbandry,
And bless the acknowledged claims of fair priority.
That moral dawning, like the natural light
Which dissipates the noxious dews of night,
Shall roll the mists of ignorance away,
And the false front of prejudice display ;

With mutual mirrors shall men's minds invest,
And each reflect his own in others' interest.
Onward it comes, with elementary force,
(Clouds of detraction cannot bar its course),
Onward it comes, and, ere your days decline,
You yet may see that glorious morning shine ;
Truth rides its wings, and, lord or tenant's right,
Truth ne'er was worsted in an open fight.

Then keep her claims alive from year to year,
Advance, accelerate her bright career !
All censure challenge, and no favour court,
But strive to leave behind a fair Report.

MY OWN FIRESIDE.

My own Fireside, where'er I be
Like magnet true, I turn to thee :
I find no sport, I feel no bliss
Pure as thy pastime and thy kiss.
Where are the social joys of life
Without our girls, and boys, and wife ?
The losel wanders far and wide ;
Love nestles near his own Fireside.

My own Fireside, when twilight's hour
Resigns the scene to fancy's power,
What dreams of loveliness and light
I've pictured in thine embers bright !
What forms fantastic seen thy glow
Fast flickering up the ceiling throw !
Through fairy land I've seemed to glide,
In reveries round my own Fireside.

My own Fireside, the world may name
More splendid fields to cope for fame,
May show the camp, the court, the bar,
To tempt us with their dangerous star ;
But ah ! ambition's glittering ray
Lures but man's baser half astray,
His better part is yet allied
To nature, and his own Fireside.

My own Fireside, of thee possest,
And family, and friends, I'm blest ;
With work I'd wear away my days,
My evenings with thy jovial blaze.

Heaven grant me still the grace of prayer,
Enough to spend, a mite to spare
Some lonely one, by lot denied,
The comforts of an own Fireside!

My own Fireside, oh let us strive
To keep domestic love alive
By cheering word, by kindly deed,
And learn each other's looks to read!
And loyal praise and thanks bestow
For blessings more than millions know,
And worship, morn and eventide,
The Saviour of our own Fireside!

My own Fireside, now fifty years
Bring half a century of cares,
And while the grey hairs, one by one,
Like Autumn's withering leaves come on,
Oh may we to our children give
Our long experience how to live,
And joyous jubilees betide
Children's on children's own Fireside.

THE CHRONICLE OF CASTEL FRAMLINGHAM.

BY MRS. E. B. COWELL (LATE MISS CHARLESWORTH).

We saw the Deben's silver wave roll gleaming through the vale,
We pass'd where Wickham's tapering spire looks far o'er hill and dale,
And pale across the dusky lea gleamed sheep and snow white lamb,
When rose against the distant sky the Towers of Framlingham.
Dark shadowing in the dim twilight their massive outline rose,
But oh! no banner's crimson fold stirr'd the grey walls' repose,
No breath of distant warder's note, no far-off bugle horn
Faint floating to the horseman's ear along the wolds was borne ;
But slow decay kept watch and ward about the Castle gate,
And ruin held the lofty place of long departed state,
And grass-grown were the entrances where knightly hoofs had rung,
And the low roof of poverty within its site had sprung.

Oh Framlingham ! grey Framlingham! thy lords have pass'd away,
On them and over thee hath fallen the mantle of decay!
Thy ruin'd walls still crown the brow where ages they have tower'd,
But in thy holy chancel aisles lie many a noble Howard.

There sleeps the Lady Margaret, and there Fitz Alan's child,
And gleams the vacant niche where once an infant image smil'd ;
And where round Norfolk's sculptur'd tomb the granite columns rise,
In marble slumber by her Lord proud Stafford's daughter lies :
Branch of a house whose graceful stem deserv'd a better fate
Than met the noble Buckingham from Wolsey's deadly hate ;
And high the Howard's lion crest looks down in ebon gloom
Above the flower of Chivalry, the gallant Surrey's tomb.

Within thy walls, in other days, held Saxon princes reign,
And round thee reav'd the pirate lords, led by the robber Dane ;
But when the Norman's iron hand ruled over hill and heath,
Then grandeur reared thy stately roofs, and splendour dwelt beneath ;
And green the park around thee spread, where glanced the graceful deer,
And slowly glided the white swan along the glassy mere ;
And through the shady avenues, the merry archer sprang,
And to the joyous huntsman's horn, the woodland echoes rang ;
And tapestry hung its storied folds around the banquet-room,
And lamps within the Chapel shrine, lit up the midnight's gloom,
And floated many a pennon fair, those battlements across,
Where only waves the wild briar now, and spreads the yellow moss.

When sorrow upon England fell, and hopeless tears were wept,
When over many a noble head the restless waters swept ;
When sank the hope of England, beneath the wild wave's foam,
And an aged King dwelt sorrowful in a deserted home ;
While o'er their head the sea gull shrieked, and the wild petrel swam,
There slumber'd low beside his prince the Lord of Framlingham.
When rose the sun upon a day, whose fame shall long endure,
That saw the bold Plantagenet in the field of Agincourt,
A single horseman fearlessly before the army rode,
And the hosts of England shouted at the signal that he shew'd :
The brave Sir Thomas Erpingham was earliest in the fray,
The Lord of Ancient Framlingham began the fight that day.

When the wild wars of the Roses were ringing through the land,
And the flowers of England faded, beneath the mower's hand,
When ruled the house of York, over moor and upland side,
In his Castle halls of Framlingham, the Duke of Norfolk died.
Earl Marshal of England, Lord of Legrave and of Gower,
Well knew the lost Lancastrian, his titles, and his power.
They bare him to his resting place, in Thetford's silent aisles,
And his young and only child they led to Westminster's proud piles,

And her hand, and her towers, to King Edward's son they gave :
But the given and the gifted met both an early grave ;
In the secrets of the tower, that noble boy was laid,
And his infant bride lies sleeping in the tranquil Abbey shade.

Oh ! a voice came o'er the border, of wailing and dismay,
From Stirling and from Yarrow side, lamenting for the day ;
Oh ! many a song of sorrow made Ettrick Forest ring
For the fatal field of Flodden, when Scotland lost her king ;
When Lenox and Montrose were slain, when Huntley fled o'erpowered
Before the Lord of Framlingham, the banner of the Howard.
He lived, as soldiers seldom live, to grey and honour'd age,
And bravely kept a noble house and knightly equipage ;
And, full of honour and of years, he calmly pass'd away,
While bloom'd along his fair domains, the pleasant month of May ;
And none could breathe of injury, or rightful claim unpaid,
By him whose grey head peacefully in Thetford's walls was laid.

He had served a reckless master, whose fiery heart and head
Had little room for gratitude, to the living or the dead ;
But a few swift years had floated o'er the aged warrior's tomb,
When again the House of Howard bent beneath the stroke of doom—
Where, like another Venice, gleaming along the wave,
Stands haughtily the tower—a palace and a grave.
Saw ye that galley flitting towards the vaulted stair ?—
Knew ye the muffled figures silently hurried there ?—
Oh ! where art thou, Earl Surrey, in thy country's hour of need ?
Oh ! where wert thou, Lord Norfolk, when thy son was led to bleed ?
Oh ! wo ! wo ! for the hour ; oh ! wo ! wo ! for the day
When the stateliest of the herd became the angry lion's prey !

A star of song, a light of Fame, a child of Minstrelsy,
In royal Windsor's woodland bowers, they marked his boyhood nigh ;
There, by the side of young Fitzroy, he trod the oaken glade,
And they are laid together now, in the same chancel shade.
In many a sunny Southern land his lyre and sword were known,
And bright in Honour's listed fields his crest of knighthood shone ;
Now in the aisles of Framlingham, no longer watched nor wept,
Though passionate love and grief were his, for ages hath he slept ;
The noble heart that beat so high, there mouldereth in decay,
And all that woke its pulses warm hath past to dust away ;
The tale of List and Tournament, the legend and worn stone,
Are all that rest to tell us, now, of faded things and gone.

Oh! parted times!—thy shadowy veil hath shrouded from our view
The splendours of forgotten years, the scenes our fathers knew;
Peace resteth on our changed land, and Holy Faith is there,
And Freedom breathes in every breeze, that stirs her island air;
And safety dwells beside our hearths, and round our calm church towers,—
A blessing on the sainted heads that died to leave them ours!
But oh! the pleasant festal rites, the feasts and customs old,
The rich and joyous pageantry, the loyalty unsold,
The grace of ancient courtesy, the worth and honour grey,
The reverent love of reverent things, that all have passed away—
Oh! broken is the yew-tree bow—the wandering harper fled,
And the lost things of parted years are with the parted dead!

And long, long, pleasant summers in silence floated on,
With flowers that all are faded now, with green wreaths that are gone,
While every breath that sighed over hamlet and lone grange,
Some tidings brought of wonder, of trouble, or of change;—
The wail above the early dead, nor youth nor rank could save,
The sorrow round the peasant's hearth, and by the martyr's grave;
But when that royal lady our island sceptre held,
For whom the winds of Heaven fought, and the dark waters swell'd;
When England all saw golden days, and spread the festal board,
Again, decay'd fortress, the tower held thy Lord;
And dark the stain of noble blood flushed on the keen axe-blade,
And Scotland unto dool and death her rightful liege betray'd.

Oh! many a summer sun since *then* hath lit that proud church-nave,
And shone across the statues cold that gleam on Surrey's grave.
The lifeless things that vainly these would shadow to the eye,
The image of the beautiful be gone for ever by!
And in our halls the sword of war hath long forgot to gleam,
And knighthood, with its stainless crest, hath vanished like a dream;
And sounds of peace float tranquilly our island vales along,
The music of the harvest-home, the early mowers' song;
And by the side of ducal tombs, and chieftains, mail array'd,
Have risen lowlier monuments, where *other* men have laid;
There wreath'd, but with love's simple wreaths, which never blood defil'd,
The pastor slumbereth with his flock, the mother with her child.

Oh Framlingham! grey Framlingham! proud record of the past,
Written by many a horse's hoof, by many a bugle blast;
By many a wandering summer-wind, fretting the ancient stone,
Sighing through niche and window-slit, all lichen-overgrown—

Chased by the silent summer shower, freshening the briar and moss,
And, trickling down the channell'd way, worn thy broad stones across;
Relic of what hath long since been, of what is with the dead,
Ages lit up by splendours wild, whose meteor-gleam hath fled!
The quiet rest of peaceful age now hangs thy worn brow o'er,
And grey-haired men sit cheerfully, each at his cottage door,
And children, chanting holy psalms, now seek the house of God,
Where once the chieftain's plume flashed by, the mail'd warrior trod.

The bloody flag of Popery was rear'd upon thy walls;
The Protestants' lone chronicler was sheltered in thy halls;
Royal and noble have they been, thy dwellers in the past;
The poor man and the homeless now tenant thy gates at last:
The bridge which hath seen leaders pass, to conquer or to die,
Is trodden by the quiet foot of way-worn poverty.
So fadeth the memorial of that which hath been high!
So worketh round the viewless wheel of human destiny!
Oh! beautiful in ruin!—most lovely in decline!
Be ours an age as ruffleless, as full of calm as thine!
And thou who *should'st* have clos'd for me my long unfinished song,
Heaven watch above thy happy home, and grant it stand as long;
Sweet quiet, with its shadowing wings, guard over its roof, keeping,
As have the solemn aisles, where thine ancestors are sleeping.*

STANZAS WRITTEN ON A CHILD'S FIRST BIRTH-DAY.

BY MR. T. W. GISSING.

The Spring was coming o'er the earth,
  And every flower and tree
Was courted by the sun and shower,
  To set its foliage free;
The wild birds carolled their sweet lays,
  When th' light first shone on thee.

Four seasons since have run their course;
  The Spring, and Summer's heat,—
The Autumn's placid mid-day skies,

* This Poem was originally dedicated to Miss Alexander, The Goldrood, Ipswich, and the "Ancestors," referred to in the last line, are those of the Alexander family, whose monuments are in the Framlingham Church.

And gilded sunsets sweet,—
And Winter's cold and chilly frosts,
    With drear December's sleet.

I've seen thy gambols on the hearth,
    And watched thee oft with joy,
As kitten-like from place to place,
    Thou'dst fling some infant toy,
And clap thy little hands with glee,
    Thou bright-eyed, laughing boy!

Thy simple prattlings I have heard,
    And striv'n to understand ;
And when in eagerness thou point'st
    Thy tiny baby hand,
Unknowing what thou wished for,
    My heart is sadly pained.

How falt'ringly thy patt'ring feet
    The first lone step essayed,
While clinging to thy trembling self
    Thou stood'st, to start afraid,
And raised thy supplicating eyes,
    That some might give thee aid.

Thy mind is like the future flowers,
    Deep hidden in the stem ;
And gaining strength with ev'ry day,
    'Twill soon expand like them,
And what is now the unseen germ,
    Will be the blossomed gem.

Thou camest with the Spring, fair child !
    When cowslips were in bloom ;
When mossy banks sent through the air
    The violet's sweet perfume !
Oh ! may thy life be like the Spring,
    Till Death shall call thee home.

MOSSES.

Where the wild world-clasping sea
Laves its shores eternally ;
Where the raging torrent swells,

'Midst the highlands' heathy dells ;
Where the stately river flows,
Springing 'midst eternal snows ;
By the brooklet's sparkling sheen,
Year by year the Moss grows green.

Where the summer sun unbinds
Th' thyme's wild perfume to the winds ;
Where amidst the boggy swamp,
Jack-o'-lantern trims his lamp ;
Where the marish flow'rets blow—
There the beauteous Mosses grow.

On the riven cliff's cold breast ;
On the mountain's rugged crest ;
On the upland's slippery slope ;
On the barrow's rounded cope ;
O'er the columns, that ere while
Stood amidst the sacred pile—
Columns that beheld the sway
Of creeds, for ever passed away.
O'er the castle's ruined keep ;
O'er its walls where reptiles creep ;
In its dungeons dank and lone,
Where each age-encrusted stone
Enclosed once to captive's groan ;
In its wide hall's shadows deep,
Where the mocking echoes sleep—
Living Mosses greenly creep.

'Midst the mighty city's hum,
Where the breaking heart is dumb ;
Where the wrecked and ruined soul
Vainly strives 'gainst Sin's control ;
Where the river's chilly arms
Gape to clasp her faded charms—
There, where passions heave and toss,
Blooms the ever verdant Moss.

'Neath the forest's shadows dim,
Where the wild bird pipes his hymn ;
Where the ev'ning breezes low
Change to music as they blow ;

Where the perfume from the flower
Sweeter comes at twilight hour—
There, amidst that wilderness,
Mosses grow in wild excess.

'Midst the rustling grass that waves
O'er the tear-besprinkled graves,
Where the dead are free from ill,
Careless of the harsh world's will;
Slander now, nor envious spite,
Dream they of in their long night.
Flowers will blow, though men may rave,
Lie bestained above each grave ;
Those beneath will never feel
Cursing tongue, or spurning heel —
On that last lone silent bed,
Mosses spring to deck the dead.

Beauty slumbers in each blade,
By no mortal hand arrayed ;
Truth and Wisdom likewise dwell
In the Mosses' smallest cell,
Nature's handmaids, fost'ring earth,
For her yearly floral birth ;
They by Nature's high decree,
Teach a lesson, Man, to thee.

THE LILIES OF JERUSALEM.

BY MISS AGNES STRICKLAND.

Fair lilies of Jerusalem,
    Ye wear the same array
As when imperial Judah's stem
    Maintained its regal sway.

By sacred Jordan's desert tide
    As bright ye blossom on
As when your simple charms outvied
    The pride of Solomon.

The lonely pilgrim's heart is fill'd
  With holiest themes divine,
When first he sees your colours gild
  The fields of Palestine;

Fresh springing from the emerald sod,
  As beautiful to see,
As when the meek, incarnate God
  Took parable from ye.

What rose amidst her fragrant bowers
  That steals the morning's glow,
Or tulip, queen of eastern flowers,
  Was ever honoured so?

But ye are of the lowly train
  Which He delights to raise;
Ye bloom unsullied by a stain,
  And therefore ye have praise.

Ye never toiled with anxious care,
  From silken threads to spin
That living gold, refined and rare,
  Which God hath clothed ye in,

That ye, His simplest works, should shine
  In such adornment drest,
That mightiest kings of Judah's line
  Could boast of no such vest.

Ye still as mute memorials stand
  Of Scripture's sacred page,
Sweet lilies of the holy land,
  And bloom in every age.

Ye've seen the terrors of the Lord
  By signs and wonders shown,
And kingly rebels to His power
  Amidst their pride o'erthrown.

Ye flourished when the captive band,
  By prophets warned in vain,
Were led to far Euphrates' strand,
  From Jordan's pleasant plain,

In hostile lands to weep and dream
　Of things that still were free,
And sigh to see your golden gleam,
　Sweet flowers of Galilee!

And ye have seen a darker hour
　On Zion's children fall,
Than when Chaldea's vengeful power
　Assailed her leaguered wall.

Ye saw the eagles from afar
　On wings of terror come,
And godless priests maintain a war
　'Gainst earth-subduing Rome.

The meteor sword, that high in air
　O'er guilty Salem swept,
And all her burden of despair
　O er which Messiah wept.

Ye bloomed unscathed, meek, lowly flowers :
　On that terrific night,
When marble fanes and rock-built towers
　Crashed downwards from their might.

Ye have survived Judea's throne,
　Her temple's overthrow,
And seen proud Salem, sitting lone,
　A widow in her woe.

Her children from that pleasant place
　Are outcasts sent to roam,
And Ishmael's misbelieving race
　Lay waste their forfeit home.

But, lilies of Jerusalem,
　Through every change ye shine,
And still your golden urns be-gem
　The fields of Palestine!

"OH! CAN YOU LEAVE YOUR NATIVE LAND?"

A CANADIAN SONG.

BY MRS. MOODIE (LATE SUSANNAH STRICKLAND).

Oh ! can you leave your native land,
    An exile's bride to be ;
Your mother's home, and cheerful hearth,
    To tempt the main with me,—
Across the wide and stormy sea,
    To trace our foaming track,
And know the wave that bears us on
    Will ne'er convey us back ?

And can you in Canadian woods
    With me the harvest bind,
Nor feel one lingering, sad regret
    For all you leave behind ?
Can those dear hands, unused to toil,
    The woodman's wants supply,
Nor shrink beneath the chilly blast,
    When wintry storms are nigh ?

Amid the shades of forest dark,
    Our loved isle will appear
An Eden, whose delicious bloom
    Will make the wild more drear :
And you in solitude will weep
    O'er scenes beloved in vain,
And pine away your life to view
    Once more your native plain.

Then pause, dear girl! ere those fond lips
    Your wanderer's fate decide ;
My spirit spurns the selfish wish—
    You must not be my bride !
But, oh ! that smile—those tearful eyes
    My firmer purpose move—
Our hearts are one, and we will dare
    All perils thus to love !

"HARVEST CART" IN SUFFOLK.

BY QUILL.

Yow, Jack, bring them 'ere hosses here—
 Get this 'ere waggin out;
I think the weather mean to clear,
 So jest yow look about!
Come, put old Jolly to, right quick—
 Now then, hook Di'mond on,
(There chuck yow down that plaguy stick!)
 An' goo an' call old John.

John bo' the " Cart shod close " we'll try
 (Get yow upon the stack);
I'm sure the whate's by this time dry—
 Bring them 'ere forks here, Jack.
Blarm that 'ere chap! where is he *now?*
 Jest look yow here, my man,
If yow don't want to have a row,
 Be steady, if yow can.

Ope that 'ere gate. Wish! Jolly—Wo!
 Cop that 'ere rope up, Sam ;
Now I'll get down an pitch, bo'; so
 Jump yow up where I am.
Load wide enough, mate—that's the style—
 Now hold ye ! Di'mond !—Wo-o !
Jack !— that 'ere boy do me that rile—
 Jest mind yow where yow goo !

There goo a rabbit ! Boxer, hi !—
 She's sure to get to grownd,
Hold ye ! Now then bo', jest yow try
 To turn them nicely round.
Don't knock them shoves down ! Blarm the boy !—
 You'll be in that 'ere haw !
That feller do me so annoy ;
 But *he* don't care a straw !

. . . .

How goo the time?   I kind o' think
   Our fourses* should be here.
Chaps, don't y*w* fare to want some drink ?—
   There's Sue with the old beer.
The rain have cleared right slap away,
   An' if it hold out bright,
Let's work right hard, lads (what d'ye say ?)
   An' clear this feld to night!

" GLEANING TIME " IN SUFFOLK.

Why, listen yow—be quiet, bo' !—the bell is tolling eight! † —
Why don't yow mind what yow're about ?— We're allers kind o'late !
Now, Mary, get that mawther dress'd —oh dear ! how slow yow fare—
There come a lot o' gleaners now— Maw', don't stand gawkin' there !

Now, Jane, goo get that 'ere coach, an' put them pillars in—
Oh ! won't I give it yow, my dear, if I do once begin !
Get that 'ere bottle, too—ah, yow may well stand there an' sneer ;
What *will* yowr father say, d'ye think, if we don't taak his beer ?

Come, Willie !—Jane, where *is* he gone ?   Goo yow an' fetch that child ;
If yow don't move them legs of yow'rn, yow'll maak me kind o' riled !
There, lock the door, an' lay the key behind that 'ere old plate ;
An' Jemmy, yow run on afore, and ope the whatefeld gate.

Well, here we be at last—oh, dear ! how fast my heart do beat !
Now, Jane, set yow by this 'ere coach, an' don't yow leave yowr seat
Till that 'ere precious child's asleep ; then bring yow that 'ere sack,
An' see if yow can't try, to-day, to kind o' bend yowr back !

Yow'll all wish, when the winter come, and yow ha'ent got no bread,
That for all drawlin' about so, yow'd harder wrought instead ;
For all yowr father 'arn most goo old Skin'em s rent to pay,
An' Mister Last, the shoemaker ; so work yow hard, I pray !
    *   *   *   *   *   *

Dear me ! there goo the bell agin —'tis seven, I declare ;
An' we don't 'pear to have got none :—the gleanin' now don't fare
To be worth nothin' ; but I think—as far as I can tell —
We'll try a comb, some how, to scratch, if we be 'live an' well.

   * The harvest men leave off at four o'clock for refreshment, which they
call their " fourses."
   † In some villages in Suffolk the church bells toll at 8 a.m. and 7 p.m.
to regulate the time for gleaning.

SONNET TO THE RIVER ORWELL.

BY MR. J. T. SHEWELL.

Orwell, delightful stream, whose waters flow
Fring'd with luxuriant beauty to the main !
Amid thy woodlands taught, the Muse could fain
On thee, her grateful eulogy bestow.
Smooth and majestic though thy current glide,
And bustling Commerce plough thy liquid plain ;
Tho' grac'd with loveliness thy verdant side,
While all around enchantment seems to reign :
These glories still, with filial love, I taste,
And feel their praise ;—yet thou hast one beside
To me more sweet ; for on thy banks reside
Friendship and Truth combin'd, whose union chaste
Has sooth'd my soul;—and these shall bloom sublime,
When fade the fleeting charms of Nature and of Time.

ON THE DEATH OF THE PRINCE CONSORT.

BY MR. JAMES SPILLING.

The wise decree is spoken ;
  The spirit hears its Lord ;
The golden bowl is broken,
  And loosed the silver cord ;
The monarch and the peasant
  Are mingling bitter tears,
Unheeding that their lord still lives
  Amid the golden spheres.

The people sip the chalice
  Their stricken Queen must drain ;
The wail that fills the palace
  Shrills up from cot and plain.
Why marvel that the nation
  Reels at the sudden blow ?
She feels her desolation ;
  She feels her Sovereign's woe.

But not for *him* she weepeth ;
  We know that he is gone
Where God's true servant reapeth
  The harvest he hath sown—
To the shining spheres of beauty,
  Where blessings fall like dew
On him who knew his duty,
  And wrought the truth he knew.

'Twas not thy high alliance
  With the Lady of the Isles,
Lost friend of Art and Science,
  That won a nation's smiles.
'Twas not the name thou worest,
  But thy spirit's patriot zeal,
The manly heart thou borest,
  Thy love for human weal !

True Husband, Friend, and Father !
  TRUE MAN—far nobler yet !
These titles, twined together,
  Form a fadeless coronet,
Worn by the star-zoned spirit
  In regions undefiled,
Who taught a future king to rule,
  And blessed the pauper child.

The wise decree is spoken ;
  The soul hath sought its Lord ;
The golden bowl is broken,
  And loosed the silver cord.
The monarch and the peasant
  May mourn, with bitter tears,
The Prince whose deeds are spirit seeds
  To grow in after years.

A VOICE FROM THE MILLINER'S WORK-ROOM.

Each thing that lives beneath the stars
  Adorns our wandering earth
With some bright ray of beauty's power,
  Or virtue's milder worth.

But far the sweetest, purest gem,
  In Nature's bounteous mine,
Is she around whose maiden heart
  Love's sacred tendrils twine.

But seldom doth her hapless fate
  Our selfish thoughts engage,
Though carefully we watch the flower,
  And tend the young bird's cage.
We think not of the weary hours
  She toils to swell our pride,
In the feverish room, till the rose's bloom
  From off her cheek hath died.

For ere the calm immortal lights
  Fade from the morning sky,
Till evening twilight melts o'er earth,
  'Mid softest melody,
She still must toil to frame the gauds
  Her haughty sisters wear,
Whilst silently the shades of fate
  Her burial clothes prepare.

Oh, sisters! think of bitter tears
  In sorrow's silence shed ;
Of pangs that rend the struggling soul,
  Till every hope has fled—
Till the noble spirit, in whose pure depths
  The love of love's impearled,
With all its worth is lost to earth,
  That fashion may rule the world.

Oh, lost to virtue, hope, and love !
  Oh, lost to life and light !
More pure than silver dew drops wept
  Upon the breast of night !
A revelation of Beauty's power !
  A beam of Heaven's own truth !
A portion of nature's fervid soul
  Arrayed in the glories of youth !

Oh, sisters! mourn the noble hearts
  That sleep beneath the clay,

And know that virtue's far too rare
    To sweep like dross away ;
And oh ! methinks your lovely cheeks
    Would blanch in your selfish mirth,
Did I name the sin of those who cast
    The BEAUTY OF GOD from earth.

IN MEMORIAM.

TO SIR HENRY EDWARD BUNBURY, BART.

BY MR. T. G. YOUNGMAN.

Droop, scattered flowers of tardy spring !
Hush'd be your songs, ye birds, that bring
Joy to our hearts, while blithe ye sing,
    Though bitter north winds rave ;
Grey be the sky, and still the air,
But let a sunbeam here and there
Look through, whilst slow and sad we bear
    A good man to his grave.

We bear him from his father's hall,
The forest giants, gaunt and tall,
Stretch their bare arms above the pall
    As slowly on we go ;
By level lawn, by wooded dell,
By lowly homes where cotters dwell,
By lane and croft he loved so well
    We bear him sad and slow.

As thus we pass each well-known haunt,
No waving plumes above him flaunt,
No blazon'd trappings' hollow vaunt
    Make up his fun'ral show ;
In this his wishes we fulfil,
In this his word we follow still,
And feel, as thus we do his will,
    A less'ning of our woe.

We reach at last the churchyard's bound,
And stand with silent awe around
That quiet spot of sacred ground
    He chose to be his grave :
With holy words, with pious care,
With loving hands, we place him there,
Then lift our hearts in fervent prayer
    To Him who died to save.

Now lightly o'er his rev'rend head,
The level, fragrant turf we spread,
And by his lonely, hallowed bed
    A stately stone we raise ;
Now on that fair-hewn tablet write,
Grave deep and strong, with hand of might,
This good man's sole, last earthly right—
    His meed of human praise.

Yes, write—but what ?   That, nobly bred,
A soldier's life be chose and led,
And gained a name for heart and head,
    From friend and foe ?
No, write not that—'tis true, but vain :
England on many a bloody plain
Such seed has sown like summer rain,
    For glory's transient glow.

That when fair youth and strength declined,
Cheerful, the war-sword he resigned,
And strode upon the realms of mind
    With no uncertain foot ?
No, write not that—his efforts there
Shall meet from time their guerdon fair,
And take of fame their rightful share,
    As flowers spring from their root.

But on his hallowed tablet grave,
Cut deep, so that your words may brave
Time's longest roll of wearing wave—
    Cut deep, and fair, and clear ;

And write that, in a sordid age,
When gold was God, and Mammon's rage
Filled social life and learning's page,
        He who now lieth here

Could o'er that heartless serfdom rise,
The lust and greed of gold despise,
Be rich, but good, and great, and wise,
        The Guardian of the poor ;
That on the acres of his soil
No man for stinted wage did moil,
Nor e'er in vain for " leave to toil "
        Ask at " his brother's door."

That earnestly he strove to give
His fellow man the means to live,
To learn, to know, to think, to strive,
        If fall'n to rise again ;
And thus, though often sorely tried,
He nobly lived, and fearless died,
And by his *actions* justified
        " The ways of God to men."

IV.

Statistical Information.

IV.

Statistical Information.

POPULATION.

In April, 1861, the population of our county, variously occupied and distributed over the surface, amounted to 335,409.

The number of the male population was 164,144, and of the female, 171,265. The women and girls thus exceeded the men and boys by 7,121; but as a number of the men were at sea, the *real disparity* was something less than this number. The excess of females was greatest in the towns of Ipswich and Bury St. Edmund's; but in Cosford, Thingoe, Hoxne, Bosmere, and Samford districts, the males exceeded the females in number. The annexed table exhibits the population of Suffolk at each Census from 1801 to 1861 inclusive.

YEARS.	PERSONS.	INCREASE OF POPULATION.	DECREASE OF POPULATION.	INCREASE PER CENT.	DECREASE PER CENT.
1801	214,404	..	..	..	..
1811	233,963	19,559	..	9	..
1821	271,541	37,578	..	16	..
1831	296,317	24,776	..	9	..
1841	315,073	18,512	..	6	..
1851	337,215	21,885	..	7	..
1861	335,409	..	1,806	..	2

E E

HOUSES AND FAMILIES.

Families are the social units that combinedly form hamlets, villages, and towns. In 1801, the number of families in Suffolk was 43,481, and in 1861, the number of separate occupiers or families was 77,543. At the commencement of the century, the number of inhabited houses was 32,805, and 155 were building; in 1861 they numbered 72,714, and 230 were building. The increase of the population was 45 per cent.; the increase of inhabited houses was 121 per cent. in the same period. At the commencement of the century there were 66 persons to every 10 houses. In 1861 the accommodation had so far increased, that the occupied houses were inhabited in the proportion of 21 houses to every 100 persons. From 1841 to 1861 the increase of inhabited houses was greater than the increase of population, and this is in many respects a good test of the degree of improvement in the county. The number of houses inhabited, uninhabited, and building at each Census have been returned thus:

YEARS.	INHABITED.	UNINHABITED.	BUILDING.
1801	32,253	552	155
1811	37,227	624	270
1821	42,773	666	No Return.
1831	50,139	1,141	259
1841	64,041	2,352	574
1851	69,282	3,107	449
1861	72,714	3,568	230

A house, as is well known to travellers in Suffolk, is a very variable unit. In the Census definition it includes the hut on the common and the castle on the hill, and the large proportion of small tenements in Suffolk is proved by the annual value of the houses. Only 7 per cent. of all the houses in the county are assessed to the House Duty. 67,000 householders in Suffolk reside in houses under £20 annual value, for only 5,394 houses in the county are liable to the House Duty.

BIRTH PLACES OF THE PEOPLE OF SUFFOLK.

An examination of the birth places of the people of this county will exhibit the blending of the people of other counties with those of our own, and show how many of the residents of Suffolk were actually born in the county.

Suffolk, in 1861, contained natives of Ireland, of Scotland, of Wales, of islands in the British Seas, of the British Colonies, of the East Indies, of persons born at sea and in foreign lands, as well as natives of every county in England and Wales. Taking the civil or geographical limits of the county, we find that 42,956 of the residents were born outside the limits of Suffolk. Of this number Wales furnished 191; Ireland, 752; Scotland, 512; British Colonies and East Indies, 439; Islands in the British Seas, 62. In foreign lands 410 of our residents first drew breath, and 27 were born on the briny deep. Looking at the contributions to the population of Suffolk from each of the counties, we find that Essex sent 7,618; Norfolk, 16,421; Cambridge, 2,836; and Middlesex, 4,749. The numbers from each of the other counties are much smaller:—Bedford, 141; Berks, 230; Buckingham, 157; Chester, 116; Cornwall, 135; Cumberland, 42; Derby, 123; Devon, 422; Dorset, 151; Durham, 137; Gloucester, 264; Hereford, 46; Hertford, 378; Huntingdon, 178; Kent, 1,160; Lancaster, 357; Leicester, 156; Lincoln, 420; Monmouth, 26; Northampton, 212; Northumberland, 145; Nottingham, 131; Oxford, 148; Rutland, 29; Salop, 94; Somerset, 254; Southampton, 512; Stafford, 165; Surrey, 975; Sussex, 404; Warwick, 225; Westmoreland, 19; Wilts, 181; Worcester, 116; York, 680. The residents born within the limits of the county numbered 294,124.

MIGRATION OF THE PEOPLE OF SUFFOLK.

Comparison of the number of inhabitants in Suffolk, and the number returned for England and Wales as having been born in the county, shows how large a number of the "natives" have been absorbed in the active operations of other counties. 337,070 persons were enumerated in the *civil* county in 1861; but 400,604 persons in England and Wales were returned as "born in Suffolk," so that the number of persons in England and Wales belonging to Suffolk *by birth*, exceeded by 63,534 the actual number of inhabitants in the county. But even this does not fully exhibit the number of Suffolk people distributed over England and Wales. The residents born in the county numbered only 294,124, leaving 106,480 persons born in Suffolk as resident of other parts of England and Wales. More recruits have, with one exception, been sent from Suffolk to every county in England than it has received in return, in many instances three or four to one. Thus

Cambridge has sent	2,836	to Suffolk, and received	4,823	from Suffolk.
Sussex	,,	404	,,	,,	1,445	,,
Yorkshire	,,	680	,,	,,	2,375	,,
Lancashire	,,	357	,,	,,	1,976	,,
Surrey	,,	975	,,	,,	10,811	,,
Kent	,,	1,160	,,	,,	6,711	,,
Middlesex	,,	4,749	,,	,,	34,090	,,
Essex	,,	7,618	,,	,,	15,334	,,

THE BLIND IN SUFFOLK.

The census of 1851 was the first that made us acquainted with the number of blind in Suffolk, and they were then found to be much more numerous than was previously supposed. In the census of 1861, the inquiry was repeated, and the number of persons returned as "blind," or "blind from birth" was, males 217, females 157, total 374. Of these, 35 (including 10 females) were described as "blind from birth." Whatever may be the influences which induce diseases in the organs of sight, it is evident that there is a larger proportion of blind people in Suffolk than in many other districts. In every 10,000 males in England and Wales there were 10 blind; but in Suffolk there were 13; in Lancashire, 9; in Cheshire, 8; in the West Riding of Yorkshire, 8; in Essex, 9; and in Norfolk, 13. In England and Wales, 1 in every 1,037 persons were returned as blind; in Suffolk the proportion was 1 in 897 persons. The proportion of those "blind from birth" to the total blind, is almost the same in Suffolk as it is in England and Wales. Of the blind females in Suffolk, 89 were 60 years of age and upwards, and 26 were 80 years and upwards. Of those blind from birth, 1 female only had reached 40 years of age, but two males had attained the age of 65.

THE DEAF AND DUMB IN SUFFOLK.

The *deaf and dumb* are much less numerous than the blind, there being 13 blind in every 10,000 males in Suffolk, and 8 deaf and dumb. The distribution of the deaf and dumb in England points to the fact that special influences, at present imperfectly understood, are in operation in particular localities, and we find that in Suffolk, deaf and dumb persons increased from 195 persons in 1851, to 247 persons in 1861. In England and Wales, the proportion of living persons to 1 deaf and dumb person was 1,640, but in Suffolk it was only 1,358. The relative numbers of the sexes exhibit disproportion; there were 8 male deaf mutes to 6 female deaf mutes. The contrast of age between the blind and the deaf and dumb is conspicuous. The numbers of the blind increase when we pass 40 years of age, but the numbers of the deaf and dumb are highest under 40 years of age. Of the 157 blind females in Suffolk, only 37 are under 40 years of age; but of the 106 deaf and dumb females, no less than 71 are under 40 years of age. Of the total blind, 85 had attained the age of 75 years; of the total deaf and dumb, only 8 had attained to 75.

OCCUPATIONS OF THE PEOPLE.

In 1861, the Population Returns were arranged by the

Registrar General into six classes, and the respective numbers of each class in Suffolk, during the first week in April in that year, stood thus:

	Males.	Females.
1st Class Professional . . .	4,200	1,932
2nd ,, Domestic . . .	59,880	138,411
3rd ,, Commercial . . .	9,947	388
4th ,, Agricultural. . .	57,195	7,751
5th ,, Industrial . . .	28,445	18,273
6th ,, Indefinite and Non-Productive	4,472	4,728

The following tabulated returns give, as it were, a bird's eye view of the number of persons employed in the principal occupations in the county:

OCCUPATIONS IN WHICH THERE WAS AN *Increase* IN THE NUMBER OF PERSONS EMPLOYED IN SUFFOLK IN 1861 COMPARED WITH 1851.

	1851.	1861.		1851.	1861.
Post Office Employes	148	188	Employed on Rail-		
Police	198	254	ways ..	251	580
Clergymen .	542	585	Telegraph Service ..	0	18
Barristers ..	16	30	Seamen .. .	1117	1424
Photographic Artists	0	40	Farm Bailiffs ..	581	743
General Teachers &	} 39	{ 79	Shepherds ..	583	878
Teachers of Lan-			Gardeners ..	1521	1735
guages, Males ..		{ 11	Gamekeepers ..	315	377
General Teachers &	} 147	{ 299	Fishermen ..	698	837
Teachers of Lan-			Printers	270	317
guages, Females ..		{ 11	Coachmakers ..	314	341
Civil Engineers .	13	19	Plumbers & Glaziers	764	879
Music Mistresses ..	23	41	Millwrights ..	98	108
Governesses ..	374	468	Butchers.. ..	896	945
Female Servants—			Fishmongers ..	125	245
General Servants .	7358	9002	Maltsters ..	540	649
Housekeepers ..	1294	1642	Innkeepers ..	751	756
Cooks ..	815	1356	Publicans and Beer-		
Housemaids ..	1000	1760	sellers ,	377	519
Nursemaids ..	696	1171	Grocers	851	1248
Male Servants—			Soap Boilers ..	9	40
Coachmen ..	93	155	Tanners	87	153
Grooms ..	295	661	Sawyers	461	514
Gardeners ..	67	155	Thatchers ..	526	544
Commercial Clerks .	169	338	Drapers, Mercers ..	496	599
Auctioneers ..	58	66	Gas Works Service .	35	72
Accountants ..	49	62	Brickmakers ..	724	873
Pawnbrokers ..	29	34	Boiler Makers ..	21	56

OCCUPATIONS IN WHICH THERE WAS A *Decrease* IN THE NUMBER OF PERSONS EMPLOYED IN SUFFOLK IN 1861 COMPARED WITH 1851.

	1851.	1861.			1851.	1861.
Protestant Ministers	130	125	Architects ..		33	19
Physicians and Sur-			Surveyors ..		25	9
geons	232	205	Carpenters ..		3155	3065
Schoolmasters ..	336	309	Bricklayers ..		2194	2126
Schoolmistresses ..	954	950	Masons		174	113
General Srvnts.,Male	1061	960	Cabinet Makers ..		441	403
Bargemen ..	229	145	Wheelwrights ..		927	900
Pilots ..	141	117	Bakers		770	739
Messengers, Errand			Tallow Chandlers ..		70	49
Boys	1195	716	Basket Makers ..		158	140
Farmers, Graziers ..	5196	4989	Coopers		258	241
Farm Servants, In-			Silk Manufacturers		650	585
door ; Male ..	2845	959	Shoemakers ..		3979	3761
Watchmakers ..	194	164	Tailors . ..		1657	1415

OCCUPATIONS IN WHICH MALE JUVENILES WERE EMPLOYED IN SUFFOLK IN 1861.

	Under 10 years of Age.		Under 10 years of Age.
Domestic Servants . .	3	Carpet Manufacturer .	1
Gardener . .	1	Silk ,, .	12
Seaman . .	1	Flax ,, . .	3
Errand Boys . .	4	Straw Plait ,, .	16
Agricultural Labourers .	515	Mat Makers . . .	5
Shepherds . .	7	Rope Maker . .	1
Farm Servants (indoor) .	3	Brick Makers . .	6
Woodman . .	1	Earthenware Manufacturer	1
Cattle Dealer .	1	Labourers . .	24
Sailmaker . .	1	Dependent on Relatives	1

OCCUPATIONS IN WHICH FEMALE JUVENILES WERE EMPLOYED IN 1861.

	Under 10 years of Age.	10 to 15 years of Age.		Under 10 years of Age.	10 to 15 years of Age.
Shopwomen	..	4	Hair Bristle Manu-		
Woollen Cloth Manu-			facturers .	17	75
facturers .	..	14	Brush & Broom ditto	24	67
Silk ditto . .	19	272	General Servants	3	1063
Cotton ditto .	2	5	Housekeeper .	..	1
Straw Plait ditto	103	271	Cook . .	..	1
Tailors . .	..	21	Housemaids .	..	105
Dressmakers	..	121	Nurses . .	5	293
Seamstresses ..	2	..	Inn Servants .	..	10
Shoemakers	..	51	Warehouse Women	..	24
Laundresses .	..	19	Agricultural Labour-		
Clothes Dealers .	2	..	ers . .	16	49
Net Makers .	..	17	Pedlar . .	1	..
			Gipsy .	1	..

LIST OF THE OCCUPATIONS IN EACH OF WHICH ABOVE TWO HUNDRED
FEMALES WERE EMPLOYED IN SUFFOLK IN 1861, AND THE NUMBER SO
EMPLOYED.

General Servants	9002	Seamstresses . .	793
Milliners and Dressmakers	4569	Tailors . . .	642
Laundresses . .	2219	Nurses (not Domestic Servants)	563
Straw Plait Manufacturers	1792	Governesses . .	468
Housemaids . .	1760	Hair Bristle Manufacturers	353
Silk Manufacturers . .	1687	Agricultural Labourers .	333
Housekeepers . .	1642	Staymakers . . .	307
Cooks . . .	1356	Grocers . .	328
Farm Servants (Indoor) .	1215	General Teachers . .	299
Nursemaids . . .	1171	Brush and Broom Makers	273
Charwomen . .	1054	Inn-keepers and Beershop-	
Schoolmistresses .	950	keepers . .	209
Shoemakers . .	820	Net Makers .	212

MARRIAGES.

The Registrar-General has shown that "the fluctuation in
the marriages of a country expresses the view which the
great body of the people take of their prospects in the world."
Such a view of the most important event in the lives of
human beings invests it with an extra degree of interest,
socially and commercially. The following table exhibits the
number of marriages in Suffolk in the years 1851—3, and
1861—3.

1851.	1852.	1853.	1861.	1862.	1863.
2,294	2,326	2,476	2,298	2,283	2,430

The Population Returns of 1861, when compared with
those of 1851, exhibit a decrease in the numbers of the
people; but the decrease in the number of marriages in the
three years ending 1863, compared with the returns of the
ten years previous, is greater than that of the population.

Of the marriages contracted in the years 1861 and 1862,
there were 3,672 celebrated according to the rites of the
Established Church. Exclusive of Roman Catholics, Quakers,
and Jews, there were 482 other marriages, celebrated at
Nonconformist places of worship, and 418 at the offices of

the Superintendent Registrars. In 1861, there were three Roman Catholic and three Quaker marriages; and in 1862, two Roman Catholic and one Quaker marriage.

There is considerable improvement in the state of education in Suffolk, as shown by the marriage registers, but the improvement is greatest on the female side. In the three years ending 1863, there were 2,121 females, and 2552 males, signed the marriage register with marks; that is, thirty per cent. of the females, and thirty-six per cent. of the males. But in the seven years, 1839—45, no less than forty-six per cent. of the men, and fifty-two per cent. of the women signed with marks.

BIRTHS.

There were 32,880 births registered in Suffolk during the three years ending 1863. This number does not, however, exactly represent the number that occurred, as the births of still-born children are not registered. The term "still-born" implies children born who never breathe in the world. If a premature infant of six months breathe, it is said to be born alive, is registered among the births, and, if it die, among the deaths. The returns for the three years just mentioned exhibit a decrease in the number of illegitimate births. Although the proportion of illegitimate children cannot, without various other particulars, serve as a standard of morality, nevertheless a remarkable frequency of such cases is, both morally and socially, a serious evil. The following table exhibits the number of births, and the number of illegitimates for the years 1861—3.

NUMBER OF BIRTHS IN SUFFOLK DURING THE YEARS			NUMBER OF ILLEGITIMATE BIRTHS IN SUFFOLK DURING THE YEARS		
1861.	1862.	1863.	1861.	1862.	1863.
10,921	10,951	11,008	888	848	865

DEATHS.

In the three years ending 1863, there were 20,759 deaths

registered in the county of Suffolk; the year 1862 being distinguished as a healthy, and that of 1863 as an unhealthy period. The mortality experienced in the summer quarter of 1863 was, in some districts of this county, greater than had been known for many years. In the year 1862, there were 6,135 deaths in this county; but in 1863, there were 7670, showing an increase of 1535 on the year, and being nearly 600 more than was ever previously registered in Suffolk in one year. We give here a table of the number of deaths in the three years ending 1863, and in the corresponding three years ending 1853 :—

DEATHS IN SUFFOLK IN THE THREE YEARS, 1851-3.			DEATHS IN SUFFOLK IN THE THREE YEARS, 1861-3.		
1851.	1852.	1853.	1861.	1862.	1863.
6,839	6,870	6,907	6,954	6,135	7,670
20,616			20,759		

On glancing over these returns, it will be observed that coincident with a decrease in the population, when compared with 1851, we have in the years 1861—3 a *decrease* in the number of marriages, an *increase* in the number of births, and an *increase* in the number of deaths.

RELIGIOUS CONDITION OF THE PEOPLE.

At the Census in 1861, an account of the religious condition of the people was not taken. Full particulars were, however, obtained at the previous Census, 1851 ; and as these Returns are important in many respects, we condense the leading facts from those relating to Suffolk, in order to show the number of persons that attended places of worship, the number of places provided for worship, and the particular doctrines and forms of the parties for whom these provisions were made.

In 1851, the population of Suffolk was 337,215. Of this

population, there were in the afternoon of Sunday, March 30th, 136,820 persons attending public worship in 719 places; of these 136,820 attendants, nearly two-thirds, 86,095, belonged to the Church of England. The largest numbers among the Dissenters were Baptists, 18,415, Independents, 18,181, Wesleyan Methodists, 6,473, Primitive Methodists, 5,822.

There were 895 places of worship in the county; and, including an Estimate for Returns, which omitted to mention the number of sittings, there were 239,403 sittings. Of these places of worship, 716, with 221,377 sittings, were open in the morning; 719, with 208,427 sittings, were open in the afternoon; and 290, with 91,756 sittings, were open in the evening.

The total number of sittings provided by each religious body may be thus exhibited :—Church of England, 157,476 ; Independent, 31,466 ; Particular Baptists, 24,515 ; Baptists (undefined), 14,304 ; Wesleyan Methodists, 14,649 ; Primitive Methodists, 7,740 ; Society of Friends, 2,380 ; Unitarians, 1,270 ; Wesleyan Methodist Association, 395 ; Wesleyan Reformers, 518; Brethren, 400; Roman Catholics, 725; Mormons, 233 ; Jews, 10 ; Isolated Congregations, 1,780.

The Church of England had 519 places of worship. Of these, 455 were open in the morning, 430 in the afternoon, and 36 in the evening. The Independents had 90 places of worship, of which 59 were open for the morning service, 61 in the afternoon, and 68 in the evening. The Baptists had 91 places of worship, and opened 70 in the morning, 71 in the afternoon, and 57 in the evening. The Wesleyans had 163 places of worship; 104 were open in the morning, 137 in the afternoon, and 113 in the evening. The Mormons had three places of worship, each of which was open morning, afternoon, and evening.

On comparing the number of attendants with the number of sittings available during each part of the day, it was found that during the morning and afternoon, but little more than *half* of the accommodation actually available was *used;* and in the evening, *less* than half of the available sittings were occupied.

The *lowest* proportion of attendants, to population, occurred in the Mutford Union; and the *highest* proportion in the Risbridge Union. In the Bury St. Edmund's, Ipswich, and Mutford Unions, more than two-thirds of the population were absent from public worship.

PAUPERISM.

The county of Suffolk has been for a great many years notorious for the extent of its pauperism; and prior to the Poor Law Amendment Act coming into operation, it was more deeply pauperised than any other county in England. The cost of poor relief per head in 1834, on the population of 1831, was, in Hoxne Union, £1 5s. 0½d.; in Hartismere Union, £1 1s. 5¼d.; and in Cosford Union, £1 1s. 4¾d. But even this exhibition of the cost in these Unions fails to show the enormous pressure which some parishes in the county were compelled to bear. In Bacton, the cost per head was £1 7s. 9d.; in Stradbroke, £1 10s. 2d.; in Whatfield, £2 0s. 7d.; and in Barsham, £3 16s. 0d. Generally speaking, the Workhouse was a large "Almshouse," where the indolent, able-bodied labourer was maintained in sensual indulgence. The lavish expenditure that characterised the provision department became notorious to the whole county. Hundreds availed themselves of this mode of living, preferring the comfort and security of residence in a Workhouse to either industrial labour or out-door relief. And that the diet table was on a scale so exceedingly liberal that the inmates were far better fed than it was possible for them to be at their own homes, the following particulars of the dietaries of various Houses of Industry, in 1834, will prove:—

WEEKLY DIETARY TABLE FOR ABLE-BODIED PAUPERS.

Parish Workhouse or House of Industry.	Ounces of solid Food, Bread, Cheese, Cooked Meat, Meat Dumplings, etc., etc.	Pints of Fluid, Nutritious Diet, such as Milk, Soup, Rice-Milk, etc.	Vegetables in Pounds.	Beer in Pints.
Workhouse, Parish of Framlingham	194	18	24	9
Onehouse House, Stow Hundred	203	10½	24	14
Bulcamp House, Blything Hundred	210	4½	16	7
Barham House, Bosmere Hundred	211	13½	32	14
Nacton House, Colneis Hundred	217	24	32	14
Eye Parish Workhouse . . .	224	21	16	15
Semer House, Cosford Hundred	233½	14	—	14
Tattingstone House, Samford Hund.	247	13½	—	12
Gilbert's Union House, Oulton	265½	12½	32	9

The pauper class is still a large class in Suffolk, but, happily, a class decreasing in numbers. In the five years ending March, 1853, the annual average number of persons relieved was 26,582; but in the three years ending January 1st, 1865, the average, annually, was only 24,027—nearly one in twelve of the entire population of the county. The cost of supporting what Thomas Carlyle calls "this army of paupers," averages about £185,000 a year. Thus, in the year ending Lady Day, 1863, the cost of indoor maintenance was £20,224; and the amount of out-relief was £83,144. The salaries and rations of the officers, including the sums re-paid to Her Majesty's Treasury, amount to £18,710 (nearly as much as the maintenance of the in-door poor). On January 1st, 1865, there were 23,944 paupers relieved: the in-door paupers numbering 2,574, and the out-door 21,379. But the able-bodied adults among them were only 587 in-door, and 4398 out-door. The following table exhibits at one view the present state of pauperism, and the cost of pauperism in the county of Suffolk:—

	First of January, 1864.	First of January, 1865.
Total number of Paupers relieved	24,113	23,944
Number of Indoor Poor	2,582	2,574
,, Outdoor Poor	21,531	21,379
,, Able-bodied Adults . Indoor	591	587
,, ,, ,, Outdoor	4,505	4,398

RETURNS RELATING TO THE YEAR ENDING LADY DAY, 1864.

Total Receipts from Poor Rate Returns.	In Maintenance.	Out Relief.	Mainte-nance of Lunatics in Asylums	Salaries and Rations, etc., etc.	Total Expendi-ture of Relief to the Poor.	Payments towards County or Borough Rates.	Total Expendi-ture.
186,764	17,012	79,379	10,253	19,026	135,775	30,546	184,721

THE COMPARATIVE WEEKLY COST OF INDOOR AND OUTDOOR RELIEF PER 100 OF POPULATION FOR THE YEARS ENDING LADY-DAY, 1852-3, AND THE YEARS ENDING LADY-DAY, 1862-3; ALSO THE COST PER HEAD OF POOR RELIEF IN 1834.

Unions.	Popu-lation in 1861.	Cost of Poor Re-lief per Head in 1834 on the Po-pulation of 1831.	Average Weekly Cost of Indoor and Outdoor Relief per 100 of Population for the Years ending Lady-day :—			
			1852.	1853.	1862.	1863.
		£ s. d.	s. d.	s. d.	s. d.	s. d.
Blything . .	26,848	0 17 1	9 6	8 11	10 2	9 2
Bosmere & Claydon .	16,174	0 17 11	10 4	11 2	12 4	11 10
Bury St. Edmund's .	13,318	*	10 10	11 8	13 8	14 0
Cosford . .	17,376	1 1 4¾	8 7	8 9	13 4	14 1
Hartismere .	17,665	1 1 5½	14 9	14 11	13 4	12 8
Hoxne . .	14,694	1 5 0¼	15 1	14 1	14 0	14 5
Ipswich . .	37,881	0 13 3½	10 7	11 4	12 11	10 5
Mildenhall .	9,595	0 14 10½	10 0	9 10	16 0	16 8
Mutford & Lothing-land . .	24,050	*	6 6	6 2	10 3	7 11
Plomesgate .	20,720	0 19 1½	12 1	13 7	13 4	12 9
Risbridge .	17,432	0 17 8½	14 6	14 2	17 0	16 6
Samford . .	12,736	*	5 11	7 0	10 7	10 6
Stow .	20,908	0 14 8¾	10 11	10 10	12 11	12 6
Sudbury . .	31,415	0 13 0½	13 3	14 1	18 6	17 5
Thingoe . .	18,224	0 16 1¾	14 4	13 11	14 10	14 6
Wangford .	13,619	0 16 11½	11 9	11 10	13 7	14 3
Woodbridge .	22,754	0 16 11¼	14 10	13 7	14 1	13 5

* The cost of these Unions cannot be ascertained, as they did not dissolve their incor-porations until several years after 1834.

The foregoing extracts from tables, kindly furnished by Sir John Walsham, Bart., exhibit the comparative cost of relief in the several Unions of this county at two different periods, ten years apart. We have also added, for still further comparison, the cost per head of pauperism in fourteen of the Unions in the year 1834.

CRIME.

There are several indications at the present time of the improved social condition of the people of Suffolk; and an opinion prevails among those best able to judge, that we may add to these indications the fact that crime has, during the last few years, decreased in this county, both in its extent and its enormity. But though this impression is strong on the minds of many persons holding official positions, it is not easy to prove it by statistical returns. The following table is compiled from Returns furnished by the Home Office, but it fails to elucidate the very point that wants to be proved.

A RETURN OF THE NUMBER OF "COMMITMENTS FOR TRIAL" IN THE COUNTY OF SUFFOLK (INCLUDING THE BOROUGHS) IN THE YEARS

1850	1851	1852	1853	1860	1861	1862	1863
472	629	609	521	177	243	243	248

A RETURN OF THE NUMBER OF "SUMMARY CONVICTIONS" IN THE COUNTY OF SUFFOLK (INCLUDING THE BOROUGHS) IN THE YEARS

1860	1861	1862	1863
1922	1930	2158	2020

Here we see that the commitments for trial have decreased in ten years from 629 in 1851 to 243 in 1861; but a great proportion of this decrease in the number of commitments is owing to alterations in the Criminal Law. The Summary Jurisdiction Act gave the power to persons charged with certain indictable offences, the opportunity of being tried at Petty Sessions, and acquitted or convicted summarily. This Act, therefore, by giving increased power to magistrates, greatly reduced the number of commitments, and will almost account for the decrease exhibited in the above Return.

The "Summary Convictions" for the four years ending 1863, are very numerous; but as the Home Office could not furnish a similar Return for the four years ending 1853, or for any one of these years, the prevailing opinion as to the decrease of crime remains, as far as statistical statements are concerned, unproved.

At the Sessions convened for the Borough of Ipswich, in January, 1865, there was not a prisoner for trial; and this singular, and as far as is known, unprecedented event in the memory of persons living, was marked by the Mayor presenting to the Recorder a pair of white gloves, to commemorate the Maiden Sessions—a Sessions at which there was no prisoner to try. Although this circumstance does not prove the absence of crime in the town of Ipswich, it evidences the absence of those violent and malicious offences against person and property which are the surest indications of moral debasement.

LITERARY INSTITUTES IN SUFFOLK.

The merest glance at the tabular statement in page 434 will show that the love of literature is not very strongly developed in Suffolk. Among the males, we find only 3,478 members of Literary Institutes in the county, although the adult males, twenty years of age and above, numbered 85,513; and, be it remembered, a considerable number of these 3,478 members are under twenty years of age. Then, again, we find only 204 female members of Literary Institutes out of 94,472 females in the county twenty years of age and upwards. According to the Census Report in 1851, there were 2,808 members of Literary Institutes; the above Return therefore shows an increase of 874 members in ten years; but two-thirds of this increase has occurred in the Town of Ipswich alone. Since the Returns of 1851, "Institutes" have been established at Debenham, Mildenhall, and Eye; and Reading Rooms opened at Wrentham and Hadleigh. That at Debenham has been very materially aided by Lord Henniker; that at Mildenhall by Sir Charles and Lady Bunbury; and that at Eye by Lady Caroline Kerrison. The "Leiston Institute" is indebted to Richard Garrett, Esq., not only for the use of the room, but also for fire and gas, which that gentleman provides at his own expense. The Mechanics' Institute at Bury St. Edmund's has also the use of its rooms rent free. In fact, several of the Institutes are not what may be called self-supporting; and those at Ipswich and Stowmarket are in a more prosperous condition than any others in the county.

Comparing 1851 with 1865, we find that at Clare, the members of the Institute have decreased from 104 to 75; at Halesworth, from 100 to 83; at Leiston, from 124 to 85; at Woodbridge, from 150 to 93; and at Yoxford, from 93 to 56. The Ipswich Literary Institute, with its 102 members in 1851, has ceased to exist. The Bures Reading Room has merged into the Parochial Lending Library; the Lowestoft Mechanics' Institute, which in 1851 had 150 members, was obliged to wind up its affairs in October, 1865, leaving a deficiency of ten pounds to be made good by the Executive; and the Woodbridge Institute had 1,400 vols. in 1851, and now, after fourteen years, making allowance for "lost" and "unfit for use," has no larger number. Were we not justified, therefore, in making our opening remark, that the love of literature in Suffolk is not very strongly developed?

F F

CONDITION OF LITERARY INSTITUTES IN SUFFOLK IN 1865.

Institutes.	Date of Establishment.	No. of Members.			Rate of Annual Subscription.	Annual Income.	No. of vols. in Library.
		Males.	Females.	Total.			
Beccles Public Library	1835	80	7	87	21s.	£90	5500
Beccles Working Men's Institute	1856	54	3	57	4s. 4d. and 10s.	40	100
Bury St. Edmund's Athenæum	1853	300	50	350	10s. 6d. and 6s.	300	7500
" " Mechanics' Institute	1824	65	..	65	10s. 6d.	70	5500
Bury and West Suffolk Library	1846	..	..	140	21s.	..	8000
Clare Literary Institute	1850	75	..	75	21s., 10s. 6d. and 5s.	60	600
Debenham Mechanics' Institute	1853	40	15	55	5s.	20	550
Eye Literary Institute	1858	91	..	91	10s. 6d. and 5s.	25 10s.	631
Framlingham Mechanics'Institute	1844	40		40	8s.	17 15s.	500
Hadleigh Young Men's Institute	1862	90		90	8s. and 4s.	30	..
Halesworth Mechanics' Institute	1850	79	4	83	10s. and 6s.	30	1200
Ipswich Public Library	1791	185	35	220	21s.	..	9200
" Mechanics' Institute	1824	605	12	617	10s.	450	7600
" Orwell Works	1830	226	..	226	4s. 4d.	49	2850
" Working Men's College	1862	653	..	653	2s. 6d.	144	1000
Leiston Mechanics' Institute	1850	..	..	85	8s.	50	3500
Melford Literary Institute	1849	91	6	97	10s. 6d. 7s. 6d., 5s., ladies, 4s.	44	600
Mildenhall Mechanics' Institute	1850	52	3	55	10s. and 6s.	25	500
Nayland Literary	1851	24	..	24	10s.	20	180
Needham Market Mechanics',	1850	51	2	53	12s. and 6s.	..	850
Stowmarket " "	1840	165	24	189	20s., 8s., and 5s.	130	2500
Sudbury " "	1834	124	6	130	21s., 12s. 6d., and 5s.	133	1100
Woodbridge " "	1836	90	3	93	10s. and 6s. ladies.	55	1400
Wrentham Reading Room	1857	51	..	51	10s. and 3s.	15	604
Yoxford Mechanics' Institute	1851	22	34	56	10s. and 5s. ladies.	25	800

There are other Libraries in Suffolk, as the Corporation Library, Ipswich, with its 922 vols., representing 659 works, but these are not at present accessible to the public; and the Library at the Ipswich Museum, which is only for reference.

Appendix.

THE REFORM STRUGGLE AT IPSWICH IN 1820 ;

OR THE HISTORY OF

LENNARD AND HALDIMAND'S ELECTION.

THE political triumph gained by the Reformers at Ipswich in 1820, and popularly known as "the Lennard and Haldimand election," will ever be memorable in the political history of the Borough. Nearly half-a-century has elapsed since that event took place, and as the passions and prejudices then excited are allayed, and the principal combatants, as well as the vast majority of those who fought under their leadership, have thrown off this mortal coil, we may now endeavour to place before our readers a sketch of the greatest political conflict that ever occurred within the precincts of Ipswich. Indeed, with the exception of the contest of Barnardiston and Parker against the son of Sir Roger North, in 1640; that of Staunton and Wollaston, against the son of the Earl of Dysart, in 1764; and that of Dundas and Kelly against Morrison and Wason, in 1835, there is nothing in the political annals of the Borough that will bear any comparison with the conflict of 1820. Thomas Carlyle has in his inimitable manner given us a picture of the election at Ipswich for the Long Parliament, in 1640, when the struggle was between Puritan and Royalist: be it our more humble task to attempt a rough sketch of an election in times within the memory of many now living, when the struggle may be said to have been between the aristocracy and the people—or Conservatism and Progress.

A consideration of the causes which led to the strong class-antagonism which largely prevailed throughout the country belongs to the province of the general historian. The local circumstances under which the conflict referred to took place, was to a certain extent peculiar to Ipswich, and may therefore properly claim our attention. The Corporate Body, according to the charter and constitution of the Borough, consisted of two Bailiffs, twelve Portmen, twenty-four Common-councilmen, and an indefinite number of Freemen. The Portmen and Common-councilmen were self-elected, each by a majority of their respective bodies, and, singularly enough, the Portmen were by this means all Reformers, and the Common-councilmen all Tories, or Blues. The two parties being politically opposed, Bailiffs were chosen from that party which happened to have the ascendancy among the Burgesses. Under these circumstances, Chief Magistrates were sometimes appointed who enjoyed neither the respect nor the confidence of the inhabitants. The freedom of the Borough was acquired by birth, apprenticeship, purchase, and gift.

There were about 1000 Freemen, but more than half of them were non-resident. A considerable majority of those who resided in the Town were journeyman mechanics and labourers. A few years after this event, it was found that of the whole of the Registered Freemen of Ipswich, only 138 occupied houses of the *value* of £10 and upwards; and of these 138, only 28 were *rated* at £10 and upwards; and of the 28, one-half were members of the Common Council. No less than 43 of the number were excused payment of rates. There were about 50 merchants and manufacturers in the Town, but only 7 of them were Freemen. There were 22 medical practitioners, but only 3 of them were Freemen. Still further, to prove that the Burgesses were among the poorest of the inhabitants, we mention that in the parish of St. Margaret, there were 92 inhabitants rated at £10 and upwards. There were 33 Free Burgesses rated, but only 3 were rated at £10 and upwards. In St. Clement's, there were 75 Burgesses on the Rate-book, but the whole of their Assessments amounted only to £229 5s.; while the total Assessment of the parish was £3,721 3s. It will thus be seen that those inhabitants of the Town who were best qualified by their education and station in society to promote the interests of the Borough, had no voice in the management of its affairs; while a body of Freemen, whose condition in life exposed them to the influence of corruption, and disqualified them for the performance of official duties, were entrusted with the election of Chief Magistrates, and were themselves exclusively eligible for the Municipal offices of the Borough. The Blues had possessed the lead in the Town for many years, and some of the most influential men of the Town belonged to that party. These gentlemen regarded the Revolution of 1688 as a dangerous innovation, and they exhibited their attachment to the principles of the Stuart family by displaying oak boughs at their doorways, on each successive 29th of May. A "Pitt" Club was formed, and held its annual dinner in commemoration of the great man's birth; and the men who would not sport "true blue" colours, or drink deep potations to the memory of the "Heaven-born Minister," were expelled from the society of their ultra-loyal fellow-townsmen. Any man who professed Radical principles was looked upon by the Tories with suspicion, and regarded as one who was continually plotting to overturn the constitution of society by pushing the *respectables* from their stools, and plundering them of their property; and to show the extent to which party-feeling prevailed, we mention that at one of the public dinners given by the Bailiffs, the following toast was given with applause:—"May the types of every Jacobin printer be converted into musket-balls, and every Democrat receive a proof impression!"

Those causes seem quite sufficient to account for the unexampled zeal and activity manifested by the Reformers at the contest in 1820. But there was another cause which, perhaps more than any other, stimulated them on this particular occasion. The Borough had long been considered as under the influence of the Government, and that, in fact, the ministers nominated the members, as the Marquis of Hertford did for the Borough of Orford, and the Marquis Cornwallis for the Borough of Eye. The Reformers had long desired to wipe off this reproach, but they felt themselves unable to do so. At the election, however, in 1818, Mr. Henry Baring, of the firm of Baring and Co, London, without being solicited, offered himself as a candidate on the Reform side, in opposition to Messrs. Crickitt and Newton. This gentleman came into the Town a perfect stranger; and though he only came the day before the election, after six days' polling and registering more than 800 voters, he was only defeated by 32. This showed to the Reformers their real strength, and prepared them better than anything else for the struggle in 1820. Mr. Baring was so pleased with the exertions of the friends in Ipswich who laboured for him on that occasion, that, before leaving them, he declared that as long as health permitted him, they should never want a candidate to support their cause. When, therefore, the decease of George III., in 1820, led to a dissolution of Parliament, the Reformers of Ipswich naturally looked to Mr. Baring to redeem his pledge, by becoming once more their leader in a political struggle. Mr. Baring, however, felt himself physically unable to bear the fatigue which, as he said, must necessarily be undergone by any candidate who would struggle at the approaching election to rescue the Borough from ministerial bondage and domestic thraldom. But though unable to do battle himself, he promised to use his utmost endeavours to introduce two gentlemen to the electors, upon whose exertions they might rely.

Thus assured of a contest, the Reformers immediately commenced working operations. Many of the leading inhabitants of the town, who were continually reminded of the necessity for Reform in Parliament by their exclusion from Corporate offices and consequent inability to take part in the management of Corporate affairs, joined with the Portmen and the Free Burgesses on the Whig side. Two Committees were formed on the plan of a deliberative and executive assembly ; and their meetings were held at the "Golden Lion." Among the members of the first Committee, were Benjamin Brame, Frederick Francis Seekamp, William Bernard Clarke, William Hammond, Henry Alexander, Thomas Green, William Pearson, Jeremiah Head, and H. Buchanan, Esqrs. The other Committee consisted chiefly of younger and less influential men, who were more likely to do the real work of the election. On this Committee were Messrs. John Head, Alfred Head, William Stephenson Fitch, John May, William May, Charles Cowell, Thomas Crawley, and Robert Gill Ranson. None of these were Free Burgesses ; and, indeed, it was remarked that the most active canvassers at this election were those who had not the privilege of voting. A London Committee was formed, who sat daily at the "Four Swans," Bishopgate Street, and the energetic H. Buchanan, Esq., of Stowmarket, was made Chairman.

On the 18th of February, the Reformers issued a placard stating that Thomas Barrett Lennard, Esq., son of Sir Thomas B. Lennard, Bart., of Bell House, in Essex, would on the following day address the electors at the Assembly Rooms, at seven o'clock in the evening, for the purpose of offering himself as a Candidate for Representing the Borough in Parliament. This gentleman arrived at William Pearson's, Esq., Solicitor, about noon, on the 19th, and, accompanied by that gentleman, immediately proceeded to call upon the Portmen and other leading supporters of the cause. At the meeting in the evening, he was most enthusiastically received by the Free Burgesses. On the following Thursday, another public meeting was held, to introduce William Haldimand, Esq., one of the Directors of the Bank of England, to the electors of the Borough. A band of music preceded the gentleman to the place of meeting, and a large number of influential supporters accompanied him. Gratified at their enthusiastic reception, Messrs. Lennard and Haldimand repaired to London for the purpose of canvassing such of the Free Burgesses of Ipswich as were residents of the great Metropolis and its vicinity. A few days only had elapsed before they declared that their success was unprecedented, and that if the Electors of Ipswich only manifested the same spirit of independence, the triumph of the cause was certain. As these gentlemen were to return to Ipswich on the third of March, to prosecute with vigour the canvass in the Borough, their friends resolved upon getting up a procession to escort them into the Town. This, which was the prelude to the magnificence afterwards exhibited, surpassed all former processions, and, in point of display, comprised all that was calculated to command a triumphant success. The Candidates were met at Copdock Elm by a numerous body of gentlemen on horseback, and the "Ipswich Journal" says that "at the 'Royal William Inn,' and at the entrance to St. Matthew's Street, so great was the concourse of spectators that it seemed as if the entire population of the Town was assembled." In the procession, a banner of immense size, of orange silk trimmed with purple fringe, profusely decorated with favours, and bearing the Arms of the Town, emblazoned and surmounted by the British Lion, was borne by 16 men on a frame, while a large body of horsemen, and a number of carriages, including those of Sir William Middleton, and other gentlemen, and containing Sir William himself, R. M. Raikes, Esq., a Bank Director, the nephew of Mr. Haldimand, Mr. Luard, the well-known friend of Mr. Baring, the Rev. Charles Fonnereau, of Christ Church, and other gentlemen, escorted the Candidates.

In the meantime, it must not be supposed that the Blues were inactive. Mr. Newton, who had in conjunction with Mr. Crickitt been elected in 1818, "felt induced, from private circumstances, to decline going again into a contest," and Mr. Round, who had previously been elected as Member for the Borough, upon being solicited by a section of the Free Burgesses, agreed to become a candidate in his stead. Mr. Crickitt having been sent by the Burgesses of Ipswich as their representative in three successive Parliaments, "felt quite confident of again experiencing a repetition of those favors that had placed him in so proud and envied a position." A Committee was formed, who sat daily at the White Horse Hotel, James Wenn, Esq., being Chairman. On this Committee, and aiding the Committee, were many staunch Tories who were not Free Burgesses. There was also a London Committee, who held their sittings in the Metropolis, and the late Mr. Simon Jackaman, a great tactician in electioneering matters, was one of its most active members. On the 26th of February, these gentlemen were escorted into the Town by a large procession with flags, banners, and music, and a cavalcade of horsemen, and each of them addressed the electors.

Tuesday, March 7th, was the day fixed for the Election. The Bailiffs were John Eddowes Sparrowe, and James Thorndike, Esqrs. The business of the day was opened by Mr. Thorndike, the Senior Bailiff, and the routine of business having been disposed of, Robert Alexander Crickitt, Esq., was proposed by the Rev. Thomas Reeve, and seconded by the Rev. Fred. Leathes ; John Round, Esq., was proposed by Major Broke, and seconded by Major Stisted; Thomas Barrett Lennard, Esq., was proposed by Mr. Wm. Barnard Clarke, and seconded by Mr. Hammond ; William Haldimand, Esq., was proposed by Mr. Brame, and seconded by Mr. Seekamp. The Blues, whose watchword was, "Church and State," selected the supporters of the Candidates from the Church and the Army; the Yellows selected four Portmen for the distinguished honour. Immediately after the conclusion of the Nomination, between two and three o'clock in the afternoon, polling commenced. The first three votes were for Crickitt and Round, viz.: Nathaniel Lee Acton, Esq., Mr. William Clarke, and Major Broke. The fourth man was a Free Burgess on the Yellow side, well-known for his bounce and splutter, Mr. Gregory Mulley, who afterwards kept the "Crown and Sceptre" Inn. More than 300 voters polled before 5 o'clock, when the books closed for the first day; and to show how vigorously the predominant party had laboured, we only need mention that among those on the Blue side were Burgesses from Wolverhampton, Plymouth, London, Greenwich, Chatham, Woolwich, and Maldon. The Yellows also had some voters from London and Bury St. Edmund's. Among the Townsmen who voted that day, on the Yellow side, were "Tom Harrison," a poor victim of election iniquity, well-known to those of a later generation as "the Blessed Man;" Joseph Bird, a poor man, whom the Rev. G. H. Greene, in his fiery and unchristian zeal afterwards publicly stigmatized as the Rohespierre of Ipswich; "Tony Breckles," "Bobby Bird," and Sir William Middleton. Among those who gave their maiden votes on this day, was a gentleman who has now for many years been elected as one of the Representatives of this Borough—John Chevallier Cobbold, Esq., who voted for Crickitt and Round. Mr. Cobbold obtained his freedom by being articled for seven years to a Reformer, William Hammond, Esq., one of the Portmen; and we believe we are right in stating that this was not simply Mr. Cobbold's first vote for Members of Parliament, but it was also the first time that any member of his family had the power of voting in the Borough of Ipswich. At the close of the first day's Poll the numbers were

Lennard	Haldimand	Crickitt	Round
157	156	121	120

One voter, Mr. William Brooks, had voted for Lennard and Crickitt. The arrival of voters in the Blue interest by the evening coaches was hailed with joyous exultations; the Yellows also had a great accession of numbers by special coaches, and the exertions made by both parties indicated a protracted contest. On the Wednesday morning, a number of the personal friends of Messrs. Lennard and Haldimand arrived in five carriages and four, and so great was the excitement, that nothing less than a procession through the principal streets, with flags and music, would suit the small fry of partisans, and to this the gentlemen submitted, amidst the shouts of an immense throng of people. During the day the out-voters kept coming into the town, some of them from long distances; and whilst on the first day of the election, the value of a vote was only about ten shillings, it had risen before the close of the second day's poll to twenty pounds, and Mr. Buchanan, we understand, has mentioned that as much as fifty pounds was given to some of the London voters. The Blues polled the largest number of voters, but the Reformers still maintained a majority. Nearly 650 voters had polled at the close of the second day's proceedings.

Notwithstanding the great exertions made on the previous day, the Blues succeeded in bringing 110 votes to the poll on the *third* day, and the Yellows no less than 117. Among the voters this day on the Blue side, were the Rev. Sterling Westhorp, George Schulen (of the Pottery), and Captain James Hallum; and on the Reform side, Stephen Abbott Notcutt, Charles Chambers Hammond, John Parish Hammond, Esqrs., and Messrs. Robert Ralph, Benjamin Hamblin, Stephen King, and George Gooding, Sen. The "Cooping of Voters" was now exemplified.

Men who had been carried away, or confined in some public-house, and stupefied by drink, were now brought up just sensible enough to give the names of the candidates. Some voters were taken to Walton Ferry, others as far as eighteen miles from the town; but even at that distance rescues were sometimes attempted, and all sorts of stratagems were put in force.

During the fourth day, the polling dragged on very slowly, fifty-nine names were entered on the Poll Book; but the difficulty now felt by both parties is shown by the fact that several who voted that day were afterwards struck off the poll as " not a Free Burgess," or " not of age." Mr. George Pooley (Alexanders' Bank), Mr. John Spooner Manning (wine merchant), Mr. Thomas Frost Goward (the father of Mrs. Keeley), voted that day on the Reform side; and Edward Bacon, Esq., Captain Wollaston, three members of the " Tuffnell " family, Mr. Anthony Dorkin, and Mr. Matthew Wing, on the Blue side. One of the candidates (John Round, Esq.) helped up the number by voting for himself, and Mr. Crickitt and Jacob Frost gave one of the few split votes, " Crickitt and Haldimand." As Mr. Crickitt polled thirty votes, and Mr. Round twenty-nine, whilst Mr. Haldimand obtained only eighteen, and Mr. Lennard seventeen, the Blues were in high spirits this evening, and paraded the town in great triumph. The expectation of ultimate success was greatly heightened by the assurances of Messrs. Crickitt and Round, who, after the procession, declared from the windows of Mr. Bacon's residence their most confident hopes of carrying the election.

The energetic assurances of their candidates on the previous evening seemed to have inspired additional spirits into the Blue party, and throughout Saturday, the fifth day of the Poll, they manifested increased activity. Their band and flags were almost constantly parading the streets. The polling, however, went on very languidly until late in the afternoon, when several Blue voters came up in brisk succession. Among those, was Mr. Crickitt himself. At the election in 1818, this gentleman had voted, but modestly enough, for his friend Mr. Newton only; on this occasion, however, he voted for " Crickitt and Round." The Reformers found that they had run nearly the length of their tether, and they polled only *two* votes this day. Their musicians and flagmen stood idly about, drinking at those public-houses that were " open " on the Yellow side. Voters, with their wives and daughters even, were staying at the " Golden Lion," and other principal inns in the town, having whatever they pleased to call for, at the expense of the party. To what extent this system of treating was carried, may be judged by the fact that the bill for tavern expenses at the " Golden Lion " Inn, amounted to nearly eight hundred pounds! Between four and five in the afternoon, a party of about three hundred persons, many of them of the first respectability of the town and neighbourhood, in the Blue interest, formed the most striking procession that had been witnessed during the election. The Poll closed at six o'clock with an addition of eleven to the numbers on the Blue side, and two only on the Yellow side. The Reformers, still determined to bring up voters, sent Mr. Alfred Head, this Saturday evening, to Bristol, after a voter; but, although no expense was spared, that gentleman was unable to reach Ipswich on his return until after the poll was finally closed on the Monday evening.

When the time arrived on Monday morning for opening the Poll, both parties felt the difficulty of obtaining voters. Every nook and corner of the kingdom where a voter was known to live, had been ransacked by either the Blues or the Yellows. The Government had brought its influence to bear, and the Treasury, the Army, the Navy, and the Dockyards had been made to yield fruit for the support of the Ministerial candidates. Each party found on the sixth day that their strength was spent ; a larger number of voters had polled than had ever been previously known. The Blues did not seem so sanguine of success as they did on Saturday. Still, hopes were entertained that, if they did not absolutely triumph by numbers, the majority of their opponents would not be more than two or three ; and they had, doubtless, already determined upon demanding a scrutiny. During the day, the Yellows polled 14, and the Blues 13 ; but of the 13 votes for the Blues, 7 were given by members of the Common Council. One voter, Mr. Thomas Hobson, was brought from Holland to vote for the Blues ; and another, Mr. George Gooding, Jun., was fetched from Paris to vote for the Yellows. Late in the day, both parties agreed to close the Poll. About five o'clock, the unpolled Common Councilmen, who generally remained as a *corps de reserve* of the Blue party, came up to Poll. These were Mr. Richard Gooding, Mr. Robert Tayer, Mr. B. B. Catt, Mr. John Denny, Mr. William Calver, and Mr. Simon Jackaman. They were immediately followed by three of the Portmen on the Whig side : Mr. William Hammond, Mr. Benjamin Brame, and Mr. F. F. Seekamp. The Bailiffs, Messrs. James Thorndike and John Eddowes Sparrowe, then voted for Crickitt and Round, and finally closed the poll. The numbers were—

Lennard	Haldimand	Crickitt	Round
482	483	474	468

The contest at the poll was thus ended, but the struggle was not over. Upon the numbers being declared, Major Broke (the gentleman who on the day of nomination proposed Mr. Round) demanded a scrutiny on behalf of Messrs. Crickitt and Round. This excited the enthusiasm and indignation of the respective parties, but the demand being seconded by Major Stisted, was granted by the Bailiffs. This move was at first supposed to be a mere feint of the Blues to break the violence of their overthrow ; but, contrary to the expectation of the Yellows, it was prosecuted with extreme activity. Major Broke said that he understood there were 70 bad votes on the Yellow side, and only twenty or twentyfive on that of the Blues, and the striking these off would give his friends a decided majority on the poll. Mr. Crickitt, however, felt it necessary to declare that it was instituted at the desire of his supporters, "notwithstanding the unwillingness of my brother candidate, Mr. Round, and myself." The Yellows, though not disposed to relinquish their vantage ground, knew that there were bad votes on both sides ; but, though they knew that the numbers would be reduced, they did not think it likely that their *majority* on the poll would be disturbed. They therefore met the proposition with cheerfulness, and immediately prepared for the struggle, Mr. Prinsep, an eminent barrister, being engaged to conduct their case.

The election closed on the 13th of March. The scrutiny commenced *pro forma* the next morning, and was then adjourned till the following Monday. It dragged on slowly, and it was not until April 14th, that it

was finally closed. During the first few days, the numbers struck off
on both sides were about equal ; but, as it proceeded, the friends of Mr.
Crickitt became filled with enthusiasm. By a series of decisions which
the Yellows declared were illegal, and exhibited the partiality of the
Bailiffs, the majority of Mr. Lennard and Mr. Haldimand was gradually
diminished, and the returning officers finally declared the numbers to
stand thus—

Crickitt	Haldimand	Lennard	Round
430	428	427	424

They thus took off fifty-five votes from the numbers polled for W.
Haldimand and T. B. Lennard, Esqrs., and forty-four from R. A.
Crickitt and J. Round. Esqrs.

Of the objections advanced by the Blues to the Yellow votes, three
only were overruled by the Bailiffs, while of those advanced by the
Yellows, thirteen were dismissed. The Yellows desired a professional
assessor to be appointed, as the Bailiffs who were the judges had both
voted and acted in the opposite interest. This reasonable request was
refused. At the election in 1818, Philip Bannocks voted for the
Yellows, and was struck off the poll because he held a place in the
Custom House, at Harwich. At Lennard and Haldimand's election he
voted for the Blues, and although on his own confession he held the same
identical office in the Customs for which he was on the former scrutiny
struck off by the Bailiffs of that year, of whom Mr. Sparrowe was one,
his vote was allowed to be good! This and some other partial decisions
determined Mr. Lennard, after consulting with the friends who had
laboured for him at the election, to appeal to a superior tribunal, and
have an investigation before a committee of the House of Commons.
This movement of his gratified his friends. Mr. Haldimand took his
seat in the House of Commons on the 25th of April, but he declined to
be chaired until the validity of Mr. Crickitt's return had been determined.

One of the episodes connected with this scrutiny is worthy of particular
notice. Information was obtained by the committee of Messrs. Lennard
and Haldimand that *three* Freemen who had voted for their opponents
received relief from the parish of Sudbourne, near Orford, and application was in consequence made for the production of the parish accounts.
Some persons in that parish and the adjoining borough, who espoused
the cause of Messrs. Crickitt and Round, among whom, it was said, was
the steward of the Marquis of Hertford, concerted measures to prevent
the fact from coming to light, and the application for the production of
the parish accounts met with a refusal. The parties, however, fearing
that they might be compelled to produce them, consulted together as to
what was best to be done, and they resolved to take a step which, it was
conceived, would have set the question beyond the reach of discovery in
any shape. An old book, belonging to the parish, in which there were
blank leaves, was procured, and the person employed to make out the
overseer's accounts was ordered to copy the correct account of expenses
into this book, but whenever the names of the pauper voters occurred,
he was to *substitute* the names of *other* persons. The man began his
work on the following morning, but information was again sent to
Lennard and Haldimand's committee of the imposition which was in
preparation to delude them. They, in consequence, set a stratagem on
foot which in the end completely counteracted the whole plot, and its

execution was confided to Mr. Oliver, an ironmonger (who resided on the Cornhill, where Mr. Ridley now lives), an enthusiast in the Yellow interest. The gentleman went to Orford, and, as the Overseer said, waited upon him, under the assumed name of "Goose," wearing a *blue* watch-ribbon, and introduced himself as an agent of Messrs. Crickitt and Round. At the time of Mr. Oliver's arrival, the assistant was engaged in transcribing the very accounts, and Mr. Oliver's tact had so far disarmed the suspicions of the Overseer, that he was permitted to assist in completing the surreptitious entries. He then prevailed on the Overseer to accompany him to Ipswich to substantiate the proof, and to take the *original* book with him. When brought before the Returning Officer, the oath was administered to the Overseer, and he produced the book in which the false entries had been made, and denied that any relief had been afforded to the three voters. He also denied that any false entries had been made in the book. The Yellows then called in Mr. Oliver to be confronted with the witness, and contradict the evidence, and the *original* book was drawn from the pocket of the Overseer, handed to the Bailiffs, and completely exposed the fraud that had taken place.

We have mentioned that Mr. Haldimand took his seat in the House of Commons, but resolved not to undergo the ceremony of chairing until it was finally determined by a committee of the House of Commons whether his friend, Mr. Lennard, should share in his triumph. Mr. Crickitt did not, however, manifest equal prudence. Elated with the result of the scrutiny, though they were aware of the rotten foundation on which Mr. Crickitt's small majority was erected, his friends determined to celebrate their triumph by a chairing, and afterwards to have a convivial dinner in honour of the event. To make the display the more effective, the ladies of Ipswich resolved to take the matter in hand: and under the leadership of Mrs. Cobbold, of Holywells, a subscription was at once opened for the purchase of a set of colours worthy of the event. The Dowager Countess of Dysart, the Countess of Linsingen, Mrs. Edgar, Mrs. Broke, of Henley, Mrs. Caroline Acton, Mrs. Trotman, and Mrs. Cobbold, headed the subscription-list; and the Blues were thus presented with a most superb set of ten colours and a banner, all of which were beautifully ornamented with silver fringe. On them the following devices were inscribed :—

"The Established Church Triumphant."

"A Constitutional King George IV. and the House of Brunswick."

"A Loyal Population—the truly Independent Freemen of Ipswich."

"Order, Good Government, and the Laws of England."

"Prosperity to the Blues."

"Fidelity to the Cause."

"Be firm."   "Be just."   "Be united."   "Be vigilant."

On the largest centre-colour, or banner, was inscribed : "In honour of those True Blue Principles which support the Throne and Constitution of Great Britain, these Colours are presented by the Ladies of Ipswich and its vicinity, 1820." These colours were consigned to the care of Edward Bacon, Esq , and were accompanied by a letter from Mrs. Cobbold, which shews the spirit of this energetic female party-leader. Mr. Bacon acknowledged the receipt of the "sacred banners" in very flattering terms, "trusting that the few individuals who have been artfully deluded from their party, will again rally round the standard of loyalty, consecrated on the present happy occasion by Female Patriotism."

Wednesday, April 26th, was the day fixed for the chairing of R. A. Crickitt, Esq., and soon after twelve o'clock on that day, that gentleman and his lady were met at the "Royal William" Inn, by a respectable assemblage of his friends, both horse and foot. A procession was formed, and preceded by heralds sounding trumpets, and a band of music. Mr. Crickitt made his triumphal entry into the town from the London Road, amidst the shouts of the multitude and the joyous greetings of numerous ladies, who had placed themselves wherever a view of the procession could be had. The procession was of a very imposing character, and in the course of it, a Regal Crown, in proper colours, was borne aloft by two men, and on an oval wreathed with laurel beneath the crown, was the following inscription :—

> "We hail our Crickitt's fourth return,
> And George the Fourth our King."

Another novelty was a group of sailors as Morris dancers; while the carriages of Admiral Page, Captain Kortwright, Mr. Kortwright, George Round, Esq., Wm. Deane, Esq., Dr. Williams, Mrs. Kerridge, etc., and a line of gentlemen on horseback wearing blue favors, closed the procession. Mr. Crickitt alighted at Mr. Bacon's Bank, and very little time was lost in preparing for the grand ceremony of the day. About twenty minutes past two, the honourable gentleman ascended a very tastefully decorated chair of blue silk, encircled with laurels. The procession then went, in nearly the same order as before, with the addition of a group of female Morris dancers in blue ribbons, three times round the Cornhill, through Tavern Street, Brook Street, St. Peter's, and St. Nicholas, to the Cornhill again, and thence to Mr. Bacon's, where Mr. Crickitt left the chair and appeared at the window, cordially thanking his friends for the high honour that had a fourth time been conferred upon him.

At five o'clock, Mr. Crickitt met a party of his friends to dine together at the Assembly Rooms. The tickets were 15s. 6d. each, and the company numbered about 170. Amongst them were Charles Berners, Esq., Major Broke, Admiral Page, Captain Kortwright, Mr. Kortwright, the Rev. E. H. Green (Lawford), Mileson Edgar, Esq., Rev. Mileson G. Edgar, Charles Round, Esq., Rev. J. C. Cooke, Rev. W. Howorth, Rev. W. Aldrich, Dr. Williams, Edward Bacon, Esq., J. N. Theobald, Esq., and many other influential gentlemen ; Mr. Round, the colleague of Mr. Crickitt, was, however, not present. Copies of the following song, "respectfully inscribed to the True Blue Ladies of Ipswich and its vicinity, in commemoration af the return of R. A. Crickitt, Esq., as one of the Representatives in Parliament of that Borough," were distributed over the tables before the dinner was set out :—

> True Blue Ladies ! mark how bright,
> How pure the bumper flows to you !
> Ladies, mark what gay delight
> Crowns the bumper now in view !

True Blue Ladies ! blithe and fair,
  To you the song of joy we raise ;
Sweet for you the vernal air
  Wafts the grateful note of praise.

True Blue Ladies ! whilst we sing
  The song your gen'rous loves inspire,
Every bosom, on the wing,
  Glows with all a patriot's fire.

True Blue Ladies ! take our hearts,
  All warm and free they beat for you :
Each to each its bliss imparts—
  Loyal hearts are ever true.

In the after-dinner speeches, almost rabid heat of feeling was manifested by the speakers against the Quakers, Dissenters, and Reformers in general ; and in a copy of verses recited by Mr. Harral on the occasion, they were denounced as—

"That recreant tribe—defilement of our land—
That worthless, heartless, soul-polluted band !
Whose aim is plunder, anarchy, and death,
Blasting and withering, like the siroc's breath."

On the 2nd of May, Mr. Crickitt took his seat in the House of Commons, and seven days afterwards, Mr. Haldimand presented a petition to the House on Mr. Lennard's behalf, against Mr. Crickitt's return. On the 11th, Mr. Crickitt presented a counter petition from some of the Conservatives in Ipswich against the return of Mr. Haldimand. The petition was signed by James Hamblin, Edward Ablitt, Robert Tayer, and Richard Bruce. The petitions were ordered to be taken into consideration on the 13th of June. As the time for balloting for a Committee of the House of Commons drew nigh, the most intense excitement prevailed in Ipswich among the supporters on both sides. It was customary, at that period, in all electioneering cases brought before the House of Commons, to exchange lists of the objections urged by both parties, at least five days previous to balloting for the Committee by which they were to be decided. The lists being duly presented on Wednesday, the 7th, were made known in Ipswich on the following Friday, and appeared to throw great gloom over the spirits of those by whom Mr. Crickitt was supported. On the Saturday evening, a select number of the Blue partisans met to consider the prospect of their affairs, and when they separated, the most unfavourable reports were circulated as to the course they felt it necessary to pursue. A communication was received by the Reformers on the Sunday morning, which they disclosed on the following day. The contents of this was, that Messrs. Hamblin, Ablitt, Bruce, and Tayer would withdraw their petition against the return of Mr. Haldimand, and that Mr. Crickitt would relinquish his seat in favor of Mr. Lennard. The effect of this intelligence on the minds of all parties was electric, and a more striking exhibition of exhilaration and despondency was not often witnessed in Ipswich. The notice alluded to having been given, the business in the House of Commons became a mere matter of form. The ballot took place on June 13th, and fifteen members of the House were selected for the Committee. On the next day, the Committee met, and Lord Althorp was chosen nominee for Mr. Lennard, and Mr. B. Wilbraham for Mr. Crickitt. Mr. Selwyn,

Counsel for the Reformers, briefly introduced the subject. He then disclosed to the Committee the notice delivered on the part of Mr. Crickitt and his friends, which would terminate the proceedings in a very short time, by leaving him to peform the easy task only of striking off four votes from Mr. Crickitt's number, so as to restore the majority to Mr. Lennard. Mr. Harrison, Counsel for Mr. Crickitt, then stated to the Committee that in inspecting the lists which had been delivered into the House, it was found that the return of Mr. Crickitt could not be supported; his advice, therefore, had been asked as to the proper course to be pursued by his clients, and under that advice the notice already detailed had been given to the gentlemen on the other side. The Committee then proceeded to strike off the names of four voters for Messrs. Crickitt and Round, viz.: WILLIAM DOBINS, *no such Freeman;* HORATIO FULLER, *not of age at the time of voting;* WILLIAM HEWITT, *not a Free Burgess,* and ROBERT KEDGLEY, *liable to the same objection.* The Committee shortly afterwards prepared their report, in which they declared that Robert Alexander Crickitt and John Round, Esqrs., were not duly elected to serve in Parliament, but that Thomas Barrett Lennard and William Haldimand, Esqrs., were duly elected to serve in Parliament for the Borough of Ipswich.

Mr. Haldimand having, with true courtesy, determined to postpone his chairing until his colleague could join him hand-in-hand in the expected triumph, the friends of Reform now resolved to celebrate the triumph of both members in a manner worthy of their cause. Monday, July 3rd, was the day fixed for the chairing, and the preparations for the *fête* were admirably suited to the importance of the occasion. All that taste, ingenuity, and invention could supply, was devoted to celebrate it with becoming splendour. During the preceding week, the county round was big with anticipation of the approaching day of festivity.

On the eventful morning, before the dawn of day, the town was all bustle and life. The bells rang merrily, the cannons roared, and other signs of joy and exultation were manifested. Such of the inhabitants as belonged to the Reform party were seen at an early hour busily decorating their houses. Amongst the most conspicuous of the decorations on the Cornhill, were those at the "Golden Lion"; the house dedicated to the personal accommodation of the Hon. Members and their immediate friends. The front of the house was adorned by a temporary alcove, tastefully adorned with olive branches, flowers, and orange ribbons, with the word "Victory" in the centre. The next object of attention was the house of Mr. Oliver, the Ironmonger, where Mr. J. R. Ridley now resides, in front of which, on the first floor, was projected a convenient balcony, for the convenience of numerous Ladies. The whole of the balcony was covered with festoons of flowers intermixed with olive branches, tastefully arranged, and the whole frunt between the railing at the top and the platform at the bottom was covered with an inscription on an orange ground, "LENNARD AND HALDIMAND TRIUMPHANT." On the house of Mr. Ranson, next door, was a banner with the words, "IPSWICH IS FREE," inscribed in letters of gold, the whole surmounted with a wreath of flowers in season, the predominant of which was the Orange Lily. At Mr. Oldacre's, where Mr. Limmer now resides, commodious arrangements were made for the convenience of the numerous ladies that graced his house on the occasion. On the opposite side of the way, the Corn Exchange was made an object of singular attraction and of interest, by a circumstance in itself trifling. Upon this building the figure of the goddess "Ceres" was transformed into the statue of "Justice," with the sword in one hand and the scales in the other, as she stood on the Old Market Cross, which was pulled down in 1812. To complete her attire, a bandage of yellow silk was now placed over her eyes, symbolical of her purity and impartiality.

The accommodation provided for the Ladies consisted of an extensive range of hustings in the centre of the Market-place, so constructed as conveniently to accommodate above 400 Ladies, who were admitted by tickets to witness the procession. The goddess "Flora" contributed her fragrant treasures to the embellishment of this interesting stage, which was consecrated to a splendid assemblage of females, amongst whom were Ladies of the first rank and distinction in the county. The whole front of the building was tastefully bedecked with flowers. On entering the Town from the London Road, the most conspicuous object which met the eye was a well-constructed arch thrown across St. Matthew's Street, from Mr. De Carle's house to the opposite building, which was profusely decorated with laurels, flowers, and ribbons, with the inscription "Welcome." As the spectator proceeded, he saw on each side of the street various devices, and other symbols of enthusiasm in the cause of Independence; flags, wreaths, waving ribbons, and a profusion of laurels expressed the joy and sympathy of a large portion of the inhabitants throughout the route destined for the procession. One common feeling seemed to pervade all that were embued with Reform principles, and each of them seemed emulous to signify the occasion with every mark of enthusiasm.

It had been announced by public advertisement that the procession would assemble at half-past nine o'clock, on Crane Hall Hill, on the London Road, as a place of rendezvous, whence it was to proceed through the town. Long before that hour, the leading streets of the town were thronged with thousands of anxious spectators. Every hour brought in fresh groups of visitors from the country in all directions, and by twelve o'clock an impervious mass filled every vacant space through which it was announced that the procession would pass. Soon after twelve o'clock, the whole order of the procession being arranged and marshaled, a discharge of artillery announced to the expecting throng assembled in the town, that the pageant had commenced its march. It would be impossible to describe the enthusiasm which the imposing spectacle everywhere excited in its progress. The waving of handkerchiefs from windows, thronged with groups of women, the shouts of applause which resounded from the countless multitude, the clangour of the trumpets, and the cheering melody of the bands of music which accompanied the procession, all tended to raise a fervour of delight. To give some conception of the nature of the arrangements, we state that the procession in its train occupied the whole length of the ground from the Barrack Corner to the top of Crane Hall Hill, being more than a mile in length. The following was the order in which it moved:

MAN IN ARMOUR,

on a Grey Horse;

TWO MARSHALMEN,

one on each side, on Grey Horses;

SEVEN TRUMPETERS

on Grey Horses, the men's jackets and caps of purple, trimmed with orange, white trowsers, trimmed with the same, and orange scarfs, trimmed with purple ;

LARGE BANNER

of orange silk, trimmed with purple fringe. The Arms of the Town emblazoned, surmounted by the British Lion, and inscribed, "The Improvement and Prosperity of the Town."

SEVENTY GENTLEMEN,

All on Grey Horses, in columns of five, each attended by two Stewards.

THE PORTMEN,

In a Carriage with four Horses.
Part of the COMMITTEE, in a Carriage with four Horses.

A CARAVAN

with a Canopy of Green and Orange fringe, drawn by six Grey Horses, with the COMMITTEE and other Gentlemen.

THE BAND.

EIGHT SILK FLAGS

with the following Mottoes :

" Liberty and Freedom ; " " Baring and Independence ; " " Haldimand and the Constitution of 1688 ; " " Harwich Invincibles ; " " Portmen and Independent Freemen ; " " The Independence of the Borough asserted 1818 ; " " London Inflexibles ; " " The Independence of the Borough established 1820."

Amongst these Flags was also one brought by the Manningtree Freemen . motto, " The Progress of Public Opinion," and also another, borrowed from the Blues, " Be Just."

A LARGE BANNER

of the Members' Arms united ; above the Arms, on one side a Lion, on the other a Unicorn, and on a scroll under the names, the motto, " Union of Patriots." Two Ionic columns formed the sides, with the inscription, " Nothing is Difficult to the Brave and the Faithful." At the top of the Banner was a ship, to which motion was given, as in full sail, and above all, the figure of Justice, supported by handsome scroll irons. [The height of this Banner was fourteen feet, and the width nine feet ; it was designed and executed by the workmen of Mr. Launcelot de Carle, and presented by them for the occasion.]

A BUGLEMAN

on a Grey Horse, on each side a Man on Horseback carrying a Banner with the Arms of the respective Members.

MR. H. ALEXANDER

in a Curricle drawn by Four Beautiful Roans.

THE MEMBERS

in a Carriage with four Horses.
Mr. BARING, accompanied by Mr. LENNARD, in a Carriage and Four.

SIR THOMAS LENNARD AND FAMILY
in a Carriage and Four Horses.
Sixty Horsemen,
in columns of five each, attended by two Stewards.
BAND.
EIGHT FLAGS.
GENTLEMEN'S CARRIAGES, VIZ.,
Sir W. Middleton's, Mr. Grigby's, Mr. Steward's, Mr. J. B. Smyth's, and
the Rev. C. Fonnereau's.
SIXTY HORSEMEN
In columns of five each, attended by two Stewards.
SEVEN CARRIAGES AND FOUR,
with Gentlemen and their Families.
ONE HUNDRED AND TEN HORSEMEN
In columns of five each, attended by two Stewards.
A numerous Train of Carriages.
WOODBRIDGE FREEMEN
In a Van, attended by a Band.
Upwards of
THREE HUNDRED AND SEVENTY HORSEMEN.

The procession in this order marched in stately measure through St. Matthew's, Tavern Street, Brook Street, Tacket Street, Orwell Place, back of St. Clement's Church, St. Clement's Fore Street, Orwell Place, Foundation Street, College Street, St. Peter's Street, Queen Street, Butter Market, Brook Street, Tavern Street, to Mr. Pearson's, St. Matthew's. This circuit took nearly two hours to perform, and about two o'clock the Honorable Members alighted to dress preparatory to the ceremony of chairing. Every arrangement for this purpose being completed, this imposing spectacle commenced its route from the house of Mr. Pearson, where the Honorable Gentlemen mounted their triumphal cars. Nothing could exceed the taste and magnificence of the splendid preparations for this purpose. It is difficult adequately to describe the beauty and elegance of the chairs. Each car consisted of a cupola, supported by eight pillars, raised upon a platform of spacious dimensions, and borne upon the shoulders of about twenty men. The pinnacle consisted of a beautiful cast of Britannia in an erect posture. The body of the machine was covered with orange silk, occasionally interspersed round the frieze of the cupola with knots of purple, and the word "Victory" was appropriately conspicuous; the supporting pillars were entwined with ribbons of the same color, exquisitely combined with laurel leaves and flowers; the platform was covered with scarlet cloth, which admirably contrasted with the prevailing tints already mentioned; the chairs appropriated for the convenience of the principal actors in the scene, were on the model of a Greek curule, and each was covered with purple satin, fringed with crimson lace. Both the Honorable Members were dressed in elegant ball-room costume, each wearing on his breast

G G

rich favors, composed of silver rosettes and orange and purple tissues. As soon as the gentlemen had placed themselves in the chairs, they were borne aloft amidst the cheers of the surrounding multitude, and a choir of trumpeters, mounted on horseback in front of the procession, announced their approach by an appropriate flourish. As the gentlemen advanced, they were greeted with the most enthusiastic expressions of popular regard. The procession went once round the Cornhill, and thence proceeded through Tavern Street, Brook Street, College Street, St. Peter's, St. Nicholas, the Butter Market, Brook Street, Tavern Street again, back to the Cornhill. As soon as it reached Tavern Street on its return, fresh objects of wonder and admiration were presented to the view of the spectators, namely, a remarkably fine figure on a pedestal of JUSTICE, six feet high, with sword and scales. This noble figure was accompanied by a splendid white flag and silver letters, motto "Justice has triumphed." There were also THE TEMPLE OF FAME, a grand and imposing device, which rose twenty-two feet in height from the shoulders of the bearers. It was three-storied. Each story was supported by eighteen Tuscan columns of brass, with silver capitals and bases. The form of the stories was not circular, but octagonal ; the diameter of the lower story was eleven feet, and its height five feet; of the centre story eight feet, and its height three feet ten inches; and of the upper story four and a half feet, and its height three feet. The body inside the pillars was of orange moreen, and the inscription on the lower story "Haldimand," on the second "Lennard," and on the upper "Baring." The tablets bore the names of distinguished persons, friends to the cause of Independence. Those on the lower story were "Sussex," "Kent," "Chatham," "Nelson," "Anson," "Lansdowne," "Erskine," "Russell," "Fitzwilliam," "Devonshire," "Milton," "Newport," "Tavistock," "Folkstone," "Norfolk," "Holland," "Albemarle," and "Grey." On the second story, "Fox," "Sheridan," "Romilly," "Ponsonby," "Whitbread," "Grattan," "Coke," "Tierney," "Smith," "Macintosh," "Bennet," "Brougham," "Wood," "Denman," "Dundas," "Darnley," "Macdonald," and "Ridley." The cornices were decorated with rosettes over each pillar ; the lower cornices had silver and purple fringe, and pine apples ; the middle cornices had three rings with the motto "Unanimity" between each of them, and the upper cornices had in the interstices two palm branches and a cable, emblems of strength and victory. Above the cornice a bust and vase alternately. There were busts of George IV., supported by those of Prince Leopold and Princess Charlotte, and those of Fox, Nelson, Wellington, Milton, Shakspeare, and Cowper. The vases were filled with laurels and flowers. The dome of lutestring—as was all the silk used as well in the temple as in the flags—was alternately orange and purple. On the top was a beautiful bronze vase, two feet in height, surmounted by an elegant figure of Fame, two and a half feet high. On each side were two profile paintings of Fame, five and a half feet high, in flying posture, bearing white flags, with the motto "Ipswich is Free." At the corners of the platform were placed four young gentlemen, Masters Hammond, Notcutt, Goward, and Coe, each of whom waved an orange banner as the Temple majestically moved along. This grand and elegant edifice was designed and executed by Messrs. Hare and Son, of the Old Butter Market. About five o'clock the ceremony of chairing was concluded. As soon as the Members approached the Cornhill, they were invited to alight at the house of Mr. Oliver; and they ascended to the drawing-room, and in a few moments presented themselves in the balcony, and each of them addressed the assembled multitude. Thus ended the ceremony of chairing, the variety, the taste, and magnificence of which surpassed almost everything of a similar kind. Much of the splendour of the scene was attributable to the Gentlemen of the Committee, *at whose expense most of the pageant was provided.*

A novelty in processions of this description added much to the interest of the scene, namely, a horseman clad in a splendid suit of mail. This was provided by a subscription among a number of young men in the town. The armour was procured from Mr. Marriott, the Ironmonger of Fleet Street, London. The suit in question was composed of highly polished brass, and when glittering in the sun, had the appearance of burnished gold. The horse, the finest grey that could be found in the district, was the property of Mr. Robert Bowman, of the "Falcon" Inn ; and the rider, a man of Herculean form, was a Mr. Chenery, who dying not many months afterwards, was said to have lost his life through wearing the armour. Considerable life and interest were given to the scene from the introduction into the procession of a group of Morris dancers who were dressed with great propriety, and whose activity excited a good deal of admiration.

The dinner was got up upon a scale of taste and elegance not inferior to anything of a similar kind. In order to provide ample accommodation for the number of gentlemen who were expected to dine, application was made for the use of the Free Grammar School Room in Foundation Street, there being in fact no other room in the town adapted for a numerous assemblage. Accommodation was provided for nearly 400 guests. The Gothic arches of the roof were adorned with festoons of laurel, alternately variegated with wreaths of flowers. At the upper end of the room, a table elevated upon a platform was provided exclusively for the most distinguished of the company. The rest of the room was occupied by three parallel rows of tables, which reached from the platform above mentioned, almost to the very entrance of the apartment, leaving space only for the ingress and egress of waiters. The dinner was served by Mr. Lappage, of the "Golden Lion," in a sumptuous style, every delicacy of the season being provided. Sir William Middleton, Bart., in the chair, supported on his right by Mr. Lennard, and on the left by Mr. Haldimand. At the same table were Sir Thomas Lennard, Bart., Mr. F. Baring, and other gentlemen of high rank. The newspapers of the day gave reports of the proceedings, and it is interesting to learn that Thomas Clarkson was present, and in acknowledging the compliment of the toast proposing his health, said in the course of his speech : "Nor is it the least of our pleasures that, when we contemplate this victory, we have in view the manner in which it has been achieved. We have never mutilated parish books to obtain it."

A song being called for from the Chair, a gentleman present sang with good taste an appropriate effusion, "THE STANDARD OF ORANGE." The words of the song were—

The battle is fought, and the vict'ry is won !
Lift the STANDARD OF ORANGE on high !
And let it, emblazon'd by Liberty's sun,
Unfold itself now to each eye.

The emblem of FREEDOM, O ! let it be fann'd
　　By the fetterless winds as they sweep ;
And fearlessly float o'er its uplifting band,
　　Like ALBION's own flag o'er the deep.

Over stormier waves than the mariners tread,
　　The bark which hath borne it has plough'd ;
And the tale of her voyage, if *rightly* 'twere read,
　　Is a record more gloriously proud.

She was launched in the port of *Good Hope ;* she set sail
　　With the soft sigh of *Freedom* to fan her ;
Her Captain was *Courage*, who never turn'd pale,
　　And *brave* were the *crew* found to man her.

O'er the billows of *Faction's* tempestuous seas,
　　Though thwarted, she held on her way ;
Her canvas caught *Public Opinion's* calm breeze,
　　And she steer'd straight for *Victory's* bay.

As she near'd her proud haven, *Corruption*, aghast,
　　Her destiny mutely deplor'd ;
She anchor'd off *Liberty's* beacon at last,
　　And the Pilot, *Success*, came on board.

Then here's to the STANDARD OF ORANGE ! and ne'er
　　May it quail to its rival of BLUE ;
Though its tint may unlovely to *Tories* appear,
　　Yet honoured by US be its hue.

A *glimpse* of BLUE SKY may be all very well,
　　But *blue*, and *all blue*, is quite frightful ;
Let the FRENCH and ITALIANS its loveliness tell,
　　Unto us ENGLAND's *clouds* are delightful !

They may sometimes seem dark, but while LIBERTY's beam
　　Can cleave them like lightning asunder,
HER BRIGHT ORANGE tints through the opening shall gleam,
　　And her VOICE shall be heard in the thunder !

This song was written by Bernard Barton, and it is especially interesting, as it shows how heartily the Quaker Poet entered into the spirit of
the Whig movement at that period.

Writing to his dear friend, William Pearson, Esq., of Ipswich, to
whose care this song was entrusted, he said, " I am informed that the
advocates of the good old cause among you are meditating a dinner.
Whether the annexed can be turned to any account on so interesting an
occasion, you can determine better than I can suggest. I do not know
how far they are capable of being *sung*, but at any rate they may be
said ; and as I suppose the event of your dining will get into the papers,
the insertion of them in such a record of your proceedings may not hurt
the cause. My entire ignorance of music renders it difficult for me to
decide on what is or is not sufficiently lyrical to be capable of musical
adaptation ; but the annexed, *read* to me as if they would *sing* * * *
As to the Ballad itself, I think it is a cut above a common election
squib ; but on that I am, perhaps, hardly the best judge."

Thus terminated this most extraordinary contest. To the Reformers
it was indeed a triumph, but the triumph was gained at a terrible cost.
The Burgesses were by this election so largely corrupted that evil

sprang up on all sides. At the time the events occurred which we have
endeavoured to depict, the Tories resorted to Bribery most frequently,
and probably to the greatest extent, because they had then the amplest
means, and their existence, as a party, depended upon the continuance
of these practices. But the Whigs retaliated whenever they could, and
political fury and universal partizanship was so strong, that there was
hardly a single individual possessing influence of any description, who
scrupled to employ it in the most effectual manner. The actual cost of
this Election will probably never be known, but Thomas Green, Esq., who
was an energetic member of the Election Committee says in his " Diary,"
" Mr. Lennard states in a letter, that his expenses here had amounted to
£12,000; at this rate the party here, including Mr. Baring, must have
expended not much short of £40,000!" We have been told that a
friend of Mr. Haldimand told the late Edward Bacon, Esq., that
Mr. Haldimand declared that he had paid upwards of £30,000 for Election expenses at Ipswich.

Mr. Crickitt never afterwards made his appearance as a candidate at
Ipswich; and not many years passed before he had to avail himself of
the benefit of the Court of Bankruptcy. Some of his documents by
that means passed into other hands, and from them we will now give a
few items of his Election expenses. The following are abstracted from
an account sent to Mr. Crickitt by his Ipswich Election Committee
when he was first returned as Member for this Borough. The account
was signed by five members of the Common Council.

	£	s.	d.
Sums paid to Ipswich voters	243	1	6
,, Harwich voters	94	10	0
,, Country voters	209	1	6
,, distant voters	721	1	0
Expenses of Country voters	361	13	7
,, distant voters	914	4	1
Loss of voyages, &c.	62	10	6
Expenses upon the Election days	474	3	2
Publicans' Bills	1,112	9	6
Incidental Expenses	1,620	18	5
Paid Mr. Freeman, on account	150	0	0

N.B.—Mr. Freeman claims a Balance of £275 17s., which remains unsettled,
as the Committee deems his charges exorbitant.

The " Expenses on the Election day " include the Admission Fees " of 47
Freemen in the Blue interest."

The sum paid to Ipswich voters was distributed among 93 resident
Freemen, of whom 92 received £2 12s. 6d. each, and the remaining one
£1 11s. 6d. for a half vote. Harwich voters received £4 4s. each,
and country voters, in most instances, the same. The distant voters
£5 5s. each, which was paid to 119 Freemen. Their expenses were also
paid.

In addition to the expenses incurred at the Election, the local current
expenses were very heavy. Among the papers of Mr. Crickitt was an
account of these expenses for two years, amounting to £1,382 19s. The
account, which was signed by a gentleman who had filled the office of
Bailiff, discloses the following payments at the bank of Messrs. Bacon
and Co.

	£	s.	d.	£	s.	d.
Election Expenses				6,617	19	2
Two years' Current Expenses				1,382	19	0
Loans, viz :—						
Osborne	60	0	0			
G. R. Clarke	50	0	0			
Beeston	40	0	0			
				150	0	0

The partisans on both sides made such repeated calls for money that the representation of Ipswich was found to be very expensive, and when in 1826, preparations were made for another election, Mr. Lennard retired, in consequence, it was said, of a resolution passed by his local committee that he and his colleague should defray the expenses of the contest for Bailiffs. Mr. Haldimand, who had subscribed large sums for various municipal contests, required as a colleague in 1826 some gentleman who could deposit £5,000. On the Blue side it was proposed to Mr. Mackinnon, who made his first appearance as a candidate in Ipswich in 1826, to deposit £7,000. This expensive system going on, the corruption of the Ipswich constituency became so notorious that at last gentlemen declined to allow themselves to be put in the nomination.

We have not much to be proud of in the conduct of our Parliamentary elections at the present day, but at least they are better ordered, and the corruption lasts for a much shorter period. Generally speaking, men have yet to learn that the elective franchise is a sacred trust, and that it is their duty to let no consideration interfere with its proper discharge. Tradesmen, too, often sell their souls for the smile of a carriage patron, or exhibit their weakness and their servility by refraining from exercising their franchise for fear of offending their customers. We shall have no honest elections whilst this timid and time-serving spirit prevails. Whether Whig, or Tory, or Radical, electors should be manly and independent, ready to point the finger of scorn at those who sell their birthright for a mess of pottage, and equally ready to award social honor to those who make sacrifices in order to vote according to the dictates of their conscience. An employer has no right to tempt any man in his employ to swerve from the path of duty; and a baronet or a squire would be as much justified in ordering his tenant to believe in the Pope, as in ordering him to vote for his nominee.

INDEX.